"★★★★★ A manuscript, allegedly discovered in an old pub, provides the focus for this extraordinary tale. Mixing fact and fiction, Jones shoehorns elements of the detective novel, a great deal of mythology and some uncommon history into what must be one of the most dazzling books ever written about Wales." *Independent on Sunday*

"*Mr Vogel* is surely one of the most remarkable books ever written on the subject of Wales – or rather *around* the subject, because it is an astonishing mixture of fantasy, philosophy and travel, expressed through the medium of that endlessly figurative country." Jan Morris

"A sprawling, genre-hopping stew of a novel that will absorb anyone with any kind of interest in Wales." Dan Rhodes

"In the spirit of Sterne (trapped on a wet weekend in Aberystwyth) or Flann O'Brien (enduring the final cure), Lloyd Jones delivers the tour-guide Wales has been waiting for: warped history, throwaway erudition, sombre farce. Stop what you're doing and listen to this mongrel monologue." Iain Sinclair

"A rambling, redemptive mystery, stuffed full of all things Welsh: rain, drink, wandering, longing, a preoccupation with death and the life that causes it. A bizarre and uncategorisable, and therefore essential book" Niall Griffiths

"Sit back and soak up the literary references, the superb metaphors and quite brilliant kindness of the writing. We need more writers like Jones." *Western Mail*

"Jones has written a novel which purports to be the story of a quest for the Vogel Papers, but it is also a memoir and a travel book. I have enjoyed it immensely. It may turn out to be the Welsh answer to Ireland's Flann O'Brien." Meic Stephens, *Cambria*

Mr
VOGEL

Lloyd Jones

seren

Seren is the book imprint of
Poetry Wales Press Ltd
Nolton Street, Bridgend, CF31 3BN, Wales
www.seren-books.com

ISBN 1-85411-380-1

A CIP record for this title is available from
the British Library.

This book is a work of fiction. Apart from
historical figures and events, the characters
and incidents portrayed are the work of the author's
imagination. Any other resemblance to actual persons,
living or dead, is entirely coincidental.

Waldo's raid on personal files at the Robert Jones
and Agnes Hunt Hospital, Gobowen, is a complete fiction.

The publisher works with the financial assistance of the
Welsh Books Council.

Printed in Plantin by Bell & Bain Ltd, Glasgow.

PART ONE

I Nennius, pupil of the holy Elvodug, have undertaken to write down some extracts that the stupidity of the British cast out; for the scholars of the island of Britain had no skill, and set down no record in books. I have therefore made a heap of all that I have found, both from the Annals of the Romans and from the Chronicles of the Holy Fathers, and from the writings of the Irish and the English, and out of the tradition of our elders.

Many learned scholars and copyists have tried to write, but somehow they have left the subject more obscure, whether through repeated pestilence or frequent military disasters. I ask every reader who reads this book to pardon me for daring to write so much here after so many, like a chattering bird or an incompetent judge. I yield to whoever may be better acquainted with this skill than I am.

Nennius, *Historia Brittonum,* early ninth century

Yntau, Gwydion, gorau cyfarwydd yn y byd oedd. (And he, Gwydion, was the best story-teller in the world.)

Math fab Mathonwy, *Pedair Cainc y Mabinogi*

THE VOGEL STORY: AN INTRODUCTION

MANY YEARS AGO a strange incident took place in this town. The event, which went unobserved by the rest of the world, would have sunk into obscurity here also, but for the scribblings of an old bar tender and dogsbody at the Blue Angel.

The Blue Angel was a tavern at the main crossroads in the old docklands. The building has long ceased to be an inn – nowadays it is an antiquarian bookshop, leaning out towards the road, untidily, like one of the many piles of books stacked inside it.

The building is shambolic, and the paint is peeling on its black-and-white timbered façade. There is nothing to indicate that once it was the main stopping point for early travellers visiting this small corner of the globe.

Only a few people know the significance of a metal badge, showing a dancing bear, nailed to the gnarled oak lintel over the doorway.

No-one remembers the barman's name nor what happened to him. It is clear that he worked there for many years. His writings came to light, quite accidentally, whilst workmen were renovating the roof. Thrust into a crevice above a purlin they discovered a rough manuscript, almost illegible, written in faded pencil on the back of tradesmen's letters sent to the inn.

There are many incongruities in the work and few people took it seriously. It was lodged in the small museum at the town hall, more as an oddity than a proper, historic archive. I read a cheaply printed version when I was recovering from a minor illness at the local sanatorium. I began to ponder – could this fragment, found in the rafters of an old coaching inn, hold any truth? Why did the author compress time so that ancient writers and travellers appeared at his bar alongside his regular drinkers, and why did cars co-mingle with horses and carts? Was the author a forerunner of the Magic Realists? Was he deluded, or was he trying to describe a timeless state of being, in which central human laws held true throughout the many ages of man?

Historians dismissed him as a fantasist fuelled by alcohol which had rotted his brain.

I became intrigued.

I searched the public records and found allusions to the central characters, which fanned the flame of my curiosity. One evening, shortly after leaving hospital, I walked to the Blue Angel and stood in the shadow of its doorway. I looked inside, through a dusty window, at the shop's gloomy interior. A stepladder stood under an open hatch in the ceiling, as if a fugitive had been caught in a mad dash for someplace to hide.

Through the murk I could see the life-size plastic pig, shiny and pink, which was placed outside the front door every morning to indicate that the shop was open for business; small children played on it sometimes while their parents snatched a few minutes looking at the books inside. This pig, which had the word OPEN painted on its side in big black letters, had been stolen once and had achieved a few hours of fame by being featured on the front page of the local newspaper.

The pig had gone missing for exactly twenty-four hours: it returned just as mysteriously as it vanished. People thought this odd episode had been the work of a prankster who had eventually buckled under the weight of his guilt.

There is a story that one of the side-rooms has been left in the same state as it was found many years ago, like a cabin in the Marie Celeste; people who have visited this room say it looks as though a great party or celebration was interrupted in mid-flow. The chamber has been left in disarray, with mugs and platters still jumbled about; chairs are skewed back from the trestle table, as if the company revelling there had turned suddenly to greet someone walking through the door – a celebrity or a great personage being welcomed back after a marvellous triumph. One old woman who had stolen into the room when she was a child recalled that something very strange had happened when she stood on the twisted oak floorboards in that long-ago room in the Blue Angel: she had heard chairs scraping on the floor, as if a host had stood up suddenly; cheers and greetings had sounded faintly in the air. She was adamant, too, that music, melodious but ghostly, could be heard behind the supernatural hubbub.

There was something else which intrigued the townspeople: it was claimed by many that the front door opened suddenly, of its own accord, on the first day of March every year, letting in a hot beam of sunshine, a token of hope for the year to come.

As I peered into the shop a spider cast the first threads in its loom, preparing to make a web in a corner of the window. I turned and surveyed the town, as the old barman must have done many times, with his broom in his hands. I wondered if his eyes, too, had admired the long arterial avenue into town as it furred over every spring with a dense green baize of leaves and flowers. I wondered what he may have looked like: a small man perhaps, in a white shirt and a black waistcoat, standing by the dusty road in his apron, studying the passing travellers; I imagined a cleanly-shaven face with a blue sheen, and carefully-combed black hair. He had a knowing and slightly detached air about him, a quick sense of humour perhaps – and he knew, like all good barmen, when to lean over the bar for a few minutes now and then every day, to put his head close to a customer at certain important times to listen to his woes and joys; sometimes a crumpled banknote would flit between them in the shadows.

I looked down at the thoroughfare and noticed, with sadness, that a robin chick – with its speckled breast – had apparently died there; I thought I saw a little body flattened into the surface of the road, like an ivory inlay in an old and blackened table.

A thunder shower broke in a crackling explosion which rolled in the hills above the town; the air smelt of sulphur, sadness, wet earth and change. I looked at the cherry blossom swirling past my feet, spinning in the eddies of the storm water before plunging into the darkness of the drains.

Looking upwards at the sky I caught sight of the dancing bear on the lintel and remembered another bear – a shabby, one-eyed teddy bear – in the barman's story.

As rivulets of electric-sharp water coursed down my neck I made a pact with the bears to follow their footsteps into the past.

There is only one place to start – with the barman's story, or the fragment of it found in the roof high above me in the heaven space of the Blue Angel. I must warn you that it is childish, with a fairytale quality, but since it is quite short – and since it is essential to our story – it must be read, no matter how fantastical or improbable it may sound to a reader in the present century.

I leave you to read the barman's tale, scrawled on faded paper which had been rolled up like papyrus and tied roughly with a rotting scrap of twine.

His jottings have become known as the Vogel Papers.

It's a crazy story. Personally, I don't believe a word of it: the way in which Mr Vogel won his fortune, for instance, is quite implausible. But I will leave you to judge for yourselves.

THE VOGEL PAPERS

INTROIT

MR VOGEL was the winner.

When boisterous spring sprayed its leafy graffiti in the trees which struggled upwards past his grimy kitchen window, Mr Vogel was given a new existence.

Like the supine earth he had been through a deep winter, distanced from the heat of the sun; he had sat for too long by his fireside in a torpor, gazing into the embers of the past as his life cooled and dimmed. Now, suddenly, the rising sap jolted him from his stupor; the jumbled fields all around him lay breathing again, like cardiac patients shocked back to life and left to recover.

Mr Vogel kept a few truths to himself but the townspeople quickly snatched his news and carried it far and wide, to every attic and cellar, every nook and cranny; swiftly forming themselves into a sinuous street collective they ladled hot gossip from their babbling furnace and moulded nuggets of news about Mr Vogel into fabulous tales for ancient, hairy lugholes and lullabies for tiny shell-pink ears. Cunningly they distorted the daily bulletins radiating from the bar of the Blue Angel and created a misty amalgam of half-truth, tenuous fact and five-pint fuddle. The streets hummed with speculation and Mr Vogel smiled with grim amusement when he heard the various versions of his legendary existence. Indeed, by the end he hardly knew truth from fiction himself, such were the cunning twists and embellishments added to the original plot.

And as the shoots of fiction grew and the tendrils of conspiracy entwined, Mr Vogel paid for the celebrations and started his quest.

After all, he had won a very large sum of money, an island croft, an elegant house, a beautiful garden and an orchard.

Mr Vogel had also won a pagoda.

THE LIKELY TRUTH

SUDDENLY, Mr Vogel was rich. For the first time in his life he was able to cast money to the wind, on a whim, without having to count his coins or fumble about in the grubby recesses of his disintegrating sofa. Though of course there remained many vestiges of his former poverty.

Previously he had visited the Blue Angel only occasionally, because he couldn't afford to drink privately *and* publicly; now he was a daily visitor to the pub, which had changed little since the eighteenth century when it had been opened cheaply and furnished frugally by a monosyllabic sailor with one glaring eye. It became Mr Vogel's second home. His new-found wealth opened new doors, as the local newspaper recorded in a special supplement; his obese bank account bought keys to new kingdoms, which he could explore with new friends.

His passage to a new life was made easy. For instance, he gained his own entrance to the Blue Angel, thanks to two ostentatiously kind 'Samaritans' in grubby overalls.

One of them was a Sumo-bellied builder and the other was his trusty sidekick, a thin and angular man who was a very poor carpenter but a brilliant mythomaniac, who spent most of his time drinking shorts and telling very tall stories.

Theirs was one of those strange, inseparable alliances, and because they drove around the town together in a battered van, the builder haggard and low behind the driving wheel, his fetch-and-carry man like a sit-up-and-beg spaniel beside him, they were called Don Quixote and Sancho Panza, after the gallant but mad Spanish nobleman – the knight of the doleful countenance – and his long-suffering squire. And that is why their van, which was indeed on its last legs, was called Rosy, in honour of Rosinante, Don Quixote's horse. His nag was nothing but skin and bone, yet he fancied it to be a magnificent steed, straining at the bit to do chivalrous deeds.

Possibly because they were basically kind, probably because Mr Vogel would feel obliged to lend them beer money for the duration of their grossly enlarged livers, the two Samaritans built a ramp from Erasmus Street to the Blue Angel so that Mr Vogel could park by the rear entrance and totter along his own little bridge of sighs, across the void between the road and the pub. This meant that he could park directly by the back door and get to the snug without looking like a 'spastic'. Regrettably, that was his nickname among the children. The Spastic.

Previously there had been many uncomfortable episodes when he or his crutches had gone flying as he tried to climb the steps at the front of the building. He was given his own key to the back door in a grand ceremony during one Sunday morning drinking session.

First, you may want to know when all this happened.

The exact moment in history is difficult to pinpoint. I'm not very good with dates.

If I asked you, quite simply, the question:

When did you last climb a tree just for fun?

you might sit back in your chair, stroke your chin thoughtfully, and say something along the lines of '*now that's a hard one, I'll have to think about that...*'

But that's when this story starts, in those warm, hazy days when you climbed trees just for fun. Certainly, it was after the Pelagian Heresy but before the Puritans came to patrol our streets, enforcing their blackouts like god-raid wardens. People still danced and played games in the churchyard.

Divisions between night and day and north and south were much clearer; the flowers of the forest could be smelt on the morning breezes, and colours moved swiftly on the landscape, as though we lived in a moving kaleidoscope of blues and greens.

At that time a king – if wrongly killed – was still worth a hundred cows for each valley in his land, as compensation to his kin, together with a plate of gold as broad as his face and as thick as the nail of a ploughman who had ploughed the land for seven years.

The Bills of Mortality were still being compiled, and the great Chronicle of the Hours was being kept, meticulously, by Gildas and his monks; a kitten was worth a penny but a good mouser in the barn was worth fourpence. This was a time of hamadryads, the tree sprites who died if the woods were cut down, and a time also of great dreams – dreams of value and meaning: a man who dreamt about the queen had to take his cows to the water so that the king could claim their reflection as compensation.

Those were the times we lived in, when people still danced and played in the churchyard, and when children knew the values of Wild and Tame.

I believe it to be a matter of honour that Mr Vogel's great journey should be recorded accurately, with as few errors as possible. I have before me the version of the story composed by his 'boy' Luther. This redaction, unpunctuated and ungrammatical with gross errors in syntax and spelling, was found in the drawer of a cumbersome writing table bought for £2 at the salerooms of Garner and Tewlitt. It is the most reliable of all the attestations concerning Mr Vogel, especially regarding his journey around the island, which the boy witnessed at first hand.

I have already digressed. I meant to tell you about Mr Vogel's vestiges of poverty, which led to many accusations of meanness, and sly comments about extinct moths falling from his wallet whenever he opened it. Well, as a regular barman at the Blue Angel I can attest that he never bought 'rounds', and he always had the exact money warm in his misshapen little hand when he paid. It is my experience as a barman that people who proffer the right amount of money every time they buy a drink are either very poor or very rich; Mr Vogel had been both, and he still showed all the characteristics of a man habitually short of spondoolics, since he was careful to give me the right money even when rich, and he often changed notes for pound coins before he left, for the gas and electricity meters. He frequently paraded 'new' clothes bought at charity shops (he was as pleased as Punch if he'd haggled down the prices) and he still did his meagre shopping at the cheapest shops in town. You get to know people quite well when you work behind a bar. You hear snatches of conversations. You see people in the raw – this is where they come like wildebeest to drink and dull their sorrows, and nearly always they want to tell you about their sorrows. Sometimes they get abusive and say nasty (but true) things about their fellow drinkers.

A word or two about the Blue Angel, my home and muse.

The doors are low and wide, in the Georgian fashion, and the walls are a yard thick, made of granite boulders with earth and rubble infill. The floors are of heavy slate flags, worn down in the main passageways, and there is a great fireplace which roars in winter and sends sparks showering towards Polaris, the great north star which is visible at night through the large square aperture of the chimney mouth.

The main bar is approached through a long, low corridor which has many paintings on either side: prints of lateen-rigged schooners, sloops, corvettes, yawls, luggers and clippers, all of which perished on the reefs which puncture the sea around us; in the porch there is a huge brown bristle-mat for foot-wiping, and an oak hat-stand which has held one solitary green hat, with a black band and a shiny brim, since the day I entered the place, and no-one knows who owns it, nor when it arrived, and from a strange superstition Jack the landlord will not remove it. Slotted into this dusty hat-stand there is a black umbrella with a wooden duck-head handle. It is as old, crumpled and wizened as the hat, and it has been there, by all appearances, since the umbrella was first invented.

The main bar is a large, square, low-beamed room with a bay window and a massive mahogany bar which resembles a church organ, behind which I pipe up my requiems and fugues for the dibbers, topers and frothblowers who treat this place as their port of call. On either side of the fireplace there are two heavy brass lanterns with red and green lights for port and starboard, salvaged from one of the offshore wrecks, and there is a single painting (with many holes in it) which shows one of the great auks which live in a small colony on our western cliffs; you will be delighted to know that this species was not hunted to extinction by mankind in the nineteenth century as many suppose – so you may disregard a report claiming that the last auk was tried by jury and found guilty of witchcraft, then stoned to death by an angry mob following a severe storm on St Kilda in the Scottish Hebrides in 1844, or another saying that the very last pair of auks were clubbed to death on the island of Eldey off Iceland on June 3, 1844, by three men hired by an Icelandic bird collector called Carl Siemsen who wanted auk specimens.

The great auk is alive and well! These happy little tales of survival against all odds are so uplifting, are they not.

Which brings me to Humboldt the parrot, who lives with me in the Blue Angel – and who occasionally attacks the painting of the great auk, in an explosion of feathers (Humboldt is responsible for those holes in the painting). My parrot arrived here with a scientist and explorer called Alexander von Humboldt, who had found him in an Indian settlement in Venezuela. The natives who had once owned the parrot had fled to an island in the Orinoco, pursued by another tribe, but unhappily they had all perished. Thus the parrot became the world's only speaker of the Atures language. Furthermore, on his travels the parrot had picked up bits of other languages from all over the world, which speckled his original tongue. Humboldt the explorer left him with me on the sole condition that the parrot be named after him, so that the German would be remembered somewhere in the world if he perished on his travels.

Finally, to complete the picture, the Blue Angel – my little kingdom – has simple tables and chairs, some stools, and I have decorated the windowsills with red geraniums because I love the smell of the plant and its warm dry soil in the summer heat; it reminds me of childhood.

Sitting on his stool the drinker will often gaze at nothingness, revealing his sordid and pitiful life, whilst averting his eyes from the dismal world behind him. Me, I watch and listen. I must reveal to you that I have a collection of leather-bound volumes hidden among the shelves behind the bar, and since I am virtually chained to my post, and unable myself to see the wide world encircling this region, I read copiously about travellers and explorers, and the strange and wonderful countries they have discovered. I also have books on imaginary and perfect lands, such as Utopia, Arcadia, New Atlantis, and The Island of Pines.

Mr Vogel reads these books with me at the corner of the bar; he is fond of fantastical stories, and knows them off by heart – he will often pierce a conversation with ridiculous comments, hoping to impress people. For instance, only yesterday, when someone mentioned that he'd seen a tramp sidling through the docks, looking for somewhere to sleep, Mr Vogel had commented airily:

'There are few beds more comfortable than a dry ditch in June. Incidentally, the law stipulates that no-one, not even a king, can sleep within fifteen yards of the crown of a road. Real tramps put fresh dock leaves in their socks every morning to avoid blisters. Was this man you saw a proper tramp, with a blue spotted handkerchief round his neck? Was he wearing a silver ring, and were his nails dirty?'

This mangled gem came from one of my books, called *The Happy Traveller: A Book for Poor Men*; Mr Vogel was quite happy to pillage my library and pass off other people's experiences as his own.

But I must tell you about Mr Vogel's good fortune. Quite simply, he was elevated from a state of penury to great wealth in one single minute. The facts are well-documented and have not, as far as I know, been disputed by anyone.

In the town there lived a wealthy man, with white hair and a huge walrus moustache, named Doctor Robert. He had retired to a large mansion on the outskirts – the one that used to be a hospital for injured soldiers during the war. This house was screened from the long flat road into the town centre by a high phalanx of trees which only brave or naughty children ventured beyond; within the old man's little kingdom they encountered marvellous sights, though they were far too young to appreciate what they saw.

I will quote here from the local amateur historian John Parker of Sweeney Hall.

Parker, who later became a priest, wrote a romantic and highly ornate version of the Vogel story. His prose is far too flowery and sentimental for my tastes, and he is prone to wander away on obtuse tangents, but he is a valuable source and he gets his facts right more often than not. Here is part of his introduction:

I heard about Vogel's good fortune on my sister Angelica's birthday – I remember the occasion well, since I had been forced to hurry home from the railway station in a taxi so that I could present her with my gift before she went to church. I had ordered a fine and expensive oriental mantle – in blue silk with a silver moon and stars – from one of the travelling merchants who supply the old families of the town. As the town's only experienced art connoisseur and architectural historian I have an eye for the beautiful and the genuine, which brings me once again to the silk mantle I conveyed to my sister that latent spring morning. I was perhaps a little flushed from the journey, which had been ghastly; mistaking my high colour for excitement, she clapped her hands together girlishly and said to me: 'I see you've heard the news John! Isn't it amazing! That strange little cripple has won the house and the pagoda. Who'd have thought it possible!'

I ushered her into the drawing room and, forgetting briefly about the mantle, listened to the first intimation of Vogel's news. As I pondered the report my sister delivered a panegyric to the beauty of the silk, and my exquisite taste, whilst fastening a scarf and prettifying herself in a mirror. Then she disappeared, wraithlike, into the white cloud of dust raised by the fleeing taxi.

Miffed that she had barely thanked me for my present, I delivered some highly sarcastic remarks to the mirror which she had used to make herself as alluring as humanly possible to a god who could have chosen from countless generations of stunningly beautiful and searingly intelligent women but was content, apparently, to waste away forlornly for the best part of two thousand years in a completely unremarkable little church waiting for Angelica. My poor sister had fallen in love with the muscular Adonis draped romantically over a cross above her misty young eyes. Unbeknownst to her this Christ-figure had spent a night in the Blue Angel after Edwin, the town carpenter, en route from his workshop to the church after repairing a split in the cross, caused by excessive heat, had himself fallen victim to excessive heat, stopped for a refreshing drink at the Blue Angel, fallen into a paralytic state of inebriation, and left Christ to sleep off the effects in one of the window seats. The following morning one of the labourers on his way to work had espied Christ, who had kept a lone vigil throughout the night in the Blue Angel, and notified the authorities, as small-minded bigots do. Edwin was incarcerated and there was talk of a trial for blasphemy, but it all blew over; Christ was reinstated soberly in the church and was thereafter called the Blue Christ. Some believe, quite wrongly, that the Blue Angel got its name from this incident.

Edwin became the butt of many jokes but was too nice a man to be punished in this life.

By now I was intrigued by the news that poor, twisted Mr Vogel had won a crackpot competition dreamt up by a strange old man, and was so overcome with curiosity that I summoned our old nursemaid, Agnes, and questioned her about Angelica's announcement. Yes, Agnes confirmed, Mr Vogel had indeed won the competition and the result had been announced from the steps of the town hall that very morning.

A full ceremony, with all due pomp and ceremony, would follow shortly.

Stop! You can halt right there, Mr Parker. You're a windbag, a gasbag. You talk more drivel than Humboldt. At least Humboldt's interesting. Yesterday he came out with a new word – *zogno*. After many hours of delving in dictionaries I found the meaning: in the Boro language of India it's the slurping sound made by mud and water when you put your hand in a crab's hidey-hole and try to drag it out. It's also the sound made by Mr John 'Nosey' Parker when he's trying to be posh. With his blue eyes and his floppy, flaxen hair he looks (speaking frankly) like a sissy. Locals call him The Professor. He likes to write about gardens and churches. He's a different sort to us, but you have to concede, he knows his stuff – he seems to know more than anyone else about the region and its history, and although he can be extremely irritating, with his gentlemanly manners and his pernickety way with words, he's the first one up the mountains in a storm, when the rest of us are running for shelter. Respect where respect is due, I say. We must endure a little more of his elegant writing, so please take a deep breath and prepare yourself for another purple passage, another dose of his yackety-yak:

What Angelica didn't know, when she gabbled the news to me so triumphantly, was that I knew quite a lot about old Dr Robert and his pagoda. As has been mentioned elsewhere he guarded his privacy jealously, and few people were allowed to visit him. We sometimes saw him driving around the town in a large car with two huge dogs bouncing about in the back seat, barking at everyone they passed. Tradesmen were met at the front gate by a manservant, called the Factotum, himself aged and stooped, who took the deliveries indoors. There was a handful of friends but they were equally reclusive and removed from the town's business, which gave them an air of mystery, heightened by the fact that they all dressed in black and still wore hats. Uncle Hugh always said that social disintegration started when hats went out of fashion.

As I say, I knew more about the pagoda than Angelica dreamt, for the very simple reason that I, also, have been young, and once played with the other children in the parks and thoroughfares of our noble town.

On one public holiday our childish menagerie, wandering aimlessly, as usual, from pleasure to pleasure, found itself in the street outside the old man's home, a gentleman's residence built of light red brick with yellow teething around the windows and doors. Architectural historians may like to know that both these types of brick were fired by Dalton & Sons at their plant on the Morda Road, and are notable for having the relief of a spread-eagled frog stamped within the frog, presumably one of Dalton senior's little jokes – he was noted for his dry sense of humour.

With a child's nose for mischief Jack, the leader of our gang by merit of his strength and daringness, challenged us all to enter the old man's hitherto 'secret' garden through a small chink of light we had discerned in the encircling privet hedge, which had appeared unbreachable until that day. We had created our own mythology about the old man's garden, since the only part of the pagoda which was visible to passers-by, the red and black japanned roof and the last few tiers, high above the garden and topping a group of sombre weeping willows, gave the place a foreign, mystical quality.

We pushed our way into the garden. I would say it was an hour before dusk and the Factotum was already pulling down the blinds in Doctor Robert's mansion, so we had only a few minutes in the gloaming to glimpse the garden. We scurried along its borders like ghosts. Part of it had been laid out in a formal, Louis XIV style with low geometric hedges and borders, fanning around a white marble fountain modelled on Poussin's 'A Dance to the Music of Time', figuring four women dancing in a back-to-back ronde and with clear, cool water bubbling from their mouths. There was also a walled garden with sweet potatoes, strawberries, scented herbs and a long espalier of fruit trees. There was an orangery, a palm house, a camomile lawn and a wooded walk through a Gertrude Jekyll garden containing many wild flowers, and also a large glasshouse, with a hipped imperial roof, housing rare and exotic plants, some hundreds of years old, lying like drowsy hospital patients cat-napping after lunch on a warm summer's afternoon. We tried the door but it was locked; instead we peered, through the condensation, at the hothouse interior, gloomy and as damply recessive as an Amazonian jungle.

There was far too much for us to take in but we were all struck by the remarkable octagonal pagoda, standing high in the air, which we could now see in its full glory. We dared not climb up its steps lest we be seen, so we contented ourselves with a brief, animated inspection. I scurried to the back of the edifice and trumped the others by finding a plaque at head-height on the rear wall of the pagoda, which said, simply:

ESMIE FALKIRK. REST IN PEACE.

At this point a door to the side of the main house creaked open and the silhouette of the old man entered our twilight world. Hiding our faces, we ran to our bolt-hole. I doubt if he saw us as human forms; he certainly did not challenge or chastise us. Perhaps he thought we were archangels gathering at that fateful moment when he would be reunited with the mysterious Esmie. I was too young by thirty years to appreciate truly his achievement in creating that garden of dreams and remembrance; it had taken him years of reverie, countless thought-maps, doodles on scraps of paper, visits to specialist book shops and trips abroad to collect his chosen flora; now, still tended like the grave of a beloved child, it gleamed with memories in the faintly rising moonlight.

Enough of your jabbering, Mr Parker! It's like listening to a bee in a bottle.

Parker's picaresque version confirms common knowledge about the old man's residence; we at the Blue Angel already knew about the plaque bearing Esmie's name, since Edwin the carpenter had put it there and divulged its existence to us during his drunken night with Christ. Speculation spread, like unseen filaments of mycelium, that Esmie was the old man's wife and that she had died in childbirth. Rumour had it that the old man stood every night in the pagoda viewing his fine plants, conveyed to him from the furthest outposts of Peru and Indonesia; the rare Alpines in their spartan quarters, and the lush orchids in the sweltering glasshouse.

'Like a bird sheltering in a tree, Doctor Robert viewed all this every dusk and sent off a cry of pain into the night,' Parker rhapsodised. 'He smelt the sadness of fronds and drooping blooms wafting on the breeze; viewed his terrible loneliness; looked downwards, from his vantage point, on the living mausoleum he had created in remembrance of Esmie and his child.'

That was the myth. The truth was even more romantic.

We discovered the real story in an obituary in the *Daily Informer* in which flesh was put on the bones of our suppositions. Doctor Robert had been a great medico, as Edwin had gathered from their brief interchanges, and the newspaper confirmed that he had been a brilliant surgeon who had saved many thousands of lives. The last paragraph revealed, as is normal in the *Informer's* obituaries, his marital status. Here was a grand surprise: he had never married and had no heir. This threw us all into turmoil. Who, then, was Esmie? And who would inherit his estate? Rumours and counter-rumours swept through the town like insurgents and counter-insurgents fighting from house to house for a foothold on the truth.

In reality, nobody knew. It was a legal document, his last will and testament, made public a few weeks after his death, which explained the riddle.

Esmie had not been his wife – but she had been the only love of his life.

The old man's solicitor had issued a terse statement on the instructions of the deceased, who had insisted on erasing all legal jargon and had worded the text himself. It read:

> Following the death of Miss Esmie Falkirk, to whom I was betrothed, whilst serving during the First World War, I disperse my estate as follows –
>
> The presents intended for our wedding on March 1, 1916, delivered to our hands and now deposited in the attic of my abode, shall be given in their whole to the first couple to be married at St Bride's Church after the publication of this statement.
>
> Since I have no heir or living relative, I wish the remainder of my property, in its entirety, to be given as the prize in a competition which has already taken place. It remains only for my solicitor to name the winner.

Here the old man's solicitor looked at the small public deputation which had been allowed into his fusty office and re-arranged the documents on his desk. He loosened his collar and allowed the meeting a moment of dignity.

'Indeed,' he said. 'You may remember that some time ago a rather mysterious competition took place in this town. There were to be 366 competitors. Everyone in the town could enter by lodging their name, address and date of birth with a solicitor. The prize was not specified. The winner would be named in due course.'

I remembered the competition quite clearly, since I had entered it myself. I had wondered what the prize could be. It was rumoured to be substantial. There was a crazy scramble as all the residents of the town lodged their names and details with the solicitor, then double checked that all their children were also entered, and their servants (many of whom were allowed to enter only if they promised to share their win with their masters). One child was so determined to enter the names of her two pet mice that she refused food until her parents pretended to relent, but only humans were eligible.

I stood up at the meeting. 'But surely,' I said, 'the attorney named in that competition was none other that yourself.'

'Indeed,' said the solicitor dryly. 'I was just coming to that. As the attorney empowered to declare the winner of the competition I will do so now. First, I would like to state that the winner was the person whose birthday fell on the same date as the old man's death. As you know, that occurred on February 29th.

'There is only one condition: that the winner shall use part of the monies to keep the estate intact and in good order, and that the pagoda must never, under any circumstances, be demolished.'

The meeting fell quiet. The solicitor held up an official, printed statement.

'This will be pinned to the door of the town hall as soon as this meeting is over,' he said. 'It announces the name of the winner.'

We craned forwards. And then came a collective groan.

THE RECORDS

THERE WAS a new mood in the Blue Angel today, jaunty and light. People are happy and excited: the great drama of spring is about to begin.

Flocks of sheep are being steered up the slopes, towards the upland pastures, like fallen clouds moving silently over the landscape. The mountain walls are newly-hatched millipedes, drying in the sun. Spring is unfurling: there is new hope in the air. That old horse chestnut in the churchyard is feathering: it's a colossal, newly-fledged chick, swaying drunkenly as it tries to stay upright. It's the first tree into leaf every year. Old eyes scan its branches keenly every day as though watching a magician; when it swirls its emerald cape the rooks shout a great *da-ra!* in the sky. And then our humours are restored, for it seems possible that we have survived another dunking in winter's cold bath of mortality.

The sun's course is changing subtly day by day. All winter it has stayed close to the silhouette of the southern hills, like a novice swimmer clinging nervously to the edge of a big swimming pool, afraid to move towards the centre. But its confidence grows daily as it floats towards its summer zenith. For me, fettered to my bar at the Blue Angel, with the universe whirring and gliding around me inexplicably, confirmation of Spring comes suddenly, when the sun changes course just enough to appear over the rim of the hills before noon: and when it comes I give thanks, I rejoice as it pours hot butter on the chimney pots above my head. This happens on the first day of March every year, if the sky is clear, and I light a celebratory fire using aromatic wood which gives off white smoke; people collect in snowdrop clumps outside my windows and point to the chimney, and they joke about it, saying that either a new pope has been elected or the old barman at the Blue Angel is sending smoke signals to Apollo again. I gashed a finger on a shard of broken glass whilst clearing up this morning. My blood spread slowly through the washing-up water, and I was reminded of nature's forces at work under the surface of the earth.

Mr John 'Nosy' Parker, as I have already told you, was reasonably accurate, though vain. He cared a little too much for embellishment, but he did try to stick to the facts.

At the Blue Angel we are given many 'facts'. We must then winnow the wheat from the chaff, but how am I, in my stifled and airless bar, to divide the wheat from the chaff, and furthermore, does not the chaff remain beautiful after the winnowing, whilst the wheat, pounded and baked, chewed and digested, becomes a revolting mess?

If Parker is fluted and scrolled in a sickly pastiche, the testimony of the boy Luther suffers from the opposite complaint. Can nothing be straightforward? Must we scrabble for the truth always? Luther is sparse. No-one will get fat at Luther's lexical table. I give you an example – and what better example than this:

My name is Luther Williams. I am twelve. I have always got a cold and sores. My bones are funny the doctor said. I have been to the school but I don't go there any more. My father is dead. My mother is Mary and I have a sister and brother. They are younger than me. We live on the Paternoster Hill next door to Mr Vogel. This is how I know him. He asked me to write this story in case he died, for people to remember our journey round the island, which we started in his invalid carriage, it was green with three wheels. I sat by him on an egg box and I could see the road through a hole. He asked my mother for me to go with him because he could not walk well and he wanted me to do errands on the journey and do things for him.

I know his name is not really Mr Vogel. This is how he got his name, he told me in the carij [carriage] one day. He got very lonely and he read in a newspaper that bad boys like me ring up people with funny names in the telephone book to upset them and say rude things, they like to call somebody with a silly name. So he said his name was Vogel so he could get calls from naughty children.

We were all intrigued to discover how Vogel got his peculiar name. And Luther sheds light on another matter. Most of us believed, wrongly, that he started his journey in the camper van which he bought with Doctor Robert's money, but after reading Luther's account I now remember seeing him drive that old invalid carriage down the hill every Saturday morning with Luther crammed by his side, peeking out of the side-window like a little owl. Must have been a strange view for the boy. Vogel had poor health, as do many cripples because of their lack of proper exercise – and he had a form of dermatitis characterised by blotched, waxy skin and terrible dandruff. He also exuded that slightly musky, goosy smell of immobile people. So this was Luther's weekend world – a vista of dandruff on a worn black jacket with its frayed collar; a balding, oily crown, and a vibrating road as Vogel's jalopy clanged along. It was as old as the hills and spluttered dreadfully, spitting gobs of oily smoke when he started it.

Humboldt surprised us with two new words today: apparently *khonsay* means to pick up an object with great care, knowing it to be rare or scarce, and *onsra* is to love for the last time. Don Quixote also surprised us with a pearl of wisdom. The Don is watchful and 'deep' – which is why he knows every morsel of the town's gossip; he is the only man I've met who can listen to three conversations at the same time and glean every scrap of information. Mostly he keeps his own company in a quiet corner of the bar, observing his pint of mild as if it were a work of art, though he has a soft spot for Mr Vogel and chats to him whenever he's in. The Don worked in the quarry for a few years in his early manhood but a combination of events halted his walks up the inclines to the wind-gutted huts high above the town.

The long hard winter of '47 had been gruelling. There had been no forewarning in January, normally the Doberman of months, as the men cut out granite cobs with hands so cold that they were devoid of feeling – numbed so completely that chisel wounds went unnoticed until thick red blood started to ooze from the cuts during the half hour allowed for dinner in a shed warmed by a cast iron pot-bellied stove. Then, in early February, there was a gale of immense ferocity. A ship was driven up on the shore and its foreign crew could be seen in a row like penguins on the stern, looking at their uncharted destination in silent disbelief.

For weeks it snowed or drifted; every day the quarrymen toiled up the inclines, only to be turned back after an hour, payless. The shopkeepers gave tick for a while, but then had to shrug apologetically; all relinquishable chattels were sold or pawned, and the men spent their afternoons combing the fields and woods for firewood and food, forced by now to gnaw turnips in the snow-hardened fields. Then came the worst blow of all. In late February Don Quixote's younger brother was killed by a hawser which snapped on the first full day of work after the thaw.

It was his birthday.

Don Quixote turned his back on the scene and descended down the inclines, never to walk on them again. He said so little afterwards that most of the townspeople think he's mute: this impression is erroneous, because if you stir him Don Quixote can talk passionately on any number of subjects. Nowadays he makes a living of sorts by gardening and bits and bobs of building work. But by night he reads voraciously, so that he has accumulated a huge store of knowledge. He is as hairy as a baboon and keeps a huge unruly dog. Between them they could fill a large sack with the hair they discard every day.

After work he calls in for a pint, silent and contemplative in the grey-blue haze of cigarette smoke, unastonished in his little sanctuary, chipping-in only occasionally. Sometimes Sancho Panza comes in with him, and he too studies his pint as if it were the Venus de Milo.

Earlier I mentioned The Don's pearls of wisdom – for he is a great observer, and drinks in more than best mild.

'Lonely,' he said one evening as we discussed the saga. 'That makes sense all right. Mr Vogel is lonely for sure.'

All eyes rested steadily on The Don. Everyone knew he was about to deliver.

Gazing into the depths of his pint, he continued slowly: 'Tell you something you all saw but probably never noticed.' Here he drew on his roll-up and thumbed the air behind him, in the direction of Paternoster Hill. 'Old Vogel, he leaves his car lights on when he goes in for the night. Sometimes he even comes out at dusk to put them on.'

Silence, then a murmur rippled along the bar. Come to think of it, one or two had noticed something in that general direction.

'Leaves them on, he does,' continued The Don meditatively, 'so people will knock on his door and tell him he needs to turn them off. Then he moiders them. That's the way I got to know him, actually. Stopped the van, went and told him. Next think I was in the kitchen having a brew with him.'

The Don winked slowly when he said 'brew'. It was well known that Mr Vogel went down early every morning to do his shopping, and that this invariably included a bottle of cheap blended whisky. Mr Vogel built up a small coterie of callers who brought their own supplies. This is corroborated by the boy Luther:

Some days we would phone Mr Vogel. Then we would hide by the window waiting for something to happen. We thought we would get into trouble like the police calling but nothing happened though we waited for a long time. Some nights Mr Vogel was stupid and left his lights on and we went and told him and he asked us in and gave us sweets. Sometimes men would call at his house on the way home from the pub with bags and bottles in them.

There is further evidence of Mr Vogel's rather endearing little ploy to get attention. Edwin the carpenter told us an anecdote about old Vogel.

'Make that the last one, Edwin,' I whispered in his ear late during the evening. I didn't want to embarrass him – though he didn't come in often, he was a great fellow, never had a bad word for anyone and he was full of silly jokes. He was over fifty but he smoked the weed, which made him a star man among the younger crew. He wasn't particularly big, but no-one would lay a finger on Edwin because he was untouchable – there are certain people who are never harmed. God knows what signal they emit, but it works. Tonight he was squiffy and getting boisterous, so I had a quiet word with him.

'Drunk?' he said to the whole bar, his arms wide open in appeal, cigar in one hand, slopping pint in the other. 'Think I'm sloshed, you lot?' They looked at him indulgently. 'Christ, you should see drunk,' he said to me through his blurred blue eyes, 'you should have seen old Vogel last night.' Here Edwin parked himself on a high chair and shook his head, chuckling to himself. 'I'll say he was drunk.'

Edwin had been sitting in his van on the hill, waiting for his mother-in-law to come out of her home. He took her shopping every Friday night.

'He came out with only one stick and he looked bloody ridiculous because he'd already changed into his 'jamas with that dirty green cardigan hanging on him like a scarecrow and those stupid tartan slippers with eyes like teddy bears.'

Edwin regaled them with the story of poor old Mr Vogel swaying from his front door to the invalid carriage. 'Don't know how he managed to get there in that state, but he bloody well did,' said Edwin. 'Saw him fiddling about inside that rust bucket of his, then he set off for the house again, but he lost his footing suddenly and went flying. Poor sod was spread-eagled in the road like a dying fly, with his arms and legs wriggling about like he was having a fit.'

Edwin mimicked a convulsion, spilt his drink on his trousers, swore, then continued:

'The woman next door, that idiot Luther's mother, came out and tried to help him, then Luther ran into the house to get his other stick, but he fell again before they got him to the pavement. Eventually they had to pin him up against the wall. Never seen anything so funny in my life. Vogel must have hurt himself because he had a hell of a job getting back up those steps. The mother-in-law watched it all with me and nearly died laughing. "Serves him right," she said. "Won't get any pity from me. Leaves those lights on to get sympathy. Fell for it myself once. Offered me a cup of tea but the place is filthy. Took him a lifetime to make it then the mug was black and smelt of whisky. Poured it into a plant." '

The boy Luther reveals somewhere in his version that he and the other children in their hovel on Paternoster Hill had stopped making their nuisance calls when their mother caught them.

She hadn't caught them outright. They usually made the calls on Sunday evenings after their communal bath, when she was cleaning the bathroom. One night when she came down she noticed water on the telephone table and became suspicious, wanting to know who they'd phoned. They never told her, but they didn't do it again.

Nothing much going for that poor woman. Husband dies and she has to drag up three children on her own. No wonder she was glad to see the boy off her hands every Saturday. At first she questioned him about his jaunts, but she gave up once she'd established there was nothing untoward going on, and knew that Luther was usefully occupied. The pound which Mr Vogel paid her was useful too. The priest had asked her why her son accompanied Vogel to the island.

'I don't know the full story,' she'd answered. Her only real interest was to know that Luther was safe, and she didn't take much notice after that. 'All he told me was that Mr Vogel wanted to find out something,' she said to the priest. 'It's to do with a cure for his condition, though God knows, we all think it's a wild goose chase, since his poor little legs have been bent like bows since he was born, and his arms are pretty useless too.'

She added, lamely: 'Old Vogel can't do the legwork himself, pardon the expression, so he wants Luther to be his fetch-and-carry boy, knocking on doors to ask questions, nipping into pubs for directions. One day he spent quite a lot of time in a graveyard looking at headstones because Mr Vogel wanted to find someone, but don't ask me who, Luther might be able to help you.'

I often caught a glimpse of Luther's mother standing in her window as I looked up from the Blue Angel. Always she was gazing out to the island, as if trying to catch a glimpse of the little invalid carriage with its two strange occupants on its rickety journey around the shoreline, phut-phutting up and down the little lanes which were used so seldom that they all had a ribbon of grass, strewn with daisies and buttercups, along the centre of the road. Luther could see the flowers flash by him through a hole in the floor of the carriage between his feet, and he could smell a mixture of hot oil and wafts of countryside smells – blossom, moist earthiness, mossy verdure and freshly-made cowpats. Or perhaps, as she looked out to sea, she wasn't thinking of the island at all, perhaps a land much further away, full of biblical milk and honey, for she had heard the Word soon after her husband's death. Her face was pasty, disfigured by margarine, crusts and lovelessness (for widowed women with three children live, often, in a garrison town, cut off from emotional supplies, preyed upon by scalping males, and consigned to long hours of waiting for deliverance).

Yesterday I came across a passage in one of my bar-room books which made me think of Mr Vogel on his strange quest around the island. It described the Russian dramatist Chekhov, dying from tuberculosis, travelling through Siberia to the prison colony of Sakhalin in a vehicle 'resembling a little wicker basket' pulled by a pair of horses.

'You sit in the basket, and look out upon God's earth like a bird in a cage, without a thought on your mind,' said Chekhov.

Travelling when you're unwell is a miserable experience, I'm told. But Chekhov still held his head up, looking around as road signs flashed by, ponds, little birch groves. He passed a group of new settlers, a file of prisoners, and tramps with pots on their backs. 'These gentlemen promenade all over the Siberian plain without hindrance. On occasion they will murder a poor old woman to obtain her skirt for leg puttees,' said Chekhov. 'Another time they will bash in the head of a passing beggar or knock out the eyes of one of their own banished brotherhood, but they won't touch people in vehicles. On the whole, as far as robbery is concerned, travelling hereabouts is absolutely safe.'

These stories fascinate me: although we have sturdy beggars hereabouts, we have no trouble from them. Courage and freedom – that's all I need to prowl the steppes among Chekhov's tramps. Perhaps you see something sad in my make-believe travel, but I say: look into your own heart to reveal your own wishes.

To end this episode, I return you to Mr Nosy Parker, and another of his purple passages:

Angelica came home from church in a state of near-collapse, such was her excitement.

I continued to sit stiffly by the window, still rather cross with her.

'My dear brother, she cried breathlessly, 'what do you think has happened?'

I surmised, wrongly, that one of the lizards who follow her every move in church had approached her mother with a view to marriage.

'My dear sister, what could possibly have happened,' I replied sarcastically.

Ignoring my levity, she replied: 'The cripple Vogel has sprung another surprise on us all. Not only has he won a fortune, he has also decreed a public holiday. There will be a great party and all the children will go on a wonderful holiday to the capital city!'

In the lull which followed, as she rearranged her hair in the mirror, I leant heavily on my writing desk, worn out by the day's denouements, and feeling not a little left out of it all.

How could there be so much excitement in one day, she trilled. To compound my irritation she ignored, completely, my star-spangled present, now spread gracefully on the table between us.

'To hell with Vogel,' I cried. 'He is a pigmy who has hoisted himself on a giant's shoulders and shines a mirror in our eyes to dazzle us.'

This finally silenced her, since she was dazzled by my own brilliance. With that I adjourned to my room, put on a fresh and cooling shirt, and walked into the countryside so that I might gather my thoughts. With me I took a stout stick and a book, Stevenson's *Travels with a Donkey*.

THE TESTIMONY

THE PICTURE is already confused. A swirling mist of gossip and misinterpretation has swept down Mr Vogel's mountainside and obscured the vale of his simple but tormented life.

How am I supposed to drag any drowning truth to safety from the great swamp of falsities created by the fabulists who seem to abound in this town? I am a simple bar-tender, heir to a mono-syllabic sailor who was down to his last eye when he came ashore (I concede that this was an extremely expressive eye, capable of oculogyric fireworks and withering glares). The socket in his left eye was filled by a green marble picked off the pavement as he passed a crouching huddle of children at play (they cried 'Oi Mister' and flapped around him when he stole their queenie, then bent back to their play, muttering. He was never forgiven in child lore and most of them never drank in his pub when they grew furtive enough to sidle into bars to buy liquor). The greeny-brown of the whorled marble contrasted sharply with the piercing blue of his overworked right eye, which glared and stared in double measure to make up for the other's shortcomings.

We found, eventually, that his heart had been broken by a native Tasmanian girl who had given him an Emu songline and a squirming fly-bed of a child, born with a scar across his left eye, portending his father's deformity by a matter of months.

Gale-savaged off the Cape of Good Hope (so named, of course, because terrified sailors had little hope of rounding it), the Blue Angel's first owner had lost his left eye in a dispute over latitude and longitude, when another drunken sailor had clubbed him over the head with a stone paperweight used to press charts onto the table-top. When he returned to Tasmania, his head still bandaged, the girl had disappeared into the brown bowels of the shanty town and all that was left of his swarthy son was a phantom memory fading fast from the retina of his remaining eye. I once met a blind woman who had lost her sight only five years previously, but who was already unable to remember the appearance of clouds. I wonder if the sailor's eye was removed by the gods, so that he should remember less of his pain.

As I have said, tracing Mr Vogel's story is like being a lost potholer following a cord back to the surface, along a maze of dark and dangerous caverns, many flooded, and through tunnels as dangerous as boa constrictors. But let us examine the evidence. Fortunately, I have many reference books and by a process of deduction I can usually glean the likeliest story. My countrymen have a great liking for the Chronicle of the Hours, which I have mentioned already. This serves two purposes: it chronicles the past year's main happenings (such as fish falling to earth and demons stalking the land), and it also catalogues major events in the year to come: it gives full lists of impending festivals, galas, hiring fairs and markets, as well as making divinations regarding the region's prospects, foretelling the likelihood of earthquakes and hurricanes, predicting good fortune and bad, the movement of the moon and stars, the most judicious times to plant crops and treat livestock, advice on good husbandry and health; in short it provides us with guidance on a host of interesting subjects. Mr Vogel crops up regularly in the Chronicle.

Since I have many empty hours to fill I have read a great deal about our region's history. As I have already told you, I am particularly interested in the accounts of travellers, since I myself arrived here a traveller, having left my home village far up the river many years ago to seek my fortune and to see the world. Up in the hinterland they still speak the old language, my mother tongue, and when I arrived here I had to learn the language of the incomers (Humboldt is retreating into silence – he's not sure which of my languages to adopt). Although I was considered to be intelligent and learned among my own people, I was given the same accord as a diseased idiot when I limped into this town, being unable to converse with the conquerors, who had power over all occupations and dwellings. Doing menial work in the Blue Angel – lighting the fire, cleaning, collecting and washing glasses, I learnt their language and might have progressed to one of the professions, but discovered that there was no great welcome for me among the rulers, who prefer to elevate their own type. And so I pass my days working, watching, listening and reading. Mr Vogel's story struck a particular chord with me because my own father was twisted out of shape by a disease brought to the region by the first missionaries, who were so anxious for us to embrace their god that they arranged for us to die quickly in great numbers so that we might meet him (it being a condition of this great honour that we perish miserably and lose everything we loved.)

Many of my kinsmen welcomed the incursors, who were much delighted with what they found.

Here is how Geoffrey of Monmouth described our region in the 12th century:

It provides in unfailing plenty everything that is suited to the use of human beings. It abounds in every kind of mineral. It has broad fields and hillsides which are suitable for the most intensive farming and in which, because of the richness of the soil, all kinds of crops are grown in their season. It also has open woodlands which are filled with every kind of game. Through its forest glades stretch pasture-lands which provide the various feeding-stuffs needed by cattle, and there too grow flowers of every hue which offer their honey to the flitting bees. At the foot of its windswept mountains it has meadows green with grass, beauty spots where clear springs flow into shining streams which ripple gently and murmur an assurance of deep sleep to those lying on their banks.

Wales Landscape

Our mountains are sublime and our rivers fluent, our air is limpid and our horizons are inspiring and august. But we are not so complacent as to think it the most beautiful land on earth, for it is the habit among many of us to have our dust divided into a hundred portions upon death and sent to all parts of the spinning globe, so that our souls can choose to remain elsewhere or to return home.

But to return to Mr Vogel.

The earliest reference to our hero, I believe, is in the *Travels* of Thomas Pennant, but it becomes starkly clear in his book that his knowledge of Mr Vogel was gained at second hand, and I know exactly why. How clearly this event displays the unreliable ways in which historians get their material, and how prone they are to error! For Mr Pennant, illustrious and interesting though he may have been, never clapped eyes on Vogel – instead he lapped up a story imparted to him by his manservant Moses, who had climbed up to Mr Pennant's chamber in the Blue Angel, heavy with porter, just before bedtime, in the light of a guttering candle, to tell him an entertaining tale about a cripple who was the talk of the entire country. This story he had gleaned from no less a person than myself! So no-one knows better the warp and weft in Mr

Pennant's story before the finished garment left the loom!

I remember that evening as if it were tonight – travellers of Mr Pennant's reputation do not lodge with us often, but since he needed quarters for his horse as well as his servant, and it being deep into dusk, he settled on the Blue Angel – after all, I heard him mutter, it was only for one night (he had the temerity to describe it, fleetingly, in his book as 'a coarse lodging').

I quickly fulfilled my role as the inn's ostler (for this task my childhood among the wild horses of the upland mountains stood me in good stead), and upon re-entering the Blue Angel I offered the grumbling Pennant, who had already downed a quart of ale, our list of victuals.

'Pah,' he said, swiping aside my carte du jour (and carte du month, for that matter). Exhibiting all the prowess of a seasoned traveller he waded past me, straight into the kitchen, past the cook and into the larder, where he examined every shank, chop and fish, before proclaiming loudly that he wouldn't give the mutton to a dying dog. He finally settled (wisely) on the beef pie and he also attempted the pickled puffin (experimentally, and such was his mistrust that he forced me to eat a portion first).

According to the *Travels*, Thomas Pennant entered this area as winter was setting in. He passed through mountainous country and descended through a boulder-strewn gorge which was so steep and hazardous he was forced to dismount and lead his horse through gorse and sessile oaks until he beheld, from the upland reaches, a widening vale gliding down to the meeting of two great valleys, and where they met two rivers conjoined in a glittering blue cascade.

On reaching this confluence late in the evening he faced seawards and followed the river to the teeming port on the environs of our town. With his eye for the anecdotal, and his serendipitous habit of stumbling on the irregular, he encountered in mid-afternoon a remarkable woman well known to us, her abode being a simple shack by the river hard by the port. I quote from his *Travels*:

> Near this end of the port lives a celebrated personage, Margaret the daughter of Evans, the last specimen of the strength and spirit of the ancient people of this region. She is at this time about 90 years of age. This extraordinary female was the greatest hunter, shooter and fisher of her time. She kept a dozen at least of dogs, terriers, greyhounds and

spaniels, all excellent in their kinds. She killed more foxes in one year than all the confederate hunts do in ten, rowed stoutly and was queen of the river, fiddled excellently and knew all our old music, did not neglect the mechanical arts for she was a very good joiner, and at the age of 70 was the best wrestler in the country, few young men dared to try a fall with her. Some years ago she had a maid of congenial qualities but death, that mighty hunter, at last earthed this faithful companion. Margaret was also a blacksmith, shoemaker, boat-builder and maker of harps. She shoed her own horses, made her own shoes and was under contract to convey the copper ore down the mountainside. All the neighbouring poets paid their addresses to Margaret and celebrated her exploits in pure verse. At length, she gave her hand to the most effeminate of her admirers as if predetermined to maintain the superiority which nature had bestowed on her.

I knew Margaret well, since I visited her to stay supple in my mother tongue, which has fallen into disuse in the town; certainly, I hear it very rarely now in the Blue Angel, which saddens me greatly, for my heart leaps when I hear it spoken and I hurry to greet the communicant. It is, I believe, the oldest language in this corner of the globe and is antique, which has caused its demise since all the new words to do with commerce, appropriation of land, legal contentions, disease and warfare have been coined by the invaders. Margaret and I delighted in pursing neglected words in dusty etymological dictionaries (she had made a pile of these in the form of a small throne and often sat on it!) and during the course of many a quiet afternoon she found no less than 39 words describing rain (including that soft grey curtain which heralds the autumn), and I found 21 cognate words for wind (you might like to know that the word hurricane comes from Hurakan, who is the God of the Storm). The grammar of our language is so precise that every sentence is unique and can never be said again. Our language also has mystical qualities, and when our ancestors learnt English for the first time they couldn't believe it was so simple – they spent many years trying to detect a secret, encoded English, a hidden version of the language which had a special, sacred force like our own, but of course there was no such thing! There are other differences: in our country it is taboo to mention anyone's name for a year after his or her death, and long ago it was possible for anyone uttering a forbidden word to be put to death; fortunately, this practice has fallen into disuse.

The history of our region and its flora and fauna were also common topics for Margaret and myself, though I feared her leviathan strength, having seen her lift an anvil high above her head to dispatch one of her ailing terriers.

There is an entry in Pennant's *Lost Diaries* detailing his night in the Blue Angel:

After pausing awhile to cut words with Margaret the daughter of Evans we rode through a dockland street which I perceived exceeding unruly and we passed on towards the town; failing to find a pleasing inn we put in at a coarse lodging yclept the Blue Angel, where we were met in an excitable manner by a native servant, who being of the worst sort of jobbing scholar, viz self-taught, wanted to know all our news and pestered us like a bee around good honey for intelligence of all degrees.

Dined upon pickled puffin, a delicacy in these parts, though tasted tough and vile as the sole of an old boot dug up from a midden. Much talk hereabouts of one Vogel, a spavined cripple who has had great fortune. It seems a doge in the town died without issue and, not knowing how to disperse his wealth, struck upon an uncommon and intriguing diversion. He decreed in his last days that the townspeople should be inveigled to lodge their names with a man of law, together with letters of credence shewing their suitability, namely their residence in the town since birth. All his fortune, his residence – including his gardens and a strange appurtenance, namely a temple building from the orient – together with a tract on an island offshore, would go to the resident whose birth date fell on the same day as his own extinction. The aforementioned Vogel, who was unable to attest in law his name or residency, was apportioned the date February 29th, for no-one could lay claim to a birth date on that day, and since he claimed that date, and feeling sorry for him, the townspeople agreed that he should have it by way of charitie. I need not describe to you the scenes of consternation and upheaval, necessitating the arming of the local militia, when the sage died on that very date, it being a leap year, and all his worldly wealth passed to Vogel, but not before a riotous assembly which was dispelled by a volley of muskets, and a hearing in chambers, after which Vogel's good fortune was declared legitimate and standing. Having gained this wealth Vogel, it seems, has embarked on a curious investigation, nothing of which is known presently save that he seeks ancestors or sources upon the island, for what reason God in his wisdom will inform in due course. He is rigging out his expedition as though he were Columbus setting off for the new world, having procured a conveyance, and is presently mustering a crew, who all have the singular mark of being debilitated in one way or another, viz deaf, or blind, or mute, or foolish. The town foments daily with rife tales about his next move, and whither he goes, and how his monies will be dispatched. Left the inn early, at daybreak, having been kept awake by unseemly mirth caused by my man Moses; reprehended him, saying I could easily find another to do the sketches for my volume. Chastened, he saddled our horses with the native servant, who gave him letters to be delivered on our journey to the hinterland, and we hastened away, with extra passengers, acquired during the night and now sucking up our blood and hopping about our limbs, viz a plague of fleas.

This extract from Pennant's journey was printed in full in this year's Chronicle, which I will revisit at regular intervals during the telling of this tale. Talking of fleas, I was intrigued to discover, only yesterday, during an afternoon lull in the bar, a reference to this ubiquitous creature in the writings of Madame Calderon de la Barca.

'We had been alarmed by the miraculous stories related to us of these vivacious animals, and were rejoiced to find ourselves in a house, from which, by dint of extreme care, they are banished,' she wrote. 'But in the inns and inferior houses they are said to be a perfect pestilence, sometimes literally walking away with a piece of matting upon the floor, and covering the walls in myriads. The nuns, it is said, are – or were – in the habit of harnessing them to little carriages, and of showing them off by other ingenious devices.'

Describing a journey in an overcrowded coach, she sat opposite a horrible bird-like female with immense red goggle-eyes, coal-black teeth, fingers like claws and a great goitre, who drank brandy at intervals. The mules could scarcely drag the loaded coach up the steep hills. They were thrown into ruts and jolted horribly. Forced to walk for a while, they reached the head of a dismal pass, where they encountered the head of a celebrated robber, Maldonado, nailed to the pine-tree below which he committed his last murder. 'It is now quite black, and grins there, a warning to his comrades and an encouragement to travellers,' she noted. 'The padre who was in the coach with us told us that he had heard his last confession. That grinning skull was once the head of a man, and an ugly one too, they say; but stranger still it is to think that this man was once a baby, and sat on his mother's knee, and that his mother may have been pleased to see him cut his first tooth. If she could but see his teeth now!'

Indeed, if his mother could but see him now; and what if Mr Vogel's mother could also see her beautiful baby now, twisted and sad, slowly drinking himself to extinction and dreaming, always dreaming of better things. But we must press on with our story...

THE GARDEN OF EDEN

WHEN I was a boy of twelve I became the owner of a buzzard –
if you can *own* a buzzard.

A family of visitors, unversed in country ways, had picked it up
and brought it to the farmstead where I was reared many years
ago, near the trickling source of the great river which flows
unswervingly through this town. I had seen it earlier in the day, on
the grass below its nest, and had left it there, as my father had
taught me, for it to have the best chance of survival. Since it had
been handled and removed from the vicinity of the nest its parents
would almost certainly reject it now, so I tried to rear it myself.

The brief life of this chick came to mind later in my own life
when I went back upstream, consumed with nostalgia for our
little white farmstead; I longed to walk through uncontaminated
fields, fragmented by the hedges into a lovely patchwork, like
church windows patterned with lead.

Once more, briefly, I felt comfortable among the crystal
streams where I had fished and played, and felt at ease within the
friendship of the language, customs and traditions. But like the
chick, once I had left the nest I too had the smell about me of
strangeness and difference, and just as the landscape had
changed indefinably, so had I.

After a while I became restless in my natal Garden of Eden,
as edgy as a young man visiting a formative but aged grandpar-
ent. I went back into exile, returning to the Blue Angel keenly
aware that I was now *déclassé*, and rejected organically by both
sides since I had consorted adulterously with both.

The chick died. I remember still the shock of sensing its death
as soon as my eyes saw, at some distance, its ragdoll proneness in
the bottom of the slatted wooden box which I had nailed
together, laboriously and clumsily. I was surprised chiefly
because the chick had shown every sign of living; it had thrived
on the strips of raw meat I had fed it, with bowls of bread and
milk, and had grown steadily from feeble baby pterodactyl to
preening and resplendent raptor-in-waiting. Years later I was told
that young birds of prey, bred in captivity, seldom survive this
phase of their development unless given essential ingredients

provided normally by their parents. So I had nurtured it as an executioner might feed a condemned prisoner, so that it would live long enough to walk to the gallows. Yesterday I entered one of the town's little churches to rest my feet after a walk through the back streets – I had been visiting some of my upriver friends who live in the town. The building was laden brimful with flowers for a festival. In the far distance I could hear Humboldt, very faintly, chattering to the customers in the Blue Angel. The heavy church door had been shut since early morning, and the sun streaming through the leaded windows (reminding me once again of the quilted landscape of my homeland) had warmed the normally cool interior. The air was suffused with the heavy perfume of the blooms, so strong as to inebriate the senses; the overpowering strength of the fragrance, almost sickly in its inten-sity, reminded me of the chick, which in the last stage of its life had exuded a cloying smell – cutaneous, oleaginous, musky, sickly-sweet.

Similar smells had come from Mr Vogel when he sat by the bar on the day of the celebration. Don Quixote had given me a meaningful look as Vogel wobbled in, propped his crutches against a wall and pivoted himself in the corner, where there was a stool for him. He was dressed in purple and black, as usual, but it was a newer shade of black, patchless and darned, since he had already started his forays into the area's second hand shops. It became a joke: surely he was writing a guide to charity shops; almost every day someone said 'Saw Vogel yesterday outside so-and-so,' or 'Bumped into old Vogel in South Street, so much stuff he could hardly walk.'

The Vogel smell was singular, and although pungent it was also endearing in a baby-smell way; it made him seem vulnerable. His scoliosis had pushed his head downwards – you saw his bald patch, which reminded me of an island marooned in a disinte-grating reef of red hair, coming at you before he levered his head upwards to talk to you, so that he was constantly looking at you from under his eyelids, as if he were saying: *Are You Sure?*

He had once been tallish, but his deformity had pushed him down, giving him a quizzical air; add to this his expressive green eyes, his haggard air, his peculiar accent, and you have a general picture of the man we call Vogel, a little bird at the end of the bar, moving his whole torso rather than his recalcitrant neck to talk to people and to sip his whisky (Vogel rarely drank beer, since this would force him to clatter endlessly to and from the toilet). It was impossible to get an impression of his body, since he purposefully bought clothes which were far too large for him – primarily because he wanted to hide his malformations, and also because he couldn't use the charity shop fitting rooms to try clothes on before buying them. He had tried once and had fallen backwards whilst putting on some trousers, tearing the curtain which hung over the doorway and presenting the two elderly women volunteers with the rare sight of Mr Vogel *sans-culotte*, as Mr Nosy Parker put it, referring to Vogel's leanings towards the political left (Parker could never resist a damp *double entendre*). What those two women saw of Vogel's maladroit legs they never recounted, making them the only discreet bodies in the whole town.

We were able, however, to discern from the general fold of his trousers that his legs bent inwards, sharply, from the knees down. His black clothes accentuated his appalling dandruff, which lay on his shoulders like a fall of early snow.

Mr Vogel had been declared the winner of the competition that morning in a formal announcement from the steps of the town hall, followed by a peal of bells from the mother church at noon. When this tintinnabulation had ceased, ships in the harbour sounded their whistles and foghorns, and drivers tooted their horns. Townspeople who had gathered in the square to hear the declaration cheered and clapped in a good-humoured way and then dispersed to the parks and pubs, the day having been declared a holiday. Mr Vogel had not yet taken possession of the old man's house and land, but he had been given a large interim payment, and his first gesture was to fund a number of street parties, a grand concert featuring all the town's rising musicians, and free food and drink – including beer and soft drinks, but no wines and spirits – in all the cafés, restaurants and pubs from six till eight o'clock. The town treated it as a massive party; the weather was warm and dry, and many people had exceeded capacity well before six, making Mr Vogel's bill far less than might have been expected. In addition he awarded prizes for art, composition, scientific invention and architectural design. The winning entries would be displayed in a new gallery, library and cultural hub to be known as the Vogel Centre. Mr Vogel wanted to be remembered, and he wanted to be liked, as do most of us (his own longings accentuated, perhaps, by his loneliness over the years). Calls of 'don't forget me in your will' and 'got a fiver till tomorrow?' greeted him when he sat in his corner, looking cleaner and shinier than usual. He asked me to put tables and chairs outside so that the boy Luther and other children could join his celebration, and he asked for crates of lemonade and boxes of crisps to be conveyed there continuously to replenish their feast. Each child was given a teddy bear or a doll. The sweet shop in the square had agreed to open its doors free of charge all day, Mr Vogel again footing the bill. No-one could accuse him of being mean or ungrateful, he said. We agreed. The boy Luther went to fetch Vogel's fiddle, and he gave us a few tunes on it; we had often heard him play *Abide With Me* as we passed his house, and he delighted us with his unexpected prowess.

Soon the party was in full swing, beer and banter flowing freely. Mr Vogel had invited many celebrated guests. I thought I saw the illustrious Mr Borrow, accompanied by a drover, a strange-looking man with a broad red face, incipient carbuncles and grey squinty eyes. This Mr Borrow, if it really was him, struck me as being exceedingly inquisitive, wanting to know everything about me and the inn, asking if there were gipsies about, and smattering his speech with so many words from foreign languages that I barely understood him. Amazingly, he could speak my own native tongue, and he told me he had learnt it from an ostler – as I am! – before he went abroad to translate the Bible into many tongues. At one point he seemed to have an animated conversation with Humboldt.

Another guest, a Mr Savage or Landor – I forget which – became inebriated and abusive, saying (cheeky rascal!) that my people were drunken, idle, mischievous and vengeful.

'I shall never cease to wish,' he slurred in my direction, 'that Julius Caesar had utterly exterminated the lot of you – I am convinced that you are as irreclaimable as gipsies.'

It was no surprise when a few of the men who couldn't handle their drink started playing up. Jack the landlord dealt with them in his customary fashion. Grasping a collar with one spade-like hand and their trousers with the other, he hurled them into the street with frightening strength. Many had suffered this indignity before, and although one or two shouted insults or shook a fist, none tried to re-enter. They knew it was useless, since Jack was famed for his quickfire temper and his strength, despite being very short of stature (he was not much bigger than a dwarf). Born on the edge of the biggest bog in our land, he was extremely clever with his hands, and a silversmith of great renown. Like myself, but quite a few years earlier, he had arrived in the town from the hinterland, dusty and wary, possessing nothing but his clothes, shoes, and his gargantuan strength.

Some said he had been a drover, others maintained he was a fugitive and had travelled here in search of a sanctuary. All agreed that when he arrived he was a firebrand and an agitator. He had quickly set up a society for those of us who speak the old tongue and we still meet regularly to discuss our history and to compete in the intricate metres of our archaic poetry. Jack had an uplands sort of humour, quite simple, mainly slapstick – for instance, when he climbed back up the stairs to the bar after changing a barrel he would bang the cellar door with his foot and enter clutching his head, as if he had walked into the lintel over the doorway – this was quite ridiculous, since he was less than five feet tall.

He spoke an old variant of our language, used in only one small valley and instantly recognisable by the guttural pronunciation of the *ch* consonant, used as a shibboleth in olden days among our shepherds and crofters to detect rustlers and vagabonds.

Jack had his own unique bartering system, and a whole day could pass without any money changing hands, depending on the nature of the task being performed for him in return for free beer. This puts me in mind of a story in one of my books about Alvise da Cadamosto, a Venetian who sailed with Henry the Navigator. When he was in Africa he met a tribe who dealt in salt – they carried huge blocks of it on their heads, to a river deep in the hinterland, and then carried out a most peculiar transaction.

Their first move was to leave the salt by the side of the river. Then they retired half a day's journey from the scene. Another tribe, who did not wish to be seen or to speak, arrived in boats and placed a large quantity of gold by each block of salt, then disappeared again. Whilst they were away the salt tribe returned, and if they were satisfied with the amount of gold left by each block of salt they took away the gold. Then the gold tribe returned and took away each block of salt which no longer had any gold by it. If they wanted to bargain further they placed more gold by the remaining blocks of salt. In this way, by long and ancient custom, they carried on their trade without seeing or speaking to each other.

In the same way a man such as Don Quixote, painting a window at the Blue Angel, would occasionally give up his task and flop silently by the bar, mopping his brow in an enfeebled way; if he had done enough work Jack would give him a pint; if not, Jack would turn his back on him and continue with his tasks.

The celebration was in full swing and I was slopping around in a squelch of spilt beer behind the bar of the Blue Angel, pulling pints as fast as I could, when I saw old Vogel and Don Quixote strike a deal. The barman's eyes are constantly on the move, keeping a register of customers and an approximation of who's next to be served – the average punter will allow you one or two mistakes in a session, but gets irritated if passed over repeatedly. So I saw them shake hands and return to their drinking, rather solemnly. Don Quixote had become animated when bar talk came round to football, and he became extremely excited when he discovered that Vogel was not only knowledgeable generally about football, but also knew a great deal about The Don's favourite player of all time, the great Brazilian winger Garrincha, who was as great as Pele himself, if we are to believe The Don.

Amazingly, Vogel knew even more about him than Don Quixote, down to his nine children, his alcoholism and his love affair with a popular singer. Vogel confided in me, when The Don had eased off to the toilet, that he'd taken a particular interest in Garrincha – known to his adoring Brazilian fans as the little bird – because he had deformed legs: his left peg was bent inwards and the right, which was six centimetres shorter, was bent outwards.

As X-rays had shown, he was a walking, running miracle, a glimmer of hope for all wobbly people. As for me, I know of Garrincha because of his drinking problem, which killed him in the end. We all have our special subjects.

During a lull in this drunken mêlée I grabbed a chance to stand awhile near Vogel and The Don to rest my own little legs, sturdy little pins which have served me well, though it has been pointed out to me by Vogel that I am slightly bow-legged from my horse-riding days. I had never noticed, but Vogel, having an eye for these things (we all innately look for birds of a feather) had espied my curvatures.

'Which family do you come from, then?' I heard Vogel ask The Don mock-innocently, pursuing the region's age-old hobby of tracing everyone's lineage. This comes partly from inbred habit, partly from a need to make sure you didn't get a clout by disparaging someone related to the person you're talking to.

The Don blew a smoke ring and left a long pause.

'You wouldn't know them.'

'Heard you were one of the L—— family,' countered Vogel, referring to a large clan living around one of the island coves, an isolated inlet hiding below a ruined castle which lurched above the ship-slicing rocks in that corner of the island. They wore a gold earring in the right ear because they believed, proudly, that they were descended from a band of smugglers. Personally, I believe they were no more than wreckers.

'Could be you're right,' said The Don, bending his head and feeling his earring.

'You got family living below the castle?' asked Vogel, like a dog who had happened on a buried bone and was unwilling to rebury it until he had gnawed every remaining scrap from it.

'Could be you're right,' said The Don again.

Vogel was alluding to an old story centred on the weather-bombed castle. Once, apparently, it was the home of a nobleman who led the happy-go-lucky life of a wealthy man – hunting, fishing, seducing his maids and getting so hopelessly drunk on market days that he had to be taken home by his servant. This servant was so strong willed that he had completely mastered his master, and laughed scornfully at any attempts to rein him in. The nobleman, who was also the local magistrate, disliked the heavy taxes imposed on the wines and spirits he so loved, so he turned a blind eye to the cove's smugglers, who repaid him by leaving crates of his favourite tipple by his door.

The high-handed behaviour of his servant troubled the nobleman and he hatched a plan to get rid of him, by paying the smugglers to kidnap him and carry him off to their next port of call, as far away as possible. His scheme worked perfectly and the servant awoke one morning with a sore head and a view of his homeland disappearing in the distance. But there's a twist to the tale. The servant's dogged and indomitable spirit didn't sink below the waves as the smugglers' vessel snailed its way along the sea's highways and byways. He showed verve and fortitude, and he became a legend; he was so popular he became leader of the smugglers' gang. Eventually the ship returned to these shores, where the servant repaid his master by doing exactly the same to him; his men kidnapped the nobleman, smuggled him on board, and sailed over the horizon whilst the servant retired to the castle. According to folklore he became prosperous and left many darkly intelligent descendants, known for their vigilance, watchfulness and cunning.

'Not unlike yourself,' commented Vogel, expecting The Don to take up the tale.

The Don stared steadily into his glass.

'Gives me an idea, though,' said Vogel. 'I need someone to help me...'

With this a noisy disturbance in a side-room took me away from their conversation.

I have to rely on the boy Luther's version of what happened between the two men in my absence:

On the day of the big party by Mr Vogel I went to the Blue Angel to see him and he got me lemonade and crisps and he left me outside and didn't talk to me because he was with the big people and too busy and when he came out he was hard to understand. He said hello boy still here then, I've got a bit of news for you we've got another one with us on our next trip to the island, need an extra pair of eyes, he knows all about the coast and the smugglers and he can drive, and he pointed to the man they call Donkey Horty who winks at me and says you're a naughty boy Luther Williams.

And you won't have to sit behind me on a box any more neither he said, tomorrow we will have a brand new bus and I will have my own seat too and there is a stove and cups and a cupboard for sweets he said and places for us to sleep.

Then I went home because the party was finished. I was given a present and I was very glad with it.

THE VISIT

MR VOGEL'S house on Paternoster Hill looked pretty and inviting when I passed it today. The front door, window-frames and pipes have been painted cornflower blue to counterpoint its glittering new coat of whitewash; mirrored in the windows I saw newly-washed clouds hung out to dry in a Constable sky. The old rose tree, subtly yellow, has been trained neatly around the doorway – in Mr Vogel's time it waved forlornly, like the arms of a drowning man, and its thorns scraped desolately on the window panes. In the evening these windows gleam and burn in the profound sunsets which roseate the bay. The garden had been a wilderness during his tenure, with celandines and dog's mercury standing side by side with spring's other promissory notes, the daffodils and the wood anemones. Now they have all gone, pulled out of the ground to make way for orderly and obedient domestic flowers.

As I passed I thought of Mr Vogel and the day he arrived outside the house with a 'new' vehicle for his quest, described beforehand as sumptuous, with a kitchen and a toilet. He went to buy it, did Mr Vogel, sure enough, but that stinginess crept in; he eyed it and wavered about it, hummed and hawed, and put it off until another day. Instead he bought a museum piece belonging to a German traveller going by the name of Julius Rodenberg, who had come to the region in search of adventure and fallen instantly and inextricably in love with a local girl on her wedding day, and still mourned for her, tethered to his yearnings like a newly-sold puppy, a-yowling and a-howling.

'This'll do for now,' said Vogel to Don Quixote after buying it in Rodenberg's yard, which was clogged with chickens and logs. The van was covered in droppings and sticky black excretions from an overhanging lime tree.

'It'll tide us over till I find the right thing. Besides, you'll be able to repair it – a new one would be so complicated, we'd never be able to mend it if it broke down.' This was said rather lamely. The Don could fix motors.

The jalopy which arrived on Paternoster Hill was remarkable – a converted ambulance, a battered old hippy bus with moss growing on the insides of the windows, and a tubercular, Doc Holliday cough which boded a quick death. At some stage it had been painted dark green by a young and idealistic free spirit who had added, in gold paint, some runes similar to those found on a standing stone in the upland mountains, a sharp, fussless script brought over the water by marauding warriors many centuries ago, long before the latest conquistadors arrived to slash and maim our culture. The inscription has never been deciphered, and in consequence has become a mystical password among those who go in search of knowledge, healing or salvation. Its unknown message serves as a perfect paradigm for all who venture beyond normal static life, in a search for something which they cannot elucidate.

This is how that old windbag 'Nosy' Parker described the vehicle:

Just as Columbus had the Santa Maria and the Pilgrim Fathers had the Mayflower, so Mr Vogel, conversely, had his waxen Icarian wings, an automobile of spectacular inappropriateness for any odyssey; many predicted that its only journey would be the two-mile trip to the scrapyard. On seeing it I remembered, immediately, Hercules. One of his epic labours was to slay the gorgon and take the golden apples from the island of Hesperides. Order was reclaimed; knowledge restored.

Perhaps my sister is right: Mr Vogel might indeed have a great goal in mind on the island, though I think he seeks more than apples. Today, after a trip to examine a gothic church in the countryside outside the town, marred only by a most unpleasant incident in which a rut of pigs chased me through a field – how I hate those creatures! – I returned homewards, and clapped eyes on the strangest of sights as I descended Paternoster Hill. Outside old Vogel's door stood an exceedingly strange chariot. The underlying nature of the craft was, I believe, a wartime field ambulance, which I demonstrated to onlookers by pointing to the faint visual remains of two large crosses on both sides of the vehicle. The wheels had been cannibalised from other extinguished vehicles and one seemed slightly smaller than the others, though this could have been an optical illusion (surely the whole craft was an optical illusion, cried Angelica). The windows were decorated with dehydrated algae, like the rim of a dried-up summer pond, which gave the panes a supernatural tinge. Every available inch of glass was covered with stickers proclaiming which countries had been honoured with a visit from this weird time machine. Inside was no better. The driver's seat had once belonged to an army landing craft. Bolted next to it was an old double seat from a closed-down cinema, once made of plush red material, now worn and frayed but still capable of giving the comfort and hospitality once prized by courting couples. The rear section had also been modified; one of the stretchers for the wounded had been retained as a bed, whilst the other had been removed. Another double cinema seat and a curious table had been jammed into the available space, with two bolted-down stools. The overhead area had been converted into a series of storage spaces for food and utensils, which meant there were frequent exclamations from people as they banged their heads on the superstructure. The contraption had a distinctive smell, a mix of rice, onions, tomatoes, herbs, incense, cannabis, tobacco smoke, and that distinctive odour which rises in foreign cities early in the morning when the streets are being washed down and fresh coffee is percolating from alleyway cafés. And now, if Angelica was right, it was being asked to realise another dream-quest, for a deformed little man who had nursed his craving in a hillside Chateau d'If for longer than is fit for a man to dream.

We all stood around the contraption – Vogel, the man they call Don Quixote, the boy Luther and myself, commenting favourably on its suitability despite our mutual misapprehensions. Luther then sat himself in one of the front seats and regarded the road ahead silently, as though preparing himself mentally for the flight home to Ithaca. Like Vogel he was crippled – though in a mental sense. Because of his brooding, uncommunicative hostility to all but Vogel, whom he treated as a dog treats a master, looking at him constantly for orders or approbation, it is impossible to assess his powers. He gives the impression of being a surly, malodorous simpleton. His hair is unbrushed, his clothes unkempt and his shoes are shoddy. Despite this he can run uncommonly fast, which is why, I believe, he was engaged in the first place – to serve as Vogel's ambulatory amanuensis.

Thank you Mr Parker, that will be quite enough for now. It would be nice to report that the next stage of Mr Vogel's great adventure went according to plan. I had envisaged a pleasant scene, something like this:

The day of Mr Vogel's first trip dawned bright and clear, without a cloud in the sky. As if to herald a completely successful day, the crew of Mr Vogel's bus met bright and breezy at seven, as most of the town still slept – Don Quixote at the wheel, silent but proudly composed, like the oarsman who steered Jason and his Argonauts on their epic journey; Mr Vogel next to him, calm, attentive, a map spread on his thin white knees; the intellectually challenged Luther by his side, near the door, ready to spring out of the vehicle like a whippet at Vogel's slightest whim. All of them sat with their bright faces set like pointer dogs towards their destination, all ready to swap travellers' tales as they scudded across the bridge to the island, a frisson of expectancy in each heart as they started Mr Vogel's odyssey.

Unfortunately, few things go according to plan, and on this morning, nothing went according to plan. Since it was spring they might, indeed, have expected blue skies but had to settle for a dull, vapid, overcast day with fine seeping rain blanking the bus's windscreen. It was then that they discovered the wipers were hand-operated, a task allotted to the boy Luther. It took him most of the journey to master this simple job, and the bus had to slow to a crawl when his energy levels dropped.

The boy had risen before his mother and was therefore magnificently dirty, mephitic and dishevelled, and a newly-hatched toe poked out from one of his tattered shoes. During the night his cold had incubated and he snivelled pathetically throughout the trip, his left sleeve acquiring a steady stream of snot which developed into a thick green slick by the evening. There was one advantage: the boy developed, slowly, a left-right rhythm between turning the wipers and wiping his nose.

Mr Vogel was starkly hungover, possibly still a bit drunk from the night before, which he had spent, thick with drink, invoking his past, crying silently, and playing his violin in a maudlin way, rather as Sherlock Holmes might have done before solving another of his celebrated mysteries. Afterwards, as Vogel's condition deteriorated, he spent an inordinate amount of time cleaning a one-eyed teddy bear he had found in the briars in his front garden, doubtless tossed there by a vindictive child gaining revenge during the regular sibling wars which old Vogel could hear in a slow Doppler shift before and after school every day.

The recovered bear had clearly fanned a smouldering ember from Vogel's past: a past which most of the townspeople handled as a trawler might treat an old mine drifting at sea – they let it drift onwards, hoping it would eventually sink of its own accord.

Eventually Mr Vogel's Argonauts were ready.

The bear was pushed into a sitting position between the windscreen and the dashboard. Its newly-washed ears rose slowly during the trip as they dried out, and Mr Vogel decided he would wet them before they set off on future voyages so that they would have a rough idea of the time as they travelled.

The Don turned the key, and after a volley of exhaust shots and a spasm of smoke, a hopeless grinding of gears and a few shudders they set off, watched dispassionately by a chatter of rooks and a passing mongrel. And so started Mr Vogel's quest in his latest chariot of fire. There are many apocryphal versions of this journey: I quote from the version in this year's Chronicle of the Hours:

Eventually they arrived at a cove and Don Quixote stopped the van by a cluster of unkempt fishermen's cottages dotted along the shore. Mr Vogel's party saw a group of men, some of them blind, mending their nets by a shoal of upturned boats. Sickly, undernourished children and dogs played among them. Mr Vogel wanted information about this cove and he sent his boy to reconnoitre whilst he quizzed the men about the coastline. At first they were very wary, asking him where he came from and what he wanted. Eventually they told him about a great calamity which had befallen them. They were being troubled by a band of witches who had landed there some years previously. These witches had been expelled from their own country for practising black magic, and set adrift in a boat without rudder or oars – they had been left to the mercy of the sea like Captain Bligh after the mutiny on the Bounty. When they landed the fishermen had tried, unsuccessfully, to drive them back into the sea. They had been constrained to a small island connected to the land by a causeway at low tide. Almost dead from thirst when they landed, they had conjured up a spring of pure water which had burst from the sands. The women lived by begging and necromancy, their menfolk by smuggling. They all wore a neckerchief, which they undid swiftly if attacked, unleashing a demon which blinded anyone harrying them. Their powers passed from mother to daughter and they had a fearsome reputation throughout the region – the women visited farms and homes with dishevelled hair and bared breasts to beg aggressively, and no-one dared refuse them. If they were turned away they chanted a terrible curse:

You will wander evermore, and with every step you will meet a stile, and at every stile you will fall, and with every fall you will break a bone.

If any of them wanted to buy animals or poultry at a fair no-one would bid against them. Each of the women was disfigured – the thumb and first finger on the right hand ended at the first joint, so they had only half a digit. This malformation was caused when the Devil slammed a door on their hands when they sneaked into his house to steal his great book of curses.

This is the boy Luther's version:

> When we got there, where Mr Vogel said there were cliffs with a cave in them, I ran along the shore to look for the cave but I did not find it, I found a little island with women on it in rags who begged me with a very sad look to give them money and when I said I did not have any they looked inside my pockets. Mr Vogel said it was the wrong place and we had gone on a fool's errand that day so we got in the bus which is not so nice as he said and I have to turn the handle to stop the rain, but Mr Vogel said we would try again soon and we went back to the town and he gave me money for my mother and some more for new shoes, he said it was because of my toes.

There's more bad news. I'm afraid to say that the van died suddenly in a fearsome clatter as they came down Paternoster Hill, and that was the end of that. It's still there now. Old Vogel wobbled in, got ferociously drunk, and told me that the whole damn fool mission had been a waste of time.

'I'll never find it,' he said. 'Never.'

It was the only time I saw him cry – sitting on the stool in his corner, after everyone had gone home. He was talking to himself, and I could see big pearly tears bounce onto the bar-top. By the time I had washed the glasses and cleaned the ashtrays he had disappeared.

When he wobbled in the next day Mr Vogel was subdued. He had all the tics of a man who'd had a heavy night – tired red eyes, shaky hands, irritability. Strangely for him, he sat down by the table in the bay window, rather than his usual spot. It was Sunday morning, and soon the praetorian guard were in – Don Quixote with his bloated belly and his big hairy dog, followed by Sancho Panza, so hung-over he was unable to talk. As usual I had to hold his glass for him as he quivered through his first drink, since he shook so violently that he was unable to hold it himself. It was one of his jokes to say 'I don't drink much, I spill most of it.'

Don Quixote and Sancho played dominoes on Sundays, ritualistically, in the bay window, first quietly, then raucously, with great clatterings and shouts as the drink soothed their nerves. Today they eyed Mr Vogel suspiciously, since he had wandered from his usual territory, and as all topers know, every drinker has a regular spot at the bar, which places him in precise relation to his peers. We need no anthropologists in this neck of the woods; alcohol is a great examiner.

So Don Quixote and Sancho were soon at it, and old Vogel watched. He wasn't being communicative, but something about him indicated that he had something to say when the time was right.

Eventually, towards the end of a game, when the hair of the dog had done its work and everyone was in high spirits again, Vogel said:

'I'm not going to bother with this island lark any longer.'

'Oh really, what a terrible calamity,' answered Sancho, getting six-pints cheeky.

'Yes, packing it in. Don't see the point of wandering about in that crate.'

'None of us saw any point in it,' said Sancho. 'Total waste of time. In fact we thought your Dick Barton impressions were bloody ludicrous anyway.'

Old Vogel smarted. 'Well at least I tried – I didn't sit around drinking gut rot and taking gibberish to the geraniums,' he replied testily.

'What you don't know,' said Sancho, tapping his nose knowingly, 'is that those geraniums clap their leaves in sheer delight when I talk gibberish. Sheer bloody poetry to them, see.'

Don Quixote slammed his last domino on the table and rubbed his belly.

'Sheer poetry,' he said triumphantly, sweeping all the money into his pockets.

Their drinks shone in the sunshine, and the pleasing amber of the bitter swirled in a miasma of blue cigarette smoke which reminded Mr Vogel of the foothills of the mountain range above them. All was well with the world. Hangovers and shakes tiptoed out through the door, bliss seeped in through the warming windows.

'Actually, I've decided to go on a great trek,' said Mr Vogel artlessly. 'I'm going to find a cure, might even go to America and go all the way out west.'

The response was entirely predictable; Sancho choked and spat out his beer, Don Quixote shouted '*what, mister?*' and a still-born silence was broken by raucous laughter, guffaws, jibes – the usual bar-room response when anyone makes a foolish remark.

'No, really, I mean it,' said Vogel, stuttering.

'Oh he really means it,' mimicked Sancho. 'I've got a better idea – why don't you bounce all the way there, like those monks you were going on about yesterday?'

Here more laughter and ribaldry.

Sancho was referring to the lung-gom-pa runners of Tibet, who complete phenomenally long journeys with amazing speed.

This is hardly the time to interrupt Mr Vogel's story, but I must tell you about a French explorer who disguised herself as a Tibetan beggar-woman and became the first European woman to enter Llasa. Riding across a wide tableland in Northern Tibet, she noticed, far away, a moving dot which her binoculars showed to be a man.

'I felt astonished,' she wrote:

Meetings are not frequent in that region – for the last ten days we had not seen a human being. Moreover, men on foot and alone do not, as a rule, wander in these immense solitudes. Who could this strange traveller be? As I continued to observe him through the glasses, I noticed that the man proceeded at an unusual gait and, especially, with an extraordinary swiftness. The man continued to advance towards us and his curious speed became more and more evident. What was to be done if he really was a lung-gom-pa? I wanted to observe him at close quarters, I also wished to have a talk with him, to put him some questions, to photograph him... I wanted many things. But at the very first words I said about it, the man who had recognised him as a lama lung-gom-pa exclaimed:

"Your Reverence will not stop the lama, nor speak to him. This would certainly kill him. These lamas when travelling must not break their meditation. The god who is in them escapes if they cease to repeat the ngags, and when thus leaving them before the proper time, he shakes them so hard that they die."

By that time he had nearly reached us; I could clearly see his perfectly calm impassive face and wide-open eyes with their gaze fixed on some invisible far-distant object situated somewhere high up in space. The man did not run. He seemed to lift himself from the ground, proceeding by leaps. It looked as if he had been endowed with the elasticity of a ball and rebounded each time his feet touched the ground. His steps had the regularity of a pendulum. He wore the usual monastic robe and toga, both rather ragged. His left hand gripped a fold of the toga and the right hand held a *phurba* (magic dagger). My servants dismounted and bowed their heads to the ground as the lama passed before us, but he went his way apparently unaware of our presence.

No-one in the bar prostrated himself before Mr Vogel; as you might expect, he was the butt of many hurtful remarks during the next hour.

But as for me, well, I saw the man's dream. We all need to have our little hopes, don't we? I have to concede, however, that Mr Vogel's dream was quite an enormous one.

He made a heartfelt speech, something on the lines of: *I might not do it, but it'll be a glorious failure. If I succeed you'll be amazed. If I fail you will have enough material to laugh for the rest of your useless lives.*

Mr Vogel clumped to his corner, ordered a large whisky, and sulked.

Standing next to him, silently, I felt a deep sympathy with him: he was trying to realise a dream. He wanted to be someone like Rocky Mountain Jim, living in a land of wild Indians and buffaloes, with new railroads girding the earth, rolling prairies, high bluffs and whirling rapids; he wanted to talk to hunters and adventurers in smoky log cabins, eat johnny-cake, squirrel and buffalo-hump. There were problems with this dream: Rocky Mountain Jim was a bold adventurer loved deeply by a horde of women, whereas Vogel had never been out of the region and had never been kissed, never mind loved – either carnally or spiritually. Who the hell would touch old Vogel! Rocky Mountain Jim was a man with Desperado written in large letters all over him, a man with a fine aquiline nose, a dense moustache and one grey-blue eye (the other had been gouged out by a grizzly bear who had left him for dead). Whereas Mr Vogel, well...

'Order!' cried Sancho Panza above the chatter.

'Order!' He stood drunkenly on the window seat, almost losing his footing. Everyone turned round, but instead of looking at his face they all seemed to be looking between his legs, straight out through the window.

He continued.

'Gentlemen. It behoves me, this afternoon, to say a few words about our gallant comrade Mr Vogel, who has announced his intention to make a great pilgrimage to be cured of all his maladies. Friends, please raise your glasses to St Jude, patron saint of lost causes, and foolish Mr Vogel, who'll get no further than the lunatic asylum if he...'

Here he trailed off, since his glazed eyes had eventually

realised that everyone was looking between his legs, and fearing his flies were open, he made an effort to adjust his clothing, whereupon he fell back into one of the geranium pots. I was glad to see that his glass had remained in his hand, and with great consideration he hadn't spilled a single drop. One of my blooms, however, was completely crushed and red petals now fluttered over the table and onto the floor. Humboldt became extremely emotional, and seizing his opportunity he made a dash for freedom through a window which had been opened by Don Quixote, who wanted to see what was going on outside.

As my parrot disappeared Sancho turned round to follow his flight, and saw what everyone else had been staring at. I myself also saw the object of their interest – a peculiar sight, since all that was visible was a head, belonging to a young woman. What I remember is that her hair was light brown and was cut in a distinctly old-fashioned bob with a blue ribbon in it; and she had a little upturned nose propping up a pair of those round glasses which make people look intelligent. She merely stared at us through the bottom pane of glass. It was very odd – I thought she must be on her knees.

Don Quixote told me later that she was, in fact, sitting in a wheelchair, which was being pushed by a man who looked as if he should be sitting in it, not her. Apparently she was carrying something, a present perhaps, wrapped in tissue paper. The woman, it transpired, was looking for someone, and soon we all knew who it was. Mr Vogel, on his way to the toilets, stopped suddenly when he saw her face in the window. He gave a cry of amazement and made a bee-line for the front door – it was the fastest I'd ever seen him move. Opening it, he [*the remaining pages of the Vogel Papers, being on the outside, had been damaged by dampness and mould, and were therefore illegible*].

PART TWO

Jorge introduced me to the company director. Antonio was the technical expert. He led me to the boardroom, where a rack of umbrellas stood against the far wall. With a deft flourish Antonio opened each umbrella and described its attributes. There were umbrellas with short or long shafts; with beech, plastic or Malacca handles; models with eight and ten ribs and one the diameter of a military satellite dish, with sixteen ribs.

'Please,' said Jorge after Antonio had finished. 'We would like to give you an umbrella for your journey.' He thought for a moment, then chose a ten-ribbed, beech-handled model with a tubular steel shaft and black fabric. 'This is good for walking,' he said, handing it to me. 'It is strong.'

As I was leaving, Jorge handed me his business card. On it was a coloured illustration showing two Galicians in local dress sitting on a bench, the man in riding boots, the woman in wooden clogs. They were kissing beneath a large brown umbrella which was being pummelled by rain. Beneath the entwined couple was the slogan

Que chova?

'In the galego language,' explained Jorge, 'it means "What rain?"'

It was the perfect apothegm for a journey which depended to some degree on self-delusion.

Nicholas Crane, *Clear Waters Rising, A Mountain Walk Across Europe.*

A VISIT FROM TASMANIA

I WAS RELIEVED when I came to the end of the Vogel Papers – I'm sure you were too.

If you've made it this far, congratulations. Reading the barman's wacky story felt like a hard slog up a mountain – somewhere like the Crib Goch ridge. Now we've reached the top of the horseshoe and it's time to turn round, look at the view, and see if it was worth all the effort. It's all downhill from here, I assure you.

It's strange, isn't it – if the Blue Angel manuscript had decayed just a little bit more we'd have been spared all that rot: a rambling journey around a make-believe colonial outpost, stuck in a time warp, peopled by oddballs. And who was our guide, the quirky barman with a taste for Dickensian English? Let's face it, the Vogel Papers don't make much sense. Not a pretty read at all – if you're still with us it's a tribute to your doggedness, your resolve to get to the end of a journey, rather than a reflection on the literary merit of the tale. But once we've started on an expedition we're reluctant to turn back, all of us, aren't we?

I'm not much of a reading man but it don't take a professor to realise that the Vogel Papers are completely fictitious. Credibility – nil. Wordy, romantic, sentimental: it's a flight of fancy, a crude fairytale. There's not much to be learnt from the handwriting either; it's a slanting, uneducated scrawl.

There's a Welsh word for the sort of man who wrote it – *gwladaidd*, which conjures up English words like rustic, yokel, bog-trotter... you get my drift.

The Vogel Papers were written by a peasant: a naive country boy with straw in his hair and mud on his boots. A man who learnt his English from second-hand, out-of-date novels. But it's a story, and I find it... what's the word – intriguing?

In those idle moments of the mind I find myself glancing backwards, hoping to catch a glimpse of Mr Vogel and his oddball crew, but of course they're never there. When the light's out and I'm stretched out in my bed I can't help wondering about the story; sleepless minutes become sleepless hours as I worm my way into the plot and become a fourth passenger, lurching about in the back of their Tardis as it wobbles through the countryside.

I'm not sure why I became involved in the first place.

With hindsight the Vogel Papers should have been left to rest in peace. But there's something about the human mind which wants to explore every possibility, no matter what the consequences. Pandora's Box and all that. And I'm a sucker for losers. Mr Vogel was a loser, and the author of his little story sounded like a loser too.

I should have walked away like Martin did. Martin was the man who lived next door to me. A strange little man with a strange little surname, which I can't remember. He was fattish, glasses, faintly sweaty. He always seemed prepossessed. He wasn't one of those people who noticed you first, more of a head-down, wait-for-it-to-happen sort of man. Always in a world of his own. We talked irregularly through a hole in the threadbare privet hedge between us. Nearly always he was alone; sometime his greying wife, her eyes burnt with some inexpressible secret, would wander slowly from the lean-to kitchen, drying her hands on something and murmuring like a chorister in a Greek play who had forgotten to exit with the rest. There were weeks when I saw neither of them. I was aware that they had two children in their early teens, but I never saw them at the back of the house, as if they were banned from the garden. At the end of both gardens there was the residue of an old granite wall which had partly tumbled into our plots.

I had masked my own broken-up boundary with a trellis.

One day my neighbour actually engaged me in conversation. He seemed jauntier than usual. We talked about his job – he was a driving instructor and he told me about one of his learners. The story wasn't particularly funny but he clearly thought it hilarious so I joined him in a hearty round of laughter.

He looked at the end of his garden and a strong silence ensued. He pointed towards it and looked at me keenly, as if wishing to pass on a coded message.

He was going to rebuild his wall, his barricade. That was to be his task for the winter, he said. He started mumbling, just like his wife. He mumbled all through November as he cleared the stones and piled them neatly, then re-dug the footings.

He was meticulous.

He measured and marked out the wall's domain with exaggerated precision. Small neat wooden crosses and strong twine delineated his winter's work.

Throughout December he constructed his wall and mumbled. This time it wasn't dry-built. He bought an orange cement-mixer and made a mix before each session.

The wall took shape, and still he mumbled. I caught the occasional word or phrase, which sounded like archaic poetry. He said things like *fate is decreed... there's not a man alive that I dare tell my tale to him... a dismal thing, deep in the chest... I cannot think about this world but memory darken my mind when I do...then this middle earth each and every day disintegrates... a haven awaits the homeless soul... the ocean's lanes...*

Was the man going bonkers?

'Middle Earth,' I said to him one day. 'I think you said Middle Earth. Am I right?'

He was passing, a gleaming spade in his left hand and a gleaming pickaxe in his right hand, both freshly cleaned.

'Yes, I think you're right there,' he said.

'Middle Earth,' I repeated. '*Lord of the Rings*? *The Hobbit*?'

'Much earlier,' he replied. 'Think much earlier.'

I thought hard, but shook my head, perplexed.

'Tell you what,' he said, 'I'll leave that with you. Middle Earth. See what you come up with. Middle Earth. We'll see, shall we?' He tried to look enigmatic.

At the town library I looked up Middle Earth on the internet and finally found a lead. Martin's mumbled phrases appeared to come from an Old English text in the Beowulf mould, from a poem called 'The Wanderer'. I figured he was either cracking up or winding me up, so I didn't mention it again. He appeared to forget about all worldly matters as his wall took shape.

I noticed that he had incorporated what appeared to be a buttress along part of it. Gradually, as the wall grew and the buttress rose, it became apparent that Martin had introduced a set of steps alongside the wall, and rising steadily with it. They looked rather nice. They almost invited you to climb them. Immediately after his last driving lesson each day Martin would change hurriedly into overalls and make a mix, then lay part of a course. Each day revolved feverishly around the weather forecast, and an evening lost to rain was an evening destroyed. I think his wife became worried about him at this stage. I could see her face, motionless, in the kitchen window, looking at him for long periods.

Once or twice I saw the children looking at him from a bedroom window.

When the wall reached the height of the small, unkempt wood which borders our little kingdoms I noticed an aura around Martin. There was a palpable mysticism about him. Finally, he capped the wall with weighty slabs and topped off his steps, which now gave direct access to the wood. The cement mixer, the pickaxe, the spade, the trowels and all the paraphernalia left over after his feat were sold at a car boot sale. The garden was cleared and tidied, and a few snowdrops and crocuses made an appearance. Spring was on its way.

Martin had done well. The wall and the steps looked as impressive as the approach to any medieval fortification. On the very next day after completion, as I tidied my own patch in a belated and slightly guilty attempt to match Martin's efforts, I saw him walking past me down his garden. He was dressed, not in his usual overalls, but in walking gear, with strong boots and a rucksack. He stopped.

'Off to Middle Earth?' I said, and he laughed a short ironic laugh.

'Something like that,' he replied.

'Off for a little wander, perhaps,' I added.

His eyes acknowledged my little morsel of knowledge.

'Something like that.' He looked back at the house and waved to his wife, who waved back at him bleakly, like a scorched letter at the edge of a bonfire.

It was the last time she saw him.

He reached the top of those steps and walked along the flags he had keyed into the crown of the wall, then he entered the woods and disappeared. I heard twigs snap for some time after, and I thought I heard a snatch of song.

It was as if those steps had been his only means of escape, like the shroud in *The Count of Monte Cristo.* The police failed to find any trace of him and he was presumed dead. His wife started an affair with one of his pupils, the one who had failed his driving test so often he eventually gave up and bought a bike.

Some months later, when I was browsing through a book on birds, I read that martins may have got their name from St Martin of Tours, possibly because the birds migrate around the time of his feast day in mid-November. Our own Martin, it seems, was a few months late on his flight into the unknown.

Perhaps I delved into the Vogel Papers simply because I had too much time on my hands that year. I had spent the winter recuperating from a minor hip operation, which had been necessary – in middle age – to correct a defect caused by a childhood disease. Once my left hip was working well again I felt wonderfully free.

I hadn't realised how static I'd become as the hip slowly seized up. Now I felt like a child again, walking about the countryside with renewed pleasure, greeting old friends and seeing once-familiar sights with fresh delight.

I hatched a great dream – a wonderful plan – to walk entirely around my country, a journey of a thousand miles or more. I would take a year off work – I was in transit between jobs anyway, having decided to become a psychiatric nurse; it seemed like an ideal time to step aside from life's teeming thoroughfares and enter the cool green sanctuary of my country's past. I would have green thoughts in a green shade.

It would be a middle-age rite of passage, a new start to life, a celebration of my newfound liberty.

When the consultant discharged me he said:

'Consider yourself lucky. A few years ago you would have been a cripple. Make the most of it!'

He mumbled an apology for using the word cripple. 'Disabled – I should have said disabled.'

I told him of my plan to walk completely around my country.

'Amazing,' he responded, almost ruefully. 'I'm so jealous. You can see Wales at first hand, and there's something magnificent about a great trek, so good for the spirits as well as the body – but don't overdo it, I don't want to see you back here with a limp again!'

The world suddenly seemed different. I stood on mountains and on sea-cliffs looking at it all. I sat in places without humans, watching the tides come and go. I had no stomach for the conventions of society. I looked at the people around me. They seemed busy, occupied. I felt estranged, but not unhappily so. Each new day I observed the small rituals of life, as my ancestors might have done: I arose, washed in the clear cold water of the brook outside my door, and took stock of the weather. (Having been a farm boy on the edge of the moors, some twenty miles inland, I am still adept at foretelling the weather. Simply by looking at clouds and animal movements – sheep and cattle snaking down from the hills, into the lee of the lowland hedges, I can see forewarnings of storms.)

I also looked for each morning's new arrivals, such as birds of passage, and I explored the hedgerows for the most recent flowers as spring strengthened and prepared for a new burgeoning, as I was. I walked and read and wrote, and shared thoughts and experiences with the people I met on the roads, on paths, on shores. No, I wouldn't work that year. Sometimes I thought I would never work again. I felt pangs of guilt, of course. But I would be dead soon enough, and I wanted to stand and watch awhile. I had two new possessions – time and freedom. That is why I read the Vogel Papers.

It seemed to me that the author was a man who had wanted to say a lot very quickly, and had failed. But there was a central, discernible, theme. A crippled man wanted to regain or revisit someone, something or somewhere, and his search involved an island, a teddy bear, and probably a woman in a wheelchair.

The author also wanted to convey the busyness, the bustle of the landscape.

The Vogel Papers were one man's attempt to convey the fleetingness, the transience of each human visit to the world. Perhaps the constantly-moving backdrop was a crude device to heighten Mr Vogel's physical imprisonment. Perhaps the teeming stage was meant as a simple juxtaposition with the cripple's immobility.

Many days I wandered on the shore with the waders as they, like me, prepared to depart. On days like these Wales feels like a Promethean rock in the ocean, visited briefly by flights of souls as they travel to and fro between birth and death.

My impending walk brought to mind the opening passage of William Langland's great fourteenth century book, *Piers Plowman*:

> In a summer season, when soft was the sun,
> I enshrouded me well in a shepherd's garb,
> And robed as a hermit, unholy of works,
> Went wide through the world, all wonders to hear.
> And on a May morning, on Malvern Hills,
> Strange fancies befell me, and fairy-like dreams.

I was weary of wandering, and went to repose
On a green bank, by a burn-side;
As I lay there and leaned and looked at the waters
I slumbered and slept, they sounded so merry.

Came morning before me a marvellous vision;
I was lost in a wild waste; but where I discerned not.
I beheld in the east on high, near the sun,
A tower on a hill-top, with turrets well-wrought;
A deep dale beneath, and dungeons therein,
With deep ditches and dark, and dreadful to see.
A fair field, full of folk, I found there between,
Of all manner of men, the mean and the rich,
All working or wandering, as the world requires.

As I made arrangements for my journey I read many essays by the masters of walking, and their words fell around me like warm chippings scattered by passing cars laden with laughing people on a dusty summer road. I started with the daddy of them all, Henry David Thoreau, and his famous opening line:

I wish to speak a word for nature, for absolute Freedom and Wildness...

I took to this eccentric American, writing almost 200 years ago. His much-quoted sentence on walking is the best mission statement I have ever read:

If you are ready to leave father and mother, and brother and sister, and wife and child and friends, and never see them again; if you have paid your debts, and made your will, and settled all your affairs, and are a free man; then you are ready for a walk.

Attaboy, Mr Thoreau Sir! I liked his attitude, right down to his last words. When a friend asked him on his deathbed if he could see into the next world yet, Thoreau snapped back: 'One world at a time...'

Here he is again:

I have met but one or two people in the course of my life who understood the art of Walking...

The word *sauntering*, he thought, was derived from idle people, fakers who roved about the country in the middle ages, asking charity, under a pretence of going *a la sainte terre* – to the holy land; or the word could derive from *sans terre*, without land or home. He was full of splendid theories. I love this sentence:

> I once had a sparrow alight on my shoulder for a moment while I was hoeing in a village garden, and I felt that I was more distinguished by that circumstance than I should have been by any epaulette I could have worn.

But let's return to the Vogel Papers. They are permanently lodged at the town museum, though last year they joined a touring exhibition entitled, predictably, *Figures in a Landscape*.

The exhibition was divided into two main themes:

1: Foreign travellers who have passed through our land, and their impressions.

2: Native itinerants, in pictures and folk stories.

Typically bourgeois reference points, you might say, but my interest was aroused because this exhibition, which started its peripatetic mission in our town, touched upon a very real interest of mine. Since I am now a travelling man myself, with that restless snail-like urge to clamp a few essentials to my back and head off somewhere, I spent many hours grazing at the museum, which housed the presentation.

I would say that my interest in the travelling folk was kindled by a roving gene among my chromosomes – and it came, by all accounts, from one of my grandfathers, who arrived here as a tramp, gentleman of the road, call them what you will. I was told this by one of my aunts, who was far from proud of our family skeleton. He was among the many itinerants who had arrived in a slow trickle in this rural backwater immediately after the Great War.

The word tramp comes from the Middle Low German for 'to stamp', and my ancestor – who had been well and truly stamped on by a roaring, monstrous world – had walked away from it all in search of sanctuary. Apparently he had wheeled everything he owned in front of him in a rusty old perambulator. There were many like him. My father told me that if they were treated humanely at a particular place they scratched a secret mark on the wall in the roadside by the house; I searched for this sign everywhere but couldn't find it. 'Ah, that shows you how discreet they are,' he said.

I think he may have been romancing – a strong trait in our family.

Later I read about the way gypsies mark a *patrin* – a trail – with small piles of leaves or bunches of hay; some tie a ribbon or a rag to a tree, and sometimes a bent twig is enough to signpost their spoor.

In urban areas the tramps were sometimes given a small amount of food and drink.

In the rural areas they were expected to sing for their supper, by doing a few chores. Many had a regular itinerary, going from farm to farm to help with certain crops. They usually slept in the stable loft, directly above the horses, who gave them warmth and company; I will not examine here the long friendship between the rootless man and his horse – you can ask Genghis Khan about that in the afterlife.

I remember two tramps who trod the lanes of my youth.

One was called Birdie. He was a squat, gingery man with a mouthful of bad teeth. He sold transistor radios from two enormous cardboard boxes lashed with twine. Occasionally, as the school bus dipped and clonked its way through the rolling Welsh countryside, we would pass him as he walked from farm to farm touting his wares. As is common with tramps, it was rumoured that he was fabulously rich and did not need to work at all. The other common fable construed around tramps is that they were once very clever but their minds had collapsed after being spurned by a lover. Old Birdie dipped in and out of my life, like the school charabanc, until he was found, stiff as a board, in a hayrick one winter. He had just a few pounds in his pockets and holes in his shoes.

There were other tramps, mainly ex-prisoners who were social outcasts, and who went from village to village begging or stealing, usually from the priests. Of course there were no social services then. Many of these men were moving around in search of work. And there were peddlers and tinkers, who sharpened knives on a whetstone driven by the chain on their upturned bikes, and there were garlic-wafting onion-sellers, who had come on ships from Brittany with their black cycles, and Indians in turbans selling carpets roped to the roofs of their vans.

My father also described a previous generation of itinerants:

wandering clerics and preachers, who led tumultuous religious revivals; clock-repairers, men selling popular ballads, men driving steam-driven threshing machines, and men walking stallions around the countryside, servicing mares.

The most unusual man he remembered was a moss-pointer, who walked around Wales stuffing dried moss into farmhouse wall-cracks in readiness for winter.

Tramps were far from my mind when I met Dr John Williams in a Cardiff hotel one day in March, 2000. It was a strange meeting; I can't remember why we struck on that particular place for our first encounter. He was over from Tasmania for a symposium on Welsh maritime history – he was an authority on the work of the Welsh shipping scholar Aled Eames. I had asked a local journalist, who had also written on the country's maritime history, for as many contacts as possible.

'Williams is one of the best authorities on Welsh coastal wrecks you'll ever meet,' he told me; it was purely by chance that Dr Williams was due in Wales only a few weeks after I mailed him the Vogel Papers with a heartfelt plea for help: *What might Mr Vogel have been looking for, if the story had any basis in truth?*

Dr Williams was a small, Humpty Dumpty sort of man with a pronounced double chin, a bald dome-shaped head and a rather strange voice which quivered between a high octave and a low warble when he was excited. He had a damp palm and rheumy eyes. He also suffered dreadfully with dandruff. I was struck by this strange parallel with Mr Vogel's story. Mr Vogel had dandruff; Tasmania was also mentioned as the country where the original landlord of the Blue Angel had begat a child.

Dr Williams echoed my sentiments: 'Funny, isn't it, that link with Tasmania,' he said reflectively. 'To be honest with you, that's why I read the Vogel Papers when you sent them – my eye happened to catch the word Tasmania, otherwise I would have thrown them away in all probability.' He sounded vaguely apologetic. I soothed him: 'This whole thing is already one big bag of coincidences,' I said. 'It'll be a miracle if we get anywhere.'

Through the window I saw spring flood the sky's arena with a delicate duckshell blue. Outside in Cathedral Road a welter of traffic was thudding towards the city centre. Above the rooftops I glimpsed the top of the Millennium Stadium. We were in an alcove window and I felt pleased with my choice. Dr Williams was excited: he was back in the old homeland, he could spend a month re-exploring ancestral fields. He was enthusiastic about post-Assembly Cardiff – it had a new vitality, he felt. This was the first time I had visited the capital; apparently it's changing rapidly now the old docks have been swept away – it has a slightly tentative air about it, as though the city was a rather wary woman who had bought some snazzy clothes for her first party after a divorce and wondered what everyone else would think.

Dr Williams wanted to help me. We sat facing each other comfortably; I had convinced him quickly that I was not a crank, and I knew just enough about the Royal Charter, the Resurgam, the Ocean Monarch and other well-known Welsh shipping disasters to kindle his interest. I turned the conversation towards Tasmania. Having known a couple of journalists over the years, I know the importance of preparation before an interview – there is nothing safer than a little knowledge of a person's circumstances to buy a little time with him. It's a discreet form of flattery.

I talked of Van Diemen and his conquest, and the apparent genocide of the indigenous Tasmanian nation, which perished finally with the death of Trugannini in 1876; the Aboriginal women kidnapped or bought by white sealers and taken to live in desperate circumstances in the Bass Strait, women who sometimes killed their own offspring as a refutation of what was happening to them; the black Tasmanians who were forced to live under different laws and in special areas until as late as the 1940s; the programme of assimilation which saw native children being taken away from their families.

'Seems the Welsh didn't suffer as badly as we thought,' I said.

Williams's response was swift and unexpected. His face tightened and his eyes hardened. 'Bloody disaster, all of it,' he said tersely. 'And now the infighting... it's like a civil war. Now it's blackfella against blackfella. It was bad enough to strip them of their land and their dignity. But to come back a century later offering them some sort of pitiful self-government was downright criminal. They just couldn't adopt white government. Their way of running things, their law is totally different... end result could be a bloodbath.'

I regretted I'd brought it up. It was clearly a cause close to his heart.

'Something similar over here,' I said as a way of giving the conversation a coda. 'The Welsh were battered by any number of invaders but they spent half their time fighting among themselves to see who would fight the invaders. Absolutely bloody mad.'

'I call it the paranoid factor,' said Williams. 'If you start feeling paranoid, which is a pretty normal sort of feeling sometime or other in your life, you start looking more closely at other people to see if they *are* looking at you. The result is that they *do* start looking at you because you're looking at *them*, so you slink off into a corner to make sure no-one looks at you. It's the same with minority cultures – they get so self-conscious and paranoid they end up half-mad with pain and either kill themselves or drink themselves into oblivion. Bet you anything you like a medical survey of fringe cultures would show an alcohol or drugs problem directly in proportion to the smallness of the culture. Innuits, Aborigines, Celts...'

We sat quietly and I thought of the Arab women I'd heard that morning on a bus to Cardiff Bay, jabbering away in their own language, a minority within a minority within a minority – they were clearly talking about their husbands, and one was volubly unhappy with her domestic situation (I don't know how I understood her, but her consternation was plain to all who heard her). I had listened, and had felt, for the first time, part of Wales...

Dr Williams shuffled about in his pockets and brought out a package.

'I've read the Vogel Papers. Very strange. Mostly fantasy, of course. I've never come across such an odd mix – I suppose the writer, whoever he or she was, might have been attempting a first novel; you'd never believe how many people out there harbour some such dream.'

'He or she?' I queried. 'It's always been assumed the writer was a male, after all it's written from the standpoint of a barman.'

'I thought we were all approaching this with an open mind,' he said blandly.

He was the scholar. 'Yes, I suppose you're right,' I conceded. 'Take nothing for granted.'

Williams opened a brown envelope and pulled out some documents.

'These might be of help. I've pondered on the Vogel Papers quite a long time, since I have a minority interest in cripples. My mother was a great fan of the Mexican painter Frida Kahlo.'

I shook my head. 'Don't know that one.'

Williams grinned. 'Larger than life character. Had polio as a kid. Then she was hit by a tram when she was a teenager and spent her life in a steel corset. Rumbustious life, had an affair with Trotsky, husband a serial womaniser – sort of put her pain down on canvas. My mother met her once and bought one of her paintings, in the early days, when they were affordable. It hung in our parlour all my childhood.'

'So much pain out there,' I mumbled.

'So much pain, and so much energy and creativity too. There seems to be a link,' he added.

We'd both had enough of brainplay so we headed for the restaurant. As we walked through I touched the document which Williams had given me, now warm in my pocket. Would it shine any light on Mr Vogel's quest, I wondered. The Ride of the Vogel-kyrie had something to do with Anglesey, I thought. And so did Dr Williams. Over the menu he said: 'The island mentioned in the papers must be Anglesey. It can be no other. The papers were found in a Welsh pub, only Anglesey has a road bridge, and that gives us just one choice.'

He ordered Conwy mussels and Welsh lamb.

I just wanted a sandwich, but I didn't want to make him look gluttonous. I made a feeble excuse... 'cholesterol problems,' I said guardedly, 'got to be careful'. Truth is, I have always been very uncomfortable about eating in public, especially with strangers. The very notion has made me feel sick in the past. I've wondered if I have some sort of eating disorder, but I've veiled the problem over the years and I've got away with it.

Williams was understanding. 'No worries,' he comforted me – 'you have what you like.'

I relaxed, and ordered the beef pie with new potatoes.

I finished a full five minutes before him.

Later, in my hotel room, I reflected on my conversation with Williams. He, also, had enthused about my trek. I had said to him as I stirred my coffee:

'Actually, I've been wondering about something recently.'

'Yes?' he answered encouragingly, but I thought I saw a small cloud cross his eyes – I think he had already seen me for what I am, a parish-pump dilettante, a jobbing scholar with a penchant for dabbling and teasing intelligent people as a flea teases a tiger.

'Yes,' I consolidated, 'I suppose I've been speculating as to why, exactly, I find Wales so lovely. I've asked a few people, and I would like your views, as a man from foreign climes. I wonder, do we love nature, the natural world, mountains and meadows and seas and lakes and suchlike because we have to? After all, if we didn't, life would be intolerable – what I'm trying to say is, are we genetically programmed to like the natural world, since we would walk about in constant pain if we didn't?'

'Get your drift,' answered Williams. 'Me, I've always put it down to the romantics – you know, Wordsworth, Shelley and all that lot waxing lyrical about it all. Seems tame now but it was a big thing at the time, people hadn't noticed how lovely the world was because they were so used to it and so busy scrabbling to get food and keep death at bay, they never thought about it. They hadn't seen towns and cities either, most of them, so they didn't have any comparison – they didn't see what a mess man can make of things.'

He looked at me, wondering if I'd finished.

'Also,' I hazarded, 'there's a possibility we've grown to like what's around us gradually, as part of our evolution.'

Williams sat back in his seat and harrumphed.

'Where do you get these ideas,' he asked (almost reproachfully?).

'Oh books, TV, you know, that sort of thing,' I told him. 'Gave up work a while ago, I've got a lot of time on my hands...'

He had gone back to his own world, and the curtain had come down on this line of thought. But my own mind had wandered off on another trail. I thought of the Japanese people who go on an annual thousand-mile pilgrimage around the island of Shikoku, birthplace of one of the big names in Buddhism. During this trip they visit 88 temples; I thought of the little churches of Wales, dotted around the land, in villages and in fields, on shores and on hillsides. I would visit them too, not for their Christian message, but for their repose and their timeless, tranquil Welshness.

Later, as I tried to sleep, city noises swished and beeped below me well into the night, and I'm not used to it. I had taken a book with me, as usual, and with my customary serendipity I came across an apt piece by Alexander Herzen, a Russian philosopher who lived in London for a while, where his home became a meeting-place for émigrés of all nationalities. He wrote, in mid-Victorian times:

Ten years ago, as I was going through the Haymarket late one cold, raw winter evening, I came upon a Negro, a lad of seventeen; he was barefooted and without a shirt, and on the whole rather undressed for the tropics than dressed for London. Shivering all over, with his teeth chattering, he asked me for alms. Two days later I met him again, and then again and again. Eventually I got into conversation with him. He spoke a broken Anglo-Spanish, but it was not hard to understand the sense of his words.

'You are young and strong,' I said to him, 'why don't you look for work?'

'No one will give it to me.'

'Why is that?'

'I know no-one who would give me a character.'

'Where do you come from?'

'From a ship.'

'What ship?'

'A Spanish one; the captain beat me a lot, so I left.'

'What were you doing on board the ship?'

'Everything: brushed the clothes, washed up, did the cabins.'

'What do you mean to do?'

'I don't know.'

'But you will die of cold and hunger, you know, or anyhow you will certainly get a fever.'

'What am I to do?' said the Negro in despair, looking at me and shivering all over with cold.

Well, I thought, here goes. It is not the first stupid thing I have done in my life.

'Come with me. I'll give you clothes and a corner to sleep in; you shall sweep my rooms, light the fires and stay as long as you like, if you behave quietly and properly...'

The Negro jumped for joy.

Within a week he was fatter, and gaily did the work of four. In this way he spent six months with us; then one evening he appeared before my door, stood a little while in silence and then said to me: 'I have come to say goodbye.'

'How's that?'

'It's enough for now: I am going.'

'Has anyone been nasty to you?'

'No indeed, I am pleased with everyone.'

'Then where are you going?'

'To a ship.'

'What for?'

'I am dreadfully sick for it, I can't stand it, I shall do a mischief if I stay. I need the sea. I will go away and come back again, but for now it is enough.'

I made an effort to stop him; he stayed for three days, and then announced for the second time it was beyond his powers, that he must go away, that 'for now is enough'.

That was in the spring. In the autumn he turned up once more, tropically divested, and again I clothed him; but he soon began playing various nasty tricks, and even threatened to kill me, so I was obliged to turn him away.

These last facts are irrelevant, but the point is that I completely share the Negro's outlook. After living a long time in one place and in the same rut, I feel that for a certain time it is enough, that I must refresh myself with other horizons and other faces... and at the same time must retire into myself, strange as that sounds. The superficial distractions of the journey do not interfere.

There are people who prefer to go inwardly, some with the help of a powerful imagination and an ability to abstract themselves from their surroundings (for this a special endowment is needed, bordering on genius and insanity), some with the help of opium or alcohol. Russians, for instance, will have a drinking bout for a week or two, and then go back to their homes and duties. I prefer shifting my whole body to shifting my brain, and going round the world to letting my head go round.

I lay in bed, listening. Little did I know that some months later I was to approach Cardiff on the shore, along the lip of the Severn. It was a day to remember, warm and happy: a day when the world left me completely alone. The muddy banks of the great estuary, all along the flatlands, lay like the huge grey gums of a dead dinosaur, mouth agape. In a moment of madness I took my boots off and attempted to cross part of Cardiff Flats in the mud, which pulled at my feet like a drunken parent sucking a baby's toes, warm and slobbery. I slithered to the oozing ravine of the River Rhymney and nearly drowned in mud, emerging like a grey, naked Druid about to shriek at the Roman soldiers as they prepared to cross over to Anglesey nearly 2000 years earlier. Fortunately, the only people who saw me were workmen sealing off the gigantic municipal tip nearby; after cleaning up I encountered one of them as he drove a huge yellow tipper past me. I got the village idiot treatment – he was a specialist in withering, pitying looks.

But that was all in the future...

THE SHIPWRECKED BOYS

I STILL get a bit excited when I open my drawerful of research papers and find the document given to me by Dr Williams in that Cardiff hotel. To put it simply, I had struck gold straight away. I hadn't endured months or years of blind alleys and red herrings like a character in a novel: I had got what I wanted immediately.

His document was a straightforward photocopy of a 1981 transaction by the Anglesey Antiquarian Society entitled *The Bone-Setters of Anglesey.*

By the time I reached the foot of the first page I realised why the venerable doctor had underscored a line heavily and written NB in the margin. This is a précis of the story, put together from all the sources I could find:

One day at the beginning of the 1700s a man called Dannie Lukie, a smuggler living in the north west of Anglesey between Cemaes and Holyhead, spotted a raft floating out to sea. It was a 'dark and stormy night' and by the time he got to it the raft was 'already sinking'.

On the raft there were two small boys. They spoke neither Welsh nor English. Most accounts say the boys were twins, of a Mediterranean appearance. One version says they were both naked.

It has been postulated that they were Spanish, or Manx – or Scottish, since this was a time of great Jacobite unrest. The Spanish theory has the most followers.

One researcher contacted the Spanish Embassy in London and discovered that there was a history of bone-setting in Spain's Celtic regions – Galicia, Asturias and the Celtic-Iberian part of Castile. But we will never know the boys' nationality nor the circumstances which led to their arrival off Anglesey's shores, terrified and traumatised on a few planks lashed with hemp rope. It seems likely that their desperate parents had tried to save them as their ship foundered.

The boys were rescued and brought ashore. One version says they were split between two families to ease the burden of sustaining them. Another story says that one boy died soon after his rescue. But one boy lived. His name was Evan, and he took on the surname of his surrogate family, which was Thomas.

Soon, Evan showed an 'amazing gift'. Starting with birds and animals, he demonstrated a marvellous ability to heal broken bones. This was well before orthopaedics became a medical science, and at a time when broken bones usually led to death or a permanent malformation. As he grew older he also grew in ability and reputation. In *Cambria Depicta*, Edward Pugh wrote:

> In this part of the island [Holyhead] I heard much of the worth and extraordinary abilities of Evan Thomas, the self-taught bonesetter... he seems to have acquired a most consummate knowledge of Osteology; for cases, desperate in the extreme, have been treated by him with expedition and success. His reputation has not only spread through his native country, but has made its way into England, where some unfortunate sufferers have happily experienced his superlative skill.
>
> This very day... I have been informed that a messenger arrived at his house from Shropshire, with a tender for £300.00 for his immediate attendance, which he has accepted. I find he has no other tongue than the legitimate language of his country.

So this 'Spanish' boy had become a monoglot Welshman. His medical ability transcended all boundaries; no-one in pain quibbles about language, and more than one racist yob has bit his tongue when delivered to an Indian doctor in a hospital casualty department.

Evan's story infused my mind the following day when I travelled back northwards.

Unexpectedly, I met Dr Williams on the platform at Cardiff Railway Station. He intended to spend a few days with distant relatives, discovered during a genealogical search of the Mormon database. I thought: how strange that this Tasmanian, chromosomally and emotionally linked to Wales, had been directed to his roots via Salt Lake City, another focal point for the Welsh diaspora. We faced each other over a train table, trying hard not to play footsie in the cramped floorspace and exchanging the occasional bon mot.

When the train stopped at Newport I had no inkling that a year later I would have strong memories of this station. On my walk around Wales I would sleep here for two nights.

On the first night I asked a railwayman if it was OK for me to bed down there. He was gentle, humane. I thought he was nearing retirement age and he had the soft, fatalistic charm of a man who had travelled for too long on the outside of life's carriage rather than within. He directed me to the small waiting room in the central area, saying it was warm but was closed after the last public train (freight trains thundered through all night, and the arrival of the mail train in the small hours was quite an event). He pointed to the main entrance hall and said: 'That's probably the warmest place in the night, though the others don't use it much.' He was Indian, or part-Indian, and I was struck by a strong irony: here was an Asian seemingly in charge of a station with white men sleeping on his platform; during the days of the Raj it would have been quite the opposite way in his homeland.

There was a genuinely downtrodden *Big Issue* seller squatting in the connecting corridor and I pressed a pound into his hand as I passed, waving away the copy he offered me. I've always felt a bit uneasy about the *Big Issue*.

Later, unable to sleep, and lacking anything to read, I went back to him. He looked wretched when I offered him the extra cash for his *Big Issue*. He stuttered an apology. It was the only copy he had, and it was months out of date. He reached into his pocket and fished out a book, saying he'd read it and didn't want it any more. Soon afterwards he was gone. People in houses hang onto their books and their possessions – people on the road pass them on to others, so they can travel light.

You may have noticed that railway stations have become increasingly populated by the homeless and the mentally ill and the addicted in recent years.

Of these social 'outcasts' the first I met was R——, a local boy in his late twenties, I guessed. He had a bottle of White Lightning with the label removed. He was very wary. Later in the night he arrived in the entrance hall and sat on the bench next to mine. He just stared ahead. My antennae detected that he was half a bottle up on the last time we met, but no trouble. Also in the room were two other men. One was well kitted out and said he was merely a bird of passage, not a down-and-out. He said he lived in Ireland and he did peculiar things like showing us a police ID badge. I stood off, since he seemed the most unpredictable. The other was a nice bloke who had left his wife and grown-up family that night. He was drunk but seemed sure of what he was doing in a grimly quiet way. He was dark, slender, and South Walian in a prototypical way; he had darkly political eyes and the beguiling physical pliancy of the fly-half. But now he had angina, not much money, and he didn't know where to go. It seemed he was going to catch the first train out, no matter where it went.

I learnt there was a coffee machine in the little taxi office alongside the station and I asked R—— if he wanted a cuppa. He did, and when I returned with his red-hot plastic cup he flashed open his filthy jacket, revealing an inside pocket crammed with Pepperoni, which he'd obviously filched. I declined but thanked him as if he were offering me riches beyond compare, then settled down to an hour of near silence with him. He wasn't the talking type. This was as close to company as he wanted. Maybe I saw childhood abuse in his eyes, but this was guesswork. In my experience 99 per cent of people like him – addicts and self-harmers – have been traumatised in childhood.

I slept fitfully and left towards Chepstow, nicely timing my arrival on the outskirts of town, in the shadow of an enormous chemicals factory, as the dawn took light.

As I walked along the Caldicot Levels that day I thought of another son of Newport, the greatest supertramp of them all, the man who coined the phrase

What is this life if, full of care,
We have no time to stand and stare.

W.H. Davies – author, poet, and roamer *extraordinaire*. A man who lost a leg jumping trains during an early career as a hobo in the newly-shaping America, and who excited George Bernard Shaw and the literary establishment with an account of his begging exploits along the length and breadth of America. Here's a sample from *The Autobiography of a Supertramp*, taken from the time he was bumming on the eastern seaboard in the late 1890s:

I shall never forget the happy summer months I spent with Brum at the seaside. Some of the rich merchants there could not spare more than a month or six weeks from business, but, thanks be to Providence, the whole summer was at our disposal. If we grew tired of one town or, as more often the case, the town grew tired of us, we would saunter leisurely to the next one and again pitch our camp; and so on, from place to place, during the summer months. We moved freely among the visitors, who apparently held us in great respect, for they did not address us familiarly, but contented themselves with staring at a distance. We lay across their runs on the sands and their paths in the woods; we monop-olised their nooks in the rocks and took possession of caves, and not a murmur heard, except from the sea, which of a certainty could not be laid to our account. No doubt detectives were in these places, but they were on the look-out for pickpockets, burglars and swindlers; and, seeing that neither the visitors nor the boarding house keepers made any complaint, these detectives did not think it worth while to arrest tramps; for there was no promotion to be had for doing so. "Ah," I said to Brum, as we sat in a shady place, eating a large custard pudding from a board-ing house, using for the purpose two self-made spoons of wood, "Ah, we would not be so pleasantly occupied as tramps in England. We would there receive tickets for soup; soup that could be taken without spoons; no pleasant picking of the teeth after eating; no sign of a pea, onion or carrot; no sign of anything except flies."

Two-thirds of a large custard pudding between two of us, and if there was one fault to be found with it, it was its being made with too many eggs. Even Brum was surprised at his success on this occasion. "Although," as he said, "she being a fat lady, I expected something unusual." Brum had a great admiration for fat women; not so much, I believe, as his particular type of beauty, but for the good natured qual-ities he claimed corpulence denoted. "How can you expect those skinny creatures to sympathise with another when they half starve their own bodies?" he asked. He often descanted on the excellencies of the fat, to the detriment of the thin, and I never yet heard another beggar disagree with him.

Please excuse me, fellow traveller, for my constant diversions. You will find that our path is long and circuitous, for that is the very purpose of my journey, not to get there quickly, but to encounter as many adventures, diversions, and amusements as possible on the way.

Already I have discovered that the author of the Vogel Papers, in trying to evoke a bustling, multifarious society, didn't have to exaggerate at all, merely fiddle about with time. And during my walk around Wales I found that time came and went with every roll of the landscape and every shift of the wind. Sometime later, on Offa's Dyke, I almost felt the physical presence of Offa's Mercians as they toiled to build the four yards or so of embank-ment allotted to each man before he could return to his own manor in the not-yet-English part of the British midlands. How they must have hated the Welsh, looking from their secret places in their savage land.

~

Opposite me on the train, Williams appeared to stare into his newspaper but I could tell he wasn't reading much. I suspected he was listening to that lilt in the Abergavenny voice, as did Alexander Cordell so many years ago. It was this place which first inspired him; he had stood in the streets of Abergavenny, in the valley below Blorenge and Sugar Loaf, listening to the thrust and vitality of the people, and he had marvelled. As we pulled out of Abergavenny I looked at the peculiar shape of Ysgyryd Fawr, the hill on my right, again not realising that this upturned keel would have great poignancy for me later in my walk as I wandered through Monmouthshire, along the Offa's Dyke Trail.

Ysgyryd Fawr had stuck up from the ground like a giant shark's fin behind me as I tacked through the fields of Llanvetherine and Llantilio Crossenney.

I'd had a 'humorous' episode at the White Castle. I arrived there early in the morning, before it opened, so I found a weakness in the fence around it and vaulted over into the grounds. I spent a stolen half hour on my own with a few birds and a squirrel in this Norman bastion and then headed back over the fence to the main entrance, where I had slung my rucksack behind a portable toilet.

But the woman who sold tickets had arrived, and I had to explain myself.

'You been in my castle, 'aven't you,' she said accusingly.

'No – I've just been for a walk round it,' I countered.

'You been in my castle, 'aven't you,' she said again. She felt very possessive about her castle, I could tell. Norman blood? Turned out she'd lived a lot of her life in South Africa. Bloody colonialists, I muttered under my breath.

'You going to pay then?' she asked.

I tried another tack.

'Actually, I'm a member of the Collwyn ap Tango Re-enactment Society,' I lied. 'We've been asked to do a re-enactment here. Collwyn ap Tango was a prince of Eifionnydd [this happens to be true]. I've been planning our demonstration.'

She believed me. She beamed. 'Marvellous! I love those re-enactments. Go down a treat. You come and do one here. My castle's doing well. Up this year again.'

She changed her mind again. 'You sure you 'aven't been in my castle?'

I tried one last throw of the dice.

'Actually,' I tried to look engagingly coy, 'I've been to the woods. You know what I mean...'

'Oh, you been for a...' she finally believed me.

I liked her, and not just because I'd won an age-old tussle for a castle. She was going to a funeral, she had a migraine, she was human, and she was guarding her castle to the best of her ability, as all those poor dead sods did six hundred years ago.

As we travelled along the fringes of the Black Mountains into England Williams regaled me with a story about Cordell, whom he'd met a few years before he departed this life so tragically. He had been found dead, with family photographs at his side, by a stream in the Horseshoe Pass area.

'Ever read Cordell?' asked Williams.

'Just the one – *Rape of the Fair Country* – though I've come across many extracts in anthologies,' I replied.

'Met him once,' he said. 'Told me a very strange story. So amazing I could barely believe it, and I've not come across it in other writings about him. He was in his early seventies when I met him – a smallish, dapper man with a toothbrush moustache. He was ex-military and looked it. He was getting tired but he was kind and he still loved Wales – it was like a love for an old flame,' said Williams, folding his newspaper and halting his story while a trolleyman sold us both beakers of tea. Then he continued:

'This is the gist of what he told me, after he had fetched out a beautifully-bound copy of *Y Gododdin* I think it was, from a cabinet. It had been presented to him as a thank-you for his lifetime's work by one of the Welsh-interest societies. Never has there been a country with so many friends! He was immensely proud of this volume.

'"I'll tell you a story," said Cordell. He had told me about his birth in Ceylon – his father was in the British Army. He talked to me in a pleasantly formal way.

'He told me that he had a daughter who had married a Scandinavian orthodontist. She came over occasionally. She'd had children of her own but she and her husband had decided to adopt a child from a third world country. So they lodged their *coincidence?*

names with an agency and after being accepted as potential parents they had been told to wait for a suitable child to come up. That could be anywhere in the world. They would have to go there immediately, when notified, to pick up their new charge. Time passed by and eventually his daughter was summoned to fetch the child – remember, this could be anywhere in the world. And so she did. She flew off and collected the baby at an orphanage in Sri Lanka, the old Ceylon. Before she left she had a picture taken of herself, holding the child outside the orphanage. On her next visit to Wales to see her father she showed him the photograph.

'"Do you know, Dr Williams," he said, looking at me with a level gaze. "That was the very building where I had been born. It was the old barracks in Ceylon, which had been turned into an orphanage."'

This incredible tale of chance had the suitable effect on me, and I had one of my own to tell, and so the journey passed swiftly through England and back into Wales, as a paradigm for the Welsh condition; so many of my countrymen have been forced to find work there, and have had such deep pangs of nostalgia when parted from their homeland, for it is true what they say, the jewel is best admired from afar. There is no greater Welshman than an exile. And some of our best friends – Saunders Lewis, Cordell, Firbank, Ffransis and Morris for instance, have either been born elsewhere or have spent long periods away.

I parted from Williams at Bangor station and made my way home. We'd agreed to meet at a church in Anglesey, near the farmhouse where he was staying. It was the parish church in Llanfairynghornwy, which I knew had a connection with Evan Thomas the bonesetter, and Williams wanted to find a memorial there too: he was still clambering up his family tree. That evening I tried to make arrangements with the vicar but couldn't get hold of him. I phoned Williams to tell him. He sounded drowsily pleased, even when I told him we would have to fly blind, since I had been unable to find anyone with a key.

The next day presaged failure. A friend let me down so I had to go by bus, and the north-west corner of Anglesey is more accessible to bears and boats than it is to buses. I anticipated, and felt, a change as we crossed the suspension bridge. It is a truth universally acknowledged by my fellow mainlanders that the island is 'different'. This difference is hard to define, even romantically. People say words like 'strange' or 'supernatural' or 'old' or 'timeless' or 'spooky'. Those who feel a sense of otherness on the island fumble for a definition. I have travelled enough to detect a commonality with other parts of the world. In passing to an island there is a feeling of detachment and passage to another time and another place. Like Arthur's conveyance to Afallon, or Orpheus's descent into the underworld, one has a sense of transportation or transposition into another realm of the senses; of a spiritual transhumance. Islands can have a fairytale feel. Often they are sparsely inhabited and one can move for hours on the landscape without seeing any human movement. Then a carrion crow will descend slowly and observe you as a specimen, silently. The wind will moan slightly in a spinney of conifers huddled like winter mourners, and remind you slyly of your own mortality. Clouds will shift and pattern the fields in a cunning re-enactment of their exact movements a thousand years ago or more, hoping you will notice. Time will have no meaning; clocks and watches will play tricks with you. The sea will wash away all memories from the shore, and the ancient chambers of man – Barclodiad y Gawres, Bryn Celli Ddu – will press you to the ground and whisper in your ear.

Islands can be Hell and islands can be Heaven. I wonder which one it was for the writer of the Vogel Papers. Was that flight across the bridge a descent into the wormhole of Vogel's personal little universe, or was it an attempt to find something – absolution, or a cure, or a prognosis?

I crossed over, below a uniform grey sky, perfectly still, as though it had been painted onto a glass cupola. I felt like a parrot whose irritable owner had thrown a grey sheet over its cage and told it to shut up and go to sleep. The landscape all around oozed sweatily with rainwater. Fields and meadows wallowed greyly in the ditches and dykes. Nature had gone to bed, and the trees stood around like hangers-on after a party. The bus rattled and felt like a crate of empties being taken away. Desperate-looking men got on at different bus stops and sat in the back, glowering moodily and picking their teeth like characters in search of a spaghetti western. An oily middle-aged man got on and talked incessantly into his mobile phone in a loud, flat, Lancastrian monotone; it was a surreal scene worthy of *Waiting for Godot*, since I felt sure there was no-one at the other end. He was infuriating. Hot ants, each carrying a molecule of hate as heavy as the universe before it banged, scurried hotly through my bloodstream. I wanted to hit him. It was a suitable day for cruelty. I imagined Suetonius Paulinus and his Roman soldiers driving nails into barrels and rolling the island's Druids downhill to their punctured deaths. The very same Suetonius Paulinus who had been the first Roman to cross the massive Atlas mountain range near Marrakesh in north-west Africa, and had reported that nearby forests harboured all kinds of wild elephants, beasts and serpents, and natives who ate their food 'like the canine race, and shared with it the entrails of wild beasts.'

I got there eventually – I hitched a bit, and walked the last two miles. I discovered there was a key with a churchwarden, Captain Roberts, but he wasn't at home. I stood by the church waiting for a bit of luck. I saw a blue estate car winding down into the half-flooded dip by the church and I struck a pose, looking at the church with my chin in my hand, trying to look interested and interesting. The car stopped.

coincidence

My luck had arrived. It was Captain Roberts with his wife, and they had the key right there with them in the car, as if they were playing the part of Providence in a Miracle Play. Llanfairynghornwy has one of those dinky little Welsh churches which look like scale models. The great cathedrals and churches of England were made to impress Man and to reach out to God. The country churches of Wales reach out to man and try to impress God – not with their magnitude, but with their smallness and vulnerability. And who would want to work all day in a snarling gale on a grandiose edifice when one could be snuggled up to God in a cosy corner of the heavenly kingdom. Wales has always prayed to the God of Small Things.

Dr Williams now hove into view and we examined the church in the late afternoon sun. I found a memorial tablet, which started:

> To the memory of Evan Thomas of Maes in this Parish who, in humble life, without the aid of education or any other advantage, by an extraordinary gift of Nature acquired such a knowledge of the human frame as to become a most skilful Bonesetter, whereby he rendered himself pre-eminently useful to his fellow creatures.

Underneath this tablet was the inscription in Welsh.

We pottered around the church and chatted with Captain Roberts, a spry ex-Merchant Navy man who had sailed out of Liverpool. He could have come straight from the Vogel Papers – he was a seafaring man, and had been treated himself by one of the bone doctors as a child. Outside, we went over to Evan Thomas's gravestone and read the inscription. As I was about to turn away and head up the path to the road a fleeting notion passed through my mind; surely the dates on the white marble tablet inside the church were different to the ones on the gravestone. I was right – there was a disparity of 22 days.

We laughed over this and I dismissed it as a stone-cutter's error. No doubt this was an afternoon job, and he'd had too much ale at lunchtime. Old gravestones have many errors of fact and grammar, with words sometimes corrected on the slate or carried over to the next line. Families of the deceased probably never noticed, because they couldn't read.

Still, it was a peculiar thing to happen, and Williams and I discussed it in his hired car – he had offered to take me to Amlwch to meet a bus. For him it was the end of the affair, a diversion, and he was off to his symposium in a couple of days, and then, after a month's adventuring, back to Tasmania.

'Hobart?' I asked.

'No – Launceston, the second city. It's at the head of the Tamar River, and it's old – third oldest city on the continent, I seem to remember,' he said. 'Quite pretty. Hilly. A few fine buildings and a nice little chairlift. Lovely old watermill complex. I divide my time between lecturing on maritime history and taking tourists along our wine route. You'll be delighted to know that I live in a suburb called Trevallyn – can't get much more Welsh-sounding than that! – and my actual address is Beaumaris Court.'

I feigned astonishment.

'Incidentally,' I asked, 'why did you start this maritime thing?'

'Tasmania's got more wrecks than most places – about a thousand at the last count,' he said. 'Comes from being smack in the course of the roaring forties. It's no place to be in a storm if you're a sailor.'

We arrived at Amlwch and he dropped me at the bus stop. After the farewells he prepared to go but then stopped the car and wound down the window.

'Tell you what, if I hear anything else of interest I'll get in touch. Got an e-mail address?'

After he'd written it down he floated off into the darkness, and I thought I'd seen the last of him. The first chapter was closed, and Williams had been a useful find. Like one of those historical characters in the Vogel Papers, he was about to disappear forever.

Or so I thought...

As I stood waiting for the bus a man walked up and joined me – it was the same man who had irritated me earlier with his *Waiting for Godot* conversation. He didn't recognise me so I played a trick on him.

'Dy'a know,' I said nonchalantly after the initial greetings, 'I'm a bit of a clairvoyant, have the gift of second sight and all that... give me your phone for a second – if I hold anything belonging to someone I can usually tell a lot about them.'

He handed me the phone, slowly and suspiciously.

I held it in my hand, closed my eyes, and regurgitated a medley from his conversations earlier on the bus.

'You have an Aunty Mary... she is very ill... you need to go to see her in hospital tomorrow... your car is playing up... you need a new exhaust... the garage can't fit you in... but I can't tell you any more... it's terrible... too horrible...'

It did the trick. He grabbed the phone and ran into the night.

Revenge can be very sweet.

I'm off to bed now, to dream great dreams. Yes, I know, I should be finalising my plans. Tell you what, you can plan the plans. Here are a few directions. I will be walking in the Roman style – three days on the road then one day's rest. I will abide by Nicholas Crane's four quadrants of survival: navigation, shelter, food and warmth.

That's enough for you to get on with. Now leave me to dream. Like Mr Vogel, I want to get out of my one-horse town, where Time is a slow puncture and Hope is heavily bandaged.

Before I go tomorrow I will plant a tamarisk tree.

Why? To see how much it has grown by the time we've finished this mission of ours?

Certainly not – hubris ain't allowed around here, my friends.

This is why I want to plant a tamarisk tree. Back at the start of this chapter, somewhere down there in the nether region of Wales, the bit that wallows like a big fat pimply buttock in the Bristol Channel, I mentioned a *Big Issue* seller who gave me a book. It was the memoirs of an American hobo called Hood River Blackie, who ran away from home at the age of 14 after some family troubles. I like this bit:

I guess it was only natural that I take to the rails, but my first ride in a boxcar was a terrifying thing. I swear, if that train had stopped I would have gotten off it and gone right back home. But after a few hours, I saw it wasn't going to jump the tracks. I also noticed a strange feeling coming over me, a kind of pleasant swelling sensation in my chest that I now know was freedom.

About a week later I piled off the freight at the little California desert town of Mecca. I had a bedroll, a packsack, and a few dollars I had been saving to buy an old car. If anyone who ever reads this ever gets to Mecca, or if you live there, walk over the tracks and look at the big tamarisk tree located at the southern edge of the town on the west side of the tracks. Under this tree on a hot September day in 1940 I met Tex Medders. Tex was probably the finest human being I've ever known. He looked rather frail to me at five foot seven and 135 pounds, sitting on a rusty five-gallon can watching a stew cook over a small fire. I can close my eyes now and still see his old face and the merry twinkle in his faded blue eyes...

It didn't take him long to get the story of my running away out of me, and to my surprise he tried to talk me into going back home and getting an education. By dark, though, I guess it had become apparent to him that I never would go home again, for all at once he looked across the fire at me and said, "Kid, let's you and me head up north to Oregon and pick some apples." I can still see the shadows of the fire flickering on his face. Never had I felt such happiness. At last I was going to be a hobo and travel with these strange wanderers.

And so started our 25-year journey across America.

When I found a picture of the tamarisk tree in a book I found something to my liking, and that is why I want to plant one in my garden. And I suppose, when I look at it in years to come, by the brook, when it whirls like a dervish in a winter tempest, when it dances to the roar, the trance-music of the storm drums, I can tap into its sap, switch off the gravitron and dance to the music of my own golden age.

AGNES HUNT

AT LAST, I can write it down:

March 1st: I start my walk around Wales. A journey of a thousand miles starts with a step! I meet a crimson fox, who watches me go by...

To begin at the beginning. It was very early (I like daybreak) when I stood by the newly-planted tamarisk tree and waited for the night's purple curtain to rise, for the footlights to come on, for my play to begin.

Far out to sea, on the horizon, the lighthouse at Penmon slunk out of the shadows like a girl sneaking away from an all-night party, sleepy and still a bit drunk, the early sun blushing her white dress with a soft pink. I stepped away from the tamarisk, like its shadow leaving it; among the millions of steps being taken all over the planet it was no different, but to me it was the most significant of my whole life. Within minutes I had met my first fellow-traveller: peeking over a hedge, which was beaded with a million glinting droplets of cold dew, my eyes met the gaze of a fox; we stood and looked at each other for quite a few seconds before he vanished into the undergrowth. His coat was a deep red, almost crimson in that light. Briefly, a million dewdrops had each held a miniature snapshot of my first step, and a million tiny foxes had quivered in tiny bubbles on the thorns; my journey had already reached epic, kaleidoscopic proportions!

A clever man like John Parker, who so annoyed the Blue Angel barman, might say something fanciful: *with that first step I tore through the placenta of my past*, for instance, but I'm not clever, and it was just a step, just the start of a walk for an ordinary mortal.

I will not plot my course by the stars, but by the people I encounter, the places I see, and the events which will come to meet me. A strange current is flowing through my body, as if I had a Gulf Stream of my own, stirring my subterranean channels; electricity fizzles in tiny blue bursts of current on my skin: a thousand miles stretch out in front of me (though I've not mentioned my journey to many people in case I come a cropper).

If you're not Welsh I must introduce you to three words (if you're not, I'm sure you have other talents!). They are *cynefin, hafod* and *hendref*.

Cynefin means your home territory, your own patch – it's the area of pastureland grazed by a particular flock, which stays there even if there are no fences. The flocks behave like this because farmers have spent centuries riding around their cynefin on horseback every morning and night, driving the sheep towards the centre of their territory. This gives each flock a Jungian collective memory of the homeland, which is seemingly passed on from ewe to lamb. The Welsh have a very strong sense of their own *cynefin*, as if an invisible farmer had also spent centuries herding them into their allotted place. This has seeped into the national consciousness, and is best put, I think, by the character Albie in Emyr Humphreys' *A Toy Epic*:

> I see life as a cage with an open door, imprisoning mice that are too frightened to run wild.

But large numbers of Welsh people – escaping poverty and religious persecution – have gone through the door in the last 150 years, and they have spread all over the world like dandelion seeds on the wind. However, I have been one of the timid ones left inside the cage. I am glad to say that today I am the mouse which roared. I will make the whole of Wales my *cynefin*.

You many wonder at my preoccupation with minorities and majorities, with borders and human movement. The reason is quite simple: I am merely following a train of thought which was put in motion by the author of the Vogel Papers – I am trying to look at the issues he raised in a modern context, from the viewpoint of the Welsh people living today, since we are quite naturally concerned about the effects on our culture of successive waves (and a recent tsunami) of incomers, mainly English people. This incoming has always created an irresolvable tension in the native Welsh, because half of their psyche wants to reject this constant and overwhelming threat to their culture and traditions, whilst the other half wants to extend a warm hand of friendship to every newcomer, a trait which is exceptionally strong in the Celt. To double this tension we have been strongly affected by English culture, and of course the language, which is one of the strongest in the world at present, and a beautiful one at that. This interracial tension is a common syndrome throughout the world, during an era when dozens of languages die every year.

There is no simple answer. The people of England are also a

collection of tribes, and since there was a huge resurgence in nationalism in the world during the twentieth century it is interesting to note that the English have largely ditched the Union Jack lately in favour of the flag of St George, so they also have felt this keen renewal of nationalism (except Yorkshiremen, perhaps).

Those other words I mentioned were *hafod* and *hendref*. Thousands of homes and farms throughout Wales bear these names: *hafod* was the summer residence, usually a crudely-made abode in the uplands, and the *hendref* was the winter residence in the lowlands. These words are the hieroglyphs of a vanished Welsh society which moved its flocks to upland pastures every spring, men and sheep first, women and children following later, thus engendering almost as many jokes as there are sheep about the relationship between Welshmen and their little woolly lovikins. I will come out of the closet immediately, to save a lot of time, by declaring myself a great admirer of sheep; they are far more intelligent than the urbanite thinks, probably more intelligent than the dolphin – all they need is a makeover by the same agency as the one used by the Dolphin Corporation.

Hafod and *hendref*: this annual movement, called transhumance, sounds like a good arrangement to me; you're living in two worlds, which must be a lot more interesting than working at a desk (school and then office) for most of your life in return for a box to sleep in and a few gizmos.

As I breeze along the two Ormes on the North Wales coast – named after the Norse word for worm or serpent, because that's what these great headlands looked like, looming out of a Welsh fog, as the invaders rowed ashore – I contemplate some of the things I am *not* going to encounter on my journey (or if I do I will hit the headlines).

Wolves. I am not going to be attacked by wolves, such as the Beast of Gevaudan mentioned by Robert Louis Stevenson in his *Travels with a Donkey in the Cevennes*, and by Nicholas Crane in the riveting account of his 10,000-kilometer walk across the mountain ranges from Finisterre to Istanbul. This is how Crane tells the story:

> ... the Beast of Gevaudan was preying on this part of the Cevennes, eating sheep and young women. Bodies were found drained of blood and partially eaten. Theories blazed along the valleys: the Beast was a vampire wearing a wolfskin, or it was a wolfpack being guided by a

crazed tyrant, or it was a lone wolf of enormous size. For three years the Beast caused panic in the isolated communities of the Cevennes, separated from one another by forest and appalling roads. The bishop of Mende ordered public prayers and hunts were dispatched by the Intendant of Languedoc. As more went missing, dragoons rode out and a reward of 6,000 livres was offered by the king. When a 130-pound wolf was shot in September 1765, the harassed population filled the churches and the Beast was sent, stuffed, to Versailles. Three months later two boys were killed near Mont Lozere. Through the winter and following spring the killing spree resumed with new ferocity until Jean Chastel found himself looking down his sights at a second wolf. After that, the killings stopped.

No, I'm highly unlikely to be killed by a wolf. One source says that Idwal, King of Gwynedd during the tenth century, was obliged to provide 300 wolfskins every year to the English crown, but Edward I – the very same delightful man who built those chunky designer castles along the North Wales coast – ordered their extermination, and the last reference to the species in Wales occurred in 1166 when a 'mad wolf' allegedly killed 22 people.

No, I'm not going to meet a wolf. Nor a golden eagle. The last was seen in Wales around 1750. Neither can I expect to be rushed by an enraged bear, like the specimen which ran 'with a relaxed, shaggy gallop, like a second-row rugby forward' towards Nicholas Crane in the Carpathians, and from which he ran with such terror that he ended up clinging to a tree, retching, after an Olympic-standard sprint, carrying a heavy rucksack, into the forest. No, I'm not going to bump into a bear either, though the borderland with England, the Marches, could still harbour a few nasty surprises I imagine. I will not, thank god, have to carry a message stick, as do Australian Aborigines who want to show that they're messengers when they're travelling through another tribe's territory.

I must take great care not to wander off the beaten track. In 695, the Kentish King Wihtread passed the following law:

> If a traveller from afar, or a foreigner leave the road, and he then neither shouts nor blows a horn, he is to be regarded as a thief, to be either killed or ransomed.

So if you meet a chappie in the undergrowth, a-hollering and blowing a horn as loudly as his lungs will allow, don't panic. It'll be me – not a madman. Honestly.

Will I be strong enough to walk all that way? My Welsh ancestors would have breezed it: I like this excerpt from the *British Gazeteer* of April 24, 1773:

> Saturday morning a singular race was run on the road between Redbourn and St Albans, one mile, between a labouring man, and a Welsh girl in her pattens, when the Welsh girl won the match.

What sort of people will I meet? Certainly not the sort of people Michael Faraday, of electromagnetic fame, encountered when he wrote his *Journal of a Tour Through North Wales* some two hundred years ago. This is how he described the Welsh peasantry:

> They are bare legged and bare footed, sometimes bare headed. Their cloathes are coarse and hang loosely and they have not the appearance at first (at least they had not to me) of being remarkable for cleanliness or order. But this erroneous judgement must be rectified. In their houses and their persons they are equally orderly and the very custom of walking bare legged and footed is a proof of it. Every girl and woman in going from their houses to the town takes her shoes and if she has stockings, them also with her. She walks however without them on, but on nearing the town washes her feet in a brook, puts herself in order and then makes a respectable appearance.

Neither am I going to be 'surprised to see a number of fine women bathing promiscuously with men and boys, perfectly naked' at Abergele, as Samuel Taylor Coleridge was in July, 1794. No such luck, I'm afraid.

Today I watched the Ursula C loading her cargo from a rattling jetty on the shore at Llanddulas, stones disappearing into her maw like grit into the gorge of a floating bird. A tiny bit of Wales is taken away across the sea, like rock from a seaside sweet stall. Two of the crew stood on the prow, looking out to land, reminding me of that ship which ran aground in the Vogel Papers. Apparently there are up to a million people in the world who spend their entire lives on ships because they can't land – they have no nationality. Wouldn't that be direful – not being able to walk around on land! Or there again, you may be a root not a branch: as William Congreve put it in *The Way of the World*: "I nauseate walking; 'tis a country diversion. I loathe the country."

The weather has been benevolent, all blue and white like an Italian nun, and I am traversing the coastline steadily and pleasantly, meeting very few people on the hoof, although thousands of mutants, all of them hiding under a shiny tin carapace, are screaming along the A55, bound for charmless houses built to replicate faithfully the suburban steppes of Middle England. The Welsh Assembly has ensured that this part of the country is completely desecrated by allowing a huge new industrial park to be built on a substantial greenfield site within a stone's throw of the sea. And these people are supposed to be on *our* side. What did Crazy Horse say?

One does not sell the earth upon which people walk.

Gannets out to sea, plunging into the water. The horizon is uncompromising, the sea cobalt and cold, and the sky is a Canaletto canopy to contain my breezy spirits.

I forgot to tell you anything about my country, those of you who have never been here, so I will provide a few details.

Wales is a small country which happens to be next door to England, and is therefore part of the United Kingdom. Cynics have likened it to a patio built onto England for the English to play on, others have likened it to an ear stitched onto England, condemned perpetually to listen slavishly for instructions. I leave it to a better wordsmith than I, Jan Morris, to describe the place of my birth:

... on the western perimeter of Europe lies the damp, demanding and obsessively interesting country called by its own people Cymru... and known to the rest of the world, if it is known at all, as Wales. It is a small country, in many ways the archetype of a small country, but its smallness is not petty; on the contrary, it is profound, and if its frontiers were ever to be extended, or its nature somehow eased, its personality would lose stature, not gain it.

You must look hard to find Wales in an atlas, for it is a peninsula not much larger that Swaziland, rather smaller than Massachusetts, inhabited by a mere 2.9 million people. Also is it so obscurely tucked away there, in the heart of the British archipelago, that many maps fail to name it at all, and as often as not people elsewhere have never heard of it, or at best assume it to be a municipality somewhere, or a lake in

Florida. Its image is habitually blurred; partly by this geographical unfamiliarity, partly by the opaque and moody climate, partly by its own somewhat obfuscatory character, which is entramelled in a dizzy repertoire of folklore, but most of all by historical circumstance.

For although Wales is a country, it is not a State. It has a capital city, but not a Government; its own postage stamps, but not its own currency; a flag, but no embassies; an indigenous language, but not indigenous laws. All this is because, though it is surrounded on three sides by sea, on the fourth its border marches with the powerful kingdom of England, and for some 700 years it has been absorbed into the political entity of Great Britain, with its seat of power in London...

... it is a wonderfully well-proportioned country. Nothing is too big, nothing lasts too long, and there is perpetual variety. It is only some 130 miles from the northern coast of Wales to the southern, only 50 miles from east to west at the narrowest point – a day's drive one way, a couple of hours the other. Yet within this narrow compass there are places that feel like India, and places not at all unlike Australia, and places that remind one of Wyoming or northern Spain, and many places that are, with their especially piquant blend of age, damp, intricacy and surprise, altogether and unmistakably Welsh.

Wales, in short, is a bag of tricks – a Russian doll, for as soon as you open one Wales there is another inside waiting to be opened. It has great natural beauty and wildness scarred only by man-inflicted cruelties.

The guy who lives in the flat below me limps up the stairs with my mail whenever I get any worth reading – he has a good eye for the dross, including free newspapers, and he leaves it all to heap up in a teetering pile, like the books in the Blue Angel bookshop. In late February it rained for a fortnight and I was housebound; I got depressed – my letters lay on the landing outside my door for day after day.

This old man and I meet on the stairs quite often and share a few words. He is urbane and well-travelled. Having the look of a hippy-trail beatnik perhaps, with a frizzled grey beard, he spoke to no-one for many months after arriving from nowhere. People took him for a sun-worshipper because he often stood for hours looking at the sky. They were wary of him. But when he announced his intention to form a society for cloud-worship he was embraced warmly by the community, though no-one joined his crazy club.

One rare storm-free afternoon, after hours of walking in the company of oyster-catchers and curlews by the lagoons on the shoreline close to our seaside town, and watching water swirl along the vermiculated mudflats as the tide moved in, I looked at my piled-up letters. On the top there was a postcard with a chair-lift pictured in the foreground. My eye was drawn to the trees in the background, which didn't have a British shape. The card had two colourful foreign stamps. The address simply had my name and the name of our town. Fortunately, I am well enough known for it to reach my door.

The message was brief.

> Cannot get in touch. Is your e-mail working? I have some news for you. One of my friends has made a connection between Vogel and Tasmania. Please contact me – Williams.

I hadn't touched the computer for days. When I get these bouts I tend to shut down all systems and wait for the bleakness to go away, or I walk it off.

Today, as I strolled along the shoreline I thought of Mr Vogel, who had never been for a walk in his entire life. I wondered how he'd felt about his confinement, how he'd coped with captivity. In an imaginary conversation I shared a few of my thoughts with him, and tried to explain what it's like to move along the land, something we take so much for granted. This is what I told him:

The natural rhythm of walking is a mild sedative. It's a fairly simple equation involving physical movement, almost musical in its pattern, followed by well-being. Endorphins released by the body during exertion give a pleasant 'high'. Presumably this is the residue of a primeval reward system which gave the hunter-gatherer a 'fix' for running about in search of food. It occurs to me that this 'high' we experience could have been much more intense – approaching a climax perhaps – when hunting was a life-or-death activity.

The moving landscape provides an absorbing diversion which frees the mind and gives us a fresh viewpoint, and we're most at ease with the world when we walk because everything is happening at a manageable pace. If we travel any faster – by car, say – the brain has to shut out most of the information it receives and is therefore in a state of conflict. Walks have been described as 'looking the world into existence.'

They have also been described as a private revolt; a journey between one's past and one's future; the creation of a story; a treasure hunt; a way of measuring ourselves against the Earth; a miniature soap-opera, and much else. Scientists believe that man came down from the trees and started walking long before his other main attribute developed: his 'big' brain. Walking can take us to paradise – but look where our brains have led us.

There had been another reason for my despondency. I had been asked by a magazine which had picked up on my story to write an article on my venture. I had done so, and as a device I had compared my little amble to the great walk by the American trail-blazer Earl Shaffer, who was the first to walk the full 2,000-mile length of the Appalachian Trail, in 1948. The hike, from Katahdin in Maine to Springer Mountain in Georgia, took him around four months. That meant he walked about 16 miles every day for 120 days, which is barely credible. Some years later he did it again, but in the other direction. Even more remarkably, he returned to the trail a few months before his 80th birthday and did it yet again to celebrate the 50th anniversary of his first walk.

The day after I sent my article to the editor Earl Shaffer died. You can't get more cussed than that. The old dog had surely waited until then to pop his clogs, just to annoy that het-up little editor who made me spend a night changing tenses (which, I suppose, is what we all do if we die in our sleep). All this hassle had left me low.

But Williams's postcard got me going again so I switched on the machine and got in touch.

Sorry, I said, computer broke, now mended. He must have kept his e-mail draft because it came almost immediately, and like the Bonesetters link it gave me another valuable lead in my bid to unravel the Vogel mystery.

This is Williams's e-mail, in full:

Greetings from Tasmania, hope you're OK and not letting this Vogel thing tie you in knots. Great bit of news about our hero. Went to a party and met a doc down on leave from the capital, expert on bones etc doing research into something called Paget's Disease, chronic skeletal disorder, reckons Vogel may have had it. We got a bit squiffy together and he got talking about a woman called Hunt who was a bit of a patron saint of cripples in the UK, fresh air fiend apparently, had the patients outside the wards in all weather, even in snow. Anyway, the mad thing is, this Hunt woman spent some of her early years in Tasmania! She wrote a book about her experiences. Get weaving mate! Can't get the book here, there's a reference to her on the internet, but only in connection with a hospital.

Keep me posted, I'd like to know if you find fresh info. All the best – Williams.

This was another nice, clean, crisp clue. Since I'd had my recent operation at the Robert Jones and Agnes Hunt Hospital at Gobowen, Shropshire, I knew immediately that Agnes Hunt had been a pioneer in orthopaedic care, and that Robert Jones was connected to the Bonesetters of Anglesey – so the bones of my story were knitting together nicely!

I sloughed off my languor and swung into action straight away. Yes, there was a book by Agnes Hunt, and yes, she had spent some time in Tasmania.

I loved the book. Dame Hunt has a no-nonsense style of writing which bustles into the reader's presence like a good old-fashioned matron and describes everything clearly, efficiently, and entirely accurately. I fancy she would have shown some pity for this weakling epistle, recognising it immediately for what it is, a chronically spavined thing, but nevertheless, from human kindness, she would have given it plenty of fresh air and hope. It would be conveniently populist to say that she could have done the work of ten modern hospital administrators, but her sharp mind and her adamantine determination surely made her a formidable force. Her brief autobiography, *This is my Life*, is 206 pages of sheer entertainment.

Her family was as eccentric as they come, and for that reason I must tell you a little about them, so let's unhitch our backpacks, sit in the shade of this magnificent ash tree, and have a bite to eat whilst I tell you the story of the Hunt family.

Agnes Hunt's poor mother disliked children intensely but was doomed to produce eleven. At the age of nine Agnes got a bad blister on her heel, but because she was terrified of Victorian 'cures' she kept quiet. The result was delirium and what was then called general blood poisoning. 'My apprenticeship to crippledom had begun, and also the great education of pain', she wrote later.

It transpired that the Hunt family had fallen on hard times after the father's death. Agnes says her chief recollection of him was that 'he laughed immoderately at any accident we had'. In search of a future, their extremely eccentric mother had attended a lecture on Australia, and had been told, quite erroneously, that an island off the coast of Queensland could be bought quite cheaply, and the breeding of Angora goats was 'a most paying proposition'.

This was quite enough to convince the idiosyncratic mater, and with missionary zeal she gathered her chicks like a hen and headed for the antipodes, as if Brisbane were at the bottom of the garden. Their adventures, during which they visited the Blue Mountains and the Jenolan Caves, are too numerous to recount here.

Eventually they arrived in Launceston, Tasmania, and headed up country, to an unfinished and 'disgusting' shack on a virgin patch of ground.

For a taste of the pioneering nature of their life, I give you this vignette which shows the dangers involved and Agnes's resourcefulness in a crisis.

One day she was helping her brother Tom to clear the great gum trees which had fallen or had been felled. They had been stacked in huge pyres ready for burning – but one of the great trunks rolled onto Tom's shoulders. She says:

> Shaking in every limb, I limped round, thinking he must be dead, or that at least his back was broken. I was, therefore, very much relieved when I heard an irate voice from under the tree trunk ordering me in no uncertain terms to remove the something, something tree. I asked him if he could feel his legs, as I had heard that people with broken backs could not, but he told me not to be an ass but to get busy and remove the tree trunk, as it was hurting him confoundedly.

Agnes rode ten miles to a ranch to get help, and Tom was freed.

> I was still obsessed with the idea that he had broken his back and could have no feeling in his legs, so, when I was changing his hot water bottles I stuck a pin into him. My mind was entirely relieved by the row he made and by the impolite names he called me.

Elsewhere, Agnes records the fate of a young man on a neighbouring ranch who, while felling trees alone, had met with a terrible death. Somehow a trunk had closed on his hand and he was found dead two months later. From the marks on his wrist it was evident that he had tried to gnaw his hand off.

I e-mailed some of these details to Williams and he replied quickly with information about the young man who died – he'd been a Welsh pioneer and his story had been featured in a book about the early immigrants. Williams sent an attachment with a picture of him. He had a youthful but full walrus moustache and a small bowler hat, a cob pipe clenched in his teeth and mournful eyes. I am intrigued by these odd twists of fate – that a picture of a Welshman should be sent, many years later, to another Welshman at the other end of the globe at the flick of a mouse. Here was a Welsh colonialist. I though: how often have I been forced to suppress dark thoughts about the incoming English in my own land, but my own race had colonised just as actively – in Australia, Tasmania, Patagonia, North America, and indeed in England itself. The Welsh Quakers had peeled off to Pennsylvania in the Lyon, the nonconformists had sailed off to Patagonia in the Mimosa, and a Nova Cambria had been established in Brazil. There was even a settlement in the Ukraine called Yuzovka (Hughesofca), now called Donetsk.

I was aware that the author of the Vogel papers had alluded to immigration as a negative force. But the English language he used so novelistically owed its power to the fact that it was an amazing meld of many languages introduced by successive invaders. Here was invasion of the body not by an illness-bearing microbe, but by a new serum; an antidote to sterility. Rationality, however, doesn't help a minority facing extinction. There is a deep sadness always there.

Williams invited me to fly out to Tasmania and stay with him, but I declined politely. I cannot travel. The world frightens me too much. I can just about cope with it in books and on television. I might easily be an agoraphobic but for my need to walk. Even this is limited to my own country.

I pulled out a book on Tasmania.

The Last of the Tasmanians made depressing reading. The aboriginals who inhabited the island believed they were alone in the world. They were wandering hunters without settled habitation or a form of government. Their wooden spears killed kangaroos and wallabies, and their boomerangs brought down birds. They had no garments, except for animal skins worn on the upper body, and no homes, though they used windbreaks for shelter.

To incoming Europeans they represented the depths of barbarism. But they were neither stupid nor miserable. Their language was sophisticated and they had a lively sense of humour. Like the Eskimo, said the author, they lived entirely in the present. They made no stores in any way for the future. They foraged on what was around for the day, and let the morrow take care of itself. With no gods, no form of worship, their only fears were raised by the 'dread voices of the constant storms, the darkness and the eyes of the Tasmanian Wolf and the Devil peering at them out of the blackness beyond the fire.'

He continued:

> They did not have the slightest understanding of the laws of the universe. They were of the earth, content with one day's food and gladness; so they lived, so had their fathers lived. Another wanderer came, another claimant of the bounding kangaroo. The aborigine saw a man like himself, but white of skin, clothed and armed with thunder stolen from the skies. But, far worse, the intruder brought mistrust and gloom to the island so long owned by the darker race.

The terrible fate of those simple people, who had lived in their own little Eden for so long, was horrific and sadistic. I wish I could say *you can't imagine what happened to them*, but unfortunately you can. 'Civilisation' has given you all the tools and all the knowledge you need to be as uncivilised as you please.

Here is an interesting point for you. Before I started my walk around Wales I bought all the relevant maps. I became interested in maps *per se*. I studied the cartography of the Greeks, Agrippa and Ptolemy. I learnt about the Roman Peutinger Table and the Antonine Itinerary, and about the medieval rediscovery of the Ptolemaic maps and Mercator's additions of latitude and longitude.

I pored over the early maps of Wales, particularly John Ogilby's wonderful strip maps. It became apparent that Mercator's lines, criss-crossing the globe, did more than make navigation much easier: they also created a vacuum. And we all know what happens to vacuums. Adventurers who studied those medieval maps, demarcating the world for the first time, knew which countries lay in some of the segments, but not in others, so they set out to fill in the blanks and complete the picture. It was like painting by numbers, and if you filled in more bits in red than the Spanish coloured in yellow you ended up with more land than they did. Early explorers were keenly aware that any land they discovered within Mercator's empty bits was theirs simply because they got there first and were bigger than the other kids.

Another point: the ordnance survey maps we use today were most certainly not first designed to help walkers – they were drawn up hurriedly to help prepare Britain for Napoleon's antic-ipated invasion.

I also became interested in human mapping after stumbling across the writings of an Innuit lunatic called Ootek. Innuit landmaps are appealing because they are unscientific, yet do their job quite adequately. No contour lines for the snow people; their maps – on skin or bark – are mostly white, and certainly not to scale. Distances are measured in 'sleeps' – the number of nights' kip needed on the way. All the important bits, such as caribou trails, rivers and camps are vastly exaggerated in size to underline their importance. Anyway, this Ootek character was quite bright and had been sent from one of those dismal camps full of snow-bikes, slinking dogs and empty liquor bottles to one of the American universities to study medicine, so that he could cure his own race of civilized maladies. He went back, not with a stethoscope and a bagful of pills, but with a newly-formulated theory which he set about disseminating with the calm mysticism of a Gurdjieff disciple. He told his people about the European discovery of DNA and illustrated the double helix with a twin spiral of snowballs.

But they had failed to detect a third helix, he said, and he illus-trated his discovery with a third spiral of snowballs dyed red with caribou blood. This third helix, he said, was the sum total of man's non-biological parts – his soul, his personality, his memories, all that made him unique. Ootek made weird and wonderful models of his own third helix, which no-one understood. I sympathised with his aims, however, for we all search for a structure to those components in us which are not scientifically accountable.

Ootek's snowballs bring to mind the antics of the 16th century British explorer Henry Morgan, who as purser of the

Sunshine accompanied John Davis on his second voyage to discover the North-West Passage, and ended up playing soccer with the Eskimos of Baffin Island during August 1586 (this was soon after the Eskimos had tried to murder a boatload of sailors with 'dartes'):

> Divers times they did wave us on shore to play with them at the football, and some of our company went on shore to play with them, and our men did cast them downe as soone as they did come to strike the ball.

This must be the first report ever of a professional foul.

I, also, was to be attacked during my walk around Wales, though not with 'dartes' – I was stoned on the Gower. Just like our hero Mr Vogel I bought a clapped-out camper van with 150,000 miles on the clock and a berth ready for it in the scrapyard. I had already slept rough often enough for my bones to complain, so I shelled out on a little luxury as I traversed the south coast. I spent three days on the Gower in weak but sap-injecting spring sunshine, and on the last day I had skirted the vast Llanrhidian Marshes, passing Weobley Castle in a fieldful of lambs. Surely these marshes, with their huddles of ponies grazing in spectral silence, must be one of the wonders of Wales: only the glinting windows of Llanelli over the water beamed me back into the twenty-first century. A friend once told me that he had seen two mature Llanrhidian ponies, realising that they were being surrounded by the incoming tide, sandwiching a foal between them and lifted it above the water (mind you, this friend has a most advanced form of the Celtic Exaggeration and Romancing Disease). Anyway, to return to my subject: at the end of the day I retrieved the camper van from Port Eynon and drove to Penclawdd in the north part, which is supposed to be Welsh-speaking. Seeking a conversation in my mother tongue, I found a solitary Welsh-speaker in a pub, but he had dementia, and he insisted on telling me – at least ten times – in exactly the same words how he used to collect cockles on the marshes with his mother and a donkey, and sell them in Morriston; soon I was sick and tired of cockles, cocklers and cockle stories, so that I wished his quaint party had disappeared long ago under the peaty waste. I bought some indifferent fish and chips – my visit to Penclawdd was not going as smoothly as I wished – and I returned to the camper, which was parked, ready for a good night's sleep, in what I thought to be an ideal spot, in a large car park in the centre of town, overlooking the river-mouth and the marshes. I nestled there with my food, feeling mellow as the sun burned a hole in the Loughor estuary.

My pleasant reverie was broken by a couple of clatters on the van's bodywork: upon looking through a side-window to investigate, I was more than surprised to discover a ragtag gang of artful dodgers, ranging in age from a snotty three to a sullen thirteen, flinging stones at my vehicle and shouting. Their precise advice was to '**** off you ****ing gypo' (pardon their English). Slightly flattered to be taken for a gipsy, I nonetheless decided that discretion was the better part of valour and beat a hasty retreat to Llanelli, where I slept near the bird sanctuary. It was a good decision, since I particularly enjoy wildfowl chattering at bedtime.

So the Tasmanians were ethnically cleansed by British settlers. As the author of the Vogel Papers stresses time and again, getting to the truth is no easy matter; each story is glossed so heavily that the truth is virtually unobtainable.

Agnes Hunt arrived in Tasmania in 1886, just ten years after the death of Trugannini, the last of the true Tasmanians. Almost exactly a century after the first white man arrived a whole race had been snuffed out. Many had been hunted for sport by bushrangers or stockmen, most of them outlaws. The native children were stolen and forced into prostitution by the sex-starved male settlers, who also took them as wives and sometimes kept them on chains like dogs. Their land had been divided into British-sounding counties – Devon, Dorset, Cornwall, Kent, Buckingham, Cumberland, Lincoln, Westmorland. And yes, on the map there were parts of Wales too... Glamorgan, Monmouth and Pembroke. Agnes Hunt makes no mention of this. Perhaps her mind was already consumed with her ambition to become a nurse – she returned shortly to Britain. I will cut corners and tell you that in 1887 she was back in Blighty and scouring the London hospitals for a job. She was told repeatedly that she was too young or too lame.

I could barely believe my eyes when I read the following sentence:

Finally, I applied and was accepted as a lady pupil at the Royal Alexandra Hospital, Rhyl.

Why, that was in my own back yard! After a round trip of X thousand miles to Tasmania we had arrived back, like a boomerang, in my own patch, a town I had trudged through on one of the less inspiring days of my walk around Wales. Rhyl is the Blackpool of North Wales, a typical British seaside resort dripping with ice cream, hot dogs and candy floss, bingo halls and flashing bauble-rooms full of coin-gulping bandits and those impossible machines with a grab which invite you to fish for a fluffy toy and never, ever, give you one. I have never heard of anyone in the entire history of seaside resorts who has succeeded in prising a single useless teddy from those machines. Rhyl is where millions of people belonging to the old working classes went on holiday before Europe was discovered. Personally I quite like Rhyl's jaded charms, but others have been less kind.

On my trek I had walked past the Alex, as the hospital is known locally. It lies isolated at the eastern end of the prom, a reminder, like some of the large Victorian houses nearby, of better days, when four railway tracks teeming with steam trains brought the first wave of pleasure-seekers into Wales. Wild Bill Hickok brought his touring Buffalo Bill's Wild West Show here in a convoy of trains, and the redoubtable Arthur Cheetham introduced moving pictures, phrenology and water electrolysis to heal those with enough time and money. It was that sort of age.

The Alex holds many memories for me. It was where my father prepared for his death. By then I had only fitful contact with him but I tried to do the right thing.

He was living in a flat in a nearby offshoot of the resort and had given up on life, spending most of his time in bed. He was yellow, and barely functioning. I never saw the flat properly, since he kept the curtains shut at all times. Every time I entered I was hit by a nauseous wave of malodour; he was unable to get to the toilet and shat on pieces of newspaper next to his bed. I had spent a great deal of my childhood cleaning up after my father in one way or another, so I rolled up those newspapers and took them out to the bins without much thought. As his liver took the final curtain he was admitted to the Alex, where I visited him roughly twice a week. There was only one subject of conversation. Whisky.

Here, in this hospital, my father was given a tumbler of whisky during my visits, presumably to keep him alive. I think that's what you call irony. He was rather like that buzzard chick in the Vogel Papers, kept alive long enough to die a certain death. So my father spent our sessions together pleading with me, not to keep him alive, but to go and get him a means to die quicker. And I did. Now you may want to know why he drank. If I told you that he'd knocked down a child and crippled him, would you believe me? That he'd turned to drink because he'd ruined the life of a child just like Mr Vogel's life had been ruined? You'd like that, wouldn't you? It would be neat, like the ending of a television play, or one of those awful American films. But no, he didn't. This is a true story, not a vehicle for sentimental parables. He didn't kill anyone. He was just a drunk.

Life on the road is the only drug I need. Old Mr Vogel would have given up the sauce too if he'd had the chance to open a door and just walk – and walk, and walk away from it all.

But we're not here to discuss alcohol. We're walking through Rhyl in 1887, to the sound of steam trains chuffing and whistling, Buffalo Bill's daredevil cowboys whooping and hollering, and demure, well-covered belles emerging from the bathing huts to sample the stinging sea waters. We're watching Agnes Hunt arriving at the Royal Alexandra Hospital to start her illustrious career as a nurse. She's a slip of a girl aged just 20 and she's a cripple. She has sampled the well-heeled life of the prosperous upper middle classes and she has sampled the meagre and dangerous existence of a British colonist in the wilds of nowhere. The photograph of Agnes on the cover of her autobiography, taken at the apogee of her career, shows a woman with an attractive oval face and the slightly hooded eyes of the intelligent, experienced observer. Her most striking feature is her mouth, which shows absolute determination, with a strong hint of temperance and fortitude. She has seen, and felt, a considerable amount of pain.

Let us join her as she mulls over her first days at Rhyl:

> It was the proudest moment of my life when I first put on my uniform and marched across the Hospital to Chapel. The Superintendent was a most awe-inspiring lady, standing five feet ten in her stockings. She occupied a sort of raised throne at the entrance of the Chapel, from which she could survey her flock and correct any misdemeanours...

The Royal Alexandra Hospital was, I believe, the first hospital for cripples that ever advocated fresh air as an integral part of treatment...

To Miss Graham's teaching I owe an immense debt of gratitude, for she taught me the paramount importance of... fresh air and happiness. She held that no nurse was worth her salt if she had not the joy of life in her, and the power of sharing it with her patients. She believed, which was unusual in those days, that God should be made manifest through joy. Certainly, the cripples of that Hospital were as cheerful a set of rascals as I have ever seen. All the children who were not too ill were carried out on the sands with their buckets, the others were pushed outside to watch the nigger minstrels, Punch and Judy shows, &c.; summer and winter, the verandas were in full use.

Agnes did not stay her full year at Rhyl – she moved on to a London hospital, and to give you a taste of nursing just a century ago, this is how she describes it:

... the nursing staff had not been touched by the finger of Florence Nightingale. The Matron was honorary and untrained... the nurses were housed in big dormitories, which they had to scrub out once a week. Their dining room was in the basement, the food was not appetizing and very ill served. Supper, for instance, was bread and cheese and beer; it was possible, however, to get a glass of milk instead of beer. The crumbs of this repast were still on the table when we trooped into breakfast the next day, and the smell of stale beer and cheese hung on the heavy atmosphere. Breakfast consisted of tea and milk and sugar, all mixed together in a big urn, thick slices of bread and butter, and an egg that had been kept too long. The meal never varied, except, perhaps, in the date of the birth of the egg. We worked from 8am to 8pm, with, if we were lucky, two hours off every other day. No care at all was taken of our health, and it was no uncommon thing for one or two of us to be warded and seriously ill... the house surgeons were not very much better off. One of them told me that the post-mortem examinations had to be done in their dining room, as there was no post-mortem room in the hospital.

At this time Dame Hunt met her lifelong companion, Emily Selina Goodford (nicknamed Goody). Theirs was one of those enduring and chastely endearing bonds forged by women in the pre-modern society when they decided not to marry – a symbiotic and loving friendship between two like-minded individuals of strong character.

Together they were sent into the hovels of Hammersmith and

Fulham to dispense aid. She says:

> The work was hard but intensely interesting. Here I realized for the first time the tremendous scope and power of the nurse's life. One went into these homes, not as 'my lady bountiful', but as a fellow human being, a friend to give personal help, to teach and to serve... nobody can be a district nurse for any length of time without realising the astounding patience, unselfishness, and bravery of the poor. Let me give one example among many. A woman was dying of heart disease, her husband was a casual labourer, and they had many children. For several years this patient had quarrelled with her next door neighbour, and their only conversation had been unprintable abuse from their respective back doors. Yet the moment this neighbour heard of the plight of her enemy, she, who in the day earned her living at the wash-tub, made of her poor tired body a human pillow for her life-long enemy to rest upon, as the invalid could not breathe unless she was practically sitting up, and no other pillows were available.

She went to work in the Isle of Wight, where she met a typical Poor Law doctor of that time, who might have stepped straight from a Dickens novel:

> He was dressed in a broad-brimmed top hat, an old and very greasy black coat and black trousers to match. He drove about in an ancient brougham, whose springs and upholstery must have dated from the eighteenth century. He had also the unfortunate habit of taking a pinch of snuff from one waistcoat pocket and applying it to his nose, and directly after from yet another pocket would appear a large piece of cheese which he ate with apparent relish! One day he asked me to help him in his dispensary. I knew nothing about dispensing but he promised to teach me. Certainly, it did not prove to be difficult, as one prescription consisted of rhubarb and soda, and the other of quinine, iron and brown sugar.
>
> He told me to make up three gallons of each, and when the patients came I was to ask for their bottles and fill them up. He added that I could tell which they had been having because there was always a bit of sediment left in the rhubarb bottle, but if they thought the medicine was not doing them any good, I could give them some of the other. If, however, there was a new patient, it would be best to start him on the rhubarb and soda. He said he was sorry he could not stop, but he had a pressing engagement elsewhere.

Agnes and Goody went off to fight typhoid in Rushden, where Agnes was nearly raped by a tramp. Together they made an intrepid pair, though Agnes suffered frequent bouts of ill-health and had to take to her bed for months on end. I seem to remember that Florence Nightingale took to her bed for many years after returning from the Crimea, as if the gift of healing on the one hand and hypochondria on the other were bedfellows, like Jack Spratt and his wife. I'm not suggesting that Agnes was a hypochondriac – it was amazing that a crippled girl achieved what she did, especially at a time when cripples were considered incapable of any form of lifestyle and were usually left to lie on pallets outside houses all day, if the weather allowed it, or forced to vegetate indoors with no expectation of them, as if they were mentally rather than physically handicapped.

At the end of *This is my Life* I felt I was closer empathically to the Vogel cause, but I was no nearer to the root of the story. I entered a period of dormancy during which the Vogel story incubated slowly. I carried on with my own busy and pleasurable life on the road, darting home whenever I needed a brief rest.

One day I struck on a ploy. I arranged lunch with a journalist friend and quickly engineered a photo-shoot and a brief article on the tenor that I was researching the Vogel Papers and was looking for any slightest recollection, or any reference in any historical papers, documents, wills, terriers, stories, fables etc. I was pictured outside the Blue Angel bookshop with one hand holding the Vogel Papers and the other pointing at the roof, where they were found.

As I expected, there was no response.

But the Vogel Story, as it went along, seemed to be a story of serendipity and quirky coincidence, and it was not going to let me down now. My next break came from a most unexpected quarter. Certainly not from the town – a blank was drawn there. Although I seldom looked at the local rag, I now bought it every week in case there was any reaction to my appearance. As I said, there was none. But one Thursday as I flipped idly through its pages my eye fell on a weekly nostalgia column by the local historian.

His article was on the traditional Welsh craft of stick-making, with the emphasis on unusual handles. I scanned it quickly. I still have the cutting in my drawer crammed with Vogel matter, and this is the relevant part:

Of course, other parts of the world have their own traditions. For instance, I can remember a most unusual type of stick, seen only once in this area. It's an unusual story. One day, some years ago, a mystery man called on a famous local surgeon – quite unexpectedly – while he was having a meal with a friend. It took some time for the surgeon to realise who this stranger was, since he hadn't seen him since he was a child. They invited him in, but he didn't stay for long: after speaking to them briefly he put hundreds of dollars on the table and then left. He wore a leather long-coat and a large-brimmed hat, and he walked with the aid of two walking sticks, their heads carved to resemble the faces of two Red Indian chiefs in full regalia. The diners, who were the renowned Doctor Robert Jones and his colleague Agnes Hunt, were surprised but amused by their impromptu visitor, who apparently represented a firm of American violin makers.

As you might expect, this snippet set in motion a fast and extremely profitable chain of events.

THE MAN FROM AMERICA

MY FRIEND THE JOURNALIST SAYS that reporters are taught to flesh out their stories however they can. No matter how trivial a fact may seem, it could be important to readers. For instance, if I say my age is 47, which was my father's age when he died, readers will have a point of comparison, and they can position themselves neatly in the age queue, like children waiting to go into class. Starting with the youngest, their eyes will travel all the way up the line to the oldest, and they will draw comfort or despair from their position as they wait for the bell to call them in for the final exam.

So this is probably the right time to say a little about myself. I am indeed 47, and in good health. Doctors at the hospital said I have an excellent constitution. I think they were implying that I didn't deserve it, and looked at me accusingly, as if I had cheated and grabbed it before the music stopped while playing Pass-the-Parcel.

I am a six-foot professional, slim, GSOH, non-smoker, own teeth, own home, sensitive, very fit, and no, I've never looked through the Lonely Hearts columns. Quite happy alone, actually. WLTM no-one with a view to marriage. Women I simply don't need.

I've been told that I'm very attractive to the opposite sex but I'm simply not ready to settle down yet. I've no need for human bondage (or should that be bonding, I always confuse the two).

I have a few inconsequential faults. Nobody could accuse me of having a well-ordered or carefully structured existence, as many people can boast. Anarchy starts at home, I say. There is something about life-planners which frightens me. Hubris? Cheek? I expect all those people who take out pensions when they're still in the fifth form and book their retirement venue at the same time as they're sorting out their gap year to drop down dead at the snap of a godly finger.

Perhaps I'm a little frugal (my less timid friends have used the word mean). Yes, I'm careful with money; I don't buy new clothes or appliances if I can possibly avoid it and I don't waste food or electricity – I make sure that everything is off before I go to bed, something which some people find irritating.

I have a scalpful of antic red hair, and green eyes. I wear unobtrusive, steel-rimmed glasses and I can spend up to twenty-four hours a day looking for them. I dress carelessly, and because I hate wearing new clothes I am kitted out in charity shop clothes, which is my only similarity to Mr Vogel, since I am unusually nimble and sprightly for my age. I have never been married (there was someone a long time ago, first love and all that, but time and distance parted us). I have no children. As I have already told you I am taking a year off, between jobs, having inherited a rather gratifying heap of cash from a rich uncle, who also left me his house. Funnily enough there is a small, modern, B&Q pagoda in the back garden.

That is enough about me for the present.

I will take you back, now, about thirty years, when I was in a hospital. I suppose you need to know a few relevant things about me. Yes, I was a patient. No, I don't want to talk about it.

The hospital had a side-ward which contained nothing but hydrocephalus cases.

During our lives we collect a handful of fundamental experiences, such as our first corpse, or our first sexual encounter, and the hydrocephalus ward was a formative experience for me. It was full of incubators, I'd say about twenty, each containing a human being with a small body and a grossly enlarged head, like those cartoon aliens with blobby white heads and tadpole bodies.

Hydrocephalus, put simply, means a gathering of water in the brain. It's a condition which is treated quickly and effectively nowadays, if detected in time, by inserting tiny pipes subcutaneously to drain the fluid. In olden days the disease created hideous forms, only nominally human, with deadened eyes. They simply lay there all day experiencing that most terrifying of states, a living death, not that they appeared to know their plight. I walked among them in awe. They looked back blankly. There was nothing in those eyes, less than there is in a doll's eyes. They could not move an inch.

To me they were the embodiment of Dante's tortured souls in purgatory; they could have been a detail in a Hieronymus Bosch. Why do I mention these zombies, these living dead? Some were children, some were teenagers, some were in their twenties, and they are all dead now. I came across them as I came across a cluster of frogs' eggs in a rut in a farm track during my trek. The eggs had been laid in an unsuitable place, because tractors drove through them occasionally and displaced the water. Some were already opaque and dead. They reminded me of those children in the ward. I walked away all those years ago, and I walked away now, as the quick walk from the dead, not with rejoicing or *schadenfreude*, but with incomprehension. There was only one difference between me and the disembodied children and the frogs' eggs; none of us had any comprehension of the others' state of being, but I could walk away.

Which brings me neatly to the man with two sticks and lots of dollar bills who walked, out of the blue, into the lives of Dr Robert Jones and Agnes Hunt, as noted by my local newspaper. I pestered the paper's librarian and he allowed me to examine his bible copies. The room smelt fusty. So this was the smell of a hundred years of history, I said to him. I came across a tiny insect scuttling slowly across a whole broadsheet page before me, like a microscopic camel in a desert of words (like me in Wales?) It was a bookworm, presumably.

'Do you know anything about bookworms?' I asked him.

'No,' he replied.

'Don't you get to know anything about them? Mechanics get to learn about rust and dentists about caries. I thought you might know the different types, their eating habits, their preferred binding glue?'

'No,' he replied again, more stolidly this time.

The incident in the newspaper column had happened at the Liverpool home of Dr Robert Jones, whom I have already mentioned as co-founder of the Gobowen Orthopaedic Hospital. I was led to a full and proper version of events in Frederick Watson's *The Life of Sir Robert Jones*:

> One day Agnes Hunt was having lunch with Robert Jones in his studio in Nelson Street when a tall young man with a slight limp was ushered in. He spoke with a strong American accent, and asked Dr Jones if he remembered a little lad from Manchester with a very bad hip disease – and added 'You came twice a week to see me and you induced a lady to give me a violin and teach me how to play it, and now I am managing director of a violin and instrument factory in the United States, and I humbly ask you to accept this small donation for

any crippled institution in which you may be interested.' The dona-
tion was a five hundred dollar bill.

As the door closed I turned to Robert Jones and asked for his story.

'Yes,' he said, 'I will tell you the story, because it can show what an
excessive influence for good a cripple child can exercise. He lived in a
wretched slum in Manchester, such a home which only drink-produc-
ing poverty can achieve. The mother, an apparently hopeless slattern,
the father earning good money and spending it all on drink; they had
but one redeeming feature, a great love for the cripple boy. The gradual
restoration of that home was what will interest you. I got a friend to
teach the child the violin, and going there one Sunday evening heard a
violin accompanied by many childish voices singing *Abide With Me*.
Apparently the whole street used to gather there on Sunday evenings to
sing hymns with that cripple boy. Finally, he asked me to have a cup of
tea with him; the tea was perfectly served and the house spotlessly
clean. With tears in her eyes the mother said that the father brought
home every penny of his wages.'

The story is very typical of Robert Jones; he told it to me because it
showed what exceeding influence for good a cripple child can exercise;
not a word of the quiet talks he had with the drinking father, not a
word of his gentle advice to and his influence over the mother.

I read this with growing certainty that Watson had hit me over the
head with the biggest clue yet to Vogel's identity. Tall man with a
limp, violin factory, *Abide with Me...* either I had a huge, smelly
red herring wafting under my nose or I had landed a whale-sized
clue. My fellow strollers, what do you think we should do next?
Read *The Life of Sir Robert Jones* from cover to cover? Job done!
Yet more clues! Robert Jones was directly linked to the
Bonesetters of Anglesey, through marriage! Here was a water-
tight connection with the little boys washed up on the shores of
Anglesey and rescued by the smuggler Dannie Lukie.

Dr Robert Jones achieved many things, and once again I will
ask you to rest awhile; let us sit on this bank on the shoreline near
Flint Castle, which stands like a child's crenellated sand-bucket,
smashed and washed up by the tide.

Dr Robert Jones (could this be the Dr Robert mentioned in
the Vogel Papers?) had also been involved in the building of the
Manchester ship canal. I quote from Watson:

It was necessary that a surgical and hospital staff should be appointed to look after the health of the 20,000 men with their wives and families in the hutments along the canal. Only a surgeon with a wide experience of accidents among manual workers could organise such an undertaking. While upon holiday in Norway, in 1884, Robert Jones attended a case in the hotel where he was staying with such success that he aroused the interest of the English people staying there. Amongst these was Mrs Garnett, head of The Navvy Mission.

He got the job. *The Provincial Medical Journal* reported:

In 1888 he was appointed Consulting Surgeon to the Manchester Ship Canal, upon which great work some 20,000 workmen were employed, and in five years over 3,000 accidents demanded his supervision. Mr Robert Jones designed and placed the hospitals. He selected the staff, which consisted of 14 surgeons.

There were three hospitals, each with a matron, house-surgeon and two nurses. During five years Robert Jones performed over 200 major operations.

The construction of the canal occupied several years. Work was both arduous and dangerous. Accidents were frequent and critical. Along its 35 miles there was continuous warfare with chance, which resulted in casualties of every type and degree.

I feel sure we are on the right track. Patience now, patience. I need an intermediary, a nuncio, in America, since I cannot leave Wales, to trace that crippled man who deposited a five hundred dollar bill on a Liverpool table. Surely he must be our Mr Vogel.

I have read about the Welsh who fled poverty, rather as the Scots fled the clearances, in the wake of the Industrial Revolution. Between 1850 and 1910 nearly 400,000 people left rural Wales for other parts of the United Kingdom. Others went abroad.

I turn to our most famous living historian, John Davies, to tell you the story:

... it seems likely that between 1850 and 1870 at least sixty thousand people emigrated from Wales to the United States... Welsh emigrants were drawn to already existing Welsh rural communities such as Cambria in Pennsylvania, Gallia in Ohio and Oneida in the state of New York, but Welsh migrants also established new farming communities, especially in Wisconsin, where the state's constitution was translated into Welsh for their benefit...

As industrialisation in the United States proceeded apace, experienced workers were in great demand in places like the ironworks of Pittsburgh and the coalmines of Scranton and Wilkes Barre. Thousands of Welsh people from the industrial areas were ready to answer the call, especially in view of the declining prosperity of the Welsh ironworks...

One of the most unusual migrations from Wales to the United States... resulted from the missionary work of the Mormon, Daniel Jones of Abergele. Jones emigrated to America in 1840 and in 1843 he became a member of the Church of Latter Day Saints. He returned to Wales in 1845 and, from his headquarters in Merthyr, he gained at least five thousand converts to his faith... in 1848, 249 Welsh Mormons emigrated to Salt Lake City in Utah, and the famous Tabernacle choir has its origins among them. It was estimated in 1949 that there were 25,000 Mormons of Welsh descent in America...

By 1872 there were 384 Welsh-language chapels in the United States and some two dozen Welsh periodicals had seen the light of day. Many of the emigrants sought to create a microcosm of Wales.

No less than 13 signatories of the Declaration of Independence claimed Welsh descent.

George Washington and Franklin D Roosevelt both had Welsh blood in their veins.

The two Welsh newspapers, *Ninnau* and *Y Drych*, printed in America for *y Cymry ar wasgar* – the dispersed Welsh in the States – have merged so I get in touch with *Ninnau*'s editor and I receive a contact in Blue Earth County in Minnesota. The contact is Anwen Marek, a psychologist at the capital city, St Paul. God help me, I think, that's the last thing I need, a bloody shrink. Still, she's willing to help and I must take all the help I'm offered. We exchange e-mails. She's doing a doctorate on the Sisseton band of the Sioux nation, which previously lived in this region – it's not so far from Little Bighorn River and Wounded Knee Creek. She mails me the highlights of a book published in 1895, called *History of the Welsh in Minnesota*, gathered by old settlers with names like Hughes, Roberts and Edwards.

I remember the Welsh myth, of a Welsh-speaking tribe of Indians discovered by explorers and traced back in folklore to Madog, the Welsh prince supposed to have landed in America some considerable time before Amerigo Vespucci was a gleam in his father's mainsail. This myth was used by Elizabeth I's astrologer, the Welsh magician Dr John Dee, to create the word Britannia and to justify British imperialism.

The conduct of the Welsh in Minnesota makes fascinating reading. Unfortunately, these particular Welshmen were the worst sort of colonialists possible. I cringed when I read:

> ... on a high bluff overlooking the river was situated the old Indian cemetery. It was formed by placing a number of crotched posts in the ground, and laying out a network of poles across from one to the other; and on top of those, wrapped in skins or blankets, the dead were deposited. This ancient burial place was cut down and destroyed as a nuisance by the early Welsh settlers. The Indian, however, was gone. For the past thirty years he has not set foot upon the land of his fathers. A mighty change has taken place; his bark villages have disappeared... his paths are obliterated... no-one can even find a trinket in the fields; it is as though oblivion has drawn its hand across the slate of their existence.

So it appears that my own race was as ready as any to walk all over anyone in its path. I am immensely sobered by this knowledge. Look how dismissive the Welsh were when they viewed the Sioux natives (it wasn't that long since the Welsh themselves had appeared 'barbarian' to English visitors):

> ... in the early days one would be quite sure to meet a troop of aborigines on the march, all walking in single file. First came the men, dressed in close-fitting pantaloons of clouted cloth or buckskin, with a wide, fancy fringe along each leg, a pair of moccasins, ornamented with beads, on the feet, and a dirty white blanket drawn over the shoulders. At the girdle hung a tomahawk, knife, and ammunition pouch, while on the arm would be carried the gun. They were a tall, stalwart looking people, straight as arrows, of a dusky red colour, with prominent features, high cheek bones, and long, straight, very coarse, black hair, often braided in two or three plaits. Behind the men came the squaws, much more haggard and squatty than their lords, because of the drudgery they had to perform. Mingled with the company would be several wolfish-looking dogs whose meat was deemed a great delicacy at their feasts.
>
> All labour connected with Indian life the squaws performed. Their duty it was not only to transport the baggage, but also to put up the wigwams, fetch the firewood, cook the meals, cultivate the small patch of Indian corn, tan the furs and the robes, make the clothing and the fancy bead-work, manufacture the household implements and hew the canoes.

The Indians were very hospitable, and would spare the last morsel, and expect others to do the same. They had but a faint idea of private property, especially in the matter of food, and thought nothing of begging eatables off the early settlers. They seldom made any provision for the morrow, but would gorge themselves with what they had at the time and wait until hungry before looking for more. They were never dainty as to what they ate. All kinds of animals, and every part of the animal, afforded them nourishment. The early pioneers remember how a dead horse or dead cow would be relished by the Indians as a big feast.

Though the braves dislike all labour, deeming it ignoble for a man, yet they are inured to the severest hardships, fatigue and bodily pains. From childhood the males were taught to despise pain, and feats of endurance were always the special feature of their feasts and dances. In a Dance to the Sun performed by a young brave named Wanotau, witnessed at Lake Traverse, the dance consisted in making three deep cuts through his skin – one on his breast and one on each of his arms. The skin was cut in the manner of a loop, so as to permit a rope to pass under the strip of skin and flesh, which was thus divided from the body. The ropes being passed through, they were secured to a tall, vertical pole. He then began to dance around this pole, at the commencement of his fast, frequently swinging himself in the air... he continued this exercise, with few intermissions, during the whole of his fast, until the fourth day at about 10am when the strip of skin from his breast gave way, notwithstanding which he interrupted not his dance, although supported merely by his arms. At noon the strip from his left arm snapped off. His uncle then thought he had suffered enough, and drew his knife and cut the remaining strip from his right arm, upon which Wanotau fell to the ground in a swoon. The heat at the time was extreme. He was left exposed in that state until night, when his friends took him some provisions.

I doubt if any of the Welsh settlers could have shown such incredible bravery (desperation?). Instead, they were happy to steal the Indians' homeland, which was beautiful. The settlers described charming valleys traversed by brooks and rills with spurs of timber jutting out across the great rolling prairie, a land bespangled by many lovely lakes and pleasant groves. The Welsh settlement was a paradise on earth, and it had been gained at the expense of the native peoples, who had lived there in great happiness until the coming of the Welsh. There was something about the settlers' description of the place, in all its lushness, which reminded me of Doctor Robert's garden in the Vogel Papers:

Corn, oats, barley, sorghum and potatoes are grown abundantly. Wild plums, grapes, gooseberries, currants, strawberries and raspberries are very plentiful. The timber of the country comprises oak, elm, basswood, maple, butternut, hickory, poplar, and in the valleys, black walnut and cottonwood.

I am minded to take you on another tangent; please bear with me – we will reach our goal eventually, I promise. Really, this is only a titchy little diversion.

In 1943 the philosopher Ludwig Wittgenstein attended a meeting in Swansea, when an academic discussed the growth of iron and coal mining in the region, saying that although the process had scarred the environment and the people, it had led to new methods and gradual progress.

Wittgenstein said that in one light it could be seen as progress, in another as decline. There was no method of weighing one against the other to justify a theory of overall 'progression'.

The academic said something like: 'Despite all the ugly sides to our civilization I am sure I would rather live as we do now than have to live as the caveman did.'

Wittgenstein answered: 'Yes of course you would. But would the caveman?'

This encapsulates the whole issue of colonisation. Native people, minorities, are best left alone. But it's too late – the last two centuries have probably seen the greatest human migrations in the entire history of mankind, and the soup is now so thick that we will never again be able to reclaim the individual constituents. Should we want to? Everything is ruled by economics; accountants are the new oppressors. Across the world, people will do just about anything to learn English, because it is the language of the web and world commerce. Just to show you how desperate things have become, there are parents in Korea who have begun taking their children to plastic surgeons for a frenectomy – an operation which snips a membrane and makes the tongue longer, so that the kids can say *right* and *wrong* instead of *light* and *long*, and so 'get on' in the world. These Korean kids spend hours every day watching video lessons in English. Chinese DJ Li Yang claims to have taught English to 20 million of his countrymen by assembling them in football stadia and getting massive crowds to shout out phrases such as *No pain no gain* and *I've heard so much about you*. Newly-independent East Timor, freed at last from

Indonesia's terrifying occupation, plans to adopt English as a vital component of the country's future. Malaysian teenagers – in their droves – buy a magazine called *Junior* which teaches them how to speak English: a recent issue featured Christmas carols and Stonehenge.

I began to understand the underlying tone of the Vogel Papers, with their emphasis on incomers who deprived an ancient tribe of its land and its health – in some North American areas two-thirds of the Indians were wiped out by smallpox and other 'gifts' from the immigrants. The Welsh, too, had suffered in the same way: the Roman Julius Agricola virtually exterminated one of the main tribes, the troublesome Ordovices, in an act of ethnic cleansing. The Irish colonised large swathes of the western seaboard, and the Vikings left their bloody tracks everywhere, having the temerity to name most of our offshore islands in their own tongue: Anglesey, Grassholm, Skokholme, Steep Holme, Flat Holme...

The Normans beat us into submission and the English swallowed us up in waves. At the end of such a thorough mauling I think it's quite natural for us to feel a little vulnerable. It's a wonder we're here at all.

I send the Vogel Papers to Anwen Marek and a précis of the story so far. She is intrigued – her own son was born with a dislocated hip, quite common, the boy's fine now. Abnormality is the norm, really.

She sounds level-headed, straightforward, sensible. She chips in with a couple of references. Have I read D.M. Thomas's *The White Hotel*, which has a Vogel and a pagoda?

No I haven't.

What about Márquez? *Love in the Time of Cholera* has a parrot, a cripple, a violinist and a one-eyed man behind the bar.

Would that be the Márquez of Anglesey? I quip.

But she ignores me and continues.

Do I know anything about Freud, who had a seminal dream (no pun intended) about his mother involving birds? The German word *vögeln* is also a (naughty) slang word for *to screw*.

No I don't know anything about Freud, but I've dreamt about him.

Ha ha she says.

Have I heard of the Sons of Mil?

Funny you should mention the Sons of Mil, I say. No.

Ancestors of the Irish, she says. According to Irish mythology the Sons of Mil journeyed through Egypt, Crete and Sicily, and when they reached Spain one of their company, Bregon, built a tower. His son, Ith, climbed to the top of this tower and saw Ireland across the sea, so they set sail to investigate it.

Sounds intriguing, I say – a view of the promised land from a tower; the pagoda could be a version of this.

I tell her that the author of the Vogel Papers was an ingénue, and that these common factors were almost certainly coincidental. She hangs fire on that.

I say I need a list of all American instrument-makers to see if we can follow the scent.

Was Vogel his real name, or are we looking for a Welsh surname? she asks.

Don't know, I say – we're working with clues at the moment, and the clues are Anglesey, Vogel and Manchester.

She contacts the American Federation of Violin and Bowmakers. Its members have names like Weisshaar, Metzler, Croen, Grugaugh, Shrapreau, Parshenov, DaCunha and Yang.

She phones round but gets nowhere. Then she spots an ad in her regional newspaper, and e-mails me.

Hi Di [she thinks this is funny, calling me Diogynes because she says that walking around Wales is just as daft as living in a tub and wandering the streets with a lamp, seeking an honest man]. I may have something for you. Man called David Roberts is giving a demo to the county's fiddle freaks tonite. For your info, the ad says it's a varnishing demonstration, if that means anything to you. Apparently this Roberts has a substantial quantity of varnish-making materials including seedlac, button lac, elemi, sandalwood and oil of rosemary. So there. I'll try to phone him, if I can contain my excitement, he may want to rub something on me. By the way, can you send a photo – sending news to a faceless computer is disconcerting, I'd like to know who I'm taking to. Ben [her son] is also interested. He wants to know why I'm spending so much time looking for a bird from Germany. He keeps pointing to the sparrows and saying 'Is that him?!' Bye – A.

The computer goes as quite as a sibyl and I go off for a few days with my small rucksack and lightweight sleeping bag. I travel very light. I take a map and warm clothing, also two candles and a lighter. I learnt a trick from a homeless man. The nights can be long and cold. If I can't sleep I light a candle and look at the flame, which is good viewing in a crazy sort of way with its oranges, blues and whites, and trees loom and waver around my igloo of light. But there's a better reason – although the flame doesn't give much heat it makes me *feel* warmer in an illusory way. A candle is good company when earthlings are dumbed by the universe and the stars shimmer coldly and distantly. The first night I sleep in a church porch at Tallarn Green. I enjoy a full nocturnal extravaganza; a pair of barn owls come and go along the yews, noisy and assertive; bats zing through the night like toy stealth bombers and there's a faraway fireworks display by a silent shower of shooting stars. The church is open, amazingly, but I stay in the porch, half out of respect, half from wanting to see the entertainment. I find Polaris and watch satellites arc past it. The Plough is my next port of call; of its seven main stars two are moving in a different direction to the rest, so the shape will change eventually. Up in Gemini the heavenly twins, Castor and Pollux, wink at me.

Castor and Pollux were the brothers of Helen of Troy, and they rescued her when she was carried off by Theseus. Castor was famous for his power over horses, Pollux was handy with his fists. They were joined at the hip, so to speak. Both of them went with Jason on his fabled quest for the golden fleece; subsequently, Castor and Pollux became the deities of seamen and voyagers. Years later Castor was killed during a war, and Pollux was so cut up he asked Jupiter if he could swap places with his brother so that Castor could live again. Jupiter gave them both a dual life, half of it below the earth and the other half in the heavenly abodes; he also rewarded their attachment to each other by placing them among the stars as Gemini the Twins.

I mull over this legend as I stretch out on a bristly doormat and sleep fitfully. Away in the fields a cow lows and the sound resonates and echoes into silence again along the frosty fields. Dogs on a hillside farm sound the alarm suddenly and answering dogs, far away, create a mystique of echoing sound effects, arriving like sonar echoes, from the blackness outside, into my submarine porch. This is the witching hour, and I share its separation from the day. It's the other side of the earth's story, told to you by an estranged friend in a candlelit room many years later.

A cynical acquaintance says I'm merely enjoying a spot of self-punishment when I sleep out at night during my walks.

'It's just manageable danger and manageable suffering – you know you can run home to mummy tomorrow'. Cow.

I'll tell you about another day's walking.

I start walking as the sun rises. I've seen off the false dawn. I walk steadily, almost dreamily, through the scurries and scratches in the hedgerows. The light takes hold and the sun rises slowly and undeferrably through the mists. I'm on a beach, walking past marshy ground, past sedges and rushes, scrambling through pebbles and shells. The walking mantra kicks in. A thought enters my head, and in tune with the rhythm of my feet it establishes a theme, then recapitulates... I find the same theme in my mind over and over again. Apparently, this constant repetition is soothing. It's automatic when I do rhythmic things like weeding or digging or walking. Perhaps it has something to do with lullabies; a recollection of my mother's rondeaux as she swayed me to sleep. The most celebrated case of this 'lull yourself to happiness' method is *The Way of a Pilgrim*, the story of an anonymous 19th-century Russian peasant who wanted to say an unceasing prayer as he walked: *Lord Jesus Christ, Son of God, have mercy on me, a sinner.*

Likewise, during my walk I may find myself thinking of a typical Welsh grouping of three: for example, as my feet hit the ground I may be thinking of three fundamental verbs – *to be, to do, to die.* You may have a different choice, such as: *to drink, to eat, to sleep.* And so on. How strangely the mind works when left to its own devices.

Today's thought is about saints. Saints walk in and out of my mind all morning like one of those tunes you wake up with and can't get out of your head. Saints. Anwen Marek has brought saints into the picture. She has sent me a small St Christopher medallion for me to wear on my walks. He is the patron saint of travellers. I infer she is religious or superstitious, which is the same thing to me. I sling it in the Vogel drawer. It has accompanying guff on the saint. He's a giant. He starts on the devil's side but defects to God after a winning streak by the man in white. As a mark of his devotion he's told to ferry people across a river; one day he has to carry a baby across the water but the child is too heavy, because the infant is also carrying the sins of the world. Ole Saint Christopher has joined the winning side, which don't endear him to me. Maybe I should go for our own St Dogmael, patron saint of children learning to walk – and according to some, patron saint of limbless children. Or St Mathurin. He's the patron saint of fools and idiots. Better still, perhaps, St Giles, patron saint of cripples. He's one of these saints from a rich, aristocratic family who takes to the woods in search of salvation. There have been many historical euphemisms for madness, and nearly every victim ends up in the woods. Lancelot the Wanderer ended up mad in the woods after his fling with Guinevere took the original route to romantic suicide. Wales has Myrddin (Merlin) the magician: he lost the plot big style and spent a lot of time talking to an ill-mannered piglet in the shade of an apple tree. It's all there in the Black Book of Carmarthen: poor old Myrddin endured twenty bouts of madness on his way to becoming a legend.

Anyway, St Giles is lurking about in his French wood in a state of abject poverty etc. when the local king happens along, chasing some poor hapless creature – this is a regular theme in saintly stories, which are thronged with nasty kings pursuing fluffy little animals into the undergrowth. The saint shields the animal or conceals it in his/her underwear, and the king promptly sees a shining light, repents, and says 'sorry brother, verily I'm a true bastard' and gifts the saint a piece of land the size of Canada, builds a church and renounces his evil ways. Unfortunately for St Giles, the ending isn't entirely happy. Nasty king comes along chasing hind. Hind jumps into thicket. Giles halts the fun and saves the deer (female, so Giles also becomes the saint of nursing mothers) but he takes an arrow in the leg, rendering him a cripple. He limps around for the rest of his life comforting himself with the knowledge that he's the patron saint of cripples. Great. His churches spring up all over the place, usually at crossroads so that pilgrims can call for a chat and a cuppa. Yes, I'll side with St Giles. We'll make St Giles the temporary saint of the Vogel story, just to please Anwen.

Hope you're still with me on this little quest of ours. You better had be. We've a long way to go yet. Let's keep on walking, with or without the saints. Round a headland, prospect of a new moon bay, fine white sand, the sea brilliantly blue and lithesome.

Unbelievable. Is this really happening? In front of me at the edge of the water there are two moonmen, like Neil Armstrong and Buzz Aldrin just stepped out of the lunar buggy, walking about in that peculiar moony walk, slowed down like a film at the wrong speed, arms out like Mr Blobby, circling a canister on the lip of the water, bending down to look at it and poking it with their gloves. Two more men come towards me with dogs, those tall ridiculous-looking clipped poodles. I hazard a wild guess – there's something about their manner and appearance – I ask if they're Londoners and by golly I'm right. I guess wildly again at south of the river, Southwalk way perhaps, and I'm bang on. We share a larf. I say *I don't believe what I'm seeing*, but I'm bleedin' right enough me ole mate, there *are* two moonmen in front of me. Someone walking their dog early on has come across a canister with a skull and crossbones on it, or one of those radiation signs, some warning anyway, and the emergency services are there, the moonmen in orange radiation suits with helmets, local firemen standing like chocolate soldiers at the top of the strand, people lurking with their hands in their pockets, the world watching this little drama unfold under a fresh morning sky with a light breeze and creation's in a welcoming mood, doorstep newly washed and gleaming, smelling nice and friendly, and I'm free to walk in and out of this soap opera, this moving tableau, whilst old Vogel there with his twisted little legs is tied like a dog to his kennel. The denouement comes: down on the shore the men in their all-over suits like neighbourhood cosmonauts jerk their thumbs in an OK sign and the firemen go down with a tractor and trailer, take the canister away, relief in the air, everyone goes, dribbling off to embroider the story, already a mini-epic forming, twisted and reshaped, given tenses and syntaxes, breaks, dramatic pauses, flourishes, climaxes, a pixel of memory glowing in the humming recesses of each brain, an anecdote to link arms with other anec-dotes across the torrent of time, a bridge of memories to the other side of being. I walk into the nearby hamlet to gather more infor-mation. The canister contained a super-condensed matter from which soap is made. Off I go, away along the shore, the event is over and my parcel of memory is wrapped and piled with the other memories ready for opening, when the time is right, or perhaps sneakily before the allotted moment.

The trip over, I re-established contact with the Marek woman.

She had been busy, as I expected, but she was just as fond of tangents as I am, and instead of concentrating on the Vogel issue she had gone somewhere quite unexpected.

I e-mailed her with the saints meditation and jokingly designated her St Christopher and myself St Giles in our impending peregrination through the Vogel morasse, which was taking on Bunyanesque dimensions.

She thought this duly appropriate, since she would be going on the great Spanish pilgrimage to Santiago del Compostella. St Giles's mother church was on this route. She was seeking absolution for provoking the breakdown of her marriage. Had I been married?

No.

Did I think it possible to gain forgiveness with an act of penitence?

No.

What was my walk about then? Was I sick and hoping for relief? Was it a secular pilgrimage? An act of repentance? A visible sign to the world that I was either disturbed or contrite?

That got me thinking.

Now she was off after another hare.

'Do you know what guides you on your way?' she asked.

'No, and I'm entirely sure it's not some crackpot divinity with nothing better to do.'

'No, I mean physically.'

'No.'

'Ha! Gotcha!'

'Don't be so bloody childish.'

'I'm not. No-one knows, exactly, how we make mental maps and how we know where we're going. But you might take a look at the pineal gland and the hippocampus, both of them in your bird-like brain.'

Getting cheeky now. I look up pineal. It's also known as the Third Eye and it has mystical qualities. Descartes believed it was the heart of the human soul. It contains a complete map of the visual field in front of our eyes. It regulates our daily body rhythms and the day/night cycle. The pineal gland is also implicated in Paget's Disease. Wow! Here was a tenuous connection with Mr Vogel!

Body
& mind

130

The pineal has magnetic material in birds and animals and is the centre for navigation. It may be important in human navigation and a number of studies are being conducted worldwide into this possible link.

The pineal, then, seems to monitor magnetic fields and helps align the body in space.

It could even be the evolutionary forerunner of the modern eye. It's large in children and shrinks at puberty. It plays a major role in sexual development, hibernation and sleep patterns. It may also be linked to psychic powers. So the pineal gland is the ideal gift for an adolescent who's about to sling his hook and head out for adventure.

Another source says the pineal is larger in men than in women, possibly explaining why men appear to be better at navigating and position-finding (remember, it's not me who's saying this).

Interesting stuff. Next I turn to the hippocampus, named (God knows why, presumably because of its shape) after a mythological sea creature which was front-end horse and back-end fish. The hippocampus is also involved in emotion and sexuality. It contains 'place' cells which construct a mental picture of our position, and it is implicated in learning and remembering the space around us. It has a three-dimensional map of our surroundings and is crucial for our ability to move around the landscape. It is here that memories are first processed and kept for several weeks before being either binned or transferred for safe keeping in the cerebral cortex. It's the major hub for all new memories.

The next bit took me rather by surprise. The hippocampus appears to shrink in people who have experienced severe trauma such as childhood abuse. That was really strange – as if abuse sufferers didn't want to know where they were going. Old Vogel seemed uncertain where he was going. I suppose his trauma was his crippledom. On the other hand, lots of us are crippled in one way or the other, either physically or mentally, I suppose. We'll deal with that later. Ms Marek has been busy and there's another e-mail waiting for me:

Hi Di. Hope you're fine. I think you need to examine why you're on this damn fool mission to walk around Wales without a reason. You gotta have a reason. Don't suppose you've come across the Aborigine songlines? They're like singing maps based on mythology and topography – if you learn the songs you can find your way anywhere in

Australia. Read Bruce Chatwin. Perhaps you're beating the bounds of your little patch over there, or walking around your territory to mark it off and put down contrary smells to warn off them other little varmint who want to steal it. You gotta have a reason.

'Do you know why I'm walking round Wales?' I answer. 'Because I can.'

It wasn't a blind, obstinate, head-down walk into any mist the future blew towards me, like Martin's walk up those steps of his. I was walking for the sheer joy of it – and to ask some questions about me, the world around me, my country, what made *me*.

I wasn't sure whether I was a child of Wales or whether I was creating a child called Wales. One thing I knew, blood's thicker than water, and I loved the place.

Anyway, cheer up she says, the violin varnisher David Roberts has been duly phoned and he has given us another lead. Not just any old lead, but a rock-solid lead worth following. It seems there's a small archive at one of the American museums concerning the early settlers, and one section deals with desertions by husbands or wives who couldn't cope with their lives in the New World, and who either returned home or disappeared into the west.

David Roberts, who himself had Welsh antecedents, had done some voluntary work at this museum and he'd noticed a letter which had been framed and put on the wall of the museum; he had particularly noticed it because there was a Welsh connection. The letter, he said, was from a woman searching for her husband.

Her name was Anna Vogel.

THE VIEW FROM HAY BLUFF

I WILL go there again, when this is over.

It will be the first place I will return to. I remember that morning in fine detail.

It was the cock-crow hour, steeped in a hundred thousand slow awakenings, when I started my walk from Hay-on-Wye to Llangattock Lingoed.

I started early from a bed-and-breakfast place I'd been lucky to find quite late the previous evening; lovely though it may be, I wasn't particularly sad to leave Hay, which has become a stilted and synthetic town, gazing self-consciously at its own self-made image as the largest books emporium in Britain. I left just after dawn in a blue haze, and this smoked around me all the time I ascended Hay Bluff, which was swathed in a supernatural stillness and silence. At a meagre 677 metres it's not much more than a pimple, but it's the highest point on the Offa's Dyke trail, which follows, roughly, the 8th century earthworks marking a boundary between Wales and England. For some reason the dyke reminds me of a batsman's mark at the crease, a weal scored in the ground by a man who expects some pretty hostile bowling. It's a massive feat of human effort, since millions of tons of earth must have been moved to create this ditch and rampart which stretches almost two hundred miles along the border between the two countries.

From a certain angle Hay Bluff looks like one of those bluffs you see in westerns, shaped like an anvil, with a line of mounted Indians gazing downwards, silhouetted against the skyline.

I laboured up its nose in a world so noiseless my ears fizzed softly as if a fuse had been lit in my head, and my boots whispered a commentary in the mountain grass; I felt as though I was inside one of those toy shakers with a snow-scene which swirls when you give it a shake, but instead of snow I was walking in powdered slate, falling soft and purple through the air, in a drowsy, pyjama-warm miniature universe. When I reached the top the sun came through and the panorama below me cleared, revealing the beautiful patchwork fields, the graceful tree patterns and the rolling landscape of the border country. I sat on the trig point on top and exulted. Childishly, I etched my initials in a brass plaque on the trig point and wondered if I would ever return to see them. Man marks his passing however he can. On another part of the Wales walk I had come across a flow of clay emerging from a headland into a bay and I had sat by it, like a nursery tot, and moulded a muddy deity, like a Celtic figurine, with little shell eyes and teeth, and hid it in the rootworks of a massive ash tree which had toppled onto the shore, leaving a small damp grotto within its base. I wonder if it's still there now.

I sat atop Hay Bluff and fermented with happiness. The only human near me was a shepherd on horseback way below me, whistling to his dogs, and funnelling his sheep towards a gate into an upland field; they massed there like fat platelets around a newly-opened wound, then disappeared slowly and left me gloriously alone.

I met a woman once who said that mountain people are up and down, people of the plains are temperamentally flat. Seems like a flat earth theory, but these old ideas, handed down over generations, often have a nub of truth. I was born on the side of a hill, and sure enough, I'm up and down like a paternoster lift. Midlanders are well-known for being unflappable and unexcitable. Could be something in it.

Me, I get silly happy on mountains. There are many reasons why people go up to look down. For me it's the magnificence of the landscape, mighty and on a far greater scale than puny man; also I like the perspective. Our own Ellis Wynne went up a mountain with his spying-glass on a beautiful summer's day in 1703 to conjure a dream about the moral state of the world below him. There is nowhere better to move around in time; by a simple act of transference one can travel back to the Stone Age, or any other age. Many diverting hours have I spent combing the hill forts for arrow heads, scrapers and other residues of early man; I have spent so many hours with these vanished tribes that I feel more at ease with them than with many living people, particularly young modern urbanites, who frighten me almost as much as the prospect of a spear-carrying primitive. A recent survey, which asked people for their ideal inhabitancy, discovered that the majority would like to live in a house overlooking a plain. 'Experts' postulated that this was a throwback to earlier times, when living high up on vantage points was essential to safety. I love that feeling of looking down on a plain and seeing its tiny movements, don't you? Many people have felt closer to their god on a mountain. I feel closer to reality, because my own little world takes on a sense of proportion; how small and insignificant I am, a minute detail on a huge canvas; and how simple and pleasurable is that feeling – for here is a true representation of our worth, in a manageable way, so that we can revel in our microcosmic pulse inside the huge macrocosmic cloud of existence, and enjoy it before we become stardust again. Being alive, being a brief collection of molecules, being a throng of atoms jostling in the marketplace of the universe is not so bad after all.

Whether we go to the mountains to get away from people, or go to people to get away from mountains, is a chicken and egg question which I'll leave with you.

I have read all the walk-and-think writers: Rousseau, Hazlitt, de Quincey, Hobbes, Kierkegaard... and Wordsworth of course, in many ways the founder of modern walking, who was reputed to have tramped 180,000 miles whilst composing his poetry (sorry, don't believe it). You can read about walking until you're blind.

Just go and do it.

On my walk up the bluff I have found a muddy postcard with an unfinished message. It has a picture of the very spot where I'm standing, so I have a little *déjà vu* in my hand. It has an address; I put it in my rucksack, dry it our later, and send it on to 'Dear Grandad' who lives on a farm near Uttoxeter; I get a charming thank-you letter. I really like that. I meet all sorts of people on these walks, from all over the world. Because we are in transit we can be bolder, more open with each other; little secrets and traits are shared in the knowledge that our divulgences will fade with every step we take away from one another. Perhaps it's better to know people briefly. We can take in a lot very quickly, and imagine the rest. These meetings are quick cocaine hits; sometimes it's better not to know all those deadweight details which sag the soul.

Talking of which, I have a little confession to make. You may find this amusing, given my strident remarks about not wanting romance in my life, but (don't tell anyone else, for God's sake) I seem to have, well, met someone that struck me as being (I mustn't use that word *nice*) – attractive. No, that's not right... striking?

She has a winsome smile, yes, a special way of looking at you...

We were in a graveyard. Pretty original place to fall in love, don't you think?

This little love story starts on the Dyke near Kington, when I met a Scottish academic and his American wife (I met more Americans on the Dyke than Welsh people). These two were animated, flowing, pulsing with life on a warm morning sent by indulgent, drunken gods; they described their day, and urged me to visit a nearby church, where I could make myself a drink, since there were tea-making facilities there. As they parted the woman said:

'There's an American couple somewhere behind us – from San Francisco – we met them in our B&B last night; if you meet them tell them about the church.'

'Of course,' I said, waving goodbye.

I reached the church, St Mary's, in a dip, nestling in a tiny hamlet called Newchurch. The graveyard contains the resting place of Emmeline, who died at the age of 14 – she was the daughter of the vicar there in the 1870s. There is nothing remark-able about that, since Welsh churchyards tell a terrible story of child mortality, but Emmeline was immortalised by Kilvert in his famous diaries, with the words:

The mountain was full of the memories of sweet Emmeline Vaughan.

Francis Kilvert was a curate at Clyro in Radnorshire and later vicar of Bredwardine, both near this little grave. Most of his diaries were burnt by a relative who was scandalised by his rather fulsome reflections on the female form. What remains gives us a lively picture of rural life in Victorian Wales; he has a lovely way of depicting the world, and daily events, the tragedies and joys around him.

As I knelt, looking at the inscription on the gravestone, I heard low voices and I swivelled round. I saw a couple talking by the porch, and as the man spoke I heard him call his partner Emmeline. Surely not. I must have misheard, I decided.

He went into the church, and she walked towards me down the path. She was beautiful.

I hesitated and faltered, but managed to say to her: 'Emmeline

– did your husband call you Emmeline?'

'Yes,' she replied softly.

'That's a most unusual name, isn't it – and what a strange co-incidence,' I bumbled, looking down, because I had just been kneeling at the grave of another Emmeline. I looked from her face to the grave, and back again. I was amazed, and smitten.

My mind raced, now, not to her bedchamber but to the Great Wall of China, and the story of two very unusual artists. The man, from East Germany, was called just Ulay, and the woman, from Yugoslavia, was called Marina Abramovic. They had done a lot of work together: in one of their projects they went to live in the Australian outback in an attempt to fraternise with the aborigines, who ignored them (but relationships improved after the couple practised 'immobility, silence and watchfulness' for hours in the scorching desert). Their speciality was physical contact, especially bumping into each other.

During the height of their collaboration they decided to walk towards each other from either end of the 4,000-kilometer Great Wall of China, so that they could literally and metaphorically bump into each other half way along, but by the time they got clearance from the Chinese authorities their relationship had ended. They decided, however, to go ahead with their project. In 1988 they started walking towards each other, from either end of the wall, nearly 2,500 miles apart. When they met again, towards the mid-part of the wall, they embraced and went their separate ways. Now that's what I call a classy farewell.

The Emmeline standing before me turned out to be the American woman I was supposed to look out for. Her husband was making tea in the church. He was much smaller than her and looked and acted like Paul Simon. I took a picture of them on a balcony at the end of the nave, and told them about my walk round Wales. The husband drifted off to look at Emmeline's grave, leaving the two of us to talk in the cool of the pews.

'Did you know there was an Emmeline buried here?' I asked her.

'No idea at all,' she answered. 'It's a very odd feeling.'

'Very remarkable coincidence,' I said.

'Yes,' she replied, 'but life seems to be one big twist of fate,' adding: 'I wonder who puts the flowers on Emmeline's grave?' There were three posies dotted around the cross.

'Don't know,' I said, 'but one thing occurred to me – the flowers aren't put there in memory of Emmeline, are they?'

'What do you mean?' she asked.

'The flowers are put there to perpetuate a myth, aren't they,' I said. 'No-one actually cares about Emmeline any longer – but they care about the story. Isn't that how myths are made?'

She was intrigued by this, and we had a close conversation. I talked about Wales, and I talked about Mr Vogel. I hadn't noticed, but by the time I finished his story she was almost crying. Yes, I could see that her eyes were misty. She had been moved by the Vogel story. I was amazed – and very apologetic.

'No, no,' she said to me, laughing off her tears, 'it's a really lovely story. Do you think you will find him?'

'I really think he must be dead by now. But I would like to know what happened to him.'

'Me also,' she said. 'Will you keep me informed? I really would like to know. Perhaps I can help in some way?'

I thanked her.

'I like your hair by the way,' she said in passing, 'my brother has red hair. I've always liked people with red hair. Do you know why redheads are given such a hard time, especially at school?'

'No idea.'

'It's because of Judas Iscariot. He was supposed to have red hair. So people with a ginger mop have been shunned ever since. Ridiculous isn't it? People are so awful – anything out of the norm and they gang up. Something to do with the herd, normality and all that.'

We sat in silence, listening to the sound of a tractor climbing down a hill towards the church, bringing with it a waft of new-mown hay. She held my hand as we walked out into the blinding sunshine.

'You look after yourself,' she said. 'Don't go too close to those sea cliffs in Pembrokeshire – I've read about them, they sound really dangerous.'

She squeezed my hand and then let go as we approached her husband, who was kneeling by the cross. He looked at us strangely.

'I really would like your address,' she said to me.

'Why?' asked the Simon thing.

'So we can send him a picture of us on the balcony,' she

replied blithely. We swapped addresses and e-mails. I was loathe to leave her, and circled the two of them, pretending to look at the graves all around. She kept an eye on me, discreetly. I knew she liked me.

My body was doing funny things to me – injecting me with strange drugs and messing about with my insides. This must be what being drunk feels like. The gypsies go to certain places for erotic love, to other places for procreation. With Emmeline I wanted both sorts of love, immediately, in a buttercupped corner of that graveyard.

I will take you on this walk from Hay Bluff, along the Black Darren, with the Black Mountains on my right and the Black Hill on my left; sounds very black indeed, but the day has blossomed into a riotously colourful cavalcade. I peek into the deep cleft of the Vale of Ewyas on my right hand, with its many buildings devoted to God, including the gaunt remains of Llanthony Priory. This valley has pulled at many men's souls, like a spiritual magnet. Walter Landor Savage, named in the Vogel Papers, lived here for a while, as did Eric Gill the sculptor and typographer; if you're into incest and depravity you should read about the antics of his strange little coven at Capel-y-Ffin.

On my left is a vast panorama, almost too much for the eye to cope with. The Olchon Valley, immediately below me on my left, and the Golden Valley beyond would take months to appreciate fully; it's all beyond comprehension, so I set off at a jaunty pace, feeling pretty damn good thank you very much, and I hope you're happy too. We're walking on a broad saddle of peaty moor with a pavement of stones put down to protect the Darren from erosion.

I'm wearing my black Hi-Tec Ascent boots which cost me £50; they're the first pair of boots I've ever felt affection for, which is probably a bit sad. I'm also wearing weathered black cords, my favourite purple pullover, and a frayed old jacket with some sort of check pattern which has long since faded into obscurity. My red frizzly mop is unhindered, since I don't wear a silly hat or have any of the other marks of a pilgrim, viz scallop shell, palm leaf, speedwell, cross, staff, badge or relic pinned to my tunic. I have my light rucksack with lightweight sleeping bag, nylon mac, medicine, two small bottles of Coke, sandwiches, chocolate, two candles, lighter, OS Landranger map 161, and a copy of Watson's *The Life of Sir Robert Jones*, which is the only non-essential item I carry today. I walk in a dream state all morning, passing no-one, since Dyke travellers all start at roughly the same time every morning and pass you in a half-hour wave, with no-one before or after them. Pilgrimage routes must be similar. For lunch I deviate off the saddle of the Darren and cut right to a col above Llanthony Priory, where I sit in the heather and eat my sandwiches contentedly like a summer cow chewing the cud in a plenitude of heat and food. I read a chapter of Watson's book, entitled 'The Crippled Child'.

There was little doubt, he said, that the primitive and nomadic tribes of prehistory had killed off their lame and maimed. He continued:

> During the Dark and Middle Ages... to be crooked in body meant to be crooked in mind. Alternate fear and ridicule represented the medieval attitude. On the one hand, Luther advised the killing of deformed infants, and on the other it became the custom to employ dwarfs and hunchbacks as 'jesters' in kings' courts and barons' castles.
>
> The psychological effect of ridicule, oppression, or contempt maturing over two thousand years needs no further elaboration. Right up to the nineteenth century to be crippled meant isolation and malignity. Of this dark background literature has left us a remarkable store of evidence. The centuries which separated Richard III from the Hunchback of Notre Dame or Scott's Black Dwarf from Dickens' Quilp show little evidence of a change in popular opinion. Even in modern fiction to be crippled is still a convenient simile for crime.

With the coming of the 'age of sensibility' in the 18th century humanitarianism was heard in the voices of men like Voltaire, Rousseau, Paine, Locke and Goldsmith – but although public attitudes softened, the lot of the cripple became infinitely worse.

> The industrialism of the nineteenth century, firmly planted in factory and mine, commenced to produce cripples in such numbers that instead of being incongruous they were in certain districts almost universal. Those were the days... when tiny children worked fifteen hours a day before returning to hovels where nothing penetrated except gin and squalor. The mothers of these hapless little ones hauled trucks in the mines at a time when the problems of Negro slavery caused every household to glow with British rectitude. Industrialism became the

most prominent contributor to the production of cripples. It was the greatest advertisement of the artificial causes of deformity – until the Great War – to be thrust upon public attention. Cripples, instead of being so rare as to cause boisterous laughter, were, from the beginning of the nineteenth century onwards, being faster and faster manufactured by industrial conditions, slums, direct infection, and accidents.

This was the background, presumably, to Mr Vogel's childhood. I have a vision of the young Vogel as a rather lanky youngster on two crutches fashioned by his drunken father from the branches of an ash tree. I imagine the scene: waiting for a wild and windy night to cover his sounds, the father takes a last mighty draw on the gin jar, then stumbles out into the darkness with his axe. He creeps through the outskirts of Manchester with a black scarf wrapped around his face, then dives into a wood, finds a young tree, and hews two branches with Y-shaped clefts which can be moulded to fit the youngster's armpits. The branches are stripped and carried away in the dead of night, back to the hovel where the family sleeps. The 'slattern' mother awaits in the kitchen for her husband's return. By morning there are two crudely-formed crutches awaiting the boy. He grovels with gratitude. He has also been given a violin. It is old, made of dark rosewood, and it has an unusual scroll, carved like a lion's head. He peers into the soundboard and wonders at the mysteries inside which create this sonorous, expressive, disturbing sound. He knows of the blind musicians. There is a blind Irishman who plays Kerry fiddle tunes and O'Carolan's planxties in a pub on the corner. The crippled and the blind, unable to do very much else, learn instruments and play music for a few pence. Now he learns to fiddle whilst leaning on a crutch. He plays with plenty of vibrato, to make people feel sentimental.

> The crippled child was regarded as a hopeless case with a right to indolence and ignorance. To be a cripple meant in town house and country cottage generation after generation of weaklings growing up with no use either of brains or limbs.
>
> Parents preferring to believe in the hopelessness of treatment were not discouraged by the medical services and general practitioners.

One doctor wrote at the time that children were often operated on needlessly, saying:

On examining the removed joint – and then contemplating the beauty of the child thus mutilated, one wondered and wondered.

Rickets and tuberculosis maimed countless little lives. Agnes Hunt describes the plight of the child cripple in this moving excerpt:

In 1900, England had no realisation of the magnitude of her crippled population, nor yet of its crying need. Some of the towns had cripples' guilds... these societies gave treats to the crippled children, and paid for convalescent treatment. Much money was also expended on splints. Unfortunately, as there was no-one to supervise the application of these appliances, they were seldom worn, though much admired and greatly prized by the parents. I have seen children with tuberculosis, poliomyelitis, with osteomyelitis, and many other crippling diseases, go into hospital, and return to their wretched homes no better, or, perhaps, with arm or leg amputated. No proper treatment, no after-care, and no hope for the future, except the gloomy portals of the workhouse – a burden to their loved ones, wretched and utterly help-less, alternatively spoilt and smacked by their people, and systematically cold-shouldered by a world which had no room, and little sympathy, for the physically disabled.

I looked down at the plain below me, and imagined it thronged with all those who had walked across it; the prehistoric tribes, the hunters, gatherers, marauding hordes, invaders, plunderers, mendicant monks, Lombards, friars, farmers, drovers, pilgrims, all pursuing their individual paths, all swirling in a medley of life, movement and hope.

In the white cottages at my feet, and beyond, in the smoke-gutted cities, there had lain children, some of them loved and pitied, most of them as unwanted as lepers, existing as a grim counterpoint to human hope and aspiration. I shuddered at my own good fortune to be treading this land. I am among the first men free to do so on a daily basis. Not a single generation since primitive man has been as free as mine to walk here, mainly because the first and only priority in life, for the mass of human-ity, has been to stay alive. Walking for fun is a modern phenomenon.

The afternoon is dwindling as I come off Hatterrall Hill into Pandy, and the mountains above Abergavenny – Sugar Loaf and

Blorenge – fade into a soft grey evening haze. Pandy looks boring so I walk the extra few miles to Llangattock Lingoed, where I find a bed in the old vicarage. It's old, big-roomed and comfortable in a classy way. I feel mellow after a bite and head for the village pub, where I am welcomed by the locals. I had expected Monmouthshire people to be English-flavoured; I am surprised to find that they look and sound like one of us, and the ground feels as Welsh as any soil I have trod.

Back at the old vicarage I phone my friend Paddy, who keeps an eye on my mail whilst I'm away. He also looks at my e-mails. He's not Irish; he's a Somerset man, and retains the soft old drawl; any explanation of his nickname has long since been forgotten. He saved my life once. He's one of those unshaven builders with dirty vests and sunburnt necks and fags hanging out of their mouths. Tonight he's drunk. By the way, please excuse his language, it really is appalling and frankly it mortifies me to write it down (the Welsh are new to swearing), but I have to tell you the story as it happened.

'Hia Paddy. You OK?'

'As fine as can be, yaroo, can you hear the whoosh in me storm drains, the hour's systolic me old peculiar. I can hear it, the blood's black and cold tonight and there's a dead fly in me corned beef sandwich.'

This is typical Paddy jibberish.

'Finnegan's awake in the larder, four eyes, and your girlfriend wants a word with you. Looks stunning. She's wagging her tail, wants to know how Mr Ulysses is getting on.'

It's a Paddy joke. His dog gives me a welcome whenever I return to the north. Paddy says I'm like Ulysses returning to Ithaca after the Trojan War.

You may remember the story – Ulysses has survived incredible odds during many adventures, and after eons he returns to his home; Penelope his wife has foiled her many suitors by promising to marry one of them when the work on her loom is finished, but every night she unravels some of it so that it is never finished; no-one recognises Ulysses except his old dog, who wags his tail one last time when he sees his master and then dies. Paddy is taking the piss, of course.

'Yaroo fuck and aye, the Frenchman blows his nose on a wet

crow and attishoo we all fall down in the woods today, the bears are unbearable this time of year it's the year of the hare.'

'Yes Paddy.'

'Ever read *The Year of the Hare*, carrot-head?'

'No Paddy.'

'Fucking ignoramus.'

'If you say so Paddy.'

'It's about a Finn who fucks off with a hare.'

'Really Paddy. That's fascinating.'

'Ho fucking ho and a pint of cold jam up yer bum, where has Spock boldy gone today anyway?'

I describe my day in a few words, since talking to a drunk is only slightly entertaining for a short while. I've never drunk in my life, can't understand why so many people want to be so very tiresome on a voluntary basis.

'Anyway me ole china, you've got a big bucketful of e-mails from that American bint and a boxful of letters from Little Bo Peep. Should keep you busy for a while. Come to think of it, have you noticed, they always land on the food if there's one of them chef programmes on TV?'

'They?'

'Flies – they always land on the food. Not on top of the telly, or in the corner, but always smack in the middle of the screen where the grub is. Know how they land? They've got little hooks on their legs and they throw themselves at the glass, hoping the hooks will catch on a tiny scratch. There's clever, whenever I try to throw myself at windows...'

'For pete's sake, Paddy, tell me about the bloody e-mails.'

'Did you know, my little ambulant carrot, that glass is quite soft really and if you held your finger against it, quite hard, not gentle like, for a few dozen years it would go right through the gla–'

'For Christ's sakes Paddy, put a bloody sock in it. I haven't got all night.'

'Ah, getting impatient are we. Hold yer horses now. Patience is a pancake. Hang on a mo. Your little lovesick transatlantic bit of fluff is desperate, she says *desperate* to get in touch. You've got to phone *immediately*, if not *sooner*. Want to take her phone number?'

'No.'

'Had our first little tiff have we?'

'Don't be ridiculous. Contact is kept to a bare minimum. She has already asked me for a photograph. What does she say?'

Paddy concentrates and pushes through the curtain of his alcoholic haze.

He explained that Anwen Marek had got in touch with a descendant of Anna Vogel, a woman called Jo-Anne Veronski, who knew the whole story. Vogel went to America, made a fair bit of money, and then disappeared. When she was winding up the estate, Veronski found a mass of documents dealing with immigration, setting up a business, wills etcetera. She also found some letters.

'Turns out these letter weren't between Vogel and his wife Anna,' said Paddy. 'Seems he had a dark secret, but the family have never fathomed it out. They want to co-operate. Marek has photocopied the letters and I have them here. They were all sent by Little Bo Peep to Little Boy Blue. It's assumed that Little Boy Blue was Vogel.'

'Thanks Paddy. I'm not sure what to do now. Don't feel like coming back yet because I want to get to Monmouth.'

'Rightyho me old Captain Invincible, onwards and downwards and all that, a man's gotta do what a man's gotta do, what's that about Wales and fields...'

Someone had once told him that true Wales was never more than a field away, no matter where you were in the land. Forever cynical, Paddy responded that true Wales was always a field away. He regarded my wanderings as bordering on the insane, but he was proud of me. 'The land won't love you back, you know,' he told me once. 'You're just a fly on a fucking big elephant, it don't know you're there and it don't care a fig if you ever lived. It's one way. A figment.'

But I got my revenge when he went all wistful about Glastonbury Tor. He's a great friend, bit of a Walter Mitty, tells amazing tall stories, drinks far too much – I often have to help him with the first pint, hold it for him because he's shaking so much. But everyone likes him. He's one of those people who can swear and cuss and blackguard people without anyone taking offence.

And so it came to pass that on the morrow I conquered the White Castle and led my imaginary troupe of vagabonds, troubadours and pilgrims through the stubble of a newly-reaped cornfield and across the exquisitely fortified Monnow Bridge at Monmouth on a day of supercilious beauty. If life is a maze and a walk is an attempt to get out of it, I want to be caught in this Welsh maze of mine, this green labyrinth, for ever. My mind, my body and the world around me have struck a perfect chord.

I attach a selection of the letters sent to me from America by Anwen Marek, together with the covering letter which came with them. It's hard to make sense of it all. This is the way I read it so far: Vogel was a little boy who was treated by Dr Robert Jones. Then he went to America, where he became manager of a violin factory. He got married to Anna Vogel but then disappeared. During his time in America he received a series of letters from someone signing herself Bo Peep. And it becomes clear from those letters that Bo Peep was a little girl who had been in hospital at the same time as Vogel in the dim and distant past, when they were both children.

The box contained 24 photocopied letters written in a neat copperplate, together with this accompanying letter:

Dear Ms Marek,

These are the letters I mentioned in our conversation. It's nice to think that we may be able to throw some light, at last, on this episode in our family history. As I told you, this man Vogel left his wife Anna in the lurch, with a young child (my Mom) and a home which was far from completed. She was a resolute person and she took on her husband's violin-making venture. She later married the manager and had two further children. Vogel disappeared without trace and was declared legally dead after the statutory period. He was never heard of again. As a family we only have a few pieces of information about him. It is said that he moved about on sticks or crutches and had a quick temper – if teased by the local children, who apparently called him Long John Silver, he became angry and threw his sticks at them. The children would then throw his sticks in the river, so he had to be helped back home by a passer-by, who often stayed for hours afterwards, and sometimes all night, listening to his music and his yarns. My mother said he was of Welsh ancestry, but came here from one of the major English cities, where his parents had gone in search of work. This Vogel was also a bit of a scruff, a drunk and a layabout, wasting away his hours playing fiddle music with his cronies in the saloon, and reciting poetry, rather than working. He always maintained that he came from a long line of Welsh bards and the small items he left behind include a framed poem in the Welsh language. Its title, we were told, means *The Song of the Shepherd*. Obviously, we do not know this because we do not speak the language, but I can give you the title, since I still have the poem – it is called *Can y Bugail*.

I look forward to hearing from you again, and I enclose a pair of gloves which I assume to be yours – I noticed them on the hallway table after you had left. This British connection of yours sounds interesting – I would like to know why he is researching the Vogel name. Let me know as soon as you find out yourself!

Yours in expectation,
Jo-Anne Veronski.

Five of the letters are reprinted below.

LETTER 1

Dear Boy Blue,

I write this letter full of sadness. It seems such a long time ago since I said goodbye to you, yet it was only this morning. My last glimpse of you at Gobowen Station will stay in my memory for ever. I feel so miserable! I don't know where you are, or whether you will receive this letter. I will continue to write to the Post Office until you have a proper address. I hope you are in better spirits, and that your parents are well. I have some news which is likely to change my life greatly! Agnes Hunt called us into her room to tell us that a Training School is being set up in another part of the hospital. We will sleep in our own little dormitories and each of us will have a locker and a nice green coverlet on our beds. We will have our meals with the matron and the servants. We will make splints and surgical boots in a workshop. Agnes Hunt is in charge, under protest, since she feels she is too old and tired, and there is no money. But as she says, work is the best medicine for us, otherwise our treatment will have been for nothing. And we can be most useful!

Miss Hunt looked tired and moved slowly this morning. I heard her crutch scrape on the yard outside my window just after dawn. When I asked her how she was, she shrugged her shoulders and said 'Every night I put a wet towel on my head and try to form plans!' How typical of her. I will do my best to help her. Our jack of all trades, the Factotum, is going to make our first surgical appliance tomorrow – from an old iron bedstead! Miss Hunt has a great plan – our Gang (pity

mentioned in Vogel papers

you're not here too!) will make all the appliances needed by the hospital, saving a considerable sum of money. It is nice to be useful after all these years of inactivity. And I get paid – isn't that incredible! My speciality is the surgical boot, which needs a nimble pair of hands. I so miss you. Another of our Gang, Edwin, is here also and he still makes us laugh with his japes and silly antics. He got into terrible trouble yesterday – it was very hot and he came in for a drink of water to cool him down. Miss Hunt asked him to go to her room to get that carving she has on her wall, the wooden one of Christ on the Cross with his robes painted blue, but Edwin dropped it and split it. What a commotion! To make matters worse he hid it so that Miss Hunt wouldn't see the damage. It was found the next morning under his bed!

I hope the journey was not too terrible for you; no doubt you were forced to lie in your cabin for most of it. Did you play your violin?! Is America as vast and dangerous as they say? Have you seen any Red Indians or buffaloes? Send me your news soon!

Miss Hunt says she has seen Buffalo Bill in Rhyl! I have picked the first snowdrops of spring and put them in a blue vase by my bedside to remind me of you leaving in the snow. Rupert is safe and well and snug as a bug under my pillow. I will kiss him goodnight every bedtime at ten, as you requested! Tonight a storm has blown in, bringing icy winds which moan around the wards. There is talk of war, all over the hospital I hear the adults whispering about it. It's horrible. Write soon!

With fondest regards,

Yours &,

Bo Peep.

LETTER 4

My Dear Boy Blue,

It is Sunday and my poor dear mother has been to visit me. I was overjoyed to see her, it was her first visit for nigh on a season. She brought me some cake and sweetmeats, and a pair of woollen mittens which will be extremely useful for my work in this cold weather. The regime is much the same as on the ward – plenty of fresh air, come rain or shine, and all the doors and windows are flung open before we start. This morning snow fell on my hair – I am immediately by the window – and when it melted the water ran like a cold knife down my neck, giving me such a shock I cried out loud! Angelica's bed was empty when we woke up. We're too afraid to ask why. Do you remember how she used to scream and cry so terribly when they injected her? They haven't taken away the little mirror they put above her bed so that she could see what was happening around her. I can't get her face out of my mind. She's like a ghost, I can still see her mass of red hair and freckles, her bent little back, and her mouth open, screaming. It's terrible. Nosy Parker is bereft. For once I feel sorry for him. Without his sister he's small and pathetic, not the swaggering know-all we're so used to.

The empty bed reminds me of that little lapwing we saw on one of the jaunts up Twmpath Lane in our beds when we were little, with the nurses pushing and teasing us. Do you remember? We had a picnic in the heather by the roadside and we must have been near a nest, because one of the birds pretended to be injured and limped about, trying to draw us away from her little home. Do you remember?

They're getting rid of those open-sided horse boxes we started off in, before the wards were built. How cold they were, but the germs must have thought so too because they never touched us!

Miss Hunt has asked me to write down all my memories (I think this is a ruse to keep my fingers agile!). Today I have written about my tenth birthday, and what a lot I had to write about! It was the year we performed our first play – The Court of Oberon.

Do you remember – I was a bat with wings made from old umbrellas! – and since it wasn't a leap year and I would miss my birthday again, I was allowed to go with the older children to Rhyl to camp in tents on the beach. What huge fun we had watching the nigger minstrels with their banjos, and the Punch and Judy, and I rode on a donkey with Goody holding me; she told me that she and Miss Hunt went out to nurse their patients in the country on two ponies called Bacillus and Germ!

I must end now because prayers will start soon and then it will be lights out as usual.

I miss you so much. So does Rupert – I thought I saw a tear in his eye last night when I kissed him and hid him under the pillow to await your safe return.

Yours etc., with fondest regards

Bo Peep.

LETTER 7

My Dear Little Boy Blue,

What a day it has been! Miss Hunt came into our dormitory in high spirits at breakfast time to tell us she had received great news – the hospital would not be used to house the injured Tommies who are beginning to return home from the first battles in France. But at 5 o'clock in the evening a telegram arrived to say that soldiers were coming on the hospital train in only a few hours! Imagine the panic as nurses ran everywhere at a gallop with sheets and blankets. The charwomen fetched out their scrubbing brushes, and I had to pack my belongings quickly since I am to be taken to a nearby farm, which may be my home for the rest of the war. I shall make a little pig of myself! Shortly before midnight there was a great commotion and we saw lamps bobbing among the trees along the drive, and we heard voices strengthen. There were 27 of them. Four on stretchers – the rest were walking wounded. They looked at the wards, completely open to the elements on one side, with disbelief but they seemed mollified when they were given plenty of blankets and hot water bottles. They have septic wounds which need careful dressing. It has brought the world to our doorstep in a sudden and frightening moment, like a gust of cold wind.

The smell of their bandages reminds me of the operations when we were little, when there was no proper operating theatre. I have written it all down in my book of memories – how we knew when children were going to be operated on the following day because the staff took all the furniture from the dining room and took all the pictures from the walls and scrubbed everything. I still remember the smell of the instruments being boiled in the fish kettles. Then they lit candles and operated on dining room tables pulled together. But Dr Robert Jones was so kind we trusted him, somehow his eyes told us that pain was on the way, but it was unavoidable and mostly for the good.

The children still greet Dr Jones with cheers and shouts of joy, and it is still considered a great honour to be operated on by him, rather like winning a prize! There have been no changes – the children are still allowed to choose their own supper on the evening before an operation, and they are still given special toys (like Rupert!) on the morning of the operation.

Today my fingers are numb because I have made an extra pair of boots for little Julius the German boy, who had a hole in the sole of his right boot, the one which drags and which used to annoy you so! Jack has been made tea boy because he is strong enough to pull the urn around the workshop, and he has taken over a little room as his headquarters. When he goes into the room he kicks the doorframe and walks in clutching his head, pretending he has struck his forehead on the lintel – which is ridiculous, since he hardly reaches the doorknob! His room has become the meeting place for all the Welsh children on the ward, who gather there like swallows waiting to return home in the autumn.

Lights out in a moment – I will continue in the morning.

LETTER 7 (CONTINUED)

Dear Little Boy Blue,

An eventful night – but I slept through it all. One of the soldiers ran away and was found in a public house at Burlton, hiding in a heap of malt. He was taken to Shrewsbury jail under escort. We are now marking out our new territory in the farm buildings. We are to rent an adjoining field for chickens, and Jack and I will be allowed to collect the eggs. Jack says he will help me along when my limbs get tired and naughty and won't listen to orders! Jack, Nosy Parker and some of the other children will help out in the garden also, so that we have suffi-cient fresh vegetables. We have a small well and the Factotum has to spend three hours every day getting enough water for all of us; since we cannot have baths we make do with bowls of tepid water and a flannel!

This afternoon Miss Hunt ordered the Factotum to harness Bobby and hitch her to the wagonette, which was stuffed full of children and we went on a great quest, calling on the well-to-do people of the area. One of the families was very rich and they lived in a big house on an island, with a moat right round it, and it had its own little bridge over the water! They gave us little presents of clothes they could spare and toffee etc. It was so enjoyable travelling up and down the country lanes. I could see a ribbon of grass with buttercups and daisies passing under-neath me, through gaps in the planking. We crossed a big hump-backed bridge and some of the children were so scared they cried and I had to comfort them. We stopped at the inn so that Bobby could have a drink. You know the place – it has red flowers in the window, and a nurse carried you inside it one day, I think you had a fainting fit during an outing in your bed.

Diphtheria has broken out and some of the children have been removed to tents on the other side of the farm. Five large marquee tents, sent by the War Office, have been put up in a field to take more soldiers. All is hustle and bustle wherever you go. Miss Hunt is adamant that our routine will not change and we still have school lessons outside on our beds in the morning. Sometimes it's so cold the nurses have to wear gloves when they're making our beds! Miss Hunt discovered Jack's little lair and ticked him off, but allowed him to continue. She said it reminded her of an incident when she was a district nurse. A local lady allowed Miss Hunt to hold a clinic in her home every month, but one day the husband, who didn't like cripples, came home suddenly and found his drawing room crammed with between thirty and forty children! He was very grumpy about it but he didn't throw them out.

Rupert is pining for you and he misses you so much that I have taken him to work inside my pinafore, where he stays all day because he would be confiscated if anyone saw him! Please write soon. I shall despair if I don't hear from you. Jack and Nosy Parker and the others send their regards, and ask if you will send them some Red Indian head-dresses and a totem pole!

Your ever loving
Bo Peep.

LETTER 11

Dear Little Boy Blue,

I am beginning to despair. I lie awake at night wondering if you ever reached America. I have a terrible recurring nightmare about you at the bottom of the ocean with your eyes open and bubbles coming from your mouth. Miss Hunt says I should persevere, since you were always a survivor, she says, and will bob up to the surface somewhere, at some time or other.

The hospital and the farm buildings are very full. I hear moaning and screams from the soldiers' marquees, and there is always a huddle of men smoking around the entrances. They look grim, but that may be because they're well enough to get out of bed for a smoke, and there-fore well enough to return to the front. Yesterday Miss Hunt faced a great conundrum. 'Esmie,' she said to me, 'could you possibly make up a cot for a poor mite of five years old who has an acute tubercular spine and is a very urgent case.' I thought for a few seconds, and then answered: 'We have enough cotton and chaff to make a mattress, and there is an old spinal chair that would do for a bed, but we have no blankets or rugs, and since your last raid on the blanket cupboard it is under lock and key.'

'Well,' she replied, 'I expect something will turn up, providence has never let us down yet, and nothing is more certain than that the child is coming and must be taken in, even if it has to share my bed.'

Gloomily we retired for the night, and sadly we arose this morning to find the snow thick on the ground and a bitter north-east wind blowing. After washing and giving the children their breakfasts, putting in fresh hot water bottles etc., we sat down to our own breakfasts in that strange brittle light after a fresh fall of snow. Miss Hunt opened her letters, and the first one, from Mrs Swann of Halston, read like this:

Dear Aggie, I have been worrying all day about your poor little children in those open sheds. Are they warm enough in this bitter cold weather? I cannot rest for fear you have not warm blankets enough, so I have telegraphed to Maddox's to send you by the first train thirteen pairs of blankets.

Miss Hunt said: 'Now you can call this telepathy or coincidence or anything else you like, but this thing has happened so often here that I humbly prefer to call it a direct answer to prayer.'

Nosy Parker is writing a history of the hospital and he goes around looking ever so important, asking all sorts of questions and writing them down with a big carpenter's pencil which looks like a spear in his hand. Talking of spears, Miss Hunt joked with me yesterday that perhaps you had been scalped by the Red Indians for your violin, but I became so tearful that she almost cried herself, patting my head and pressing a handkerchief into my hand. As a consequence she gave me a book to read, which is rather dry but since it was owned by Dr Robert Jones I treasure it and read a page during my last few minutes before prayers nearly every night. It is a book by a man of long ago, called Thomas Pennant, and is a tour of Wales, where Dr Jones lives. It is a land full of princes and poets and strange people, including a very strong woman who builds boats, makes harps, beats all the men at wrestling, and has a pack of hounds for hunting! No doubt your new home is also strange and wild! Today as I worked in the workshop someone delivered a dog cart as a gift, to be used as a conveyance for our children. Inside it I found a small enamel disc with a dancing bear embossed on it, and thinking immediately of Rupert I took it and polished it – you will find it enclosed within the folds of this letter. I will continue to send letters, though you don't answer. Even if you don't care for me any longer, I still wonder at your progress among the heathens – are their pow-wows and war cries stunned into silenced when they hear Abide With Me? I do hope you have not taken one of the squaws as your wife and settled in a tepee. Edwin has been quiet of late and I am worried about him, for very little dampens his spirits usually. He has confided in me that the cause of his ill-humour is the soldiers, for his own father was a soldier also and ill-treated him terribly, causing his own son's malformations. I feel sorry for Julius – his family is interned somewhere, he does not know where, and he still cannot speak our language, but he has lovely eyes, big and blue, and he follows me around like a little puppy all day, so that we are the cause of much mirth all along the hospital. One night I woke up to find him in bed beside me, his little arms around me, as if I were his mother. I let him be, but shifted him to his own bed on the other side of the partition as dawn broke.

I will end with a loving message from your own dear Rupert, whom you must miss more than anything in the world!

COME HOME SOON I NEED YOU!

You are forever in my thoughts.

Bo Peep.

LETTER 18

Dear Little Boy Blue,

Greetings from a lonely voice across the water. It has been an inestimable time since I saw you, and since I have not heard from you I must accept, reluctantly, that you have either perished or failed to reach America. Miss Hunt said you were a survivor; I offer up my earnest prayers that I shall see you again one day. For the present I will desist and wait for a sign that you are there, it is more than my heart can bear to write into this void which separates us. Perhaps the war is responsible – perhaps my letters are not reaching you on the other side. I wish it so; nothing would grieve me more than to know that you are reading my letters, yet not replying. You have that side to you. I remember when little Luther came to us, with his simple ways. His mother would come to see him every month, and as soon as she made a move to leave he would ask her to fetch one of the newspapers from the corner. She always did so, without understanding why he wanted such a strange thing – after all, he was simple and could not read. She noticed that often he held the newspaper upside down. Her inquisitiveness grew too strong one Sunday, if you remember, and she returned to see what he was looking at. He was crying. He wanted the newspaper so that he could hide his tears when she left him. You were the only one who was not affected. You just lay in your bed and looked at him, without a tear.

We are already tired from the war. I fear that 1915 is going to be a tiresome year, and a wet spring has given way to a dismal July – it is the fourteenth – covered over by grey skies and black thoughts. The hospital is clogged with mud and limping soldiers. Miss Hunt tells me that Dr Robert Jones is performing heroic deeds with his medical teams at the front. His new splint has saved thousands of lives.

Jack sends his regards. He is confined to the dormitory for a month because he was caught smoking with the soldiers. Luther has learnt to spell his name at last, and he won all the prizes at the sports. He is very quick and he does not seem to notice the pain he must suffer in his spine. Nosy Parker has finished his history of the hospital but is cross because he must wait for Dr Jones to return from the war before he can complete his great work. I am generally well, though I have two callipers now instead of one, and my walking is going through a difficult phase. Little Julius goes with me everywhere. This morning, for the first time since he arrived, he was not by my side when we walked to the breakfast room. He had simply vanished. I searched and searched, and eventually found him in the tent which remains from the diphtheria outbreak. He was playing with a little girl, the sole remnant of the epidemic. He had felt sorry for her. I chided him and dragged him away, but because of his language problems he did not understand that the area was out of bounds. I hope he has not caught it. Strangely enough, I am not feeling so grand myself tonight, so I will seal this letter, my last, with loving kisses from myself and your ever faithful Rupert, who looks very dandy because I gave him a clandestine bath last night when no-one was looking. His fur is soft and sweet-smelling and his eye has an extra lustre. In accordance with your wishes I have not sown on another eye to match it.

May the winds of the ocean blow a thousand kisses to your sweet lips.

I will be your everlasting friend, as I promised you that Christmas Day long ago. Goodbye my sweet. I shall see you in heaven if not sooner.

Bo Peep.

LOST AND FOUND

SO, my friends, our story takes a step towards its final resolution. Are your feet hurting yet? After all, a long journey such as ours wouldn't be the same without a bit of pain, would it? Irish pilgrims walk up Croagh Patrick barefoot, do they not? And there's a far more arduous pilgrimage, ending in Tibet, in which thousands of penitents travel for up to 2,000 miles: 'They prostrate themselves on their faces,' noted the Everest mountaineer John Noel, "marking the soil with their fingers a little beyond their heads, arise and bring their toes to the mark they have made and fall again, stretched full length on the ground, their arms extended, muttering an already million-times-repeated prayer.'

Let's face it, this hajj of ours is a breeze.

We learn a lot from the Bo Peep letters, I believe. If you're still stumbling along behind me on this madman's trail you will have noticed that Little Bo Peep lets slip in one of her letters that her real name is Esmie.

Esmie Falkirk? Surely she must be the same Esmie Falkirk whose name was inscribed on that plaque on Doctor Robert's pagoda many chapters ago. The Bo Peep letters contain other names from the Vogel Papers: the Factotum is there, and Edwin, and Angelica, and Nosy Parker. They're the same people, but they've been taken to another time, another place – they're in a children's hospital, and it's wartime.

The Bo Peep letters also contain an incident in which a wooden figure of Christ splits. Edwin mislays it for a day. Ring any bells? And Jack, the landlord of the Blue Angel is there also, with his daft 'I've hit my head' routine.

You're quite right, this book has more freaks than a Fellini film.

There's a one-eyed teddy bear, just as there is in the Vogel Papers, and there's another common factor – Bo Peep reveals that her birthday is on that most freakish of dates, which was also the date on which Doctor Robert died and Mr Vogel won his fortune – February 29th.

And what has Mr Vogel got in common with that date, February 29th?

I think you'll agree that they are both anomalies – blips, deviations, irregularities.

But let's look at it another way.

They are also additions – little extras.

They are enhancements and elaborations – and they are both means of correcting a slight imbalance caused by too much regularity.

Normality can never walk normally unless there's a flaw to walk on.

Do you know what? I've a sneaky feeling that the Vogel Papers were a complete fiction – a fairytale construed around actual events which happened many years previously, real events which took place on a children's ward.

But enough of conjecture – we'll follow that trail later.

There's a blemish in my great trek, and I put it there.

A tiny little kink, which means that you – yes, that's you, the tethered herd lowing in the urban cowsheds of Little England – can never follow exactly in my path. Well, not legally anyway. This is how it came about.

I had been walking alongside the river Dee all day. A bore had swept upstream (I will allow you some sarcasm here), flicking cormorants into the air.

I stopped at a village called Holt, on the Welsh side of the river, which is linked to the English side by a fine red sandstone bridge. The river doodled below me in a lazy, Sunday morning in bed sort of way, and I crossed over to visit Farndon on the English bank. These two villages rub along pretty well nowadays, though some people can still remember unpleasant scenes outside the Saturday night dances when mixed race partners left hand in hand. I called into a pub for a drink, and inquired about Pickhill Hall downriver. This impressive old hall has a dinky accompanying bridge over the Dee in its grounds. I figured this route would save me a few miles if I could get across the bridge, but there was no public access marked on my map.

'Don't worry,' said the pub lady, 'my husband used to work there and you're allowed across the bridge.' I checked with another person on the way: his story was different. I chanced it anyway.

When I arrived at Pickhill Hall I strode up to the building purposefully, since lurking about is bound to get you noticed (and usually disliked). There was an old geezer kneeling by a door, painting it, and I asked him for advice. He was very pleasant, and as it happened he'd cycled around Wales in his salad days. We swapped reminiscences.

'Strictly speaking, you're not allowed to cross it,' he said in a fatherly way, 'but I don't suppose anyone will bother trying to stop you today. Mind the ha-ha, though.'

I minded the ha-ha and reached the bridge, one of those old bolted steel affairs, with rotting planks and barbed wire strung all over it like Christmas decorations. I found a point where I could climb the superstructure and worm my way through the barbs, then I dropped down on the other side feeling more daring than a Colditz escapee. It took me ages, however, to find a way out to a road without exciting the interest of local farmers. Still, if the SAS want any tips they know where to find me.

It's time for one of my blind diversions: up a gully, through trees, and along a steep path to that vantage point over there, where we can view the world's crowded forum again. Let's put the map away, rest for half an hour and observe dots moving in the distance and gaze at faraway smoke plumes, admire puffy little clouds perched on those far-off peaks like old men's wigs, while I take you into the parallel landscape of the mind. My topic during our respite this afternoon is Running Away (there's a possibility I may wander off myself occasionally – my mind is consumed by a certain Emmeline).

Every year more than a quarter of a million people are reported missing in Britain. Of those 250,000 troubled souls about 100,000 are under 18. They are from all age groups, ethnic origins and income groups, and from all areas.

Of the people reported missing no less than 8% are found dead. Some have been murdered, others have committed suicide, and others have met with accidents.

All these troubled souls have upped sticks and gone, taking with them their reasons, which range from problems at home and at work to long-term stress, general unhappiness, debt, redundancy, illness, injury, alcohol, glue-sniffing, drugs, various addictions, school, foul play, abuse and bullying. Although not cited, I suspect that pregnancy is there too somewhere.

In newspaper parlance, it's a terrible indictment on modern society.

Enough to make you weep. A contemporary of Chaucer's, Margery Kemp, who was quite obviously doolally by modern standards, spent the latter part of her eventful life going on pilgrimages, and her speciality was crying.

She even sought a licence from the church to *wear white and weep*. I really admire people who go for it. No half measures.

The 'disappeared' are not dissimilar – they walk and they weep, internally or externally. I've shed a salty tear or two on my country's mossy and maternal shoulder.

The freedom to open a door, step outside and carry on walking is the last true freedom we have, except the freedom to kill ourselves, of course. In an over-governed and constrictive state we can still get the hell out of it. The consequences can be pretty dire, and not for a moment will I romanticize them. But the choice is there in its stark simplicity.

I've wasted many words so far and got pretty well nowhere. No doubt some of the starters will have given up on our little quest, saying *sod him, he's pissing in the wind – I've got bigger fish to fry* etc. and they will have peeled off from the little group which started off on this pilgrimage. I won't chivvy you along, and I've no holy grail to promise you. If you want to come, come. The quest is there for the quest alone.

I have, however, prepared a little surprise for you.

I'm not a great one for celebrations, but I think we must mark the end of our quest somehow, when it comes. Some sort of party – a band perhaps, something upbeat and cheering, like a *ceilidh*. You don't walk round Wales every day. Actually, I've arranged something already. You'll never guess where it is – I'm sure you'll be tickled pink.

The Blue Angel – where else!

I had a word with the people who run the antiquarian book-shop there – gave them some guff about 'end of a mission' and 'suitable place' and 'accomplishment' and 'a fitting time to say thank-you to all concerned'.

They fell for it hook, line and sinker. They're even prepared to allow a bar on our big day. So when we end this walk of ours, and hopefully end the Vogel mystery too, we can have one hell of a party. You can, anyway. I'll enjoy watching. I'm not a drinker, as I think I've told you already, and parties are never quite the same with a Coke in your hand. But hey, what a time we'll have, and it'll be great to see everyone all together.

I've been musing while plodding along the contours of my beloved Wales. In the way celebrities on *This is Your Life* or *Desert Island Discs* listen to the highlights of their lives, or their favourite music, I've been pondering over whom exactly I'd like to have with me on the night of the party – except for you lot, of course, the ragtag rabble who have followed me so far. I want the others to be there too, if we ever find them – Mr Vogel, Esmie, Edwin, Don Quixote and Sancho Panza, the one-eyed landlord with a stolen marble in his left socket, the simpleton Luther, Julius Rodenberg, Thomas Pennant, Mr Nosy Parker, Angelica, the whole damn lot of them like spectres at a feast.

I will invoke them, one by one, to see if they will walk through that doorway under the dancing bear. It would be nice to see them all. At the end of this chapter I will have chosen my first guest. I can picture him already, seated quietly in what was the snug, away from all the noise and hubbub. He will have a bottle of stout before him, and he will engage the barman briefly and crisply in a conversation about a disfigurement which also marked the original landlord at the Blue Angel, namely a gammy peeper, a wonky watcher, a pooped planet swimming about in a black hole.

What is self & how does time effect it.

The preamble is over and we're on the home straight. Let me say a few things about myself. I am a child of my times, and in the patois of my times, I will tell you that I go on this quest to *find myself*. No, don't panic. I mean the words quite literally, for somewhere along the way I *lost myself*. I am retracing my steps, for I have been parted with a number of items.

First, my physical self. As I have told you, I am 47 years old, which means that there is virtually nothing left of the infant born so many (yet so few) years ago. Less than ten per cent, in fact, such is the rate of our cellular degeneration and regeneration. About 87% of me is less than ten years old. So I am not the person I used to be.

Second, my spirit, my soul, my persona, call it what you will – that has also been borrowed by various people, so that very little remains which is mine. I am a collection of other people's memories and anecdotes, little else. I thought I knew everything about myself – it turns out that others know far more. So I have borrowed back what little's left of me for this final jaunt, maybe so

We are what we are interested in → Culture/Sub cultures

that I can have a few memories just to myself – a little share option between me and the public corporation which is Me Dot Com.

Those memories. They're beginning to fade already. Talking to fishermen on the banks of the mile-wide Dee at Connah's Quay, with the giant Corus steelworks laid out over the river like a sleeping giant, Gulliver dressed in blue and tethered to the alluvium. The fish have voted with their fins, I am told mournfully.

I will go back to meet myself at different points, to renovate and repaint each memory... I will go back to a sloping field along Offa's Dyke, near Presteigne, to see the most spectacular rowan tree I have ever seen: so perfectly proportioned, so magnificently berried, so fully leaved that I sat and looked at it with complete admiration, suspecting that this was the idealised mother of all Welsh mountain trees: the original matrix and progenitor, which if pulped and made into paper would provide us with all the lost words and all the lost stories of Wales, words appearing magically on the seagull-white quires.

We have reached a watershed in the Vogel story.

America has been mined and our ship has returned, laden with ore. Mr Vogel had undoubtedly been to America, where he had started a violin factory and got hitched. For an unknown reason he then fled, abandoning a wife and an infant daughter.

We do not know where he went. We can be certain, however, that at one stage in his life he was a patient at the Robert Jones and Agnes Hunt Hospital at Gobowen in Shropshire. Gobowen is a rapidly-growing village near Oswestry, about two miles from the Welsh border. Oswestry was one of those border towns which the English and Welsh fought over for centuries, like two dogs scrapping for a bone, and one can still hear Welsh spoken there, occasionally, on market days. On the outskirts, to the north, there is a completely magnificent Celtic hill fort. To the south is Sweeney Hall, home of a very real John Parker, who became a minister in two Welsh parishes. He was one of the early Welsh travellers and a great lover of our little country. If he was 'nosy' it was in a very nice way, and the author of the Vogel Papers did him a great disservice. I wonder why? I'm told there was a real Julius Rodenberg too, and that he wrote a charming book about his visit to Wales.

~

I think we need to tie up some loose ends before we pursue the young Mr Vogel, relentlessly and unflinchingly, to Gobowen Hospital.

I started the story of the Bonesetters of Anglesey on the island's shore, after a storm, with the smuggler Dannie Lukie rescuing two small naked boys. One of them, Evan Thomas, became famous for curing animals and people of bone maladies. He treated the high and the low, the rich and the poor, on a 'pay what you can' basis. Evan's gift passed on to his son Richard, and we have an anecdote about him too:

> On one occasion a passenger, a man of some substance, travelling on the Holyhead to London stagecoach, suffered an injury while the horses were being changed at Gwindy. Advised by a bystander of the prowess of Richard he sent a message summoning him. However, when the bonesetter arrived in his home-made tweed suit and mounted on an ugly old mare, the passenger was shocked by his dishevelled appearance and curt manner and refused even to be examined by him. Whilst the local people were protesting to the stranger about his illogical attitude Richard, unobserved, left the scene to return home. At last the injured man was persuaded how foolish he had been and someone was despatched to try and catch up with the bonesetter. When they did so they failed completely to entice him back. No-one, not even the monarch himself, would be forgiven for treating him with contempt.

Richard's seven children all went on to practise bonesetting in one degree or another. Two of the daughters emigrated to the United States and practised their art there, according to Hywel Jones, an authority on the bonesetters.

The whole lot of them were proud and quick-tempered, and all of them had an exceptionally strong grip. Some doctors recognised their talents, but most were antipathetic and this hostility honed the family's proud temperament. They were intensely religious and had dominating characters with a sardonic sense of humour. They were quick to take offence and long in forgiving. The family had a physical characteristic – a defect in the little finger. This was generally described as a crooked little finger. Hywel Jones says:

I had some interesting correspondence with a lady from Wisconsin, USA, who was anxious to claim herself as a direct descendant and was overjoyed when I told her about the anomaly, for she had a crooked little finger.

Richard's son Evan walked the hundred or so miles to Liverpool, with the apparent intention of emigrating to America, but whilst still making up his mind he found work in a foundry. Here, accidents were so common that his abilities were soon called upon and he eventually set up a practice. Again, I quote:

It was a time of great industrial development in Liverpool, particularly in the area of the docks and his work increased rapidly. At first his patients were mostly dock workers, seamen and labourers but his reputation soon spread and people of all classes were before long to be found sitting on the bare painted wooden benches in his drab waiting room. He was a dour, silent man with no trace of humour and his command of the English language was so poor that normal conversation with his patients was at a premium. The Anglesey bonesetters were always regarded as hard men, impervious to the suffering they caused... but Evan did at least attempt some form of alleviation. In order to try to distract his patient's attention from the inevitable pain he was about to evoke he had his own musical box and, as he prepared for manipulation, his manservant would wind up the machine in readiness for the moment of action. Another counter attraction was the parrots. Evan had one or two of these birds in his consulting room and one can imagine their competing with the shrieks of the unfortunate patients.

Other doctors became jealous of his success, and since he was unqualified, they set out to make life difficult for him. Nine times he appeared in court, accused of malpractice, and each time he was acquitted. He was arraigned on a charge of manslaughter, and was again acquitted; the people of Liverpool, incensed by the malicious harassment he had suffered, met him as he returned home from court to congratulate him. When he stepped from the ferry at Seacombe he was met by a large crowd and a brass band playing *See the Conquering Hero Comes*. He was carried shoulder-high to his carriage. But Evan realised that the day of the unqualified practitioner was over and that his five sons could not continue the family tradition without a formal qualification.

His eldest son, Hugh Owen Thomas (whom I will call Hotty,

because of his initials) was to take the family into new territory. He was brought up in Anglesey, and whilst walking on the beach at Rhoscolyn he was hit in the left eye by a stone which permanently maimed him; consequently he wore a peaked cap to hide this disfigurement. After schooling he went on to qualify at Edinburgh, at roughly the same time as Joseph Lister, whose pioneering work with antiseptics saved many lives.

Hotty went on to set up his own practice in Nelson Street, Liverpool. Incidentally, he was an agnostic, which was most strange given his family history.

He was a busy man, having been appointed medical officer to many clubs and societies such as the shipwrights, ironworkers and boilerworkers and he also treated many seamen. He devised ingenious splints, was violently opposed to superfluous amputations, and believed strongly in the powers of complete rest and fresh air. I particularly like this description, by Hywel Jones, of this amazing little man, who worked like a Trojan to save those around him.

> ... he was a striking figure commanding attention more by his personality than by any personal attributes. He was small in stature, thin and pale, with dark grey eyes capable of great expression and a slight dark moustache and pointed beard. No description of Hugh Owen Thomas would be complete without mentioning his peaked cap, to shelter his tender eye, his closely buttoned frock coat and the inevitable cigarette dangling from his lips. Today it is fashionable to criticise doctors who smoke, but he would have refuted such an attitude as monstrous. He firmly believed that his miraculous escape from contracting cholera whilst he worked day and night in the ghastly slums of Liverpool during the great epidemic of 1864 was attributable to his habit of continuous smoking. This may be the one and only instance where his beliefs proved to be incorrect! He was rapid and sudden in all he did, as if there wasn't a moment to lose. He would fire questions at patients in quick succession and sometimes, if particularly hurried, would start his interrogation even as he ascended the stairs. Though abrupt in manner there was an overlying tone of kindness in his voice and he was beloved by children.

We have a description of 11 Nelson Street by the American surgeon Dr John Ridlon:

I was in a narrow room with shelves of medicine bottles on the left, and a stained counter-shelf below on which sat a crying child supported by its mother, whilst strapping the child's feet into iron splints was a thin, sallow little man dressed in black, with a cap with a glazed peak cocked over one eye, thick lensed spectacles, a ragged brindle beard and a cigarette in his mouth.

When the child stopped crying I stepped forward and handed him my card. He read it aloud and asked: 'What can I do for you? I am Mr Thomas.'

I said: 'Mr Thomas, I have read your book on the Hip, Knee and Ankle, and I have come three thousand miles to find out whether I am a fool, or you a liar'.

There was a twinkle behind the thick lenses and then he said: 'I think we'll find that out in half an hour.' Thus began two wonderful days...

Hotty was childless. He needed someone to continue the tradition, so he and his wife 'adopted' Robert Jones, who would go on to revolutionize orthopaedics, save thousands of lives in the Great War, and help found a hospital. Robert Jones was Hotty's nephew.

Hotty was the last of the Anglesey Bonesetters. But, miraculously, the gift brought to these shores by two shipwrecked boys now passed, like the Olympic torch, to a new bearer, who was to prove himself the fastest runner of all.

Today, 11 Nelson Street is revered as the birthplace of modern orthopaedic surgery in Britain. In Hotty's day it was an extraordinarily busy place. At six o'clock in the morning he was already on his rounds, riding behind two beautiful horses. He visited a dozen patients before his breakfast, always a cup of tea and a couple of bananas.

During the morning he saw 30 to 40 patients. Long experience enabled him to make a quick diagnosis, and his examination, though rapid, was very gentle. Hotty had a blacksmith at work in the smithy, a saddler finishing off various splints, and others making plasters, bandages and dressings.

There were other cases to treat in the afternoon, and after his evening meal he hurried from the table to see his evening flock, who continued to come until eight o'clock. In spite of his strenuous day he remained bright and cheerful, and he loved to chat. At eight he went on his last round, and from 9.30 to 12 he either worked in his lathe room – fitted with the most up-to-date machinery – making new surgical implements or repairing old ones, or he went to the library to read and write.

It's wondrous how he could work under such pressure for over thirty years, for he never took a holiday, even on Sundays, when he had his free clinic, attended by up to 200 cases from all parts.

Hotty died at the age of 56 after travelling to Runcorn to attend a patient; he had a fever when he started, and a long wait in a cold railway station brought on pneumonia. The *Lancet* mourned him thus:

> A grief so profound and widespread as that which was manifested in Liverpool on the tenth instant when the remains of Dr Hugh Owen Thomas were laid to rest, is seldom witnessed. There can be no more eloquent or touching testimony of the worth of a man's character than the tears of the poor among whom he lived. The toilers at our docks and warehouses are not insensitive beings, and the daily struggle of their lives is too earnest to admit of much display of sentiment. To see thousands of these, then, men as well as women, as anyone might have done in Liverpool last Saturday, stirred to their very depths by an emotion that found expression in passionate sobs and tears, as they lined the streets or pressed forward to gaze into the open grave, proves that its silent occupant had won his way to their hearts.

Dr Hugh Owen Thomas, I invite you to be the first guest at our party.

THE MYTH OF THE CAVE

THERE IS A TRADITION in Welsh poetry called *canu llatai* in which the poet sends a bird, an animal or a fish to salute his lover (only the birds can talk, however). Sometimes, but not always, he has been hindered or imprisoned and cannot get to her. Mostly, though, it's a literary device, the medieval equivalent of sending a kissogram.

Today I sent a letter containing a poem and a tormentil – that beautiful, unpretentious little yellow flower which shows its sunny yellow head all over Wales – to my Emmeline across the sea.

I was devious, as was Dafydd ap Gwilym (the greatest of Welsh poets) over 600 years ago, when he was up to the same tricks, fooling credulous husbands.

This is what I did: I put myself on the Wales Tourist Board's mailing list, implanted my message in one of the board's promotional letters, then re-stickered and re-posted the envelope with Emmeline's name and address – clever eh?

You may remember the prioress, Madam Eglentyne, in the Canterbury Tales, who wore a brooch bearing the words *Amor Vincit Omnia*. Love Conquers All.

Unlike poor timid cowering Mr Vogel I will pursue love gloriously, I will sweep Emmeline from her brattish little husband and marry her in my own Welsh paradise.

Dafydd ap Gwilym sent a seagull, a woodcock and also the wind to woo his beloved. Another of our poets, Cynan, famously dispatched a goldfinch from his purgatorial hellhole in the trenches of the First World War, pleading with it to visit his home in Anglesey. The beginning of the poem is an exercise in nostalgia:

> *Nico annwyl, dos yn gennad*
> *Drosof hyd at Gymru lan,*
> *Hed o wlad y gwaed a'r clefyd*
> *I ardaloedd hedd a chan*

(Sweet finch, be my go-between with Wales, sweet dominion, Fly from blood and wounds to vales of peace and harmony.)

The earliest example of a bird-messenger in Welsh literature is an episode in the Mabinogi when Branwen sends a young starling from Ireland to alert her brother, the giant Bendigeidfran, that she is being treated cruelly at the Irish court.

Later, after her rescuers' poignant return and Branwen's death from a broken heart on the banks of the river Alaw, they arrive at Harlech and hold a feast lasting seven years, during which time the three magical birds of Rhiannon sing a song of enchantment.

And a scintillation of memories return to me, of the birds I have met on my walk. Goldfinches everywhere in thistledown flocks, carried on the wind like antic dots, their reds and yellows and blacks merging into a drunken amalgam of whirring brilliance. Wheatears and stonechats in the uplands, watchful in the heather and the gorse. Brown pipits plebeian in the aeolian grasses. Larks tremulous on the wing, singing a song of enchantment over Wales. And every crow was Arthur returning from Afallon to lead the Welsh nation to glorious resurgence.

The choughs of the west coast, sentinels of the cliffs, chiding me, their bright orange beaks an emblazoned badge of their special status. In mid-Wales I saw red kites hold sway over their dominion. On the cliffs south of Aberystwyth, on a cloud-phalanxed morning of breezy, unrepentant optimism, I had been attacked by a buzzard; there was not a tree in sight, but sometimes they nest on cliffs, and presumably I was near its chick. The first intimation I had of its presence was a great whoosh and a feathery flick on my head. It was really scary. The noise created by its Stuka-like descent had a thrumming, vibrating reediness as the wind passed through each strut of its feathering: every primary, secondary, tertial, covert and scapular. I grew increasingly scared; this bombardment created a paranoia and a sense of oppression and fear – later my thoughts went to the countless ambushes which took place in old Wales.

Gerald of Wales, in his famous tour of the country with Baldwin, Archbishop of Canterbury, in 1188 to drum up support for yet another futile crusade, records many such incidents:

A short time after the death of Henry I, King of the English, it happened that Richard de Clare, a nobleman of high birth... passed this way on a journey from England to Wales. He was accompanied by a large force of men-at-arms led by Brian de Wallingford, then overlord of this area, who was acting as his guide through the pass. When they reached the entrance to the wood, Richard de Clare sent back Brian and his men, and rode unarmed into the forest, although this was much against Brian's wishes and, indeed, against his express advice. Richard was foolish enough to imagine that the trackway was safe. Ahead of him went a singer to announce his coming and a fiddler who accompanied the singer on his instrument. From then onwards things happened very quickly. The Welsh had prepared an ambush for Richard. All of a sudden Iorwerth, the brother of Morgan of Caerleon, and others of their family, rushed out from where they were hidden in the thickets, cut down Richard de Clare and most of his men, and made off with their baggage which they had seized in this savage way. Just how ill-advised and foolhardy it is to be so presumptuous is made only too obvious by disasters of this sort. We learn to be careful about the future and to exercise caution even when all seems to be going well. To rush on regardless is simply false bravado. It is at once rash and inconsiderate to take no heed at all of the advice given by those who are trying to help us.

The buzzard on the cliffs harried me for well over a mile. I have a favourite walking pullover which was purple once. Now it is old and washed out, with a hole where I snagged it on the barbed wire at Pickhill Hall. I knotted it about my head like a babushka and tried to keep an eye on my attacker, but he raided from behind every time and frightened me damn near to death with his great swoops and menacing wing sounds. My heart was ticking madly by the time he eased off and let me go.

I saw other lone flyers: a yellow-hammer on Anglesey, flashing absurdly through the trees; a greater spotted woodpecker on the banks of the Dee; and I heard green woodpeckers on the Dyke – how glad I was to greet the yaffle, which has seemingly vanished from my home territory.

And the footsteps I have followed!

Famous and feeble, ancient and modern. I have a picture of footprints made by three walkers in the Usk estuary over 6,500 years ago, still perfectly preserved in the ossified mud. I will ask you to do a little experiment now. Get up and take a step. Did you step out with your left or your right? Bet you've never thought about it, though you've taken countless steps. Me, I'm a left footer usually. There's a left-leaning in walking. Walkers naturally drift to the left when they're covering long distances. Many of the great left-leaning thinkers, radicals and libertarians of history, have been big walkers. The left hand path is said to be solitary, individualistic, personal. It can also lead to danger, and some people associate it with Satanism. Mr Vogel was said to be a little leftie. Bless him. I will teach him all about politics when I find him; I will invite him to my parliament of crows on St Anns Head to show him the tankers entering and leaving Milford Haven. I will invite him to stop one, or to influence its passage in any way. Observe, I shall say, how ships come in and ships go out, day by day, plying rich black money from one deep pocket to another. Observe, I shall say, that neither the ships nor the money nor this deep sound, the second best natural harbour in the world, belong to the nation of Wales. That will be enough political knowledge for poor fuddled Mr Vogel.

Stop press... News just in from Dr Williams in Tasmania. He's very, very excited: an expedition led by one of his academic friends may have found the long-lost Thylacine, the Tasmanian Devil, which was hunted to extinction by farmers – the last known specimen, Benjamin, died in Beaumaris Zoo near Hobart in 1936, though there have been many unverified sightings since – is this going to be the greatest comeback since the resurrection of the Great Auk in the Vogel Papers? A search party has stumbled across a lair with two live cubs deep in the Tasmanian forest. *'Hold on to this news,'* he says in an e-mail. *'The world's not ready – media would be down here like a pack in their infernal helicopters. Will confirm the news when it's appropriate.'* I'm delighted for him – it's not every day an extinct species is rediscovered!

I must summon one last emissary to conduct my affairs in another land, for as you know, I cannot leave Wales (I will try to tell you why later, if I have time).

We must seek out those children mentioned in the Vogel Papers, and in the Bo Peep letters – in tracing them we will most certainly find that cunning old fox Mr Vogel, who has taken us on a loping trail across the wilds in an attempt to lose us, only to lead us straight back to the henhouse.

Somehow I must get my talons on the hospital records, and I have an excellent candidate to do my nosing around. His name is Waldo, and he's a little worm.

There's a word for the microscopic deposits left by burrowing insects after they've carved their neat little tunnels through your best furniture – frass.

And this little corner of Wales is covered in Waldo's frass.

Waldo is a small pot-bellied Welshman, a builder with a battered van, and he has an enormous dog which is exactly the same size as him. I don't know what breed it is – something to do with Ireland and bogs and hunting. Both of them have equal amounts of fur and mud stuck to them, with the exception that Waldo's pelt ends in a furry line around his neck, like that part of a lawn which is next in line to be cut. Waldo is lively, animated and talkative, and he can listen to three conversations going on at the same time in different parts of the room. Despite his Neanderthal appearance he is a walking encyclopaedia and a huge repository of local gossip. Talking of Neanderthals, Waldo is convinced that he's a throwback, and indeed, there is evidence that *Homo sapiens* and Neanderthal Man did have a little fling. Neanderthals were given a bad press, says Waldo. A longer gestation period and a slightly smaller pelvic girdle was all that held them back. Waldo is aware of my interest in the pale land of watersheds and crossovers.

'Them Neanderthals were just like us Welsh, just a bit different, but it was enough to get them rubbed out. Life is just a matter of rubbing out everything that's smaller and different,' he said once.

As I said, Waldo is a builder, but he's interested in everything, and he has more information crammed into that seedy little brain of his than the British Library and the World Wide Web put together. Mostly he puts it to bad use, because Waldo is a naughty man. His mind is muckier than his beat-up Wellingtons and his moral fibre is tattier than his overalls. Waldo has never been 'official' – he doesn't have a National Insurance number and he's not on the electoral roll.

That's the way he likes it. He used to work in the quarry on a cash-in-hand basis until the manager wanted him on the books. Waldo is strictly off the record. He and Paddy the Pisshead – already mentioned – are major chums, and they've worked together since time began. One of those odd friendships, but it's lasted.

As I pondered how to broach the subject one evening he

happened by, in that serendipitous way of his, whistling the Welsh song *Myfanwy* by way of recognition as he walked under my window. The usual obsequies over, and my face slavered on by his hound, we got down to business.

'Waldo, my old friend...'

'Uh-ho. So we're looking for a favour are we.'

Waldo had espied my intentions immediately and sat there grinning inanely with a face like a big cheesy moon. His weathered mien glowed like peat burning on a fire and his eyes puddled into two black holes ready to suck in any matter which I or the universe could blow in his direction.

'I wondered if you might possibly...'

'Spit it out, don't bugger about.'

A thrush lingered and sang, briefly, of great sadness, in the branches of the sycamore outside.

'I want you to take part in a little deception for me.'

'Good.' He rubbed his hands and adjusted himself so that he lay back in his seat with his legs straight out in front of him, with his chin on his chest and his hands clasped on his huge beery stomach, as if in prayer. He closed his eyes.

'I need to gain access to all the records of the hospital at Gobowen in Shropshire and I need you to find out some information for me.'

'Righty-ho. Is that all?' He seemed vaguely disappointed.

'It's important to me. I want you to do some ferreting about for me. You know what I mean.'

'Righty-ho.'

Waldo fussed his dog and waited for more, but I let the silence linger and we listened to the thrush's wavering little solo outside, like a choirboy attempting the *Piet Iesu* for the first time.

'I've prepared the ground for you,' I continued placidly. 'I have gained an alias for you to smooth your way. Your name will be John Parker.'

Waldo looked unimpressed.

'It's been used before, in the Vogel Papers.'

'Yes, I know, but it's quite authentic.'

I gestured to a black and white postcard on the mantelpiece, next to my teddy bears. It was creased and had a large cross in biro over one of the buildings in a large complex.

'That's Gobowen Hospital about fifty years ago. You'll see a large chimney just off centre – that's the laundry. If you follow the road alongside it you'll come to the playing fields. Along the border of the field you'll see a set of wards, one of them with a cross on it. That's Ward 2 – the old children's ward. It's the staff social club now. You'll pretend that you were a patient there in the late '50s. That will be your angle. A few years ago a Japanese specialist who was conducting a major survey into Perthes' Disease invited surviving ex-patients to Gobowen where they were X-rayed to evaluate their medical progress and to gauge the success of their treatment. The Japanese consultant, a deceptively young, handsome man of somewhat larger proportions than the average Oriental, had poor English but you gleaned the information that you had suffered from a mild form of the disease and that your hip bone had held up well to forty years of wear and tear.'

'Righty-ho. I've got that. Can you tell me something about myself?'

'Indeed so. Perthes' Disease attacked the ball and socket joint in your left hip, so your first symptom was a slight limp when you were five years old. This worsened until your parents decided to take action. However, they were not convinced that your limp was genuine; for some reason they thought you might be shamming to gain sympathy, so they devised a little test for you.'

'Good God man, that's a strange story. Why would they think that?'

'I don't know. Anyway, this is the test they devised. One day, when you returned from school, they suggested that you join them in a ball game. You all stood in a triangle in the yard outside your home, tossing the ball to each another. Then, deliberately, your father threw the ball beyond you. They figured that if you still limped while running after the ball your affliction was genuine. You did limp. They took you to a doctor. Very soon afterwards you were taken from your home and sent to the hospital at Gobowen. They had to import a nurse from Wales because you couldn't speak any English: you became very attached to her. She had long brown hair, dark eyes, and you loved her. You don't remember her name. Got it?'

'Yes, I've got it. But have you made this up? Will it convince them?'

'Trust me. It's all true. You're merely taking the place of

someone who really did experience all this. OK?'

'OK – though I've about as much chance of carrying it off as those two up there.'

He nodded towards the two teddies on the fireplace. Both had been found on my great trek – one on the beach at Newborough in Anglesey, one-eyed, one-eared, sunbleached and coming apart at the seams; the other – filthy and covered in oil – I'd found in the roadside grass at Pentrefelin near Criccieth. I had mended them, put them in the washing machine, and watched their little faces coming in and out of the suds like slightly alarmed children on an out-of-control funfair ride. They had become talismans and took pride of place among the ephemera which I had brought back: a giant yellow tooth which I told everyone was a woolly mammoth's; a Dutch ship-to-shore fax message matted with fine emerald-green seaweed, now framed in my lounge; lustrous metal fragments from Burry Port, inexplicably light and silvery-blue, as if they had dropped from a spaceship; beautiful birds' feathers, mainly pheasants'; a plank from a shipwreck, with two white crosses painted on a faded blue background.

'Dya know something,' said Waldo reflectively in the gathering gloom. The thrush had ended its solo and now a blackbird was jabbing the air with its alarm call.

'Your walk around Wales is all about comparisons. I think artists call it *chiaroscuro* – the interplay between light and shade, which creates a sense of drama. Is that what you're trying to do – create a bit of drama in your dull little life by playing with darkness and light, like a child with a torch?'

'You may have something. I've never thought about it much.'

'Have you ever heard of Plato's myth of the cave?'

'No. Should I have?'

'Not really. It's a dialogue between Socrates and Glaucon, and it's about a cave in which a group of humans are kept chained by the neck and the legs. They have been there since childhood, so they have never seen the outside world. All they have seen is shadows – the shadows of men and objects, on the wall of their cave.

'One of them is liberated and shown the real world. He is blinded by the glare, and is distressed. Eventually the shadows he saw previously turn into reality and he is enlightened. Feeling pity for his cavebound comrades in the grotto, he returns to tell them

Allegory of the cave

the truth. But when he gets there he can no longer see the shadows as well as his comrades do, because his eyes have become accustomed to the light. And because he is perceived as being blind he is ridiculed – they say *he went and came back without his eyes.'*

Waldo ruminated for a few seconds, then continued.

'Do you remember that bit in the Vogel Papers when the author says he no longer feels he belongs to the land and the people of his childhood, because he has left them and has become estranged, whilst he will never be accepted in his new home either?'

He went through the Vogel story, which had used the word *déclassé*. It's a state of limbo, and although those in limbo are spared the eternal suffering of Hell they are also debarred from Heaven.

'Is your perverse interest in cripples also related to this state of peripheral existence?' he asked.

I was struck by his words and fell silent. I sat there and let my mind grapple with Waldo's outburst. He was a very perceptive man, but I wasn't used to this directness.

'Yes,' I fumbled, 'I think you may be on the right track. It's true, I am somewhat engrossed in the condition of those who aren't mainstream, who aren't typical members of society, if there are such things.'

'Could this do with you being Welsh?'

'Yes, I suppose so.'

'We're not that small a minority – there are nearly three million of us,' he replied.

'I realise that. I'm more concerned about the half a million or so who speak Welsh, not that the rest are any less Welsh of course. It's just that there's a poignancy about the language and its fate.'

'Any idea how many languages there are in the world?'

'Wow – now you're asking. Five hundred? A thousand?

'You're way off. About six and a half thousand.'

'My God – as many as that.'

He told me the statistics. Half the languages on Earth – over three thousand – have less than ten thousand speakers each. They really are small. They make the Welsh language seem prosperous. And 28 per cent of all languages are spoken by fewer than a thousand. Yes – more than a quarter of the world's languages have fewer than a thousand speakers apiece.

'Puts things in perspective for you,' said Waldo. 'So we're not such a washed up bunch after all.'

'Yes, but you know what I'm driving at. No matter how optimistic we try to feel, we all sense that tide of uniformity washing over us. How many major languages are there?'

'It's true – a few major languages are making huge gains, especially English. Ten major languages account for half the world's population. And the big boys are gaining all the time.'

I knew the major causes – urbanisation, westernisation, global communications and marketing, population movement and discrimination. Most languages are facing extinction and linguists say that over half the world's languages are moribund and will not be passed on. We and our children are living at a point in the history of the world when the majority of languages will vanish within two generations. Imagine all that history and experience down the drain, all those nuances lost, all that diversity and difference, everything which has made the world interesting, attractive. We're looking at a one-stop shop peopled by identikit humans grazing on a McDonalds/Coca Cola axis in identical high streets and supermalls, with not a whit of difference between Bangor and Bangalore, Cardiff and Korea. Doesn't that really mess your head up? Doesn't that make you want to weep for all those languages which will be eradicated by men in suits who are as indifferent to our collective fate as the raiding, looting, raping, murdering armies of the past?

It was almost dark in the room. We looked into the fire, and I remembered my childhood, when looking for shapes in the embers was a major pastime. This was before television, before domestic electricity. How naive we were.

Tornelaian Finnish, Asturian, Aragonese, Catalan, Basque, Galician, Occitan, Romany, Sami, Mirandese, Frisian, Low Saxon, Ladin, Sardinian, Luxembourgish, Aromanian, Vlach, Pomaki... these were just a few of the languages which would disappear. And that was just in Europe.

'Enough, enough!' I said with a slight laugh. 'Indeed. We all know what the situation is.'

'Look at it this way,' said Waldo, 'there are dozens of dialects and ways of life which have disappeared from Wales without our knowing, and we're none the wiser. Perhaps, after we've reached a mono-state with one world language, one culture and one colour, we will explode into a zillion fragments again, a human equivalent of the Big Bang – perhaps that's the essential pulse of the universe. One thing's sure. We won't be here to see it.'

With this Waldo got up and prepared to depart.

'Among all this linguistic carnage I have one positive story to tell you – every massacre has a survivor,' he said. 'In a tiny corner of Lower Saxony there's a slip of a language called Sater Frisian which is spoken by about 2,000 people in just three villages – and it's growing. Look on the bright side!'

He added, with a trace of sarcasm: 'When do we put Plan A into operation then?'

'Next Monday. I've arranged for you to see the hospital administrator. He's a very nice man. Very accommodating. He's looking forward to meeting you.'

'You knew I would say yes?'

'Yep. By the way, here's another little bit of information for your factfile. In your first week at Gobowen you were strapped onto a metal frame which held you tight and which made movement almost impossible – you were effectively tied down, like Gulliver, for over a year, but you could move your arms and your head. You had two leather straps around each leg, in your groin, and you still have the marks of those straps on either side of your unmentionables. A weight was attached to your left foot to act as a drag, to encourage your left hip to regenerate. The frame was called a Jones Frame, after its inventor, Dr Robert Jones, who believed that immobility and plenty of fresh air was the best cure for cripples. He was right in your case, because you have no after-effects of Perthes' Disease and you have been spared a lifetime in callipers, or having to walk in a clumpy shoe with a built-up sole. The only physical mementoes you have of that year in your life are small white scars on your hips, the result of corrective surgery, the white strap-marks, and an over-correction in your left leg, which means that it points straight in front of you when you walk, rather than at a quarter to three like the rest of the yokels round here.'

Waldo smiled and went through the door, his hound leaping and bouncing after him. They left me sitting in the dark, with my teddies and my memories.

The next stage of the search for Vogel was in place.

There was one thing left to do before I headed for my bed, and that was to choose the second person to join us at our last supper in the Blue Angel, following the end of the quest. I had no doubt who it would be. Doctor Robert Jones, who would sit alongside doughty old Hotty, Hugh Owen Thomas, at a table in the snug so that they could talk about the old days at 11 Nelson Street.

Robert Jones, with his white hair, droll walrus moustache and his studious, steel-rimmed glasses. I have an immediate reference point: he was born in Rhyl, although he was brought up in London. I have a picture of him in my mind: his eyes have seen many profound experiences, and in those pupils I see a deep compassion.

I think I have told you enough about Dr Jones, but let's imagine a few snippets from his conversation with Hotty after they have received warm greetings from their ex-patients, who have shuffled into the snug to greet them, smiling but unsure what to do next. Robert Jones will want to catch up on family news; his father was a journalist, and he has a knack of gleaning information quickly. Robert Jones went to live with Hotty and his Aunt Elizabeth in Liverpool when he was seventeen.

'I've never told you this,' he'll say, 'because I thought you might tick me off for gadding about when I could be ministering to your patients in Nelson Street. Do you remember that week when I passed my primaries in anatomy and physiology at Lincoln's Inn?'

'I do indeed, Robert... after all, you were only a boy, and quite carried away by your own brilliance.'

'Well I'm afraid Daddy and I were quite outrageous and spent three days on the town. We saw Moody and Sankey, Dr Joseph Parker, the Royal Academy, the Albert Hall, Crystal Palace, Patti at the opera, Salvini the great Italian actor, and the Archbishop of Canterbury. What a week that was.'

'Tell me Robert, what were those Navvies like on the Manchester Ship Canal? You must have had a devil of a job with them, drunk and riotous...'

'They were like warriors Hugh Owen, like soldiers at the front. The dangers they faced were almost as great as facing battery rounds from the German trenches...'

'Tell me Robert, how did you get hold of that X-ray contraption? It changed our craft for ever...'

'From Mrs Wimpfheimer, that fussy woman who helped us at the Sunday clinics, actually – she translated an article from the *Frankfurter Zeitung* and I crossed over to the continent immediately. I think I'm right in saying that Dr Holland and I were the first to use the X-ray in this country... we used a little tube and developed a photograph of a small bullet embedded in a boy's wrist.'

Robert Jones was physically exuberant, a keen all-round athlete – an excellent shot, a cricketer, a horseman and a boxer. He liked organising boxing bouts with his friends and had a huge collection of books about boxing.

'Tell me Robert, what was the name of that American boxer who cried in terror and ran out of the surgery when you tried to treat him... Sullaman or something.'

'It was John Sullivan. Saw him again when I was staying in a hotel in Washington. Massive man. Saw Dempsey beat Carpentier too, and Jimmy Wilde go down before Pancho Villa. One of those big boxers came to me once and I made him lie on the floor ready for treatment. I said to him, *I seem to have seen you in this position before my man...*'

'Very droll Robert. But I think it was teaming up with that little Hunt woman which was the making of you.'

Robert Jones first became involved with Agnes Hunt when she took some of her young patients in a home-made handcart to his clinic at a hospital in Liverpool.

'She was a rare bird, that one,' he murmurs.

He visited a new home at Baschurch in Shropshire, set up by Agnes and her mother – the first open-air home for crippled children. Through sunshine and storm, snow and sleet, one side of the shed or ward was always open.

'It was an inspiring sight to visit the children,' says Robert Jones. 'Such rampant gaiety. Infectious diseases rarely spread, not even the dreaded pneumonia. I went there every Sunday morning by car with my dogs in the back.'

'Ah well, Robert, you certainly completed what I started. Well done my boy. But don't forget, you ate up all the knowledge of the bonesetters too! And you borrowed one of my little ideas, I seem to recall, to save all those soldiers in the war, aint that so?'

It was so. The Thomas Splint, strapped to the soldier's leg immediately after the injury and before the victim was taken to a clearing station, reduced mortality in compound fractures of the femur from 80% to 20%. It was close to a miracle – many thousands of lives were saved.

'My dear chap, I hear the war made you a household name throughout the world,' says Hotty, shaking his head with pride.

That shipwrecked boy sōwed the seed of modern orthopaedics, and Robert Jones, in the post-war years until his death, attempted to take all the lessons learned from the war to the civilian populations of Britain and America, to treat every potential cripple. It is Dr Robert Jones, more than anyone, who rid our city streets and our country cottages, gleaming white in the sun but concealing a dark secret, of all those wasted lives.

Dr Jones, please join us at the Blue Angel.

THE PHOTOGRAPH

WALDO came whistling down the path with a triumphant, supercilious look plastered all over his face so I knew he'd found something. He wore a voluminous white coat stretching down to his feet; fortunately it hid most of his pendulous midriff – that blubbery mass saddling his central regions like a glob of glacial moraine. His attempt at a shave looked like the residue of a child's experiment with a magnet and iron filings. As soon as he stepped inside my door he whipped off the top layer, exposing his usual coating, a frayed and emulsion-speckled pair of overalls, which somehow reminded me of a Papuan native in full war paint. He had a large black and white photograph in his hand, which he waved with a childish and idiotic gesture – he was Chamberlain wagging his bit of paper from the plane steps. But though exuberant, Waldo played me like a fish before giving me his catch.

'Tell me, my old friend, do you intend writing about this peregrination of yours before shuffling off the mortal coil? A few ruminations? Will you be our new Baedeker, the latest Theroux, our own Dr Johnson? No, not Johnson – he hated the wild bits of Wales didn't he. Something modern and provocative, another *Landor's Tower* perhaps. No, you couldn't manage that, could you?'

'Just shut up, Waldo.'

I was in a foul mood. Emmeline hadn't replied to any of my love-ciphers.

No cheeping bloody starling had arrived on my windowsill with a message tied to its wing, leg, wherever you tie messages to starlings. Neck perhaps.

During that day on the Dyke I thought we looked great together, side by side: hadn't Wales been joined to North America once upon a time, hadn't we leant on each other like two plates in a washing-up rack, in the kitchen of creation, when Baby Earth was still pumping volcanic squitters into its crusty nappy?

If Wales and America were drifting a couple of inches away from each other every year, me and that American temptress, with her too-wide smile and her scented city chit-chat, were moving apart at a million miles a minute. She'd given Wales a good push with her oar when she left and sent me flying. I was really *mad* with her.

She'd told me that the hedges of Wales reminded her of Clark Gable's moustache in *Gone With the Wind*. By now I hoped a hurricane had sucked her into the sky, like Dorothy in *The Wizard of Oz*. Curse her, and a pox on Wales too for allowing us to meet in the first place.

Waldo persisted. 'Well, what's the answer? Where will you begin? With the Red Lady of Paviland perhaps, or with that tooth from Pontnewydd Cave?'

'Come on, let me see it Waldo, don't fool around.'

'Perhaps you'll start with the dinosaur footprints at Sully,' Waldo droned on.

He was trying to be really smart. Waldo my great chum, my old pal, was roaming around the room like a clockwork troll high on Duracell.

My mind flitted to some of my high-points: those towering south Glamorgan cliffs, once under a shallow Mediterranean sea, or perhaps the Pembrokeshire coast, which had been higher than the Swiss Alps in the world's infancy.

'Come on, give me a clue,' said Waldo.

He sat down in his usual chair with his legs right out and his chin on his chest. In that position his belly reminded me of the burial chamber at Bryn Celli Ddu, a large grass-covered mound in Anglesey. One day, while I stood regarding the chamber, a mole had started rising on it, creating a little animal pimple on a bigger human pimple. It seemed neat, almost allegorical.

'Let me see it Waldo.'

'You will see it, my man, you will see it indeed, but not before you've answered my question. Two can play the guessing game. And you've kept us all waiting long enough for just a clue about your interest in this Vogel character. Don't try to tell me, for one nanosecond, that your sole interest is the Vogel Papers. Because I can sniff you as well as my dog, and I know that you're hiding a bone. You want to see this photograph far more than a mere bystander would, and your pediculous rovings through Wales's private parts betray a man who has seen a pirate's map and wants to reach the treasure as soon as possible. So, speak – where will you start your story? I intend to give you one morsel of information for each titbit you give me.'

I saw that my rotund little friend was in frolicsome mood, so after a few hums and a few haws I answered his question.

'All right, Waldo, I will play your little game. My first choice would be a little place called Portskewett in the shadow of the new Severn Bridge. It's mentioned in the Anglo-Saxon Chronicles – some obscure king, Caradog Freichras or someone like that, put himself out to grass there. Viking cloak-fasteners found on the foreshore. It's that place where a few men still fish for salmon on rocks in the river, with bigger versions of those pole-nets that kids use on the beach. Lots of Parliamentary soldiers were drowned there when they were tricked by the ferry-men who had taken Charles across and wanted to give him a head start. There's a large Iron Age fort on the banks of the Severn, with one edge nibbled away by the river – it reminded me of a jam tart which has been gnawed on but returned hurriedly to the pile by a child who's heard his mother's footsteps in the hall. Apparently the estuary is fairly new, if you know what I mean, and the Severn Channel was a shallow valley when the hill fort was in use. The really striking thing about this fort is that there's a football pitch smack bang in the middle of it. The whole thing's a metaphor. New gods for old. Let me put it like this. If an Iron Age man walked through that door now, teleported from the past, the first place I'd take him would be Portskewett. He'd be astounded by the river and the new bridge, the cleaving of England from Wales, and the coming of a massive henge to bear people from one bank to another. He would be intrigued by the ruins of a gothic church. He'd be bowled over by the waterworks, which look as though they should house a crazy eccentric's tele-scope, and the houses and the cars and the clothes and the televisions and the computers would also astonish him. There, Waldo. That's where I'd start it all, with a football game in the middle of a hill fort with an Iron Age Celt standing next to me on the touchline. Does that answer your question?'

'Bet that Iron Age hairball would know more about football than you do mate,' he answered cynically. 'Or he'd smack his head with his club and say *Jeez, what a cracking idea, we've built thousands of these but didn't know what the fuck to do with them* and leg it up the valley to sell tickets to his mates.'

'Very amusing, Waldo.'

I have warned you about the language, haven't I? Waldo and

Paddy use swear words in spadefuls.

Waldo finally condescended to give me the picture, which although musty-smelling and torn in one corner was the work of a professional – it was sharp and clear, and it was also quite large. It looked like a press photograph which had been given to the hospital after publication.

It showed a group of beds and a chair, all with children in them. Standing around them were adults, two men and two women. Altogether there were twelve.

There was a fine-looking man with a walrus moustache – Robert Jones of course. There was a serious, formally-dressed woman in beige, very tired-looking, with a crutch – Agnes Hunt, and in the background a slight man with a damaged eye and a funny little cap – Hugh Owen Thomas. There was also a nurse with long hair, very dark eyes, and a big warm smile.

It wasn't obvious at first that the photo had been taken in a hospital, but the conclusion was inescapable, given the number of beds. All the children were dressed up in costumes. A couple of multi-coloured streamers and a balloon on the wall indicated that it was probably Christmas, though there was no tree. All the children were named on the back of the photo in a bleary biro writing, sloping to the left and fudged in places. The names were written directly behind each child, so that there could be no confusion as to whom they all were. There were eight of them.

In the foreground there is a little boy, the only one sitting on the side of his bed. He has a robe on, and a turban with a big paste jewel in it, and a funny beard made from cotton wool. His scruffy shoes and turned-down socks peek out from under his costume. The boy has a flattish nose, a rash of freckles and cold sores around his mouth. He has a distant, almost blank look in his eyes, and the nurse, stooped by his side, has her hand firmly on his shoulder, as though restraining him. In this get-up he may be one of the Three Wise Men, or a great potentate of one sort or another, which may have been a little joke by the nurses. His name, on the back of the photo, is Luther Williams. His face is artless, to match his character in the Vogel Papers. It's ironic, isn't it, that his religious mother named him Luther without knowing that the German theologist advocated the culling of all handicapped children. Luther in the picture has no visible handicap.

Agnes Hunt has a bed before her. This has a piece of wood

rising from the headboard, which looks like a miniature gibbet, but instead of a body hanging from the extending timber there's a small square mirror angled towards the camera. In this mirror I can see a little face – a button nose and two eyes, gazing intently at the lens. Her thick hair is frizzled, probably red, and she has a slightly twisted face, with the right side higher than the left, and one eye smaller than the other. Because her body is malformed she is unable to show her full face to the camera. Directly behind her on the wall there is a fairly large wooden crucifix; the Christ figure, which is ivory-white, and has a loincloth which might be coloured blue. Draped on her bed is a counterpane or mantle which shimmers in the light; it has a silver moon and stars glinting on it. The Christ figure, the mirror and the moon-and-stars mantle all match up with the story in the Vogel Papers. A big plastic spider hangs from the mirror, and on her thigh there is a bowl with a spoon in it. She must be Little Miss Muffet. She must also be Angelica – I flip over the photo, and I'm right. What's more, her surname is Parker, so she must be Nosy Parker's sister, as she was in the Vogel Papers.

In the bed next to her there's a thickset, dark-haired boy, with lively eyes, who somehow looks older than the rest. He has a plaster on one of his legs, and draped over this he has a leopard-skin outfit which makes him look like a pocket version of Fred Flintstone. He has one of those bars with two balls on each end, like the ones weightlifters hoist over their heads, only his must be papier-mâché because someone has painted 1,000 lbs on each end. An exaggerated curly moustache has been painted on his upper lip to make him look like one of those peculiar French strongmen. He is holding his head and grimacing, as if he has just walked into something. I have no doubt who this is – Jack, and his surname is Jones. He has the facial features of a dwarf.

Part of a bed can be seen in the left hand corner, and propped up in it is a little boy with long fair hair and pretty features. He's wearing a schoolmaster's gown and a mortar board, and large spectacles which have been borrowed from a grown-up. They make him look owlish. He holds a cane in his right hand, which he points to a blackboard beside his bed. On this is written, in childish writing, THE PROFESSOR.

On the reverse side he has the name John Parker.

There's a little boy standing by Parker's bed, dressed as Oliver

Hardy. He has a puckish face, with a couple of teeth missing, and what appears to be a giant fake nail sticking through his head, and a massive hammer in his hand. Round his neck he has a board which says: THAT'S ANOTHER FINE MESS I'VE GOTTEN ME INTO. His name is Edwin – Edwin Summers, Edwin the lovable, laughing carpenter who leaves Christ sleeping in a pub overnight.

There are two beds facing the camera in the centre of the photo, one with a boy in it and the other with a girl.

Between them there is a wicker chair with wheels, and swathed in it there is a small boy, the smallest of them all. He is the only one not looking at the camera – his eyes have slid down to the floor in front of him. He has a little hat with a skull and crossbones on it, a black patch over one eye, and a wooden sword resting across his legs. This is Julius Rodenberg, the son of interned Germans.

The girl on the left of Julius lies inside her bed but her upper part, above the folded-down cover, has a brocade dress with bows, and she wears a bonnet. There is little of her face to be seen, but it appears regular and attractive, with a wariness in the eyes which I associate with the physically maimed. Her hair is cut in a bob and she wears a ribbon in it; she has a pert, snub nose and she wears those round glasses which make people look intelligent. She has a small shepherd's crook festooned with ribbons, and she holds up a cardboard depiction of a woolly sheep on a stick. This is Bo Peep. The back of the photo bears the name Esmie Falkirk.

The boy on Julius's right lies flat on his back and his legs are below the coverlet, but on his torso he has a shimmering tunic and a matching cap with a pointy peak, of the type you see Robin Hood wearing in films. He has a cowhorn draped around his shoulders on a leather thong and he is holding it to his lips, as though he's blowing into it. This is Little Boy Blue, who has come to blow his horn. On the back of the photo his name is given simply as Vogel! with a big exclamation mark.

Here, in one photograph, were almost all the characters in the Vogel Papers. My hunch had been right – the Vogel Papers were fictional, but had been based on actual events. Who had written the papers? Surely the author had to be one of these children in the photograph.

Waldo looked at me with lizard eyes throughout my perusal. There was a lengthy silence after I had propped the picture between the two teddies sleeping on my mantelpiece. He made no effort to retrieve it.

'Cuppa?' I suggested.

He nodded and went into the kitchen. I heard him fill the kettle and prepare the mugs. He knew I took tea with a half-spoon of sugar. He takes coffee with five spoonfuls of sugar, which partly accounts for his corpulence.

'Got what you wanted?' he asked when we settled again. His dog lumbered into my side-table and knocked my tea, spilling liquid over the carpet. Waldo mopped up, wordlessly. The carriage clock ticked and tocked resolutely and we both looked through the window, out over the water, at Wales in her small vastness, as an equinoctial sea roared into the shore, attacking us with all the weight of accumulated anger, in churning billows of great white froth-water – a mad cavalry charge, flooding in on a roaring, rearing, bit-champing, nostril-flared gallop, wide-eyed and spumed, onto a shore dulled and waiting to surrender. The sky behind this huge sea-gob had unconvincing patches of bright blue and looked like a newly-painted film set with clouds still drying and slithering on the canvas.

The sudden knowledge conveyed to me by that photograph electrified my skin; my flesh felt taut under the goose pimples.

The cloud factory was in full production: a ragged convoy of inkstained cumuli glowered in from the west like vast bursting toadstools, splattering wetly onto the window, and I contemplated what was going on in the world around us: the fields behind us, clambering towards safety, swimming in a raw umber stew of mud and mould, drenched sheep bobbing on the surface like dumplings; moles passing like thrombotic clots through their sinking, creaking submarine gangways in the ground below us.

A man walked like a crooked nail through the field nearest us, with his dog, and I could see the field seep into him, insinuating its nucleic acids, its genetic information – its fairy rings, pre-Christian cowpats, murders, eyeless lambs, raven-picked bones, rusted ploughshares, its Durex-bursting Springs, its countless footprints criss-crossing the weave of time.

'What's that field called out there?' said Waldo, as if reading my mind.

'I think it's called Maes.'

Every field in Wales has a name – I presume it's the same in England.

'If you had a telephone directory with every field name in Wales I suppose it'd be that thick,' said Waldo, holding an imaginary brick between his thumb and forefinger.

'Which reminds me, I know how Vogel got his name. It was nothing to do with telephone books and choosing an odd name so that naughty children would make nuisance calls, as the Vogel Papers say.'

'Really?' I said. 'I've got so used to his name that I couldn't imagine any other. D'you mean to say he had an ordinary name? I find that quite disappointing.'

'Yes, well, we must expect these little disappointments. It's going to be very difficult to make any sense out of all this – someone has deliberately smudged over the truth, to make everything sound romantic and strange.'

I waited for further illumination.

'His real name was *not* Vogel. It's in his notes. His father was a Welsh hill shepherd until they decamped to Manchester, and he was known as *Ieuan Fugail*, John the Shepherd. But when the boy was taken to Robert Jones's Sunday clinic that German woman who helped out, Mrs Wimpfheimer, the one who translated the article on X-rays from the *Frankfurter Zeitung*, kept calling for *Vogel* instead of *Fugail* – and it stuck. Apparently she referred to him as "my little lame sparrow". So the reason for the name is quite prosaic.'

The crooked nail man urinated against an oak tree in the corner of the field and his cur squatted by his side. I imagined it quivering, anxious for a quick return to the fireside.

Waldo looked at him through the window.

'By Christ,' he said, 'it's the man below you, the cloud-worshipper. He's got himself a dog. Don't think the dog is much of a cloud-worshipper though.'

With the wind grinding its gears outside we formed a plan for the coming weeks. Waldo had been granted special dispensation to use the Health Sciences Library at Gobowen, but unbeknownst to everyone he was melting in and out of the records room with a lock-pick. On his first visit he had managed a cursory look at

Vogel's papers and a proper study of Julius Rodenberg.

Little Julius, inquisitive and interested in his new surroundings, had been 'adopted' by Esmie, as her letters to Vogel had hinted. They had become close friends – perhaps she reminded him of a sister, or his interned mother. His parents had not been allowed to see him for security reasons, Shropshire having a number of military bases which they might have seen. Such cruelty. Julius had a club foot and had come in for a small corrective operation, scheduled for Dr Robert Jones's attention. But Julius had a tendency to wander and get lost, and one day, whilst searching for Esmie, he had wandered into a tent. Inside it lay the sole remaining victim of a diphtheria outbreak, a little girl who was well on the way to recovery. But there must have been a few lingering bacteria, because within a day or two he was displaying the usual symptoms – fever, weakness and throat inflammation. The growing concerns of his nurses are chronicled in his notes, as his disease was first suspected and then confirmed. Julius was sent to isolation in a part of the hospital called Harley Street, ironically named because it was extremely spartan. He had been ministered to by a lone nurse, probably spending many hours on his own. I find it particularly sad that so many children have lost so much in one fleeting moment, either through accident or infection; I have thought long about this supremely decisive moment in our lives, this shivering of the human ship on rocks, when a momentary action or accident changes the whole course of our existence.

The First World War, which was a war waiting to happen of course, was sparked by the assassination of the Archduke Ferdinand in Sarajevo. The Archduke was delivered right to the hands of his assassin by his driver, who took a wrong turning in a tiny lapse of concentration. That war alone cost the lives of about 20 million soldiers, and led directly to the Second World War, which cost at least 30 million lives. So a few seconds of bleariness, maybe caused by one last glass of beer the night before, or a row between the driver and his wife before leaving home that morning, killed off 50 million people. I know it doesn't quite work like that, but you know what I mean. I've come across a number of lives which have been blighted by one little act, one tiny action. Perhaps you too can look back to a fulcrum, a hinge in your life which changed it for ever. Julius paid dearly for his few minutes of wandering.

The last line of his notes says merely: '*Parents informed. Funeral on Monday. Wooden cross made by the Factotum.*'

There was a great stillness and silence in the world when I awoke the next day.

The sea, now passive and calm, looked almost embarrassed, like a hung-over partygoer who had behaved crazily the night before and needed to send out a number of apologies. Waldo had left me to it. No doubt he wanted to catch up on local news, since he is the local Reuters and chronicler, having an encyclopaedic history of the town and its environs. Nothing, but nothing, gets past him, and he's the first to know about any goings-on or misdeeds.

I had the wanderlust again. It sent hot bubbles through my blood. I had to get going. I felt like Princess Marya in *War and Peace*, feeding pilgrims as they passed her home, and longing to go with them:

> Often as she listened to the pilgrims' tales she was so fired by their simple speech, natural to them but to her full of deep meaning, that several times she was on the point of abandoning everything and running away from home. In imagination she already pictured herself dressed in coarse rags and with her wallet and staff, walking along a dusty road.

I knew it was time to continue my walk around Wales. As the Mongols say, better a wandering fool than a sitting scholar.

I can have a proper row with Emmeline whilst I'm on the road. It's easier to have a good shouting match with someone, especially if they're not there, on a lonely shore, miles away from anyone. I've been caught quite a few times, once by a young man walking his dog; I think he was more embarrassed than I was, and he detoured me in a wide arc. Wordsworth taught his dog to warn him when people were approaching, so that he could avoid being taken for a lunatic.

Enough said.

Since we Welsh have a great liking for the number *three*, and group things in threesomes, or triads, I must choose a third Healer to join us for that shindig at the Blue Angel. The choice is quite obvious – Agnes Hunt, who will sit next to her old friend

Robert Jones (my, how she adored that man!) in the snug. I don't think there's much more I need to tell you about her.

Let's see now. Born to a landed family in Shropshire, large household, eccentric mother 'who pursued her family and friends with malignant fidelity' and, after the death of her husband, took her family Down Under to seek a new life. As you know, Agnes was crippled as a young girl – when she got a blister on a heel she was so afraid of telling anyone it became infected. Here was another person whose life had been decided in a few hours.

Agnes Hunt had experienced pioneering adventures in the outback, cooking kangaroo tail soup and roast wallaby, and returned to study nursing at Rhyl and various English hospitals. Her training was sporadic, due to breakdowns in her health, or further mad quests with her mother.

Then came the Baschurch adventure in Shropshire. They found a property, aptly named Florence House, and turned it into a home for crippled children.

Water came from a well under the scullery floor and the drains were faulty, but it was the first open-air orthopaedic hospital in the world. This is the epicentre of our story.

This is the Jerusalem of British cripples; the matrix of their deliverance – and it was only a century ago.

Florence House was a success. I quote:

> A curious fact appeared: the Home exerted a magnetic attraction for cripples, for whom it was in no way suited. For instance, the staircase, leading up to the two large rooms, ambitiously called wards, was never meant for the transport of cripples. After carrying down one particularly helpless child, Goody said to me: *This is much too dangerous. We shall probably kill some of these infants, and most certainly ourselves.*

They built a shed in the garden and Agnes slept there with the badly crippled, whilst the more able slept upstairs. Agnes transported children to and from the hospital in a contraption which she described as a perambulator so that the crippled children could travel cheaply. She describes one trip thus:

> The journey was two hours by train and then over the ferry at Birkenhead... whilst taking a party of twelve children of all ages and stages of crippledom across the ferry I was accosted by a lady, who in a voice of horror demanded if I were responsible for all those children. I

blushed to my ears and bashfully replied that I was, whereupon the lady
sternly pressed a tract into my hands and left. The title of the tract was:
The Wages of Sin is Death...

In 1921 all patients were transferred to the Shropshire
Orthopaedic Hospital which was established on the site of an old
military hospital at Gobowen. Hundreds of thousands of people
have been treated at this hospital, and it is world-famous. A great
pioneering venture, after-care, spread into the neighbouring
counties, including Wales, and Welsh children went there in their
droves. 'Goody' died in 1920 and a chapel was built at the hospital in her memory. Her motto had been:

> Do the work that's nearest,
> Though it's dull at whiles,
> Helping when you meet them
> Lame dogs over stiles.

Agnes had one last task to fulfil before she died, and that was to
establish the Derwen Cripples' Training College in a nearby
house to train the stream of cripples issuing from the hospital, so
that they could earn their living and lead as normal a life as possible. This is where the Bo Peep letters were written. Agnes Hunt
was well ahead of her time in so many ways – she abolished visiting hours and encouraged parents and relatives to drop by
whenever they wanted to.

Agnes Hunt achieved everything she did with few rewards,
and despite being a cripple. Agnes, your presence is requested at
our party!

THE CHASE

A SIMPLE farmer steering his cart through the rutted mire of a country lane anywhere in Wales two centuries ago might have encountered some very strange noises coming from a very strange man.

The farmer, knowing only one language, might have said *Bore Da*.

The stranger, knowing 35 languages, might have answered *Bonjour, Guten Morgen, Buon Giorno, Goddag, Buenos Dias, Good Day to You Sir*, or he might have simply astonished his fellow wayfarer by pulling out a ram's horn and bellowing the Songs of Moses in Hebrew.

This strange person, Dic Aberdaron, will be my fourth guest at the Blue Angel feast, as a representative of all the people who have walked around Wales throughout history. I know there will be quibblers, and I sympathise with their misgivings. Why not one of the itinerant court poets, someone like Dafydd ap Gwilym, or a drover, or a saint? No, I want Dic. He was quite spacky, completely off the wall, but I like them unconventional. And he certainly was that.

He had a mop of black hair tied back with a green ribbon made from ferret skin. His face was covered in hair and on his head he wore a 'Davy Crockett' cap made from the skin of a hare. He was called the Welsh Jew, and draped over his shoulders was a shawl-like garment embroidered with quotes in Hebrew and Greek.

His multi-coloured coat had numerous pockets into which he stuffed his many books. Dic Aberdaron was a walking ency-clopaedia and during a lifetime of wandering he became famous for his outlandish appearance and eccentric habits. He had an extraordinary talent: he spoke up to 35 languages, both ancient and modern – and it was said he could summon and command devils.

With a cat by his side and a ram's horn slung around his neck he travelled the length and breadth of Wales and England.

If we leave the highways and byways of early nineteenth century Wales and travel back to the present we can still marvel at the feats of Dic Aberdaron, or to give him his proper name,

Richard Robert Jones. The son of a smallholder and carpenter, he was born 'when the sun was in cancer' in a mud-walled house at the tip of the Lleyn peninsula in 1780.

As a child he loved books, and although unschooled he could speak his native Welsh from an early age. He was fluent in English by the time he was ten, taught himself Latin by the time he was 12 or 15 (accounts vary), Greek when he was 18 and Hebrew the following year. Poor Dic was naturally averse to work and spent most of his time pursuing languages; this failed to impress his father who eventually threatened him with a poker. Dic was forced to seek gainful employment and he headed for Caernarfon and then Bangor, where he was befriended by the bishop.

But he neglected his job, tending the bishop's garden, and he was forced to head for Anglesey, where he found time to learn French and Italian. He went to live in Liverpool in 1806, by which time he had developed an enviable range of eccentricities. He had an instrument carved from a ram's horn with which he used to sing the Songs of Moses in Hebrew. When it was not used for this purpose he kept his money in it. Someone gave him a cat which followed him everywhere; this cat was called Miaw and always received the first bite at meal times. Dic could not sleep unless she was by his bed, and his books were covered in pictures of her.

He also carried a small harp, a telescope he had made himself and an enormous map of Wales tied to a pole. He wore two sets of spectacles with an additional device, attached to the lenses, to further improve his view.

He failed to get regular work at Liverpool so he went to London (which he hated) and then Dover where he was given breakfast, a chest to keep all his books and 2s 4d a day for working in the Royal Shipyard, where he learnt Greek.

He returned to London but fell on hard times again, forcing him to sell his books. He returned to Wales and two Bangor clergymen attempted to make him into a printer but he failed at this also.

Dic would have picked up a restraining order these days: because of problems at one set of digs he upset everyone by playing his ram's horn loudly, and during another sojourn in Liverpool he went round blaspheming in every conceivable language when all his possessions, including his books, were taken from him in lieu of debt.

In a letter to *The Times*, a Liverpool paper, a publisher and book-seller called Efan Llwyd from Mold claimed that Dic could speak 35 languages including Hebrew, Welsh, English, French, Spanish, Piedmontese, Ethiopian, Irish Gaelic, German, Syrian, Georgian, Russian of the North, Russian of the South, Armenian, Low German, Arabic, Coptic, Classical Greek, Modern Greek, Portuguese, Persian, Breton, Dutch Low German, Swedish, Manx, Scots Gaelic, Latin, Danish and Gaulish. Some of the other tongues he listed are untraceable, but Dic's ability with languages was undeniable – he was frequently summoned to the Liverpool Corn Exchange to translate for the merchants. There is also evidence that an Oxford scholar, Doctor Parr, questioned him and came to the conclusion that he had a thorough knowledge of the Greek language but had little comprehension of what he read. He seemed to have no interest in literature, reading his many books with little appreciation for their contents. Dic died at St Asaph whilst returning home from Liverpool after a breakdown in his health, and is buried at the parish church. I went there once to visit his highly unconventional bones but failed miserably to find them. Without any doubt whatsoever I choose Dic Aberdaron, linguist and walker *sans pareil*, to first-foot our triskelion.

Last night I dreamt I was walking through high lonely mountains, rising, like knees in a bath, from a perfectly still, emerald-green sea far away, in another universe, and I knew with great sadness that someone I loved had passed by only recently, and that I had missed my only chance in the whole of time to see her again. Was it Emmeline? Love comes to me only in dreams. She hasn't replied. Perhaps that poisoned dwarf of a husband has intercepted my letters.

I am scuttling around the land again. Next time you're outside a shop buying postcards of Wales take a good look through the rack; somewhere in one of the postcards you'll see a tiny black dot moving slowly on the landscape, like a paper mite. Take care! Don't crush me with your clumsy thumbs – I have many more postcards to pass through before they drag the stand through the door and lock me inside the shop over winter.

I am in Dyfed, in the magical realm of Pembrokeshire, which

pokes out into the Atlantic like a pig snouting its trough; this is the only part of Wales with direct access to the Otherworld in Welsh mythology – it's a portal to an ancient, dangerous fantasy game. This is where pigs, magical creatures, first arrived in Wales, gifts from a pantheon of gods living in a Celtic Valhalla, and linked to this part of my country by a time corridor. Teetering on a cliff, a stupendous incision cut into the rock – as if a slice has been taken from a Christmas cake and I am a little pearly decoration left right on the edge – I await the sonic boom of the great boar, the murderous man-devouring *twrch trwyth*, pursued from Ireland by Arthur and his hosts in their ship Prydwen. This bristling, enraged monster-pig carries a mirror, a comb, and shears between his ears (all these items are needed by a boy born in a pigpen who wants to marry a giant's daughter). The boar arrives in a ravening whoosh of water below me in Porth Clais. I hide as his enraged porcine retinue disappears into the woods. For a long time, as I pass northwards, I hear warriors, bugles echoing in the trees, surges of sound – roars, screams.

Back home, sleeping in my safe little piggy bed, my mobile phone trilled by my head on the pillow one morning. I'd no idea how it got there.

It was Paddy, and he was already pissed.

'Twas the rusty nail wot done it, with a demi-twist of lemon, me ole' china. Better get your skates on rapido cos there's another loony right behind you and he's treading on your tail. Get my drift? It's time to do the high fandango and hit the trail of the lonesome pines, *si*? Knot them seven league boots on your plates of meat and get goin' or the hare will be past you whoosh, me little tortoise. Seen the papers?'

'Christ Paddy, I was sleeping.' My voice crackled. I was disorientated and grumpy.

'It's in the *Western Mail* me contumacious old codger, a celestial body wot is fleeter than you and younger and handsomer is flitting up the coast behind you. Says he's walking round Wales, and he's going to be the first person to do it. No chance, you've less chance than a Cadwalader's ice cream in the burning pits of hell. What's more, my jinja ninja, you know him. Have a guess! Never in a million years! You're buggered now – might as well turn over and stay in bed for ever.'

I gathered my wits as well as I could. People loomed in and out of the fog of my sleep chamber. Someone I knew? I groped about uselessly as Paddy talked nonsense on the other end of the line.

'Go on, tell me!' I urged him shrilly.

Paddy, being a merciful and compassionate man, put me out of my misery.

'It's the giant who built a causeway and hopped over to another world. You know, Martin, the man who built those steps at the bottom of his garden and went looking for fairies.'

I was dumbfounded. I sat in my bed looking at another strange being who was looking straight back at me from the dressing table mirror, a man with badly-cut red hair trying to make a frenzied escape, and a mouth as slack as a village idiot's about to deliver a gallon of dribble. Initial shock gave way to blind panic. And anger. Who the bloody hell did he think he was? A bloody Englishman about to circumnavigate my own blessed country, when it was right and proper that I should be the demi-god to accomplish the feat? Blood and bollocks, it had taken me over forty years to realise that walking around Wales was the only pathetic un-Olympian feat I had ever really wanted to accomplish, and here was an interloper with nary a midge's cognisance of what he was doing or what holy ground he was treading, what famous company he was keeping, stealing my little bit of thunder, admittedly not much more of a noise than a child rattling a tray, but as close to making thunder as I would ever come. He had stolen the one glorious act I had set myself to perform in my whole life, a quest I had spent a lifetime preparing for; this bastard chasing me up the Welsh coast was about to embezzle my inheritance, whip away my own little Excalibur, which admittedly was closer to a plastic prong from a chip shop, but it was bloody well mine and, figuratively speaking, because the ceiling is quite low, I was prepared to brandish it above my head in the Blue Angel on the night of the party and declare myself a rightful successor to Llywelyn ap Gruffudd, Owain Glyndwr, Collwyn ap Tango or any other man, great or small, who had shed his blood over a patch of ground no bigger than God's fireside rug, but which nonetheless bore the imprint of His immaculate feet.

'Still there?'

Paddy defibrillated me back to life and I gave the bedclothes an almighty kick, but succeeded only in winding the coverlet around my leg so completely that I was virtually unable to move.

'A wee bit narked are we? Going to do the usual Welsh thing – throw all your toys out of the pram, quarrel with everyone, declare yourself a complete failure and offer to carry Martin's rucksack?'

'You fucking bastard! Destroyer of dreams! I hate you!'

I cut him off and prepared myself in a whirl of action, pissing, dressing, finding my rucksack and maps, purple pullover (in the wash, never mind, grab it), sleeping bag (still smelly from the last jaunt), faded coat (only one button left now), medicine (is there enough?) cheque card and money, bits and bobs, and I'm ready in half an hour to claim back my kingdom, as quickly (I thought) or quicker than one-eyed Dafydd Gam when he girt his loins and shouldered arms ready for Agincourt. I had to get to my own Agincourt on the west coast, Abersoch, as quickly as possible, so I phoned Waldo at the pub, where he did light duties in the morning (an excuse, more than anything, to gather news drifting in on the first tide).

'Waldo?'

'What d'ya want now, Amundsen?'

'It's like this, Waldo.'

'It's like what?'

'There's someone after me.'

'After you? You been a naughty boy? You can trust me, won't tell anyone about it.'

Heavy irony.

'No – he's in Aberystwyth, and he's trying to catch me. I've got to get to Abersoch as soon as possible or he'll beat me. He's English.'

I told him the news.

'What – he's trying to walk round Wales too?'

'Yes'.

'Well bugger me. As if it wasn't enough having one lunatic on my hands. Does he know about you? Cheeky English twat. I'll sort him out for you. Plenty of cliffs around Aberystwyth.'

'No Waldo, I want to beat him fair and square.'

'Don't be a fucking idiot – he's English. He'll walk through the night singing psalms with God by his side if he thinks there's a garden shed he can overrun by the morning. He'll have partitioned *wakes view of England* [handwritten annotation]

Anglesey by breakfast and set up a Zionist state on Holy Island by noon. You don't understand these people. It's in their genes. You don't get to conquer half the world by saying *after you* in the nursery milk queue. You're talking about the race which invented double yellow lines.'

'Listen Waldo, there's a bus at ten. Are you going to carry on all day?'

The phone slammed down and I knew he'd be climbing my stairs in a matter of minutes.

He was.

'Ready then?'

'Yes. Thanks.'

'Don't mention it. I've got a cousin in Llanengan and I'd like to see her anyway. Ideal. By the way, Paddy's coming along for the ride. He's abnormally pissed.'

Waldo's truck was outside. It's a coal truck which he bought for next to nothing and did up, though you can still see the company logo beneath a coat of green household gloss, which Waldo found in a skip. He's handy with mechanical things and he's cleaned it up nicely, though the wipers judder and grind terribly, sometimes giving up the ghost altogether. *like the Ivans moss* [handwritten annotation]

The cab is full of odd mementoes from his travels; he's tied a large plastic gorilla to the rear-view mirror and various other plastic animals dangle from the ceiling. They're from all sorts of places – cereal packets, fairs, burger joints. Things he has found on his travels – marbles, coins, a dried-up toad, owl pellets, a broken toy – are scattered on the dashboard. The windows are covered in stickers: RNLI, Save the Whale.

We headed off across North Wales, with Paddy between us, towards the peninsula, and settled into our routine motoring conversation, which because of Waldo's concentration and Paddy's inebriation was a disjointed and sporadic affair.

Today the fields stretching out on both sides looked like a huge jigsaw puzzle newly completed by a giant, who had promptly spilled his drink all over it. Wetly, we followed the configurations of the puzzle, towards a large blue bit on the edge of the fractured picture – the sea.

By the time we reached the end of the Pentir road Waldo had debriefed me about yesterday's visit to the hospital at Gobowen and his latest delvings.

'Incidentally,' he said with an earnest sideways look, 'I think I need some more anecdotes to drop into my conversations. I don't want them to become suspicious. Have you got a few more tales I can tell them?'

I thought for a few minutes as the fields passed by and the road asked its usual metaphysical questions.

'You got any scars on your hands?'

'Course I've got bloody scars on my hands. Everyone's got scars on their hands.'

'Got any on your fingers?'

He thrust his left paw in my face, forcing Paddy to take evasive action, and wiggled it. He had a handful of scars.

'You don't build walls and fiddle about with cars for fifty years without getting a few scars,' he said.

'OK. Pick out a thin, long weal, you know, a white one which looks like an old knife cut. Say you were pushing a glass urine bottle down your bed one day and the lip shattered, cutting your finger. Waggle your hand about just like that and describe gallons of blood, they'll believe you.'

'Fine. Anything else?'

'Say you have a picture of yourself with two famous stars of the day who were visiting the hospital. I'll give it to you when I get back. You're in your hospital bed, as usual, and you have a tatty little case containing all your toys and books by your feet. One of the celebrities visiting you is Winifred Atwell, who was a very well known blues and honky-tonk pianist. She is quite plump and black and has a knockout West Indian smile. She's wearing furs and one of those dinky little black hats perched miraculously on the side of her head. The woman with her is statuesque, drop dead gorgeous in a blonde way, and she is also all mouth and teeth. She's Betty Driver, once a well-known star of Coronation Street (as if I needed to tell him). She was behind the bar of the Rovers for years, can't remember her screen name.'

'Betty, she was called Betty on the telly too,' said Waldo immediately, Waldo the man who would never in a month of Sundays admit to watching soaps.

'Ask them if they can find out when Atwell and Driver were there, because you're sure the picture I've just described appeared in the *Liverpool Daily Post* and you'd like to see it.'

'Great – that'll do fine,' he grunted, and huddled over the

wheel. He drove us into Pwllheli where we stopped just long enough for me to grab my usual two bottles of Coke and something to eat on the trek. We started off again, having located Paddy and lugged him out of a pub called the Mitre. Didn't take much guessing where he was.

'Well shiver me timbers, we're in Polski land,' said Paddy a few miles out of town.

He was beginning to slur. 'See the double-headed eagle?' He pointed to a small sign by the road as we passed. 'There's a big Polish settlement up that road, hundreds of them, all talking Polish and meeting for meals in a big canteen in the middle of the camp. Went there once for dinner with an ex-pilot I met. By Christ, had *he* seen a few things. Anyway, there I was with him in his cabin and a bell started tolling, and before you could say Jack Robinski hundreds of us were filing down concrete paths to the canteen. It was like one of those films about people being taken over by an alien power. It was dinner time, and we all sat around huge tables with gleaming white tablecloths. It was incredible – like being whipped over to Poland suddenly. Gave me a hell of a welcome. They had a lot of sadness about, what with their war memories and a miners' strike going on in Poland – they all had Polish newspapers.'

Paddy's face wobbled towards mine. He was beginning to flush, and he was getting more lucid, which usually happened in the last few minutes before he started falling over things and breaking them.

'You're into minorities, people of the bloody fringe, whatever [wipes his mouth and burps, I can smell the whisky], well look at that lot – they're a minority within a minority within a minority within ad bloody infinitum. Like those ever decreasing bloody needles in *The Third Policeman,* you can't see the smallest, only feel it. You might as well call yourself a minority of one, declare yourself an independent nation and have done with it man. I need a piss.'

Soon we were in Abersoch, one of a collection of Welsh resorts which have grown from fishing villages into fun havens for a fairly limited number of well-off English families who bought second homes and boats there a couple of generations back. They're mostly from the Liverpool-Cheshire-Manchester belt with a sprinkling of Brummies; they make good money from hard-nosed business ventures at home so they can frolic in the Welsh surf. These jetski colonialists are quiet Gold Card-bearers with pretty, spoilt daughters and lanky, grungy sons who have expensive guitars and surfboards. In olden days it would have been pink gin territory; now it's lager-and-car talk at the local bar. Welsh affairs are strictly interdict – a lesson learnt from pioneering parents – so as not to agitate the dwindling band of locals. There are more ways of killing a cat than with cream.

I sit watching the girls with Waldo – they look like seals in their wetsuits and are strangely sexless. But Waldo looks so long and hard at one blonde-streaked Venus gyrating behind a boat that he drops his ice cream on his trousers, which has unfortunate visual connotations, so I get him another one whilst he calms down. Paddy has gone to a pub behind us, but has been turned away and is now shambling towards us with a Spar bag and more supplies.

'That bloke's on a mission,' said Waldo. 'His last liver function test was either appalling or they mixed him up with George Best. Can't you have a word with him? Perhaps he'll listen to you.'

Both of us knew he'd listen to nobody. He had the Celtic curse.

'Whilst we're talking about hopeless cases,' said Waldo, 'I've found out a bit more for you. Yesterday I managed to get hold of Luther's file. Not very happy reading, I'm afraid. His father died from tertiary syphilis and passed on the disease to Luther. That's why his mother was so depressed in the Vogel Papers – she was under a sentence. Those freckles on Luther's face aren't freckles at all – they're a rash which is common in kids born with inherited syphilis. Other things too, quite horrible. Fissures around the lips and somewhere else I don't want to think about.'

'That's strange,' I interrupted, 'there was a programme on TV last week about Hitler. Apparently his own Howitzer was a bit abnormal and he was convinced it was caused by genetically inherited syphilis.'

'You don't say,' said Waldo. 'Anyway, one of the early symptoms is a constant snuffle, often accompanied by blood, which explains Luther's 'cold' when they set off on the quest to Anglesey. The terrible thing is that babies appear perfectly normal at birth, but the disease is eating away at their liver and their brains. The list of effects is endless according to his notes – exfoliation of nails, loss of hair and eyebrows, irritability, eye disease, notches on the teeth, it's all too horrible. Sins of the father – it's all there. And there's worse to come.'

'But what was he doing at an orthopaedic hospital – surely he should have been in general,' said I.

'No, as I said, there was worse to come. Luther wasn't showing any further symptoms yet, which is probably why they liked to keep him on the move, but in time the disease would attack his skeletal structure, leading to bone malformations. He was probably there short-term for an evaluation. Poor little Luther. His brain had already been eaten into. Poor little boy. One stupid act by his father. What a price to pay. Try believing in a god who does that to children.'

'No siree,' chimed in Paddy who was laying into a half bottle of cheap whisky.

'No mercy on the menu up there in the celestial boardroom when Luther went up for his interview, was there? Ole Hera must'a been on a heavy period and Zeus must'a swigged a rake of ouzo the night before. Bad business, boys, I don't mind telling you. I'm glad as hell I turned out as normal as a squid in a tent. Bent me pegs on the morning dew and tied me groundsheet to a periwinkle's knickers, but I'm right as rain.' Here he drivelled on for some time as we watched the nymphets on the shore.

'Time to get going,' I announced, and I got ready to go.

'Too fucking right,' said Paddy, who started slinging pebbles at me, so Waldo wrestled him down and told him to behave. Seeing that the party was getting boisterous I headed off towards Bwlchtocyn (ah, what poetry in that name) but had my head so full of mud I went way off course, wandering about like a man in Paddy's state, and ending up at a farmhouse door asking for directions. A complete false start. By now, of course, the day was dwindling so I headed for the Sun Inn at Llanengan, where I could while away the late hours jangling with the locals and keeping myself warm, before heading for a night on the dunes. Well alackaday, the first thing I see outside the Sun Inn is Waldo's wagon; Pedro his dog is sitting up in the driver's seat and Paddy is slumped by his side, sleeping. Waldo is having a jangle inside with his cousin, so I join them until they go, then try to find the 'visitor' spot in the pub, which I get wrong (not a good day) and end up listening to a group of settlers drinking wine and Being Intelligent.

Then a group of young Welshmen come in but two are pretty

out of it and they're talking mainly chainsaws, so I go into shut-down mode and just sit there, wondering about tomorrow and trying to be pleasant until 11 o'clock, when I head for the dunes and find a nice sandy slope in the shade of the maram grass, where I can lie back in my sleeping bag looking at the stars and listening to the tush of the night-surf in Porth Neigwl, the great skillet-bottomed bay called Hell's Mouth.

It's great to be out in the amphitheatre of the night, waiting for the play to begin: the shadows will form a chorus around the bay and I will lie in the auditorium with the shorebirds and the snuffling creatures of my nocturnal world. It's not too cold to sleep, and I'm nodding off when the mobile goes off in the ruck-sack under my head, startling me. I've forgotten to turn it off, so I scrabble about and answer it.

'Hia me old peculiar. It's me. Paddy. Just phoning to say good-night.'

I didn't even answer. In the next four hours I got sick and tired of stars and nature and longed for a nice warm bed. Nature's all right when you're in the mood.

AROUND THE WORLD IN A DAY

I DRIFTED in and out of the night, like the waves lapping a short way from my head.

When I woke properly, stiff and cold, under an inky sky seeping with new light, I found that I was damp with dew, and my sleeping bag was blubbering with water.

I shook off what I could of the wetness and stuffed everything into my rucksack. I had slept in my boots, so there was little to check. I stepped out of the dunes into a gimlet dawn and started along the lip of Hell's Mouth, with the breaking waves gleaming toothfully by my side. I felt like a fly crawling along the lip of a huge saucer.

I would like you to daydream with me, as the dawn's eyeball rolls feverishly in the night's black socket. I am a wrecker with a lantern, luring ships onto the shore, like the 18th century wreckers of Crigyll on the west coast of Anglesey. I thought wreckers were illiterate ruffians living in caves until I read about these Welsh mooncussers: on the contrary, they were upstanding members of the community – a farmer, a weaver, a tailor, a housewife, and children were among them; a chapel elder discovered some of his own congregation at it.

If you visit Beaumaris Courthouse you will learn about the famous case of 1741 when four of the robbers were arraigned before the island's chief justice, Thomas Martyn, who also happened to be a notorious lush (like that magistrate in the Vogel Papers, who was kidnapped by pirates and taken across the sea). The wreckers' families disrupted the trial and Thomas Martyn made a drunken hash of things, so the men got away with it. But the wreckers had committed a particularly heinous crime, and they had a grim avenger on their trail. William Chilcott, captain of a sloop called the Charming Jenny, had been lured onto the rocks in a storm and had witnessed the wreckers murdering his wife by holding her head under water until she drowned. They broke a finger to remove her gold wedding ring and her body was stripped of valuables. Despite setbacks, Chilcott eventually got the men tried at Shrewsbury, and two were sentenced to death (although only one seems to have been hanged). When I first read this story I thought of Paddy, lured onto the rocks by his addiction – while we were forced to watch, helplessly, as he drowned in alcohol.

But back to the present. I am walking on a beach, and the dawn is seeping in from the east. There was a time when the seashore communities and the farmers inland had virtually no contact with each other – they were separate nations, almost.

Walking alongside this wine-dark sea has another connotation: there was virtually no travel by land in pre-medieval times, it was simply too dangerous, so humans moved about almost exclusively on water; the Irish sea on my left was their main artery, and the long shoreline of West Wales, my walkway today, was the equivalent of a motorway hard shoulder.

When the light took hold I discovered that the tide was coming in, and I eventually had to traverse the muddy, fissured falls of earth which had been dislodged from the shoreland. It wasn't enjoyable, especially since I had to scurry along the edge of a long field in full sight of a farmhouse before I reached a road near the pretty National Trust house at Plas-yn-Rhiw. Farmers have had too many bad experiences with walkers to wave at everyone cheerily; I have been directed peremptorily to the nearest footpath on more than one occasion, despite my Welsh greetings. I sometimes feel a bit guilty, swanning around the country decadently while they're doing proper work. The farming families are the real core of the country, the spine. They are the respirator which gives Wales its deep, ancient breath. They're the real people; in comparison I feel so ersatz, so poorly reproduced on the great photo-copier of my nation's genetic pool.

As I walk slowly up the steep hill from Plas-yn-Rhiw, with the bay descending down an escalator behind me, I consider my next guest at the Blue Angel party, who will be another walker. Will it be the first person to walk around the Earth, Dave Kunst? Now there's a man I tip my hat to. Dave set off from Minnesota with his brother John and a pack mule called Willie Makeit (get it?) on June 20, 1970 – but only Dave returned. John was shot and killed by bandits in Afghanistan. Dave resumed his trek after recovering from his wounds, this time accompanied by another brother, Pete. They crossed India and went on to Australia, where their third Willie Makeit died in the desert. An Australian teacher,

Jenni Samuel, volunteered to haul their baggage behind her car and guess what – she and Dave fell in love. They married when he completed his walk on October 21, 1974. He got through 21 pairs of shoes and took about twenty million steps. What a hero.

Not to be outdone, a god-fearing man called Arthur Blessit (no, I'm not pulling your plonker) has circumnavigated the globe carrying a full-scale cross. And of course there's Ffyona Campbell, who walked the 1,000-mile length of Britain at the age of 16 and then marched around the world at the rate of 50 miles a day.

But the one who really wins my respect is a great-grand-mother called Doris Haddock (you couldn't make it up, could you) who decided, at the age of 89, to walk across America in a campaign for political reform. She became a celebrity, with big-name Republicans and Democrats joining her on her 3,200-mile meander from Pasadena in California to Washington DC. Doris, standing a mere five feet tall, had emphysema and arthritis. She got through four sets of shoes and had to ski part of the way because snow threatened to disrupt her trip. Way to go, Doris.

There are other freaks – Gary Hause belted round the globe in turbo-charged style: he 'did' America in 87 days and Europe (yawn) in 147 days.

No, I'm not going to choose any of those.

Here we go through Rhiw, home of that cantankerous old genius R.S. Thomas, who made great word-potions from the glistening trail of a glow-worm in his bosom-bower, and who had all the synonyms for sadness nestling like butterflies' eggs under the leaf of his tongue.

The day's fine and I'm hitting my stride, though there's a slight panic frosting my spirit; will the Englishman beat me to my finishing point near Bangor? How much Norman blood has he in his ventricles? How much desire has he to seize my terrain and plant my head on a fencing post, leaving me there like a trophy mole?

I reach the top of Mynydd y Graig and wander in the heather, stepping on whitened rocks which surface on the path like whales in the fish-lanes of the Atlantic.

The sea glitters; my eyes follow the contours of my country, along her headlands and her coves, and I am smitten by her seemliness, her gleaming grandeur. She appears through the veils of her morning mists to welcome me, and to lead me to sweet anchorages on this wayward journey of my heart.

So, I'm a jollyman now, hoity-toity and a-swaggering on the dusty road like Dick Whittington with all my worldly possessions wrapped up in a polka-dot bandana on a stick swung over my shoulder like a cartoon character, and I'm getting sea-drunk and fizzy with bubbles of glee blown landward specially for my own consumption, and I'm hawking my happy pills down through a Marie Celeste farm, large but abandoned, above Porth Ysgo, wondering: what happened here, why was this tribe scattered to the four winds, what became of the children who said naughty words by the duckpond and fell about giggling and dizzy in the hayrick after doing too many headstands?

Onwards, into the day, and I find an old roadside church high above, looking down on Aberdaron, a charming little church which would look great in a film set on a stormy west coast with a crazy priest who's a cross between Trevor Howard in *Ryan's Daughter* and a Welsh ranter with a name like Easter Evans, white-haired and red with Christ's blood swigged secretly from a bottle hidden in the organ, preaching to the seals all sat up like a regular congregation down there on the rocks.

I sit in the churchyard, with the dead, and share the sun with them. My sleeping bag steams on the headstone of an old Welshwoman who would have been flabbergasted by my sleeping bag and by my dissipated notions.

Who, in God's name, I ask my captive audience, will I invite to the ball?

Who will be my second walker?

I might, I might just choose an oddity. How about William Gale of Cardiff, who recorded his greatest walk in the late summer and autumn of 1877, when he covered 1,500 miles in 1,000 hours. He walked for six weeks solidly at the rate of 36 miles a day.

Or how about the great American temperance leader Weston, who set himself the task of walking 5,000 miles in 100 days, in a non-stop trek during 1884. On his final day, when he walked from Brighton to London, he was cheered by large crowds patrolled by mounted police.

I've a liking for Foster Powell, who covered his first high-speed trek, a 50-mile endurance test along the Bath Road, in just seven hours. To make it more interesting he wore a heavy greatcoat and leather breeches. Powell did a 402-mile ramble from London to York and back in six days, and he walked the 112 miles from Canterbury to London Bridge and back in 24 hours, with thousands of astonished spectators awaiting his arrival. He became famous throughout Britain and decided to attempt the Canterbury walk in a faster time, but lost his way and felt so ashamed of his failure that he went into a decline and died a bitter and disappointed man.

We must feature a Scotsman, and who better than Captain Barclay? One August morning he started from the house of a colonel friend in Aberdeenshire at five o'clock and walked at least thirty miles to shoot grouse in the mountains. By five in the afternoon he had returned to dinner, and then he set off for his own home sixty miles away. He walked it in 11 hours, without stopping once for refreshment.

In the days when ordinary people couldn't afford stagecoach travel many had to go long distances on foot. I rather like the tale of a Keswick woman, known only as Molly, who walked all the way home from London carrying a small table. It is recorded that she said "I's niver sa tired of anything in my life as that auld table" when she finally got to Keswick.

In the same league we have Old Mr Eustace, who at the age of 77 walked from Liverpool to London in four days. Pow!

Perhaps I should choose one of the 500 or so ramblers who took part in the 1932 Mass Trespass at Kinder Scout in the Peak District as part of a growing campaign to gain open access to mountain and moorland. Confronted by the Deputy Chief Constable of Derbyshire and his men, they sang the *International* and other revolutionary songs as they set off. They were met by a posse of gamekeepers with sticks, who battled with them but who were disarmed (a couple got a taste of their own medicine). Later, after their upland victory, six of the ramblers, chosen at random, were tried at Derby Assizes, charged with unlawful assembly and breach of the peace; pro-rambling witnesses were too poor to attend and the jury were mostly country gentlemen and military types. It was a farcical political trial and those found guilty were meted heavy sentences. Similar rallies became common, and those pioneers of freedom eventually won the day. We have a lot to thank them for.

No, as I sit in the churchyard, I decide it will be none of these.

I start off again, down to the little fishing village of Aberdaron, at the end of the old pilgrim's way, which starts at Clynnog Fawr. Three pilgrimages to the offshore island of Bardsey were considered equal to a pilgrimage to Rome in the Roman Catholic world. The nearby church at Pistyll, of which more later, had leper huts within its enclosure to harbour those seeking a cure, or preparing to meet their maker. Salvation lay over the water, on Bardsey, reputedly the home of 20,000 saints. It is a dangerous channel, though I have never seen any records of the hundreds who must have drowned during the crossing. That turbulent stretch of sea, which boils like a great cauldron, is a suitable Welsh place to represent all the other aortic valves between life and death, ranging from the Styx to the Ganges. Pilgrims were regarded as a different breed to the rest of mankind; they lived *secundum Deum*, and were therefore aliens in this world, belonging to the city of God rather than the temporal world.

The point I make, in a secular world, is that the pilgrim, in transit between a previous state and a new condition, is irreversibly changing his life either for better or worse, and in temporarily removing himself from worldly matters he is suspended in a state of deferment or adjournment. He is also attempting to escape from mundanity, to free his spirit, to forget that he is merely a channel for excrement, as Leonardo put it. Leonardo was a man who bought cage-birds in the market place and set them free – the pilgrim, romantically speaking, wants also to rise from Leonardo's palm.

My mobile trills as I walk down the slipway by St Hywyn's Church. I squat by the sea wall, and the shingle hurts my bottom.

'You OK?'

It's Waldo.

'Fine.'

'Where are you?'

'Getting a numb bum on the beach at Aberdaron. What about you?'

'In the disabled toilet at the hospital library. They loved your story about the photo with those celebrities – they checked it out and found it pretty quick. Impressed them no end. The scar on my finger went down pretty well too. Can't talk for long in case someone comes in. I've got a few more facts for you. Jack, the little strongman, was suffering from dwarfism. He was actually quite a few years older than the rest of them – have another look at his face in the picture.'

So Jack was one of the Little People. My memory handed me pictures of the dwarfs who had crossed my path: real ones, not Disneymen or Diddymen; a man in my home town with a wonderful sense of humour; actors in the film *Willow*, partly filmed in Snowdonia and starring a reluctant dwarf who saves a special baby from an evil queen.

Mythology has its fair share of dwarfs, such as the Nibelungs, northern dwarfs in a German epic whose king had owned – and then lost – a great but cursed treasure trove of gold and precious stones (Tolkien's dwarfs came from this family, quite clearly). Dwarfs are people with average-sized bodies but small-scale arms and legs, whilst midgets are all in proportion but much smaller than everyone else. Dwarfs tend to suffer more as they grow older, I seem to remember, when their skeletal structure starts paying the price for their unusual shape. Famous dwarfs include Snow White's little friends, who are common figures in the folklore of the world. Traditionally, dwarfs are short and stocky with long beards and they work in mines, digging for minerals and metals. They are exceptionally skilful with their hands and make beautiful objects which greatly surpass man-made objects. Norse mythology has two famous dwarfs – Brok and Sindri, who made many magical objects including Thor's hammer and Odin's magical ring.

'You still there?'

'Yes Waldo.'

'I've got something on Edwin too. Poor little sod was being knocked about by his father, a former soldier. Very difficult to read between the lines. Edwin had a number of old fractures when he was admitted. There's a line in his notes which says something like: *Disturbed family background. Father injured by nerve gas during military service, unable to co-operate. Mother very nervous, unwilling to volunteer information.* That's all I can find. Edwin seems to have been a deceptively happy boy. Might have been happy because he'd been saved.'

'Or he could have been one of those kids who tried to joke their way out of trouble,' I replied. 'Sometimes abused children have a black sort of humour. You know the ones. There's always one in the playground, joking and messing about, but you know he's having a bad time at home.'

'Could be you're right.'

'Thanks Waldo. Any news about Martin? Is he catching up?'

'Nope. Don't know where he is – I've been tied up here. Can you meet me tomorrow? I'm going to half-inch Esmie's file and bring it to you. I think you need to see it yourself. Bit sad. Where will you be tomorrow morning?'

'Reckon I'll be near Tudweiliog. I'm stiffening up, I'm not fit enough. I'll give you a ring.'

'OK. Keep it up. Bye.'

I sit on the little hump-backed bridge in the centre of Aberdaron, looking at the farmers' wives roaring up to the Spar store in their mud-spattered cars. Their eyes flicker over me as their husbands' eyes scan their flocks and herds, to see if there's anything wrong with me... looking for those traditional signs of a sick animal – a crooking of the back, a lack of interest, a lowering of the head, a slow detachment from the rest of the herd, then the lying down. Sick animals are the ones on their own in a corner of the field. Perhaps this self-isolation is autonomic, to lessen the chance of spreading a disease; perhaps it is an attempt to find a sanctuary to wait for recovery or death.

I have no time to dwell on Aberdaron's tired pilgrims. Like them, I am anxious to reach my goal, but I am also aware that in reaching it I will burst the bubble and wake from my dream. If the Sleeping Beauty's year-long sleep is an analogy for a journey to the otherworld, then the prince's kiss, or the return to reality, is indeed bitter-sweet. With that fillip, or shake of the shoulder, utopia is dispelled.

I hurry up the hill towards Uwchmynydd and pant up the little concrete ribbon road to the top so that I can sit by the coast-guard station. Here I can see the giants' sea-soup coming to the boil, threatening to lift and topple Bardsey Island like a saucepan lid. Below me, in Bardsey Sound, the water seethes. The island lies serene and mysterious, aloof in her divorce. A lazy giant toys with the sea like a broken mirror, a buccaneer's bauble washed up on a drumbeat shore, catching slivers of spring sunshine between the cracks. All around me the hills slumber like huge and unkempt trolls sleeping off a pagan feast, their fading green and brown costumes bulging with ancient dog-eared manuscripts, their pockets stuffed with all my country's records and histories.

I hear a bell clang, and the island seems to make a subtle shift to starboard. I will land there one day, if I can.

I lie in the springy scratchiness of the heather, a flea in a beard, and follow the seagulls, air-surfing, choirboys running with their arms stretched out, all clean and white in their gowns, looking for a puddle to dive into.

I think about Edwin. We have something in common, though I'm not the jokey one in the playground, I'm the moody one. A little matter of childhood memories. There's one thing I've felt during this walk, and it has taken me a thousand miles to feel it, and it's a fine feeling, to match the blue of the sky and the outbursting, popping brilliance of the yellow on the gorse, a new feeling to go with the great rushing realisation of spring, the surging sap, the birds changing their song and the animals quickening in a dance of exultation and exuberance. I feel it now. I have realised something – that all those little secrets locked up in drawers and bolted inside the bulwarks down there in my creaking hull must join the rest of me. They are part of me and my making, they are bubbles in my seaside rock, inkstains on my school desk, holes in my shoes, shit in my clouts, semen on my sheets. They are among my components, and I have grown used to them, those internal birthmarks which stain me in lichen blotches, and since they have been with me for so long I will take them with me and discourse with them about our common ancestry, so that they can join the rest of my whirring molecules, where they belong.

My mind clouds over and my judgement is impaired by Martin's chase. I decide I have no time to hug the coastline, as I normally do. I head off straight for Llangwnnadl along the B road, which is quiet enough for me to enjoy the hedgerows. Wales appears and disappears on the other side of the hawthorn hedge, like a naughty child playing peekaboo. A bank of primroses gives me a sudden surprise; that sublime yellow – I stand stupefied by that yellow against the variegated greens of the backdrop.

I walk now, steadily along the fringe of grass by the roadside, among the daisies and the pineapple weed, and other common wayfarers of my ilk. The pineapple weed, which is extremely common in Britain, is a pilgrim in its own right, having started its journey in Asia. It was introduced into Britain – via the state of

Oregon – in Victorian times. Since then it has marched along our roads at a sprightly pace.

Whilst we're on the subject of plants, I'd like to tell you about common comfrey and greater stitchwort. Comfrey roots were dug up by medieval herbalists and boiled to a sludge which was used like Plaster of Paris around broken bones – its name comes from the Latin *conferre*, meaning *to bring together*. Turning to greater stitchwort, which has easily-snapped stems, this plant was also used as a medicine to heal broken bones; made into an infusion with acorns and wine, it was further used to cure a stitch in the side, hence its name.

Have I chosen my next guest at the Blue Angel bash? It's time I decided, isn't it?

For a long time I was tempted to take our Old English friend, The Wanderer, with his eye for detail:

> The friendless man awakens and sees
> Dark ways before him, sea birds
> Bathing and spreading their feathers,
> Hoar-frost and snow falling...

But I decided he'd be too mournful for the company:

> Thus I, so often weary with sorrow,
> Deprived of my native land,
> And far from my kinsmen who are free,
> Have to fetter my heart's secrets.

No, that won't do at all. I think we need an entertainer, a troubadour, a jongleur or a trouvere who will make us laugh and remind us not to take ourselves too seriously.

If you've forgotten, I'll remind you that troubadours and their troupes were itinerant entertainers who thrived mainly in Provence in the Middle Ages – they moved from town to town and made a parlous living by treating the peasants to impromptu dancing, conjuring, acrobatics, singing and storytelling – they were the ones who brought us courtly love, the gusto and bawdiness behind *Carmina Burana*, and some of the coarse comic tales which inspired Chaucer.

I can just imagine the arrival of a jongleur at a fair or a market place – it must have been a stirring event. I would join the heaving, noisy, sweaty crowd to hear him sing, accompanying himself on a lute, or performing a *chanson de geste*, which was a song about great deeds of chivalry. His stock in trade would be comic stories about lustful priests, lascivious women, and young men who were quick-witted and adept at fooling rich merchants and bedding their gullible wives. I would join in, making rude noises and wanton gestures, like the rest of them!

The troubadours first came to prominence in the eleventh century when they joined forces with wandering clerics to sing songs and tell tales which attracted pilgrims to shrines. Many were aristocrats, some were kings. They were also an important source of information about wars, politics and fashions. I once met a minstrel called Roland, who was a man in their mould. He performed in the public places of Wales, and I met him outside Harlech Castle on a fine day for putting money in a cap. He wore a Basque beret when it was fashionable to do so, and he had a fine head of curly auburn hair, and a laughing cavalier growth on his chin, a gold ring in his ear. He wore the garb of a hobo or road monkey. He knew the lampooning interludes of Twm o'r Nant and could perform them rudely and comically with puppets. With a fiddle he played jigs and reels, and he delivered short satirical poems about the company around him. His teeth gleamed like a pirate's and his body was made to boast of amours. Like me, he was a great contrast to normality, but in a much more interesting way. How I wish I was that man. Roland will join Dic Aberdaron and myself to represent the three walkers in the public bar of the Blue Angel. Dic can sing his *Song of Moses* in Hebrew, Roland can play his fiddle and I will pass the hat round.

I make good progress and I decide on a slight detour to visit the very beautiful church at Llangwnnadl, which has an atmosphere of sheer tranquillity. I rest awhile, a pagan in a Christian shrine, feeding like a mutant on other people's peace. Nothing wrong with that. Get a fix while you can. I decide to end the day at Tudweiliog, and it's dusk by the time I get there. I have enough bread and cheese to see me through the night. It's going to be cold; the sky is clear and Venus is already beaming away like an interstellar lighthouse. I unfurl my sleeping bag in the porch and rest on one of the stone slabs on either side, having lifted the bristly doormat onto it. After a short nap I wake up. People are walking by, probably returning home from the pub. They chat boisterously and then their voices fade and I am left to the night. It is going to be a very long eight hours. As I have told you, I always carry two candles and a lighter in my top pocket, and I light one of them now, and try to warm myself, mentally, cupping its multi-layered flame with my hands. As I move my feet something rattles on the floor and I squat down, fumbling for the cause. It takes me ages to find it – a round disc, about the circumference of a coffee mug, with a raised edge. It is bluey-black and made of enamel or gunmetal. On it there is a dancing bear, painted in bright red paint. A little token from Little Bo Peep all those years ago, and it's nearing its final destination. I had so nearly lost it, on the final lap of its journey.

That night in the porch of Tudweiliog church seemed like the longest of my life, even if I did have an old bear to keep me company. I shivered for most of it. I was mighty glad to sense the dawn coming along, I can tell you. That's one of the things about sleeping rough. You're bloody glad to see another day, another sun.

ESMIE'S STORY

A PULSE went through me when I heard Waldo on the mobile.

Dawn was still an hour away, and I was freezing.

'You still alive there boy? Where are you?'

'Yes – just about. Tudweiliog Church porch.'

'I'm on my way down in the jalopy, should be there by first light. Got a guest, but you may not recognise him – he's sober. Bye.'

After that, every second of time made a personal appearance in the porch and gave me a long, lingering look of incredulity and pity. I packed my stuff and stamped about. The dancing bear jingled in my pocket.

Waldo arrived after a couple of centuries. I huddled next to Paddy in the cab, warming myself, my teeth chattering and my fingers tingling.

'Why do you do this to yourself?' asked Paddy censoriously.

'Just shut the fuck up, Paddy.'

He looked like an extra in *Night of the Living Dead*.

'Why are you sober, anyway?'

'Shops are shut. Poor time management.'

We all sat there like crash-test dummies, whilst I came back to life.

That night was the coldest yet. A near death experience. Waldo fished out a battered Thermos from somewhere and put it in my hands.

'Thanks Waldo. Thanks very, very much.'

I drank his hot sugary coffee, thick and tangy. After a while he gave me another present – an envelope file in a sickly Love Hearts colour. Inside it was another file, which was much, much older. It may have been blue once; it was so faded and thumbed and frayed it needed a berth in a museum. Clipped onto the edge was a computer print-out.

'I found that for you,' said Paddy, as if he'd found the meaning of life.

'Thanks Paddy. Thanks very much.'

'On the internet. I thought it might be useful. Though I don't see why I should help you when you don't give us the slightest hint what's going on. What about this Emmeline? Who is she? Sounds the emotional type – why does she want you to fly over to America as soon as you've finished your walk?'

I was suddenly paralysed, as if a giant goblin had clamped a frozen hand on the back of my neck, as bullies do at school, until you nearly wet yourself, with that strange tingly feeling all over you.

'Emmeline? She got in touch?'

Paddy detected my excitement.

'Ooo, I've hit a nerve, haven't I?'

I squirmed, and he knew it.

'Tell me, Smurf-face, what's going to happen now?' asked Paddy. 'Never left Wales in your life. Can you do it now? Don't see it myself. Reading between the lines, troll-features, I reckon you cowered under a bridge somewhere nice and quiet until a hapless victim came by. But you'll scarper back into your hidey-hole as soon as she says *come and kiss me big boy*'.

I shivered, thinking about it all.

'By the way,' Paddy added, 'your old friend from Tasmania and the Marek woman want a word. They think you've let them down rather badly.'

I gazed guiltily at Paddy's print-out, feeling like an alien. I'd forgotten about Williams and Marek, and the help they had given me. They seemed far away and irrelevant. I asked Paddy to e-mail them, telling them about the end of the walk. I'd get in touch afterwards, when I'd recovered.

The print-out was headed *And They Shall Walk Again*. It said something like this:

For twenty years Eleanor Roosevelt had been the most admired woman in America. But in a 1952 poll she was edged out by an Australian nurse, Sister Elizabeth Kenny.

Sister Kenny had fought an amazing personal crusade against the crippling disease poliomyelitis, with a unique treatment scorned by the medical world.

America suffered its worst epidemic in the history of polio during 1952, and hospitals were full of infected children.

Born on a farm, Elizabeth Kenny was educated at home. As a typical Australian girl she enjoyed helping out on the land, tending the animals, and playing in the great outdoors.

In 1907, when she was 27, Elizabeth decided to become a nurse, and after getting herself a uniform she tended to the people on her home patch. She had no formal qualifications. She dealt with all the usual ailments and farm injuries, but in 1911 she came across her first case of polio.

Called out to a small cabin in the hinterland she encountered a little girl of two whose limbs were 'painfully deformed'. Shocked, Sister Kenny jumped on her horse and rode to a place where she could send a telegram asking for advice.

The response she got, apparently, was: *Infantile paralysis. No known treatment. Do the best you can.*

Sister Kenny had nothing to fall back on except her own intuition.

The little girl recovered completely.

Elizabeth Kenny became an army nurse during the Great War but returned to treating polio victims in the early thirties, when polio became a worldwide epidemic.

By 1950 polio had taken a grip on the world and there were a number of devastating epidemics in Europe and America. The disease was associated with summer and autumn, and as panic grew more and more children were deformed, swimming pools were closed and people shunned public places and events.

Sister Kenny had great success and people took their children from all over the world to her clinic in Australia.

Her methods were dismissed by the medical establishment, but her supporters arranged for her to visit America, home of the world's most famous polio victim, President Franklin Delano Roosevelt.

'Didn't know Roosevelt was a polio victim,' I mumbled in the cab.

'Christ yes, and many more besides,' said Paddy, as if he knew everything about polio. 'You want some famous names? The film world's full of them – Mia Farrow, Donald Sutherland, Francis Ford Coppola, Alan Alda... singers, now let's see – Ian Drury, Joni Mitchell, Neil Young. Sportsmen – Jack Nicklaus and Chandrasekhar. Authors – Sir Walter Scott and Arthur C Clarke. Emperors – Claudius. Royalty – Lord Snowdon. They're all over the damn place.'

'OK, OK Paddy, that's fine. Just let me finish this.'

By the early forties immobilisation was on the way out and the Kenny system was on the way in. As the polio toll rose, many hundreds of doctors and nurses were trained in her ways, and splints became obsolete – in 1947 a stockpile of more than 10,000 of them was sold for scrap.

Sister Kenny became a mega-star, with crowds flocking to see her. Hollywood made a film about her, starring Rosalind Russell.

With hindsight it was difficult to know what part Sister Kenny played in the war on polio, since her methods were obscure, and were disputed by many. But like Florence Nightingale and Agnes Hunt she became a beacon for those wishing to rid the world of a nasty disease which attacked perfectly normal children. It left a small percentage of them badly crippled, usually in the legs, and a small minority dead. So, before I even opened the file on little Esmie Falkirk, who was commemorated on that pagoda in Doctor Robert's lavish garden, I knew we were dealing with a polio victim. But I had no idea that her condition was so tragic. Darkest Fate had found a malign and obscure curse to change Esmie's life for ever.

The light was gaining strength, so Waldo extinguished the cab light and I finished off the coffee. It was time to go. Reading my thoughts, Waldo confirmed the bad news I was expecting: 'He's at Pwllheli. You've got to have a good day today.'

'Have you finished at the hospital?' I asked him.

'Not quite.'

'There's one last thing.'

'There's always one last thing with you. Go on then.'

'That photograph of all the children in the hospital. Try to find out more about it. I think there's more to it than Christmas. There are some presents on Esme's bed but none on any of the others. And that teddy bear on Vogel's bed. Dr Robert Jones looks as though he's presenting it to him, as if it were a prize. Will you try?'

Waldo started the engine. 'As good as done, chappie.'

'In the bag, no problem,' said Paddy, adding quietly: 'Can you spare a few pennies till Friday? Spar's open soon, and I need some medicine. I wouldn't ask, only...'

'Yes Paddy.' I scrabbled around in my top pocket, realised I'd lost my lighter, jumped out and felt about on the porch floor. I found the lighter – and my money too. They'd dropped out in the night, with the dancing bear. I handed a tenner to Paddy and said: 'Seems it's my lucky day, and yours too. Don't ask for any donations at your funeral. We've all paid in advance.'

Off they trundled, and I started off towards the glorious bay at Porth Dinllaen with its red pub, inaccessible to traffic. The pub had been built by a Dutch sailor, I seemed to remember. When I started my journey around Wales I had thought of my country as small and introverted, brooding, nostalgic, darkly recessive.

I had thought of Wales as an embryo which had become joined accidentally to England and the rest of the world like a Siamese twin; and as with all Siamese twins, the union was paradoxical – both natural and unnatural at the same time.

Like my forbears, it was easy for me to see Wales as a mother, and myself as a cell lodged in another period passing through her reproductive system, her womb. But it wasn't like that really. Wales was an area of land which people like me became fond of through usage and association. It wasn't ours, it most definitely didn't belong to anyone at all.

Here was I, a Welshman by birth, passing a pub built from ballast brought by ships returning from Holland, on a particularly lovely strand which had narrowly avoided being despoiled by an English MP, who had wanted to create a great port on it; as I descended to the pub I walked through a golf course which regularly saw people of many nationalities playing a game invented by a Scotsman. No, I felt Welsh not because I had any more right to walk in this place than any of the other earth-mites around me, but because I had a huge jumble of facts and fictions about my birthplace amalgamated in my poor overheated cranium, a massive fable of stories and memories and pictures, a mosaic of small miracles and great cruelties, or great miracles and small cruelties – this is what human love is made of, give or take a few hormones. I felt a kinship with all the souls who had fought for and loved this little tile in the floor of the universe's vast, echoing cathedral.

When I fell overboard and my little country sailed on like a beautifully crafted pinnace, its lights and music fading, I would disappear quickly like all of them, and another would take my place at the side-rail; there would be no wide sweeps and calls on the still sea to find me; but ah, what a fine voyage it would have been along the towering cliffs, terrible and beautiful like life itself.

I darted into a shop in Nefyn and got myself some victuals, then thudded along the road to Pistyll. I would break bread outside the astonishing little church there, sitting against the graveyard wall, close to Rupert Davies the actor, who once played a famous TV detective, Maigret. It's a tiny church which still marks the Lammas feast, now a rarely-observed Christian festival celebrating St Peter's deliverance from prison on August 1. But it has more of the appearance of a pagan festival when you open the door of this tiny little church above the sea. At Christmas, Easter and Lammas the whole building is decorated with boughs and twigs, and mosses and ferns, all suffusing the church with an intoxicating mixture of aromas, and there are flowers (for this old feast was once a harvest festival) and fragrant plants; in this fairy world of delicate green lights and subtle shades I have stood in wonderment, truly transported to another time, when lepers gathered in huts on the seaward side, and pilgrims fished in the nearby pond, now discoloured and fishless.

I sit awhile by Rupert Davies, eating. I open Esmie's file and withdraw its contents. A robin flits onto Rupert's headstone and regards me, his head tilted sideways.

There is a photograph. She has rounder features than the face under the Bo Peep bonnet; perhaps she is younger here, but it's the same girl. Her haircut is farmhouse kitchen, pudding-basin plain, with one strand held sideways with a small ribbon. She has dark, glittering eyes and a cheeky little nose. Her smile is crooked and charming. There are no round specs, as yet. Her small shoulders are wrapped in a heavy cable-stitched cardigan from which the collar of her gingham blouse juts out, askew. There is no name on the back. There is a slight rust mark on the photo where the paper clip has held it onto her file. Esmie looks sweet, in an old-fashioned way. Children had a different look in their eyes then.

The first letter is from her doctor to the registrar of a hospital in Wales. I read it:

> I would be grateful if you could arrange an examination for this little girl, who has had repeated tonsillitis and a more recent attack of quinsy which greatly distressed her – severe breathing difficulties.

The next letter I open is the registrar's reply:

> I have examined this girl. She shows signs of poor diet and I advise a course of vitamins and trace elements before tonsillectomy – I will arrange surgery as soon as possible.

Then there is a note, some months later, from a house doctor:

> Please keep a close watch on this girl today. She complains of headaches and a sore throat. Nausea, vomiting and diarrhoea. Alternatively restless and drowsy. Complains also of back pains and stiff neck, muscle tenderness.

Next, there is a consultant's report:

> I am very concerned about this little girl – she is the third to develop these symptoms on the children's ward since we closed to admissions.
>
> She has developed abnormal sensations and is sensitive to touch, experiences difficulty in urination, constipated with bloating of abdomen, swallowing and breathing difficulties, high fever. Positive Babinski's reflex. Sputum and faeces tests. Close observation essential.

There is a gap of a day, then:

> Poliomyelitis confirmed: paralytic, partial bulbar and respiratory. Inflammation of anterior horn seems likely, since lower limb muscles are flaccid and unresponsive.
>
> Other cases on the ward are improving, but I fear we have permanent damage in this case. We are trying to discover the cause of the outbreak. Tests on all relevant staff.

There is a dossier of medical data, test results and indecipherable jottings, then a discharge note from the registrar:

> I regret that this child, although recovered from immediate symptoms, will be permanently crippled. Please break the news to her parents.

Reading between the lines, I realise that the cause of the outbreak had been a new nurse on the ward, who'd been in contact with the disease elsewhere. She'd worked for just one shift, and had only momentary contact with Esmie, when she moved her from one cot to another. The discharge note continued:

> I need not draw your attention to the sadness of this case. The girl seems generally well, and the reality of the situation has not sunk in yet. I have arranged for her to be admitted to Gobowen, where she will get specialist treatment.

I sat in the spring sunshine and watched a three-masted ketch with rusty red sails cleave the waves, struggling through the water with frequent tacks. I felt slightly nauseous, either from the greasy sausage roll I'd just eaten, or Esmie's tragedy. Such a lot of misfortune for such a little girl, and here was I sitting in a place dedicated to a god who allowed such things to happen. Esmie, a perfectly normal little girl who had a minor problem with her tonsils, had been given a crippling disease in hospital, and to increase the irony, her infector was a nurse, and to make the whole thing black, black, black, contact between nurse and patient had been just one movement of the hands as the nurse lifted her from one cot to another. Just one tiny second on the endless plain of time had kicked Esmie's little legs from under her.

I fastened my rucksack, said goodbye to Rupert Davies and the Robin, and set off on the road, saying farewell also to the tricorn peaks of The Rivals with their famous Iron Age settlement, Tre'r Ceiri – the township of the giants – and onwards into the day, which was settling slowly like sediment along the roads (the tide was in and I couldn't scramble along the boulder-strewn shore). Under the shadow of Gyrn Goch I went, remembering one particularly evocative spring day, unseasonably hot, when I had climbed it with a friend, young and carefree in the sheep-walks, meandering among the sedges and the sphagnum bogs, accompanied only by wheatears, pipits, larks, stonechats and ravens. We had become thirsty, like Coleridge's ancient mariners, and we had longed for water. I had heard the faint whisper of running water under my feet, and plunging my hand through the turf, had found an underground rill of peaty but cool potability. It was on a headland not far from here along the coast that Samuel Taylor Coleridge had also travelled one hot day; his coach had broken down, and he and his companions had walked up to the higher ground, as I had done with my friend. With throats unslaked and black lips baked Coleridge's group had searched for and found a spring, and had drank gratefully of the sweet water; the episode was transposed, later, into a passage in the *Rime of the Ancient Mariner*. Coleridge, Shelley, Wordsworth *et al* had rhapsodised about Wales's sublime features, forgetting to mention in passing that they were here only as an alternative to the Grand Tour, which had been called off because the damned French were making a nuisance of themselves. And over there –

that wall snaking up the mountain was quite possibly built by Irishmen who worked for their food and beer money, and slept (with their wives, who collected the stones) under stone slabs, or perhaps it was built by prisoners of war or soldiers who had returned to a destitute and jobless Britain after the Napoleonic Wars, and had been put to the task to prevent insurrection. Here, in this single vista, I have Coleridge and his fops gadding about with soldiers, blunted and dispirited, and here to join them comes Eben Fardd, who has just written one of the best odes ever to win at the National Eisteddfod, *The Destruction of Jerusalem*, and is on his way to his little classroom in the great church of St Beuno's at Clynnog Fawr below us to teach his clutch of monoglot Welsh children; here comes a farmer, carrying his wife on his back to church, as was common, to keep her Sunday best clean – his dogs slink behind him (in St Beuno's there is a pair of dog tongs to jettison unruly animals during services); here comes a seventeen-year-old youth, Edgar Christian, from Clynnog, who went in search of adventure in the wastes of Canada in 1927 and died in a log cabin with two other pioneers – his diary is a classic; and thither, in the time it takes a cloud to pass silently over us, we espy the silent war party of *Llywelyn ein Llyw Olaf*, Llywelyn the last true prince of Wales, filing over the ridge towards Bwlch Dau Fynydd, to do battle with Llywelyn's brothers Owain and Dafydd at Bryn Derwin, one of the defining battles of Wales; yonder, on the horizon, I can see the first yacht ever seen in Britain, the Mary – in a few minutes she will be shipwrecked on the Skerries, a jagged line of rocks off Holyhead: survivors will salvage planks from the wreck and make a fire; they will catch a sheep and roast some mutton, they will divide a small cask of whisky between them all. The 15 surviving passengers and 24 seamen will be rescued on Sunday and taken to Beaumaris...

The Mary was the first royal yacht and Charles the Second originated yacht racing in her. The *jacht*, a Dutch naval vessel used for fast patrols, had carried nobility around Holland's canals in peacetime. Charles fell in love with the Mary while exiled in Holland, and brought her back with him; she became the ancestor of today's yachts and dinghies. Her remains lie shivered on a Welsh coastline.

I think it's possible, don't you, that the author of the Vogel Papers had a purpose in introducing the image of the shipwreck into our innocent minds. This was a story about a cripple, after all, and he could find no better metaphor, in the parsing of a cripple's life, than the imagery of the wreck – the vessel destroyed in a few minutes by ill fortune or carelessness.

This may be a pot noodle theory, but perhaps it's worth considering.

I think the answer to Vogel's quest lies in that photograph on my mantelpiece. There is something about it: I know, somehow, that the little group of crippled children pictured at Gobowen holds the key.

As for me, I will sit in St Beuno's church, now that I have reached it. I am very fond of this church, with its quirky side chapel along a corridor. An elderly man is pottering about. We talk. He has a flat cap and the unlit remains of a roll-up behind his ear. He is a belt and braces man in a clean white shirt and gargantuan corduroy trousers hanging around his legs like corrugated iron sheets. He is avuncular, a man of the people, and he has 'adopted' the church – he spends much of his spare time here, mending broken bits, painting doors, sweeping, washing out vases. We sit on opposite sides of the nave, he a child of his times, with his household god, and I of mine, with my selfish genes.

'Do you know something, I think I'll try it,' he said to me cryptically.

He held up a small object and I went over to look at it.

The man held a small rusty key.

'Found it in the vestry,' he said.

Then he lumbered past the rood, and I followed him like a dog.

He stood behind the altar, studying the wall, and it took me a while to see what he was looking at, a small square in the stonework, something that looked like a safe or a cupboard.

'No-one knows what's in there,' he said. 'It's a puzzle to all of us.' He held up the key, dropped his fag end, picked it up again, popped it back behind his ear, and wriggled the key in the lock.

The safe opened easily and quickly, and we both looked into the cavity behind the little iron door. Standing there was a most beautiful silver chalice, and the man took it from there and polished it with his sleeve. We both admired it; it had a quirky lack of regularity which made it look very old, and we quickly saw that it was, for we could make out a year which started with 16--, and

coincidence 226

a Latin inscription. Later I saw a magazine article about the chalice, which was indeed very old and precious, and had been presumed lost or stolen centuries previously. And I was there at its discovery. How fine that made me feel! Finer than anyone standing around when the Gunderstrup cauldron was lugged from its Danish bog.

Sitting there in the church at Clynnog with a host of motes, ancient and modern, swirling and dancing in a beam of warm spring sunshine which filtered through the windows, I too felt like one of the motes, warm and impossibly amalgamated, caught in tiny unseen currents, but here to share the moment in the vast molecular swirl of time, and I wished for this miscellaneous exis-tence for ever; suddenly I cared not a whit for the race to the finishing line, nor of Martin's victory. Let him have the laurels. I would join the cripples' retinue and travel with them; we would make a merry band with our sticks and our crutches. We would be the last to reach heaven; it would be full and we would look through the lepers' window, from outside, at the great and the good within. Jack would blow up his muscles and pretend to lift the pearly gates above his head; Edwin would get a bag of sweets from St Peter for telling silly jokes, and we would share them; Luther would dash around the perimeter looking for a place where we could all sneak in; clever Nosy Parker would thumb his pocket Bible and find an appropriate quotation which might sway St Peter's judgement; Vogel would blow his horn like Little Boy Blue and summon the lamb of god for Esmie to play with. Yes, we would be the last to arrive outside the gates of heaven, and we might be locked out with all the sinners and all the animals, but that would be fine because we had all of us had some experience of being punished at random, and since the gods or mankind liked to punish someone as an example to the others, it might as well be us. It was slightly better than being one of the chosen few inside, looking out at the damned peeking and staring in through the windows.

I said farewell to the old man and his holy grail, which was shining now thanks to a good clean. He came to the door with me and stood there, watching me leave his temple.

I decided to leave the road. I'd had enough of the ways of man; I veered onto the beach and made my way towards the fort at Dinas Dinlle, half-eaten by the sea like that fort on the other side of Wales at Portskewett. I had always wanted to go to Dinas Dinlle. There I could sit and look at Caer Arianrhod, the rock in the sea where the mythical Lleu had been mysteriously returned to his mother. She had cursed him, saying he would never have a name, nor a wife, nor his own weapons. The magician Gwydion had fashioned him a name and weapons, and a wife made from flowers, called Blodeuwedd. But she was unfaithful, and was transformed into an owl. Paddy had told me this story – his head was so mushy with romantic notions that he had once written an entire novel for a lover, and had burned it in front of her as soon as she had finished reading it, so that no-one but she would ever see it. She had thought him quite mad and had escaped with great alacrity.

I reached the great tumulus at Dinas Dinlle, a third of which is missing on the sea side as though the giant playing with his sea-mirror by Bardsey had got up suddenly and given it a great swipe with his boot, like an angry farmer sent mad by an infestation of moles. Here I welcomed the evening. I would not make Caernarfon that day, so I decided on a bed in Foryd Bay, for it looked likely to have a bird hide, which makes a good perch for travellers in the night. By now weary, but sublimely content as I neared the end of my journey, I entered the bay in a glow of reds and lambent yellows as the sun dipped into the ocean. As a child I had wondered if it fizzed and made the sea boil when it touched the water. The tide was out and the mudflats rippled away from me like the hide of a hippo emerging from the ooze. A curlew cried mournfully and I could see shellduck wandering like amnesiacs along the flats.

The bird hide was locked, so I gathered armfuls of dry grass and reeds, and made a bed for myself on a bank in a straggly copse overlooking the bay. I snuggled a shape for myself and lay there, looking at the shadows deepen in the water gulleys which spread like capillaries in the mud.

I phoned Waldo, and told him where I was.

'What the bloody hell are you doing there?'

I explained as briefly as I could. I think he understood.

'Come and join me for the last day,' I begged him. 'Get Paddy to drive your wagon back to the Blue Angel – surely he can stay sober for that long. I'd really like you to be with me. You've been with me all along, and you and Williams and Marek have made this possible. Have you learnt any more about the photo?'

'Yes.'

'Well?'

'No – it's my turn to keep you guessing. I'll tell you tomorrow.'

'Aw, come on Waldo...'

'It's no use. I want to be with you anyway, to see your face when I tell you. I know the ending before you do. Or do I? It's a nice feeling, my little friend, and I want to see you dance. Bye.'

And he was gone.

I looked at the celandines clustered in a yellow sheen around me in the grass and felt sorry for crushing some of them; they and the wood anemones are among my favourite flowers, for they herald the full glory of spring. The celandine seems brighter and fresher than its cousin the buttercup, which was once hung in bags around the necks of lunatics to cure them. But it would take more than a few buttercups to cure me of my own brand of madness.

The alfresco bed was a good idea. I slept like a baby that final night.

THE END OF A MISSION

I AWOKE with the dawn and lay there like a weasel, sniffing the air. A sea breeze ruffled me and a gust of mortality went right through me, coldly, and I felt, looking across the grey sea, that I had only a short time left; my ancestors were nearing me with their bronze vacuum cleaners, ready to suck me into their big bag of dusty history. As I lay there I heard someone dislodge pebbles on the shore. Once, I had lain waiting for death, for nights on end, and I had felt the force of death close to me, circling me slowly, waiting. I was not afraid of him; both of us waited for the other to make the first approach. Death, when I met him, was quite different to the death I had expected. He had appeared to me as a young man, very good-looking, sleek, well groomed, detached yet close, humorous, experienced, warm in a controlled way; death had behaved like one of those Italian-looking men you see in glossy magazines, sitting in a street café, smoking alone at a table, waiting for someone to charm. The smoke curls from their cigarette, slowly and beautifully, as they consider the finer points of art and philosophy; they are the ones who get the pretty girls because they never try.

I saw a figure appearing on my left, scrabbling along the shoreline scree, and it most certainly wasn't death. It was Waldo, I recognised his girth and his Neanderthal lurch from afar. He had someone with him. I waved and hallooed. They saw me and changed direction, rattling the stones and sending a covey of ducks winging away from the capillary creeks. And who was that man with him?

Sweet Jesus! It was Martin!

'Hello Waldo,' I said, staggering to my feet.

'Hello Martin,' I said, and my trousers fell down. I had undone them in my sleeping bag because the dancing bear in my pocket was cutting into my leg.

I looked ridiculous.

'Hello there,' replied Martin, studying my alabaster limbs. 'Don't know how you got round Wales with them,' he said, nodding at my legs. His own were brown and hairy and manly.

'You were lost in thought there,' said Waldo. 'Anything interesting?'

'I was thinking about death, actually.'

'I'm not surprised,' said Martin, still looking at my legs as I hiked up my trousers.

'Martin's going to join us for the last day,' said Waldo with a subversive wink.

'Oh,' I said abashed – I suspected that Waldo had used his cunning and wiles to scupper Martin's run for the finishing line. 'Why's that Martin? You'd have been there by now, nearly. Could have been the first to walk round Wales.'

I petered off rather lamely, because I felt like crying. I had so desperately wanted to be the first. There was no denying it.

'Actually,' said Waldo, sitting on a large boulder and rolling himself a cigarette, 'Martin was fascinated by your story and he wants to be one of your guests at the Blue Angel.'

'Why, you're welcome Martin,' I said. Secretly, I wondered how Waldo had pulled off this little coup.

'Sort of walk in together, you mean,' I quavered.

'That's fine with me,' said Martin. 'I'd love to be one of the twelve at your last supper. Waldo said it would be fine with you. He said I would make up the numbers, because you're one short.'

'That's right,' said Waldo, cutting in quickly. 'It's like this, isn't it,' he said, winking madly at me, 'we've got eleven at the moment, and twelve would make it a nice round number. Now let me see.' He stuffed his roll-up in his mouth and held his hands in front of him, to increase the dramatic effect, sticking his fingers in the air, one by one, as he spoke.

'We've got three healers – that's old Hotty with his gammy eye, Doctor Robert Jones with his big moustache, and Agnes Hunt with her crutch – seems to me the healers need more attention than the rest,' he quipped.

'Then we've got three walkers – let's see now – there's yourself,' he said, pointing to me, 'there's Dic Aberdaron and there's the minstrel, Roland.

Then there are three cripples – Edwin, Luther and Jack. That's because Julius is dead (he looked up at me quickly and made a sign for me to shut up), Vogel and Esmie we can't find, and Nosy Parker and his sister Angelica, well, unfortunately they're unable to attend. Indisposed, as it were...

'Now then, we need three *helpers*,' he said, accentuating the word, though he seemed to be scrabbling about a bit here –

'there's me, if I'm allowed (big wink at me), Paddy can stand in for Anwen Marek our American ambassador, that's if he can stand of course, and you Martin, I'd like you to stand in for our Tasmanian friend Dr Williams, who can't make it because he's too far away. That makes twelve. The Last Supper! Couldn't be better. Sorted!'

Waldo's voice crackled under the strain of his connivance, but it seemed as good a plan as any, so I joined in the conspiracy by pulling the dancing bear from my pocket and handing it to Martin, saying: 'There, you can nail that into the doorframe of the Blue Angel when we arrive, to mark the end of our journey. Whadya think?'

'That's great,' said Martin, who seemed genuinely grateful to be involved in all this nonsense.

'Well that's agreed then,' said I, labouring the point as usual.

Waldo went into headmaster mode and got me going, stuffing my sleeping bag into my rucksack and tidying up whilst I splashed some water on my face in a nearby burn.

'Time to go!'

We skirted the wide Foryd Bay in the early morning light, and I felt weightless, as though a pressure valve had been released steamily into the Foryd mists; we chatted and strolled pleasantly (sometimes one of us fell back a little to enjoy a private reverie, as walkers do). I thought of the great early actress Sarah Siddons walking through Wales with Ward's Strolling Players, on just such a morning as this, her ears ringing with last night's applause. A jenny wren darted across my path, chiding me angrily: and then my mind went to the Stephens Island wren, which had lived in peace for many millennia on a small green island off the coast of New Zealand. Without an enemy in the world, it had lost the ability to fly, which proved fatal: when a lighthouse was built on the island along came a lighthouse keeper, who took with him – for company – his cat Tibbles. The last Stephens Island wren disappeared down this (vastly experienced) feline gullet in 1894. Nature, red in tooth and claw...

As the rising sun warmed my body and flooded my soul, I caught up with the others to share my tale.

Waldo laughed and pointed at Fort Belan near the bay's mouth, built by the super-rich Sir George Assheton-Smith so that he could play soldiers. His family had plundered the slate of the Vaynol Estate, all 33,000 acres of it, and had lived opulently in a mansion on the banks of the Menai Straits, waited on by fourteen unmarried servants. I remembered that the very same Sir George had been in contact with a character mentioned in the Vogel Papers – the super-strong Margaret daughter of Evans, builder of boats and wrestler of men, who had thrown Sir George from her boat into a lake when he had pretended to make advances to her, supercilious young parvenu. That was the way to deal with them. I was about to say something along the lines of 'we've been milked long enough by those bloody leeches' when I remembered that Martin was English, so I buttoned my lip and made fair conversation with him about the flora and fauna around us; he turned out to be a bit of an expert (he would, wouldn't he?) and I mumbled 'yes' and 'no' as if I knew what he was talking about when he identified each flower and trotted out its Latin name like some bloody memory man let loose on me for the day. We spotted a little church in the field alongside us and we detoured to browse in its ancient curtilage. 'These little churches in the middle of nowhere are the gems of Wales, aren't they,' said Martin, and I could see Waldo miming the words and mincing about behind him. I looked down at a gravestone and studied it as though it were my own, hot about the cheeks with embarrassment at Waldo's antics.

I sat on the gravestone and picked my teeth with a long grass-stem.

'That's sweet vernal grass,' said Martin. 'It's responsible for the smell of new mown hay. Used for bonnet-making once...'

Waldo stood behind him, on a grave, holding a pretend boulder above his head.

'Waldo,' I almost shouted, jumping from the gravestone and stumbling painfully against a slate tomb, 'Waldo, did you get anywhere yesterday? Any news about the picture?'

Waldo did a mock stage entrance and produced a folded slip of paper from his pocket with an absurdly dramatic flourish. It was a letter.

'Come on, you can read it whilst we're walking,' said Waldo, who offered to take Martin's rucksack for a while (I think he was mocking me) and declared archly:

'Of course, common cottongrass used to be made into candle-wicks and is excellent as a *stuffing* for pillows and

233

mattresses.' Waldo emphasised the word *stuffing* and looked back at me with an idiotic look.

I opened the letter, which had become torn along the folds. It was typewritten, and some of the letters were half red and half black because the ribbon was worn. It was from Agnes Hunt to Robert Jones:

Dear Robert,

I shall expect you on Sunday, as usual, to operate. We have a busy schedule, so please leave the dogs at home, since the Factotum is tired of cleaning after them!

I wonder if you might provide your services for a few moments on the children's ward after completing your duties. One of the new girls, Esmie Falkirk, celebrates her birthday on the 29th of February, and since we do not have a leap year on our hands, I have devised a stratagem to give the child a treat on a date close to her birthday. I have arranged a celebration for the first of March, which is this Sunday, in the form of a fancy dress party for the children, as a special treat for Esmie. I have organised a number of competitions, and since Esmie is very bright, and clever with her hands, I am sure she will carry off most of the prizes. I would be most grateful if you could drop in at some point to present the children with their prizes and to help us sing Happy Birthday to the girl, who admires you greatly and holds your book on Thomas Pennant as a prized possession. Perhaps you will be able to spare a small prize to add to our haul – the little boy whom they all call Vogel is due to have his first op soon and I would like you to give him a little present, as per usual. Goody has a scheme which sounds very grandiose and I think it would benefit from your advice, since the travelling involved would be very hard on some of the younger ones.

Yours etc, Agnes Hunt.

'I told you so,' I called to Waldo as I struggled to catch up with them. I was breathless, and waved the letter at him. 'Told you.'

'OK clever clogs, you were right – it wasn't Christmas in the photo. I suppose we might have guessed something from the vase of daffodils on the table in the background,' he added dryly. And the presents at the end of Esmie's bed were all the prizes she'd won. It was all very plain now. And the teddy bear, Rupert, mentioned in the Bo Peep letters: was he the present which young Vogel received from Dr Jones that day so long ago? I was beginning to think so. Was receiving the teddy bear – such a small present, really – so momentous an event in the boy's life that it became the equivalent of a great treasure, equal to the fortune won by Mr Vogel in the Vogel Papers? My brain prodded this new information as I followed Waldo and Martin towards the open sea. Waldo was rambling in more ways than one: as we turned eastwards he was telling Martin about the vagaries of the Welsh language. The ever-brilliant Martin responded with a story about the Lokele people of the eastern Congo, who rely on tone to give different meanings to the same word or phrase. For instance, he said, *liala* meant *rubbish dump*, whilst *liAla* meant *fiancée*. Likewise, *aSOolaMBA boili* meant *I'm watching the riverbank*, whilst *aSOoLAMBA boIli* meant *I'm boiling my mother-in-law*.

'Fascinating, *absoLUTEly FAScinating*,' said Waldo with wafer-thin sarcasm. He turned to me and waved me on, urging me to catch up.

Caernarfon Castle, that magnificent badge of our subjection, loomed into view as we came alongside Abermenai Point.

Martin was ready with some more information; the bastard knew more about Wales than I did. Knew it like the back of his hand.

'This used to be a ferry point,' he confided in us. 'Many years ago the ferry sank twice in a short period of time and on both occasions everyone was drowned except for one man – amazingly, it was the same man who survived both accidents. Kinda lucky, don't you think?'

I felt left out, so I elbowed in with my ha'p'orth.

'Ferrymen were cruel sods,' I said, still out of breath – both of them were quicker than me, even though I'd walked a thousand miles. It really pissed me off. 'Yes, some bloke, English I think, was told by the ferry blokes that he could walk over from the island, but of course he couldn't, so they just waited for him to drown and then rowed out to strip his corpse. Think there was a court case.'

'Scottish.' Martin looked at me pityingly. 'He was Scottish.'

Here Waldo pretended to be a bagpipe-player and did a silly walk over the little swing bridge that crosses the river Seiont. We were in Caernarfon.

'Quick,' whispered Waldo whilst Martin was in the toilets, 'let's get him out of here before he starts. Can't stand the castle anyway, so let's grab some grub and get him onto the other side.

He's doing my head in.'

'What the hell was all that baloney about the last supper and twelve of us at the Blue Angel?' I asked.

'Had to bait the hook, or he'd be there by now. You deserve it. It means a lot to you. To the victor his spoils. It was only a little white lie anyway. You are having a party, after all. Paddy's already there blowing up the balloons. Well, maybe not. He's promised not to get legless before we arrive. Cheer up! It's a great day for us! Why the long face?'

'To tell you the truth Waldo, I'm not looking forward to it. You know what I'm like. There's a black hole waiting for me the minute I step out of that place and go back to normality. I just can't imagine how I'm going to come down slowly. It's scary.'

'Well think of something else then – do something else that's daft and meaningless,' said Waldo. 'Fly round Wales, or sail round it, or follow all the river to their sources – endless possibilities. Huge! You've only just started!'

Fair play to Waldo, he's a good mate.

'And there's more, we're coming to the end of this little play of ours, aren't we?'

He waved his arms around, pretending to be a ringmaster: 'Take your seats please, ladies and gentlemen, for the greatest show on earth (trumpet impression)...'

Martin came out of the toilet and looked at him.

'OK Martin?'

'OK'

'Sure?'

'Sure.'

'Positive?'

'Absolutely bloody positive,' said Martin. His face reddened.

'I thought we'd get some rolls and eat out of town,' said Waldo. 'Caernarfon's great and all that, but I'm just not in the mood for history. Stuffed with it. Could do with a good party.'

Martin was tensing up, I could tell. He was looking at us in a different way, and sat slightly apart, legs dangling over the wall as we rested on the quay. We watched the boats on the river, and a small crowd gathered as the bridge swung open for a party of fishermen. I could smell the gutted fish, and a few gulls harried the deck as the men eased into a berth.

'Hey Martin,' I said, 'you can go ahead of me if you like. I don't mind. It doesn't mean anything to me.' Liar.

'No, it's OK, we'll go in together,' he nearly whispered, 'anyway, I'm going to carry on right round, hope to do Britain. Want to join me?'

'Might do just that,' I lied again.

'You might get some more muscle in those chicken legs of yours if we do,' he added.

We bought rolls and moved on, but then we made a curious error, because I missed the cycle track on my map and we headed out of town on the main road, which was a big, big mistake because it's narrow and there's no pavement, a real death trap, and we had to walk Indian file on a hostile stretch of road with drivers glaring at us. We were mighty glad to turn off on the B road to Port Dinorwic, and walk along the Straits again. By now it was steaming hot and we were beginning to tire – road walking is twice as hard because the surface has no give, and stress levels rise because you're always on the lookout for loony drivers. We were all hot and bothered by the time we reached a little bird hide on the little-known National Trust reserve on the Vaynol Estate. We stopped to eat, and to rest. Walking around Wales hadn't been a bowl of cherries throughout – trudging through industrialised Newport and Cardiff had been boring at times, and unsightly caravan parks had dampened my spirit along the west coast.

I turned to Martin.

'What was the best part for you?'

He didn't take long.

'I really liked the Dyke, and the leg from Hay Bluff to Pandy was out of this world.'

'Yes, I think that was the best bit for me too.'

'Also the whole of Anglesey,' I said, 'especially the north. It felt really wild in places, like stepping back in time, and the wildlife up there was really good, better than anywhere I think.'

I enthused about the seals, and the gannets with their scintillating orange-buff heads plunging into the whipped sea on a blue-breezy day, and the porpoises in Bull Bay surfacing in the water in front of me suddenly and shockingly, like eels in a bucket. He waxed lyrical about meeting no-one for days at a time. Walking around Wales can somehow herd everyone into the middle, like a dog rounding sheep: people retreat and look at you, full of interest, wondering if you're going to bite them. Most are really kind. I'll never forget the welcome I had at the Prince of Wales in Kenfig. In a pub above a lost village in the sand dunes, where I slept that night with Port Talbot steelworks all lit up like a huge spaceship about to land, I had been feted and fussed by the locals, as travellers should be in any self-respecting country; it's a basic sign of culture, after all. News from afar. Strange tales. A chance to be magnanimous, generous. Personalities, and hopes and losses weighed up quickly. Everything in microcosm, speeded up; the journey from cradle to grave, humanity, deaths and entrances – all condensed into a play, a masque on a magnificent set, in which I, forever an understudy, had been the principal actor for just one performance. I had finally lodged my shaky fingerprint in the huge index of humanity; I had done something which was just slightly out of the ordinary. I had built a small and invisible monument to my passing.

A fly buzzed and droned around us in the hide. We were quiet, happy. A bunch of military types were being taught to sail in cockleshell dinghies on the water in front of us. We could hear someone barking orders and screaming when anyone made a mistake. That was all over for me. I would never obey orders again.

'Coming then?' Waldo stirred slowly. I could see he fancied a pint and a nice nap.

'Tell you what, I said, let's go over the two bridges. It'll be slightly more interesting.' They agreed.

Crossing the Britannia Bridge was no fun, since it's a main arterial road now. The expressway through the region has changed it for ever, opening it up and making the hinterland much more accessible. It has made North Wales more of a playground than ever, a lawn for middle England to party on during sunny days. No-one can blame them for coming; our country is beautiful. And of course there are benefits. But it has sounded the death knell of old Wales. I have seen its passing. Somehow we have moved from medieval times to modern very quickly, in my lifetime. Never mind. I know where to find Wales still, in her secret bowers.

We headed jauntily towards the suspension bridge with the Swellies – a dangerous channel for sailors – writhing below us. We could see Bangor Pier: the end, a little beyond, was nearly in sight. We paused in a lay-by, looking at the water between us and the mainland.

Waldo fetched another letter from his pocket and handed it to me. This one was hand-written. It was from Robert Jones to Agnes Hunt. It had been written in ink; I could smell its pungent power on the page. Communication was different then too – the medium, after all, is the message. Ink is for courtesy, dignity and wit.

Dear Agnes,

Splendid news – we have made excellent progress with the frame which will treat Perthes children. I have devised soft leather thongs to immobilise the upper leg; they will cause discomfort at first, and we can expect some tears when the little ones are first strapped down, but they will get used to it. We shall see what results we get when we try the prototype.

Your party was an excellent idea and Esmie had a wonderful time, well done. I'm glad that my 'teddy' was appreciated, no doubt the Vogel boy will like it, since he will need a comforter in the months to come – as you suggested, after presenting it to him I broke the news that he will be operated on after the proposed holiday, though I fear I can make only minor alterations; he will be bed-bound for quite a while. The teddy bear seemed to soften the blow.

Finally, Goody's plan seems an excellent one. By all means take your little protégés on holiday, I think London is within range providing you go by charabanc rather than rail. I think the Board of Education will allocate funds if I have a word with Miss Kenyon. I would suggest, however, that you keep sightseeing to a minimum, and spend as much time as possible in the parks – Kew Gardens might be an excellent choice. Since you are so good at arranging competitions, might I suggest that the holiday is couched as another 'prize' since we cannot afford to let the children believe that this is going to be a regular event. Incidentally, you and your merry band might like to call at my home, which as you know is just inside the border here in Wales, on your return, for a celebratory tea. I should consider it a great honour. The children can play in the garden, weather permitting, or we can go in the greenhouse if it rains.

I will see you on Sunday, as usual.

Fondest regards etc., Jones.

I re-read the letter and handed it back to Waldo, who made a great show of folding it up again and putting it back in his pocket, as though he were a great illusionist who was mesmerising me with subtle magic.

He arched his eyebrows and said: 'Nearly there, aren't we? I think we can work out what happened. We all understand now, don't we?'

I walked on.

'I'm still rather foggy, actually, Waldo.'

I noticed that Martin had made a start, so we ran after him. We couldn't let him get away now. Waldo would sit on him, I knew, rather than let him beat me to the Blue Angel. I hoped the party wouldn't be a flop. I wanted friends to be there to make a fuss of me and take photographs so that I could look at them years later. I would frame a big picture of me arriving and hang it above the bears on my mantelpiece.

'Got it?' asked Waldo.

'No. A bit, but not all. I understand part of it. Vogel in the Vogel Papers won a large house with a pagoda and a fortune.'

'It's all simple, really,' said Waldo, who was running out of patience.

'Agnes Hunt arranged a holiday for the children in London, and she arranged a 'competition' which the children thought they'd won. Vogel was given the traditional gift for a child about to be operated on, a teddy bear, because he needed all the good news he could get – he was about to be tied down to a metal frame for a while. It doesn't take a genius to realise that a child tied down to a frame for months on end is going to suffer. He's going to have pain. He's going to have indignity, with bedpans and bottles and bed-baths and nurses looking at his willie. He's going to develop physical weaknesses – his muscles will waste through lack of use and his stomach will blow up like a famine baby. He's going to have a lifelong phobia about being held down or restricted. It says so in his notes. He will suffer extreme claustrophobia and he will always want doors to be open. He will not want to sit in the middle row in the cinema, he will want to sit in the end seat so that he can walk out whenever he wants. He will feel sick and panicky if he feels he can't get up and walk away from any situation. He'll need more freedom than the average person.'

'I understand that Waldo.'

'I think you understand it very well,' he replied. 'It's going to be a pretty traumatic experience, isn't it?'

'Sounds bloody awful, if you put it like that,' I replied.

'I'll explain a bit more,' said Waldo. 'Vogel the child was made to believe that his ward had won a great prize, which was a trip to London. They saw great sights. They went to Kew Gardens, which has one of the most famous pagodas in Britain. On the way back they called at Robert Jones's home and had tea in the garden. Do you see it now? The whole experience fused together in Vogel's childish mind, and that is what we read about in the Vogel Papers. Got it now?'

I *had* got it.

We had to lunge forward again to catch Martin. Slimy little bugger was trying to slip away.

My legs were beginning to feel like lead as we walked across the Menai suspension bridge.

'Know why this was built so high above the water?' asked Waldo.

Martin knew.

'Yep. To let sailing ships pass underneath.'

'Right as usual,' said Waldo sarcastically. 'Do you know why Mr Vogel also won a croft on an island and a few fields overlooking the sea, Martin? Do you know the bloody answer to everything?'

'No, don't know the answer to that one,' said Martin, who had detected a hint of mania in Waldo's voice and was looking at the ground as hard as he could.

'Because he thought he was one of the Bonesetters of Anglesey, that's bloody well why,' said Waldo, getting too close to him by far. 'For some reason he thought he was one of those two boys washed ashore on a raft and rescued by Dannie Lukie – the boy who vanished from the records. Do you understand that? Do you get the sodding irony?'

I had never seen Waldo like this.

'Christ, I get it now,' I said, jump-starting my ten-ton legs into action and leaping into the lead. 'The quest round the island, I get it now – he was searching for his past, for his twin brother...'

The Vogel Papers made sense, at last. But what was all that stuff about second hand clothes and Vogel's legendary meanness? I asked Waldo.

'Dunno,' he answered in a tired voice. 'Perhaps he was from a poor family who depended on hand-me-downs – that was normal then, wasn't it?'

'Or perhaps the Vogel Papers had something else in mind – remember, the two little boys had no clothes when they landed in

Wales, and they had to be dressed in other children's clothes – strange clothes – after they'd been saved,' I said.

'I don't know,' said Waldo. 'I don't suppose we'll ever know.'

We walked onwards in silence. We had made some sense of the Vogel Papers, and it felt good. We had no definite proof, it was true, but we had a likely scenario, and that was good enough for me.

'We're nearly there now Martin,' I said with false jollity in my voice. 'Got the dancing bear ready?'

'I'll find a stone to knock it in,' said Waldo. He found a handy chunk of granite on the verge and kept it in his hand. Martin looked as though he got the message.

I could see the Blue Angel, down by the docks, and its door was open. There were people outside with glasses in their hands. They had their tops off and they wallowed on the walls like albino seals on a stony promontory. I could see Paternoster Hill climbing away from them. There was an old camper van parked half way up. I wondered if the lights were still left on at night.

'So, Waldo, tell me this,' I said as we walked down towards the pub. Someone had seen us. It was Paddy. He waved, and fell backwards into the doorway. I could see his legs wiggling, pathetically and slowly, like a near-dead fly.

'What was Vogel looking for then?'

I looked at Waldo, who was looking at Martin.

'OK Martin,' he said, and he stepped in front of him. 'That'll do for now. No hard feelings or anything. Nothing personal. It's quite simple. I know what this means to my friend. I couldn't stand it if he was beaten. I know it's wrong of me. But there you are, the English have won every race so far. I think we could do with a little victory. You can wait here for a few minutes while we go on ahead. There's something I want to tell him before we get there. We'll wait for you in the doorway, and you can walk in together. That's only fair, isn't it? Here's the stone. You can do the business with the bear.' Waldo looked at me. 'Come on.'

Faced with this mountain of a man, Martin sat down on the verge, sulkily.

'The end is like this,' he said to me, and he put his arm around me as we walked the final hundred yards.

'Mr Vogel wasn't searching for something important or valuable.'

'I understand,' I said.

'He was looking for something that had been very important to him once.'

'What was that?'

'Do you remember that teddy bear, the one which was given to him by Doctor Robert Jones?'

'Yes, I remember it very well.'

'It became more than a teddy bear to him. It became his best friend during that very long time he spent in bed. It was his mother. His father. His brother. His pillow. His pet. His confidante. His handkerchief when he cried. He held it. He smelled it. He kissed it goodnight. It comforted him. It stayed with him all those endless nights when he was alone in a bed many miles away from his parents. That bear gave him all the love that was missing from his life.'

'Yes. I understand that.'

'Then came the day to leave hospital. There's a cryptic note in his records, which says that Vogel was extremely upset when he left, not because he was going home, but because of a decision by his father.'

'Yes?'

Waldo stopped me and pulled me round so that I was looking at him.

I could hear people shouting and cheering. I could see arms waving through the blur of my tears.

'The father,' said Waldo, 'went to get Vogel from hospital. And as they left he made the boy leave his teddy bear on the ward for the other children. He thought he was doing the right thing. He thought the other children would appreciate the teddy. But he was taking away from his son the only thing that was valuable to him.'

'Yes?'

I was blubbering, almost. Martin appeared like a tadpole in the pond that was my left eye. Someone with a camera appeared in the pond that was my right eye. And then a sudden gust of recognition swept through me. No, surely not. Could it be? It was! The person behind the camera, smiling her lovely wide smile, was Emmeline. I was overjoyed; I was so excited I trembled, my body quaked.

'Vogel never forgave his father. Of course, there was nothing he could do about it. The teddy was taken from him and left on the ward. He went home. Years later, when he saw for the first time how certain wrongs, however small, can be as important to a child as great calamities, he decided to search for the bear. He created a fantasy about it. He wasn't well.'

Waldo gave me a squeeze and a great big brotherly smile. I turned, and walked towards my friends. There was a banner over the door, saying *Congratulations*, and another over the whole street saying *Welcome Home*.

With his arm around me, Waldo guided me towards the door.

'The bear – what happened to the bear?' I asked.

Waldo hugged me extra hard.

'We'll find the bear. I'm sure of that. We'll find the bear.'

Martin walked up to us, and we watched him hammer in the dancing bear. It gleamed against the black of the lintel. There was a hush.

I turned round and smiled at everyone, waved.

Then I walked in through the door of the Blue Angel.

PART THREE

And at the end of the seventh year they set out for the island of Gwales, where there was a fair royal palace, with a great hall, overlooking the sea at Pembrokeshire.

They went into the hall, and two doors were open, but the third, facing Cornwall, was closed. Manawydan said: 'That door, yonder, we must not open.'

They spent the night there and they were joyful. They could remember nothing of the sorrows they had seen with their own eyes, or had suffered themselves, and they remembered nothing of all the sorrow in the world.

And in that place they were eighty years, and they were unaware of having spent a time more joyous and delightful.

Every day was just as perfect, and none of them looked any older...

Then, one day, Heilyn son of Gwyn said: 'Shame on me if I do not open that door to see if what is said about it is true.'

He opened the door and looked on Cornwall and the Bristol Channel, and when he did so they all became conscious of every loss they had sustained, and of every kinsman and friend they had missed, and of every ill that had befallen them...

And from that moment they could not rest.

Branwen, daughter of Llyr, *The Mabinogi*

THE FIRST STEP

AS SOON as one door closes another opens.

That's what the old people say, isn't it?

Just when you think you've reached a dead end, with nowhere else to go, something always seems to happen.

That's the way it was with me that afternoon. It was a dull day, grey, with occasional leaks from a sky bulging with water, an old man's body bloated with oedema.

Tied to my post, and untroubled by customers – who grow fewer by the day – my mind had wandered abroad, to visit an old friend of mine. He had strapped a knapsack to his back when we were still young, waved farewell, and tramped all the way to Istanbul, crossing Europe as Hitler came to power. His name is Patrick Leigh Fermor, and he lives in Greece now. You may have heard of him.

It was then, in my mind's eye, as Patrick Leigh Fermor and I opened Rabbi Loew's door in Prague to see the rabbi's famous man of clay, the golem, being brought to life with words fed into his mouth on slips of paper, that my own door opened suddenly and in lurched a wet and bedraggled thing, a dripping homunculus come to life.

I'd given up all hope of finding Mr Vogel, in fact I'd pretty well forgotten about him. And to explain how and why he arrived in my shop, in a swaying, gasping moment of alarum and confusion, I must take you back to the very beginning of our tale.

I need to mop up a bit, if you'll pardon my little joke, since Mr Vogel left a sluggish spoor all along the floor as he struggled towards me, before falling into the seat alongside my desk. I'll leave him there for a few minutes, rasping bronchitically, and looking around him dazedly, whilst I swab the decks.

I introduced our story, the story of Mr Vogel, by telling you about the scribblings of an old bar-tender and dogsbody at the Blue Angel, a tavern in the old docklands.

As I told you, nowadays it is an antiquarian bookshop, the very shop I stand in now as I mop the floor – as that old barman must have done too – in the wan light of a small desk-lamp, with the shadows of books rising in jumbled towers all around me, teetering skyscrapers; no, more like Tryfan and Glyder Fach stacked in granite cobs on either side of me in a white spring mist below Bristly Ridge.

I told you, right at the beginning, about a small badge or token, showing a dancing bear, nailed to the black oak lintel over the doorway. It is there still.

I told you that I had read a cheaply printed version of the Vogel Papers when I was recovering at the local sanatorium.

I had become intrigued, and one evening, shortly after leaving hospital, I had walked to the Blue Angel bookshop and stood in the shadow of its doorway. A thunder shower had broken in a crackling explosion which rolled in the hills above the town; the air had smelt of sulphur, sadness, wet earth and change.

And then nothing, simply nothing, had happened.

Some of you, the ones with long memories, the pedants, the finicky and the querulous, will put this book down now and mutter awhile, saying something like: hang about, haven't we been dragged the whole way around Wales, lugged along an ill-lit and poorly-signposted path through a deranged mind, looking for a figment of a man called Mr Vogel who had an invalid carriage, who left the lights on every night so that people would knock on his door, who had his own little bridge of sighs to the Blue Angel, who mysteriously won a fortune, and who went on a quest around an island? Didn't we traipse across three continents behind this wanderlust-infected fool, didn't we travel through time to find a hopeless little alcoholic with dandruff and bent legs?

And I would understand, completely, if you wanted to know exactly who it was that slept in the church porch at Tallarn Green and watched the bats and the shooting stars, walked along Hell's Mouth like a fly along a saucer rim, and had his toes sucked by the Rhymney River Mud-Monster.

My answer to you is – wait: wait awhile, and you will understand. If your own life is simple then lucky you; we have a rather tangled skein here, and I'm trying very, very hard to unravel it.

With your permission, I will continue.

When I recovered from my operation I sought a job, and fate, like a pedagogue, led me to the Blue Angel bookshop. A pedagogue was a slave who led children to school in ancient Rome: that's what my work does to me – I am enslaved by books; I am trapped among a restless and jostling crowd of words trying to break through the book-covers, covers which restrain a mob of sentences like baton-wielding policemen at a protest rally. Each of us has his own chains; I too have my fetters, but I have journeyed in other people's fables – on foot, on ships, on trains, on clouds – to release me from my deskbound enthralment.

This is the truth for you – the absolute truth.

I had spotted an advert in the local newspaper, *The Daily Informer*, seeking a bookshop attendant for the Blue Angel, and because I am supple in the mother tongue, and knowledgeable about the history, fauna and flora of the region, I got the job.

I needn't tell you the consequences: here I am, within its ancient walls, dreaming daily of the scenes depicted in the Vogel Papers, when it was an inn. Business is poor. I have too much time to dust the tomes and to read pages at random; if it's a love story I'm adulterous, sneaking a few stolen moments with one of the lovers, or if it's a travelogue I become a pilgrim, enjoying conversations with people I meet on cliff tops. If plots have got dogs I bark at the moon, if they've got bears I eat honey and roar. With sanyassins I talk in tongues in the shade of the banyan trees, and when my eyes gleam white in the night I tremble and groan: I am the incubus who haunts your midnight shadows.

The man who wobbled into my bookshop was confused, and he looked ill. I realised, immediately, who he was. I succoured him; showed compassion, listened to his twisted and convoluted story. Even then, on the first day, the footings of friendship were laid in our muddy trench. I began to understand him; I began to comprehend the forces driving this frail little man. Friendship, in its early moments, relies heavily on intuition, and I knew, straight away, that Mr Vogel had certain dimensions, rooms in his mansion – which I wanted to explore. In time I came to realise that Mr Vogel's life was an endless corridor onto which thousands of doors opened, each chamber jammed to the ceiling with letters, postcards, journals, diaries, keepsakes, mementoes and other desiderata, all those little things which give us pleasure.

Certain dreams of his, which he made known to me during our early association (little knowing, then, that I would be like a father to him eventually) revealed that he had no real grasp on reality. It seemed as if he were in a completely different world to mine; indeed, by the end I hardly knew what had actually happened and what had been imagined. As an example I will tell you the first nightmare he recounted to me:

> I was directed, in my dream, to a bookshop near the old docks. It was
> a Wednesday – February the twenty-eighth according to a calendar on
> the wall; this had an eerie and supernatural significance. The date
> glowed on the page. The shadows swirled around me and the books
> were alive, moving, clamouring for my attention. In front of me I saw
> an unwritten scene from *Great Expectations*: in the corner Miss
> Havisham stood by her husband, and their peculiar offspring sat
> behind the Blue Angel counter, cobweb-garbed. Two book dealers were
> rifling the shelves like cannibals picking their teeth: one was called Billy
> Silverfish, the other Dryfeld. They whispered a great conspiracy in my
> ear. I was impelled to get rid of them. My ruse was perfect: I took them
> to the American section and persuaded them to orchestrate one last
> concerted hunt for the great white whale Moby Dick; I offered them
> Queequeg, the novel's massive tattooed savage, alive again as a helper,
> then directed the three of them to Moel-y-Gaer fort near Mold, from
> where a ley line would take them straight to Hay-on-Wye. I told them
> a distressed author was searching for them, needing them in another
> book. By now a tempest heaved the street outside. A great oak tree with
> an eagle in it threshed and cracked behind the shop; various buildings
> had sunk or were sinking, their keels bubbling downwards into the
> void, all except one shop, a liquor store bolted to the pavement, yellow
> light fanning perfectly outwards, lamping the dismal night...

Naturally, when I realised he was confused as to *whom* he was
and *where* he was, I called the authorities, since we all need, occasionally at least, to know who we are and where we're going. What
else could I do? It's easy to blame me now, with hindsight, isn't
it? Was I supposed to let him sit there for ever, looking at me
mulishly, talking himself into Bedlam, driving away the few
customers who ventured in?

Mr Vogel, the man who stumbled into the Blue Angel bookshop, thought he'd come to the end of a glorious quest, a
magnificent walk around the whole of our country, Wales, fairest
of all lands, Kohinoor in the encircling diadem of Britain's shoreline. Upon my instigation, and perhaps I regret it now, he was
taken to a place of safety. Soon enough he saw it as a prison.

I went to see him nearly every evening, and our friendship
began – I say friendship because I am unsure which word to use:
Liaison? Fellowship? Comradeship? Brotherhood?

Since he had wandered into my domain like a lamb in a

storm, I felt partly responsible for him, rather like someone who has taken an injured animal, found by the roadside, to the RSPCA; I wanted to know why he had wandered away from the herd, and how he was faring. In dribs and drabs, he told me his entire story – the truth, the whole truth, and nothing but. I decided to write it all down.

Now there was one very interesting thing about Mr Vogel. For although he wanted his story to be told truthfully, he also wanted it told *his* way.

He would grasp my arm with his bent little hand as I sat by his bedside and say:

'For God's sake Gwydion, tell it like a story-teller. Don't make me sound ordinary. Make it all sound interesting. I want people to like it, to read it to the last word, and to smile when they close the last page. Who cares if there's a slight blur here or there? Accuracy never filled a sack in the Celtic granary, we all know that. Give it some verve, some pizzazz. Will you do that for me, Gwydion?'

I asked him exactly what he meant, and he sighed, then thought for some time.

'Look at this room now,' he said, sweeping his withered paw around the place.

There was something quite appealing about him: the way he looked at you; because his back was so bent, and he was so hunched over, he always seemed as if he were peering over non-existent glasses, asking everyone, *Are You Sure?*

'You've read plenty of books – give it atmosphere, tell it how people really see it but can't describe it. Don't tell any lies. Tell them how I feel inside, not how I look or act.'

For days, as I tended my flock of books, I pondered how I could paint another man's grass greener. I made a fumbled effort, threw it away, then tried again.

I could write it black and biblical. Start every sentence I would with a verb.

'No,' said Mr Vogel, the sound of blood bubbling in the back of his throat.

'Only joking,' I said in a soothing voice. 'I'm only teasing you Mr Vogel. I'm not going to throw in any choirs or chapels or boyos or butties, honest.'

'Thank God for that,' he growled, 'I thought you were going

to give me hymns and rain.'

I told him my story also, accidentally. It was padding; I threw him sprats to catch a mackerel. I gave him my own scraps as I tried to tease information from him. He was sharper than I thought. He noticed things, clung to throwaway lines and cobbled together a crude overview of my life. He realised that I, too, was addicted to something, as we all are, in one way or another...

Finally, I found a style which invoked the quale of Mr Vogel's life rather than its every nut and bolt. He liked it.

'That's it,' he said with a flamboyant grin. 'I want you to take the attar, the essence, and create a new flower from it. That budding, unfolding, will be the story of my life.'

I thought of the tormentil, so common in the uplands of Wales – so unremarkable, inconspicuous almost; tiny and yellow, it was a member of the rose family, yet it was so much more delicate and subtle than its showy domestic cousin. That was his message: create a lovely mountain blossom from the most slender of fragrances, the essence of Mr Vogel, not his crippled and crushed human form.

My next move was audacious by any standards. After preparing myself carefully: ripping my clothes, lathering my hair into a bouffant frenzy, blacking my teeth and rubbing grime into my pores, I feigned madness by running into the street and flinging my arms around the neck of a passing horse, talking wildly about the Antichrist; to seal matters I told the horse repeatedly that I loved it and wished to marry it. This had the desired effect and within the hour I was sitting next to Mr Vogel in the institution, taking care to utter regular protestations of love for my horse. I expected the staff to be surprised by my sudden descent into madness, but they thought nothing of it: as one of them said to me, most of us have at least one bout of mania in our lives. That night I slept soundly, waking at dawn to a troubled vision of Caligula steering a seventeen-hand stallion past my window with Nietzsche behind him, sleeping, his arms looped fondly around Caligula's waist. Perhaps I was the mad one, not Mr Vogel.

It was still peaceful when I awoke from my first night's sleep at the institution. I walked through to the day room where I sat silently, watching the weak early sunshine quicksilvering the windows. Most of the patients were still asleep, and the only sound I could hear was a soft shuffle coming from a pair of moth-eaten slippers in the shape of two furry little animals with beady little eyes staring at me. They belonged to Sylvia, a little woman of indeterminate age and mixed race – nobody could deny that she was very mixed up – who was mousing up and down the corridor, collecting small fragments of litter and carpet fluff, and putting it all in a battered and bulging envelope. She would send it to Downing Street later that morning, as more proof that unseen forces were about to invade the world. Sylvia asked everyone she met to take her to Downing Street, but no-one ever took her there. She whispered the *Nunc Dimittis* to herself in a quiet rustle as she hoovered the corridor for madness. Myrddin, the new schizophrenic, was beginning to bang about in his room, so trouble was brewing.

A young and very pretty nurse whom I came to know as Debbie had just come on duty; she nestled into her chair in the staff station, cradling a mug of coffee, still blushing with a soft radioactive glow after a night of flooded sexuality, and very tired in a tingly sort of way.

Donovan, her lover of three nights, sat opposite her, looking like a young steer who had cleared a fence and found himself in the Elysian Fields among a thousand young and attractive heifers. She nestled a foot in his crotch and gave him a gentle nudge.

'Tired?'

He grinned comically and lolled his tongue out. 'Fancy a quickie in the linen room?'

'Don't be ridiculous,' she said, thinking about it seriously for a moment.

'Good God,' said Mr Vogel when I showed him my notes, 'it's good, very good. Is that what life is like, really? Sounds extremely realistic, actually, but why the canoodling, for heaven's sake – are you a sex maniac or something?'

'Look at it this way,' I said to him as the blood returned to his face, 'you've had none in your own life, as far as I can make out, so we need to make this story real for the real people out there who really do have sex.'

He mused over this, and replied:

'Well just go easy on it, that's all, I don't want to die of shame before we've even started,' and he added smartly: 'Welsh people didn't get where they are today by having sex all over the place.' I think he was joking, though he had a very straight delivery. I realised, eventually, that the workings of his inner mind were far more complicated than was apparent to those around him.

'OK, go on,' he continued, waving his hand at me regally.

The breakfast rattled in on a trolley. Porridge in a big aluminium canister and corn flakes. On Sundays the patients helped them-selves when they rose. No matter how daft they were, I noticed, they always managed to feed themselves, the ones who wanted food. Many didn't. Many were there in body alone.

Sylvia knocked on the door of the staff station and gesticu-lated. She wanted a fag. Donovan gave her one and she shuffled through to the dayroom where two silent figures were waiting for a staff member to put the cable back on the television – it was removed every night in case someone used it to hang them-selves, though the staff mumbled that it was something to do with lightning.

'Got a new one,' said Debbie. She looked at a fresh folder.

'Found agitated, kissing a horse, outside that old bookshop near the docks. Wasn't that lame fellah Mr Vogel found there too? Is there something about the place?'

Both men had been disorientated and angry, she said.

Donovan looked out at the dayroom. In the corner, by the almost empty book-case which held, inexplicably, part of a German guide book to Wales which had been torn in half, the lame patient had laboriously dragged twelve chairs into a circle.

He sat, now, in one of them, looking at the room around him. The room had a very distinct smell, a smell he had never encoun-tered before. It frightened him slightly. Mr Vogel felt very lonely. The sounds were different. People walked differently. They didn't talk like other people.

Mr Vogel stopped me by tapping on my sleeve.

'Lovely touch,' he beamed, 'lovely – the twelve chairs, they're for the twelve people invited as guests to the Blue Angel at the end of the great walk around Wales, right?'

'Of course,' I said, proud of my ingeniousness.

'But the German guide book?' He frowned. 'What's that about? Needless detail, surely?'

'Well actually, no. I thought I'd work in a reference to Julius, that little German boy you told me about – you know, the one who followed Esmie Falkirk around the hospital like a puppy and died of diphtheria.'

'Of course,' he said, 'poor little Julius. He was in the bed next to me for a while at Gobowen. Poor little mite, with those big blue eyes, and his parents weren't allowed to see him, must have been a nightmare. We teased him too, we did Nazi salutes and made little moustaches with our fingers. Children are so cruel, don't you think? Even crippled children, we were also cruel you know. Little fleas have little fleas upon their backs and so *ad infinitum...* I'm ashamed to be human, sometimes.'

'Don't get maudlin, for God's sake,' I said to him.

'All right,' he gestured approvingly, 'that'll do for today. I'm still a bit weak you know. Need some sleep now.' He closed his eyes, and went to sleep immediately, like a child.

When I saw him the next day Mr Vogel was just full of himself. I sat by him, and noticed that he had a glob of jam in the corner of his mouth, and a pile of toast crumbs in his pullover folds. He also had a big pile of Calypso orange cartons by his side; he drank them steadily, and with relish, at regular intervals.

'Come to the window,' he urged me, grasping my arm a little too firmly, since he doesn't realise what a very strong grip he has after years of handling crutches and sticks; our deficiencies, so often, are compensated for in other ways, sometimes marvellously.

'Look,' he said, indicating the scene below. The infirmary is on a hill, overlooking a plain, and the view is quite spectacular; we could see activity everywhere, with people whizzing to and fro, and lorries and cars zooming hither and thither at crazy speeds – but behind it all, behind all this frenetic human activity, we could see the earth, the soil, the rocks, the grass, the graceful trees, the crooked little rivers, and the faraway mountains of Wales, blue and misty, filling us both with longing.

'Lovely, eh?' said Mr Vogel. We stood and watched, until he grew tired. Below us, in one of the oaks, we could see a treecreeper hoovering the bole for insects. Another bird, much larger – a buzzard perhaps – nestled in the upper branches.

'Got any further?' he asked me when we sat down.

'Got any further? How can I get any further if I don't know what happens next? I can't just make it up you know. I seem to remember that this is your story as well as mine, Mr Vogel my man, so I think you'd better tell me some more, don't you?'

And that's the way we did it: every evening I would listen to him, and the next afternoon I would read out what I'd written. It wasn't all plain sailing, mind you: we were held up for days at a time whilst he nit-picked about my version, or remembered something else which he wanted to include, or corrected inaccuracies. He was a pretty hard task-master, actually. But I enjoyed it. It gave me a purpose in life, I suppose.

Like Don Quixote and Sancho Panza we needed one another for our own reasons: he wanted his story told, and I wanted to occupy my hours, to ward off the phantoms. We moved on with the story, and this is how it developed:

Donovan studied the lame man. An odd-looking fellow. He had green eyes and a thin residue of red hair plastered onto his waxy scalp. He wore a faded purple pullover with a hole in it, and baggy black trousers. Even at this distance Donovan could see a halo of white around the man's collar – he obviously had terrible dandruff.

'When's this Vogel character being seen?' asked Donovan, flicking through the night report.

'He's first on the list,' said Debbie. 'One of the general doctors will do a physical later. Dr Jackson will see him at twelve tomorrow. We should have the blood tests back by then. They had a hell of a job getting blood from him. He wasn't very co-operative.'

A chair came sailing out of the breakfast room. Donovan sighed and went to sort it out. It was going to be a long shift. As he went through the door his pager went and he broke into a run. Trouble on another ward. The chair-thrower would have to wait.

'Why all the detail?' asked Mr Vogel, irritably. 'Can't you get on with my story?'

'Actually, it's my story now as well,' I answered huffily. 'I've always wanted to know what it's like in a funny farm.'

Mr Vogel looked round, as if he was seeing the place for the first time.

'You mean I'm in a mental hospital?'

'They're called psychiatric units now, and you're here just for a while because they need to assess you. Come on now, you'll soon be out.'

'You mean I can't walk out of here right now?

'Not just yet.'

'Christ, I thought I'd just walked to freedom.'

'You have Mr Vogel, you have. By the time we finish this story you'll be as free as a bird, don't worry. We're just unlocking the last few doors. Understand?'

He was mollified for now. I continued his story.

By the time a doctor arrived from the general hospital, stethoscope trailing from his pocket, there were three sitting in the circle of twelve chairs. Debbie pointed to the one in the middle.

'He's the one.'

They looked at him. He seemed to be talking to his new companions. Sylvia the Hoover sat by his side, head upturned, like Mary Magdalene looking at Christ in a Florentine altarpiece. This was particularly striking because above her head there was a depiction of Christ, mawkishly Catholic, which had faded and turned almost blue in the sunlight.

On Mr Vogel's other side a man with a huge walrus moustache sat slumped in his chair. They looked like friends lounging about, talking and laughing softly in the shade.

Mrs Williams stood looking out of the window, towards the island. She was thinking about her children, when they were small, playing on banks of daffodils and cowslips and wild garlic in the wood behind her old home on the hill. They had all gone, visiting briefly on wet Sundays with their cheap flowers from motorway service stations, and their fall-and-cry children. She wished them all away; she felt as if she was being pulled downwards into a vortex of guilt; she shied away from their mental and physical anorexia, the famine of their childhoods. Her husband had been a wastrel and a fool, but she had put up with him; not until the children were grown up did she find out what he had done to them. She felt sick to her core. What a terrible waste; what a terrible mistake she had made.

Sunday morning ground on, and everyone was beginning to avoid Peter, whose sole mission was to go round in a continuous circle greeting everyone and shaking their hand; this became wearisome after a dozen or so times.

Mr Vogel was talking to the man with the walrus moustache.

'Absolutely amazing,' he was saying, 'I thought I was in the middle of a war. Lovely day, spring in the air, and I was walking – do a lot of walking, you know, in fact I've walked right round Wales, first one to do it actually – I was walking along the Caldicot Levels – that's on the coast between Chepstow and Newport – when gunfire broke out right by me, just over the hedge. Threw myself to the ground – I thought I was being shot at. Guns going off everywhere, *drrrrrrrrr* [he tried to make the noise of a machine gun], hellish loud, I know what it's like now to be in a war – I thought I was going to be shot to pieces.'

The walrus man nodded, pretending to listen. He looked wise and professorial, but his eyes were blank.

'Anyway, turns out I'm in the middle of an army firing range, missed the red flags warning people. There was a big bank of earth between me and the soldiers. But it certainly had me worried. Then I walked up to a checkpoint and there were two young Ghurkhas standing around, just kids really, and I shook hands with them and talked for a few seconds, but their English was very poor, and they certainly couldn't speak Welsh. Big smiles though, then they told me to walk through the fields, right round this shooting range. They're all over the place down there – got to be careful where you go. Thought I was a dead un!'

Mr Vogel fell silent, but only for a few seconds. Then he jerked back to life.

'Reminds me of the time I was in Paraguay, actually. Friend of mine, police inspector, was bathing in one of the rivers, not a care in the world, when out of the blue he was attacked by a shoal of piranhas – took him completely by surprise. Anyway, these piranhas, nasty little buggers, chewed him in such an unfortunate place, if you know what I mean, that he immediately swam to where his clothes were on the shore, got his gun out and shot himself through the head. Man's man and all that. Couldn't face the shame. Not a very nice ending at all.'

The walrus man nodded sagely.

The doctor sat in the staff station, an empty chair between him and the rest of the staff. They rarely spoke to each other, the medics and the nurses, and when they did so it was in a tersely professional way. Protocol hasn't changed much since Hattie Jacques swept around the wards behind James Robertson Justice in the *Carry On* films.

'I've examined the lame man,' he said to Debbie and Donovan. He was a Muslim, and could smell last night's alcohol exuding from their skin.

'Rather odd chap, I think. Do we know who he is?'

'No, he's not talking normally,' Debbie answered. 'He seems to be reciting Welsh place-names, mainly.'

'They all seem to be places by the sea,' Donovan added helpfully. He would quite like a stethoscope dangling from his own pocket. Stethoscopes had magical powers, he had noticed, to which females seemed especially susceptible.

'We need to know who he is, so I can get his medical records,' said the doctor. 'Run a check on him and get in touch with the police – ask them to follow up the usual lines, and if that doesn't work ask them to get the local papers involved.'

The doctor's hand scurried away on the medical notes, already thickening with information on the latest arrival.

'He seems to have a nasty limp, but I'm not sure... he could be putting it on for my benefit,' said the doctor. 'I wonder if some sort of test could be devised?'

They all sat there, trekkers on the bridge of the USS Enterprise, waiting for Spock to beam them a bright idea.

Debbie looked around the station and had a bright idea. In the corner was a giant cuddly toy, a large fluffy teddy bear which was being raffled among staff and visitors. They had to guess its birthday.

'How about the bear,' she said, pointing to the toy. 'We could take it into the day room and start messing about with it. Perhaps you could drop it a few feet away from the Vogel man to see if he reacts, Donovan. If he gets up easily and walks straight up to it we'll know he's OK.'

The doctor pondered for a while.

'Seems worth a try,' he concluded eventually, rather gloomily. They sortied onto the ward with the bear, chatting and laughing amiably, which marked them out immediately as staff. They formed a rough triangle as they mingled with the patients. Seeing that Mr Vogel's shoes were undone, Debbie knelt in front of him to refasten the Velcro. When she finished she patted his knee and said: 'There you are, that's better isn't it?' But his eyes were fixed mesmerically on the bear.

Debbie got up and sat in one of the empty seats, next to Sylvia the Hoover, and winked at Donovan, her swaggering paramour of three glutinous nights.

Donovan took his chance and pretended to throw the bear to her, but he miss-threw deliberately and the bear landed a yard or so in front of the lame man. The ploy worked perfectly. Mr Vogel hurried to his feet to retrieve it, but stopped with a cry of pain as soon as he took a step, and tottered towards the bear clutching his left hip, wincing as he went. There was no doubt now – there really was something wrong with him. Debbie, Donovan and the doctor looked at each other with wise looks, like three poor actors in a village play. They wended back to the staff station, Donovan carrying the bear by one leg. They closed the door.

'Well that's that then,' said the doctor. 'I'll arrange X-rays as soon as possible.'

After a longish scribble in the endless note-taking – he often felt more like a novelist than a medic – he looked out, and was startled to see Mr Vogel's face pressed against the reinforced glass just inches from his own face. He was squinting at the bear.

Debbie followed his gaze, and talked to him slowly and loudly in idiot-speak through the glass:

'It's a raffle. RAFFLE. The bear's a prize in a RAFFLE. You have to guess its birthday. Got any money? HAVE YOU GOT TWENTY PEE? You can choose a date if you like. YES, YOU HAVE TO GUESS ITS BIRTHDAY.'

Mr Vogel shook his head and returned to his seat.

'I'm sure I've seen him somewhere,' said Donovan. He looked at the man's face. He was rather distinctive, and Donovan tried to imagine him with a mop of frizzy red hair and glasses. In a bar perhaps? Had he seen him in one of the town's many pubs?

Dinner rattled in on a trolley and the doctor went. Debbie and Donovan shepherded the patients into the dining room, those who were willing to go. Some remained in their rooms, hiding from the world. It was a quiet dinner. There was no small talk on the ward. Small talk is a sane pastime. The patients, generally, were either very quiet or highly voluble. There didn't seem to be an in-between. Mr Vogel cried silently; big pearly tears splashed into his grey plastic tray, which had individual indentations for each course and his drink. He cried through the meal, tears trickling softly down his cheeks. His glasses steamed up and he sat silently like a man in a fogged-up car on a wet and miserable day in nowhere. In the dayroom the television droned on, alone in the corner, showing a film to no-one. It was *Forrest Gump*, and Forrest was still a little boy, running down a track, away from a gang of boys throwing stones at him. The callipers on his legs were falling off as he escaped.

When Debbie went up to him to reassure him, and to cajole him into eating something, Mr Vogel said in an elaborately polite way:

'I'm very sorry. I don't seem to be hungry. Walking does that to me. Most people get hungry, don't they? But no, not me. If I walk all day I seem to lose my appetite.'

A couple of extra big tears bounced off the lid of his food tray.

'I hope you don't mind. Would it be all right if I went now?'

He looked at her expectantly.

'It's the party, you see. I really must be there. They're all expecting me. They'll wonder what's happened to me. I'm really looking forward to seeing them all again. Agnes Hunt will be there, and Doctor Robert Jones, and the old man, Mr Hugh Owen Thomas. It's going to be quite a do. And I really need to go because I must pay the band.'

Debbie patted him and parcelled up the tray.

'Never mind. Don't worry, perhaps you'll be able to manage some toast later,' she said kindly. 'You like walking then,' she added, stooping so that her eyes were looking directly into his. 'Do a lot of walking do you?'

'Right round Wales,' he said seriously, and a bit of a smile broke through his tears.

'Right round Wales – the whole country. That's why I'm tired. Can I go now?'

Debbie looked at him with her great brown eyes.

'Can't go yet – you'll have to stay until you're better. WE'VE GOT TO MAKE YOU BETTER.'

Later, in the staff station, when she was updating the patients' notes – as the staff seemed to do endlessly, leaving them little time to spend with the patients – she noted in her large, looping handwriting:

Mr 'Vogel' rather unsettled, didn't eat lunch. Tearful but pleasant. Possibly delusional – says he has walked around Wales, and wants to go to a party. Most of the time he sits with Gwydion, talking. They have asked me if they can get some books, and they have given me a long list. I have agreed to help them.

Debbie looked at Donovan and asked him for his opinion on Mr Vogel.

'Mmm, that's hard... bit early yet, don't you think?' he answered. 'Seems to be in a fantasy land. Says he's walked round Wales. Keeps going on about a party he's missing. Don't know what the likely story is. Crackers probably. Alzheimer's? Some sort of dementia? Alcoholic fantasist?'

They both watched Mr Vogel through the glass. He was thrusting his hand down all the backs of the seats as though he were searching for something. Suddenly he straightened, with a small object in his hand between forefinger and thumb – he held it up to the window, and then turned towards the staff station. He lumbered up to the station, holding his hip. Soon his face was up against the window again, and he tapped the glass with the newly-found item – a twenty pence piece.

'The bear,' he said. 'The bear.'

Debbie guessed first.

'You want to guess the bear's birthday?'

'Yes – the bear's birthday.'

She opened the door, and he tried to limp in, but she put the palm of her hand against his chest and said: 'Wait there.'

He did.

Debbie got the tray with the competition paperwork.

'Right then,' she said, twisting a biro from a plat in her hair. 'You've got twenty pee, so that's just one go. What's it going to be?'

'February 29th,' he replied immediately, breathlessly.

She looked at the list, then looked up at him.

'There isn't a February 29th on here,' she said. 'They only happen on leap years, you know.'

Mr Vogel stood there, quivering. He just stood and looked at her. He was a freakish man who wanted a freakish date, but that was what he wanted.

'Oh what the heck,' she said. 'I'll add it to the list – after all, it could be a leap year couldn't it?'

'It *is* a leap year,' said Donovan behind her. They both looked at the year planner on the wall.

'So it bloody well is,' she said. 'They're out of order. They should have it on here. That's made my mind up. I'll put it in between February the twenty-eighth and March the first, and underline it so they won't miss it,' she said. 'And I'll put a little note in the margin saying it's a special request from Mr Vogel.'

He limped back to his chair in the ring of twelve. He sat there for the rest of the evening with Sylvia the Hoover and the Walrus Man.

Later, when Donovan removed Debbie's bra swiftly in the linen room, she said: 'We're bloody crackers doing this here.'

'A lot more fun than walking round Wales,' he replied as his mouth sped down towards her.

'Very nice,' said Mr Vogel when I read this little episode to him. 'Very nice. Can't wait for the next bit. Any more sex?'

He'd changed his tune. I tut-tutted him: 'Don't be naughty,' I said reprovingly.

Looking at him there, lying in his hospital bed, with his two hands on the folded-back sheet in front of him, like a little dormouse, I was consumed with guilt. Having got him in here, I had to get him out.

He smelt slightly waxy and milky, like a baby. My little lame friend.

'Have you ever read Culhwch ac Olwen?' I asked him, wanting to while away a few more minutes, so that I didn't have to leave him alone to gather unpleasant thoughts.

'No.'

'It's the very first Welsh story. There's a giant in it, and he's got a beautiful daughter called Olwen – she's so beautiful that white flowers spring up in her footsteps wherever she walks. Anyway, the hero of the story, Culhwch, who was born in a pigsty, falls in love with her and asks for her hand in marriage, but the giant's having none of it. Culhwch is set a number of impossible tasks which involve King Arthur, incredible bravery and guile, and a chase around Britain and Ireland after a wild boar who has a comb, a mirror and shears between its ears – these are needed to trim the giant's hairy bits ready for the wedding.'

'What's this got to do with our story?' asked Mr Vogel suspiciously.

'Just bear with me. One of the tasks is this: the giant demands a white head-dress for his daughter on her wedding day, but any old head-dress won't do – it must be made from flax seeds which the giant sowed in the ground many years previously, but which failed to grow. One day, as a warrior involved in Culhwch's quest journeys over a mountain he hears wailing and lamentation. The noise is coming from an ant-hill, which is being engulfed by fire. The warrior saves the ants, and in gratitude they recover the flax seeds from the ground, so that a fine head-dress can be made for Olwen. But what I like best about this story is the final line.'

'What's that then?' asked Mr Vogel, his interest aroused.

'By the end of the day the ants have recovered the flax seeds, all except one. And that last seed is brought in by a lame ant just before nightfall.'

'That's me!' cried Mr Vogel. 'The lame ant! – that's me, isn't it!'

'Yes of course it is.'

A thought struck me.

'And you, Mr Vogel, will bring in the last seed of our story.'

He had another terrible nightmare that night. Again, the date February 28th had a special significance. All hell was let loose, he said. His ruse had gone terribly wrong: the two booksellers he dispatched along a ley-line to Hay-on-Wye went awry and ended up in Milford Haven where they activated the Quaker Whaling Fleet; this was now in pursuit of Moby Dick northwards through Ramsey Sound. But the whale had wreaked a terrible revenge – many men had been lost overboard, among them Captain Ahab (his peg leg devoured by the Gower Worm); all the crew had stood like penguins on the starboard rail, looking at Wales and singing (to the tune of the national anthem):

> Whales! Whales! Bloody Great Fishes Are Whales –
> They Swim Through The Sea,
> We Eat Them For Tea,
> Oh Bloody Great Fishes Are Whales.

Their voices were reedy in the wind; the whale's gigantic spume-geyser spurted between the shark-finned rocks of the Bishops and Clerks. Billy Silverfish tried to harpoon Great Auks. Mr Vogel would be arraigned for this, hanged from the yardarm.

~

He told me eventually, of course. Mr Vogel couldn't keep that sort of secret.

I had already guessed, after a fashion.

He was afraid of the yellow fan of light outside the off-licence, or 'liquor store' as he called it. It was a warm, inviting wedge in the darkness.

He feared that if he stepped inside that light ever again he would be lured onto the rocks by the wrecker's treacherous lantern, swaying drunkenly in the wind. Walking through that fan of light would require just three steps. And then he could keep on walking. For ever.

THE SECOND STEP

THEY yearned for April, the sweetest month, when the days would be young, lithesome and warm, and pilgrims would gather once again to take their paths to enlightenment. People would have a spring in their step. The hedgerows would welcome a new wave of flowers; the fresh and verdant banks would greet them like flower-girls, cradling primroses and violets, and wood anemones and snowdrops.

Enthroned on a large boxful of books brought to him by the helpful Debbie, Gwydion wrote of alexanders landing under their light green parachutes; birds hurrying through the fragile air with bits and bobs in their beaks; blackbirds singing plangent cadenzas, thrushes warming the earth's blood with their absurd promises. April was a good time to be alive.

Mr Vogel was beginning to grasp reality again; he had given up all hope of his party, and after taking stock of the world around him he was beginning to make plans for the future. His dream world hadn't vanished completely. A new set of night pictures swamped his mind, including this sleep-fable:

By February 29th the southern fisher-folk of Milford Haven were becalmed in Cardigan Bay; the dark and volatile inhabitants of the western seaboard swooned in great numbers, overcome by the sweet fragrance of Moby Dick's ambergris which floated offshore, a perfumed island. Now the Anglesey whalers left Holyhead to join the hunt, their dervish compass sent whirring by the mirror, comb and shears held between the ears of a monstrous boar cleaving the waves between Ireland and Wales. Calamitous divinations were uttered by the Aberaeron Soothsayer: his fishbones augured a great battle and much blood – only one would survive, a mermaid would reveal all…

Gwydion watched, amused, as the normal people – the hospital staff and the authorities – compiled a history for Mr Vogel. They had traced his medical records on the same day as a small piece appeared on the front page of *The Daily Informer* under the heading: *Mystery 'walker' puzzles hospital.*

While his medical files flitted to and fro along the highways of

Wales in search of him, Mr Vogel rested and contemplated. He looked at his fellow humans, scurrying around him in pursuit of meaning and purpose. He looked through the windows, at a world which mocked them all by having no meaning and no purpose, in vast amounts.

In this ampleness of time he fell in love.

His choice was supremely bizarre and couldn't have been predicted by anyone, least of all himself, as is nearly always the case in matters of the heart. To complicate matters she was married – and she was extremely suicidal, even before she met him. Her husband was small, inoffensive, and devoted to her. Mr Vogel cared not a whit. He courted her avidly.

Anna was most definitely not the prettiest girl in town. Anna was sad.

Anna sat in her chair in the corner all day, trembling and smoking, and harming herself. She had livid weals on her arms where she scratched herself, and old white scars where she had cut herself with knives. They reminded Mr Vogel of the zig-zag patterns cut in the stones of a Neolithic tomb on Anglesey. He had sat outside it, watching a gaggle of dirty, aggressive, near-naked children twittering in an ancient language whilst they collected frogs, toads, snails, fishes and snakes for a miraculous potion – such a concoction, desiccated and withered, had been discovered by archaeologists, poured onto a hearth there; this was hard fact, not a figment of his imagination as the children had been, garrulous and quick-moving above him on the mushroom mound.

Poor Anna. Her story was too terrible to imagine. Mr Vogel found her engrossing, and her story so sad that he cried vicariously and alone on the toilet, his tears a salty palimpsest dripping between the operating scars on his scrawny legs. Never before had a woman touched his heart so. He had seemed unable to love. He put this down to childhood experiences which he had never discussed with anyone. He, also, had been tormented by his father, whose special cruelty was to put little Vogel on the kitchen table and take his trousers off so that visitors – anyone – could see his puny, curved legs. He also removed the boy's underpants so that they could see his operation scars. Vogel's cheeks still burned with indignity and shame.

Now he spilt out his pain to Anna, and their bond was formed. It was first love in middle age, and Mr Vogel had never felt such feelings; they burst inside him like hot sherbet lemons.

He felt as though he were in a dream. None of it seemed real. He had taken on the smell of the ward, of displacement and dislodgement, pain and fear; now a new smell joined all the others, the smell of newly-ploughed love.

Anna told him her story. She had been one of three children; the other children, her two brothers, had been treated lovingly, normally. Unaccountably, the parents had developed a steely and icy hatred for their only daughter, and had treated her terribly. From the age of about eight onwards she had been prostituted by them, forced to sleep with men from the town. One of them was a magistrate. This was the truth. Mr Vogel knew she was telling the truth. He realised that many of the people around him held stories which were very frightening, almost beyond the comprehension of normal people.

Anna developed a terror of those men who used her. She would hide under her bed, screaming, when they came. One day a new 'customer' had been taken to her, but she had refused him. He had threatened her, and told her that if she continued to refuse him he would kill her pet tortoise – her parents' sole concession to her childhood (it had belonged to her brothers). She had believed him incapable of a crime so despicable, and had continued to resist him. He had returned later that day and had jumped on the tortoise before her eyes.

Her sexual servitude had continued throughout her child-hood. Eventually she had escaped. She had married, but her first husband had been a monster who had beaten her mercilessly and terrorized their children. It is common for abused children to pick abusers as their partners; Anna wasn't to know this. In time he was jailed. Her life reached a more even keel with the arrival of her second husband, who was close to being a saint. Periodically, however, the past revisited her. She would retreat into caves of fear and howling coldness, tearing herself on the stalagmites and stalactites of her memories; nightmares descended on her in vicious wolverine packs, ripping at her sanity. Her husband knew where to find her: hiding under the bed. Twice she had tried to hang herself. The guilt ensuing from these attempts at suicide added yet more to her next bouts of depression and self-loathing. It was then that she came to the hospital. It was why she was here now.

At one stage Anna had become religious, and had gone to church up to three or four times every day. She had prayed and prayed to be left alone, to be cleansed. Once she had taken a small figurine of Christ from the church and had kept it under her pillow until her guilt grew too strong, and she had taken it back to the priest. He had castigated her, telling her not to go there again.

It was then that she knew there was no God. She had pleaded with Him in the small hours of her childhood as the shadows of tyrants climbed the stairs to her bedroom; she had implored, begged for a miracle, wet herself with fear, but there had been no voice of pity, no help. She knew, now, finally, that there was no God.

Anna had a special bedroom. Every wall was covered in mirrors. Every square inch.

Every so often she would go there with a knife and cut her wrists, then smear her blood all over the mirrors. This alleviated her pain for short periods.

Mr Vogel was indignant on her behalf. He felt angry. Things like that shouldn't happen in real life: he wasn't at all sure if they should happen in stories, either.

He felt like going to her parents to accost them. Were they still alive? Had she seen them since leaving home?

Anna told him that they were both still alive. Yes, she had been to see them once. They had behaved as if nothing had ever happened, as if they had destroyed all mental records of their crime. When she had asked them to account for their vile behaviour they had told her not to be a silly little girl. Nothing had changed. She had left. She had fitful contact with her brothers, who were unsure whether to believe her story. After all, these were the parents who had shown great love to two of their children, given them plenty of toys and affection; how could they have treated the other so very differently? Surely it was impossible.

Mr Vogel was in love. He desperately wanted to win the raffle so that he could give her the giant teddy bear. It would make up for all the teddy bears she had never played with when she was a little girl. Perhaps she would stop hurting herself. It would make everything better.

Mr Vogel didn't win the raffle. The bear was won by the doctor with the trailing stethoscope, who gave it to the children's ward. Mr Vogel was so upset he cried on the toilet for hours, and the staff removed his belt.

The article in the *Daily Informer* resulted in a trickle of calls: Mr Vogel was quickly identified as David Jones, an eccentric and often drunken disabled man who lived in a scruffy house on a hill near the centre of town. There were a few visitors, most of them from the fringes of society. One was caught trying to smuggle a bottle of whisky onto the ward. The chief guests were a Sumo-bellied builder and his trusty sidekick, a lean and angular man who stayed on the ward only briefly, and who spent most of his time sleeping on one of the benches in the garden outside the entrance to the psychiatric unit.

An interregnum set in; the passing days became weeks as Gwydion and Mr Vogel worked on the saga, their fabulous version of Mr Vogel's life and times. Gwydion sat on his ever-rising throne of books while Mr Vogel sat in a chair beside him.

Mr Vogel's tall stories now became formal set-pieces, glorious renaissance buildings which housed myths of perpendicular beauty – sheer and poetic. Gwydion enjoyed listening to him as he held forth:

'I remember HM Stanley rather well – we were brought up in the same workhouse, the one in St Asaph,' he was telling Sylvia the Hoover, who was cat-napping (her dark little head, in an African-looking bandana, had slipped onto his shoulder).

'Met him years later and he told me all about that famous encounter with Livingstone in Africa. When he arrived, apparently, he was met by a huge mob, and he was forced to walk down a living avenue of people, until he came to a white man with a grey beard. Livingstone looked pale and very tired, apparently. Stanley said he felt like running up to him and embracing him, but he was scared of having his pride dented so he tried to be dignified – he walked to him deliberately, took off his hat, and said: *Dr Livingstone, I presume?*

Yes, replied Livingstone with a kind smile, lifting his cap slightly (Mr Vogel lifted an imaginary cap). They both grasped hands, and then Stanley said aloud, for all to hear: *I thank God, doctor, I have been permitted to see you.*

Sylvia gave a loud snort in her sleep and a jolt went through her body, then she went back to sleep.

'Nice story,' said Gwydion as he glided up to Mr Vogel and sat down.

Mr Vogel hardly turned a hair, and embroidered his outrageous fib, looking Gwydion full in the eye:

'Your face reminds me of a man I knew in Africa,' he continued, his hands waving about expressively as he described his experience. 'He was bitten by a snake when he was asleep. I tied a string tightly around his leg and since I didn't have any caustic I put some gunpowder in the wound and exploded it. I cut out the bitten part with a knife and burnt the area with a piece of white-hot iron, then I instructed the porters to keep him awake at all cost whilst I went to sleep – I was too tired to stand by now. If the patient goes to sleep he'll die: he must be kept awake at all cost.'

'Come on,' said Gwydion, 'we'll go and put that down on paper.'

'Incidentally,' said Mr Vogel airily, 'Dickens loved getting out and about before writing – nothing he liked better than a long walk at high speed.'

Mr Vogel got up and limped to his room, Gwydion following.

Dr Jackson, or Wacko as he was known on the ward, the consultant psychiatrist, eventually got to see Mr Vogel. Everyone seemed to know when it was the consultant's visiting day. There was expectancy in the air; Sylvia the Hoover washed and tidied herself, and tried to behave normally – in fact everyone seemed to behave far more normally than they usually did. This mystified Mr Vogel. He sat next to Anna and asked her:

'If I get you a teddy bear will you stop harming yourself?'

'I'll try,' she said. 'I'll try my best.' And she meant it.

Dr Jackson discussed Mr Vogel with his coterie in the interview room.

'Seems we have an interesting case here,' he said in an overly interested sort of way. He was very well dressed and immaculately groomed, with bright blue eyes and long blond hair waving stylishly around his impressive head. His peers at medical school had called him The Professor. He looked excessively powerful. Donovan thought: That man looks so absolutely right for the part, with his nice hair and his white teeth and his sparkling eyes and his £300 suit and his shiny brogues. Donovan thought illicit thoughts; would the consultant get the same reverential treatment, would he have passed the same exams, he wondered, if he'd been small, lame, ugly, bald and had a couple of teeth missing? No, though Donovan, not bloody likely; people still liked their leaders to look the part. He had noticed that the hospital administrators mostly seemed taller, bigger, smarter, more confident than the ward staff.

Dr Jackson's voice took on a carefully modulated tone.

'There's nothing much we can do about his physical state, since he's permanently lame – his adventure stories are a complete fabrication. His exploits and escapades are castles in the air, he's tilting at windmills. For one reason or another he's living in a fantasy world and our job is to rescue him and bring him back to our world, to reality.'

A slow series of nods from the gathering indicated that they agreed, though Donovan thought it might be better to leave Mr Vogel in cloud cuckoo land, wherever that might be – beyond Blaenau Ffestiniog, on Pumlumon maybe, in the fifth dimension.

'Now,' continued Dr Jackson. 'Debbie, I believe you have been his personal helper. What's your opinion on this?'

Debbie was still a bit new to the heady atmosphere of the case conference, but she took a deep breath, as her mother had taught her to, pretended she was alone, and read (slightly nervously) from her notes.

'The patient has settled well on the ward. He was upset and agitated at first, but now accepts that he must stay here until he is allowed to go. He seems confused and often says that he cannot be entirely sure what has really happened to him, since the real events of his life have merged with his fictions and his dreams. He's rather dotty and says strange things. He says that truth has changed continuously since he was born, and he is no longer certain which version he should believe, or whether he should believe anything at all (whatever all that means!).'

Mr Vogel had told her his theory: that all experiences, bad ones especially, were constantly replayed by the mind, like a video, and edited slightly every time to produce a version of our personal history which was acceptable to the mind.

'That's all we do throughout our lives, really,' he told her. 'We join up with a good story and write ourselves into the script, otherwise it will all have been for nothing.'

He said that every country on earth has constantly doctored or re-edited its own history, so why shouldn't he?

She continued: 'Mr Vogel says that everything becomes mixed up as you get older, and it doesn't really matter eventually if it happened or if you dreamt it. He is sociable and polite, and now that he uses his room he likes to sit in it with Gwydion for long periods. They seem to be writing a story and Mr Vogel laughs and cries quite a lot when they're talking about it. At first he seemed very scared in case we restrained him in some way, or locked him in, but he has now relaxed.'

'He has a strange little habit, hasn't he Debs,' Donovan added. 'Go on, tell them.'

Debbie reddened and hesitated; now that her delivery had been broken she became quite shaky.

Dr Jackson soothed her. 'That's fine Debbie. You're doing fine. Please tell us about his little habit. I hope it's not too offensive...'

They all tittered dutifully.

'Well, it's like this,' said Debbie, before taking a mouthful of water. Dr Jackson looked at her lips around the rim of the glass and created immediate video footage of a pleasing sexual act. He would edit the clip to his own advantage later. She continued:

'He likes to sit in his room on his own, but he also likes a bit of company. We noticed one night that he always left his light on after everyone else had switched theirs off – it's a trademark of his. He's fine after one of us has gone to talk to him for a while and tucked him in. But he'll put that light on and leave it on until someone's called on him. It's quite endearing, really.'

'Quite a little character we have here. I'm told by Donovan that he believes he's walked *completely* round Wales, and pigs might fly,' said Dr Jackson superciliously.

'Got anything against pigs?' asked Donovan, who was irritated by Dr Jackson but could never fathom why. He was so unshakably certain about everything, he seemed to approach everyone as an imperial power might approach a tiny colony.

'Absolutely hate them actually,' said Dr Jackson, 'they're revolting and I'd quite happily erase them from the face of history. I was chased by one as a child.'

'No point giving you one for Christmas then,' said Donovan, with the slightest hint of malice in his voice.

'This walk round Wales, it's not completely impossible you

know,' said Debbie, defensively. 'People do amazing things. And he does seem to know his country very well. Stranger things have happened.'

'We'll leave it at that,' said Dr Jackson. 'Miracles do happen, we've seen them before on this ward.' Dr Jackson turned to Donovan and asked him for his impressions.

'Really strange person, never met anyone quite like him before,' Donovan answered. 'He won't wear new clothes – we took him shopping but he wouldn't go anywhere near the proper shops. He dragged us into a charity shop. He's formed a close friendship with Gwydion and also with Anna – seems very intense and we've got to keep an eye on that one. He pretends he has lots of money but he doesn't have a credit card. Says he's got plenty of friends, which probably means he hasn't got any at all. Wants to get in touch with Esmie, whoever she may be.'

'Righty-ho,' said Dr Jackson. 'I'll have a look at him myself now. Thank you both for your help. Could you call him in now?'

They went back on the ward and told Mr Vogel the doctor was ready to see him.

But Mr Vogel didn't like the idea at all.

'Doctor?' He was extremely suspicious. 'What does he want with me? Are they going to operate again? I'm not going in. I can't do it, I...' he was in a terrible spin.

They calmed him, but it was no use. Wild horses wouldn't drag him into the interview room. Dr Jackson had to go into the dayroom and sit in one of the twelve seats. They sat away from the rest whilst they chatted.

'I just want to talk to you for a while,' said Dr Jackson in his most calming voice. 'Just a few minutes, after all, we want to get you out of here as soon as possible, don't we?'

Mr Vogel gazed at him with his Are You Sure look.

'Now I understand you call yourself Vogel, is that right?' he asked gently. 'Though you have another name too, a proper name. Would that be David Jones?'

'Yes, that's right.'

'And which name would you like me to use in future?' asked the doctor, looking at his watch.

'You can call me Mr Vogel,' he answered. 'It started off as a bit of a joke, but it sort of stuck, and I'm so used to it now... it was the children on the ward you see.'

'It was your nickname?'

'Yes, at Gobowen. There was a German lady at the clinic and she said that I looked like a little bird because my legs were so spindly after being in bed for so long.'

'And the German word for bird is *vogel.*'

'That's right. All the other children started calling me Vogel. That's how nicknames come about. Funny isn't it? And when I'm not feeling very great, not on top of the world, I tend to talk to Mr Vogel about the old days.'

'Understand completely,' said Dr Jackson, adding:

'I'm told that you speak Welsh – can't speak it fluently yet, but I'm trying, going to lessons and all that you understand,' he said.

'Yes, I speak Welsh,' answered Vogel, who was beginning to warm to his subject.

'In fact I speak two minority languages quite well.'

'Two?'

'Yes, Welsh and English.'

Dr Jackson searched his mind and looked for the obvious catch.

'Don't quite get your drift,' he said guardedly.

'English as she is spoken, the King's English is a minority language now. Your mother tongue is dying slowly. All the other types of world English, especially American English, Australian English and Indian English have taken over, they've superseded her – all the new words come from abroad now. BBC English will have gone in a century – you'll hear a medley of estuary English, Americanese and strange regional accents, distorted by new immigrants. Ever thought of that? Ever thought what it's going to sound like, living in Britain then?'

Dr Jackson looked a long hard look at him and finger-combed his lion's mane of blond hair. He reminded Mr Vogel of someone else, someone from his past.

'Surely you mean the Queen's English,' parried Dr Jackson.

'No, it's called the King's English after the King James Bible, actually,' said Mr Vogel. It was nice to know more about the English language than the English themselves sometimes – after all, they seemed to know a damn sight more about Wales than he did.

'I see I'm going to enjoy talking to you,' said Dr Jackson. 'Will I be talking mainly to Mr Vogel or to Mr Jones?'

'Both in equal measure,' said Mr Vogel. 'Incidentally, did you know that your name, with the 'son' at the end, shows that you're from Scandinavian stock, and that your family lived north of a line between Chester and London?'

'Fascinating,' said Dr Jackson with a skipful of sarcasm, 'it's nice to know where we're both coming from.'

'Touché,' answered Mr Vogel.

Later, when Donovan went to Mr Vogel's room, the last to have its light on as usual, to tuck him in and say goodnight, Mr Vogel was reading.

Donovan bustled around him for a while, closing the curtains and tidying Mr Vogel's clothes and desk, ready for lights out. Having finished, he slumped in the chair by Mr Vogel's bed and watched him as his eyes flickered along the lines.

'What are you reading?' he asked.

'The *Mabinogi* – Gwydion brought it for me. Told me a story about a lame ant yesterday, so I thought I'd catch up on all the old Welsh stories. Would you believe it, I've never read them.'

Donovan yawned and wondering if Debbie would be down the pub after work, waiting for him. 'Did them at school, but I can't remember a thing about them now. Which bit are you on?'

'The bit about Pryderi and the pigs.'

'That's a strange coincidence,' said Donovan, fighting another yawn and settling back in the chair. 'Second time today that pigs have flown past the window.'

He closed his eyes and rooted about in his memory, trying to remember the Welsh word for pigs. After a while it came to him – *moch*.

'Pryderi and the pigs – wasn't that the story which explained all the places in Wales called Mochdre?'

'Something like that.'

'Go on, remind me of the story.'

Mr Vogel looked at him sideways from beneath his pool of light.

'Haven't you got a home to go to?'

'It was something to do with war, wasn't it. That's it, Gwydion the magician was trying to start a fight with the South Walians, wasn't he?'

'Yes.'

'Well go on then, remind me.'

Mr Vogel sighed, closed his eyes, and went over the story.

Gwydion – the fictional Gwydion, not his new friend – indeed wanted to start a fight with the South, and he hit on a cunning plan.

Pryderi and his southerners had been given a strange and wonderful gift by the king of the otherworld – pigs.

Gwydion and his party of twelve northerners travelled to the court of the southerners pretending to be poets. They feasted, and Gwydion (who as well as being a magician was also the best storyteller in the land) entertained everyone with mind-boggling tales. Afterwards he asked for the pigs as a gift. But Pryderi wouldn't consider it – the porkies had to stay put. So Gwydion came up with a ruse. Using the dark arts he created twelve splendid stallions and twelve elegant greyhounds, each of them with bridles and saddles and collars and leashes of gold. He offered them to Pryderi in return for the pigs. The deal was done; he was given the pigs and he started to herd them homewards; wherever they stayed overnight was subsequently called Mochdre (pigtown) or had '*moch*' in its name. But Gwydion's spell lasted for only a day: the stallions and the greyhounds dematerialized, and the southerners mustered their troops, ready for war.

Mr Vogel looked round and thought Donovan had nodded off.

'You asleep?'

'No, just thinking. Great story.'

Donovan got to his feet, tucked in Mr Vogel's bedspread, patted his shoulder and offered to turn out the light. Mr Vogel accepted.

'Perhaps you should tell that story to Dr Jackson,' said Donovan's silhouette in the doorway.

'He hates pigs and he doesn't believe a word you've ever said.' Mr Vogel was sitting on the ward, and he was feeling better.

He was eating again, and he was drinking Calypso by the boxful.

He drank some water and it tasted elemental, of mountains and minerals, melting snow and spent volcanic forces. He put it to one side – it was too early to touch such a simple power.

He breathed the air, feeling its invisible companionship, like a friend holding him up, supporting his weight in a moment of giddiness. The ground had new solidity under his feet, and he swayed less. His eyes cleared, slowly, and the green of his irises contrasted anew with the white of his corneas. His skin looked healthier, even his dandruff became less obvious. There was something else, too. He wanted to end his tall stories. He didn't want to ornament his fable any longer.

'For pity's sake,' he said to the mirror, during a long and carefully considered conversation with himself (a dialogue which was becoming calmer by the day).

For pity's sake, he wanted to let go now. He didn't want to fabricate any longer. He wanted to be himself, to enjoy the taste of water, the primacy of air.

He had hoarded enough stock now. Why conflate and distort, he asked himself, when the facts of his existence, pure and simple, were wonderful in themselves?

He had been in the wilderness for some time. Mr Vogel was beginning to merge with David Jones again. It was a good sign. He was never completely at ease when Mr Vogel went off into the woods and became feral; he never knew what Mr Vogel might do – he was capable of great emotional excesses, frightening in their intensity.

He sat quietly in the dayroom and started making a mental will. The time had come. He had already decided on a humanist funeral; now he started mulling over his choice of music, and poems and readings. He would have to have a piece of violin music for sure, but it most certainly wouldn't be *Abide With Me*.

The Mendelssohn concerto, perhaps, for its delicacy, or the Elgar for its sheer romantic sentimentality; no, something simple perhaps... *The Lark Ascending*, that was it, something plaintive and relevant – *The Lark Ascending* would do fine.

There would have to be some Mahler. That was easy – the second movement of the *Resurrection Symphony* would be perfect. His friends would get the joke.

Something for Paddy – Tom Lehrer perhaps, something to amuse the rabble and to shock the chapel-goers; and then perhaps a good old standard blues number, something like *Freight Train* for his hobo friends...

The dinner trolley rolled in and Mr Vogel headed automatically for the dining room. It was amazing how quickly one slipped into the rhythm of the ward; food and pills marked time as well as any clock. He was ravenously hungry and ate one of the absent patients' dinners as well as his own. Debbie patted him affectionately and said: 'Well done Mr Vogel.'

He went back to his seat and waited for the pills trolley; it was like waiting for communion in church when he was a child. He'd soon turned his back on all that: he'd decided quickly that he couldn't possibly believe in a god who was stupid, mad or evil enough to create a man like his father, who spreadeagled him on the kitchen table, like a frog for dissection, and showed his naked distortions to all who wished to see. Sometimes Mr Vogel was cruel to himself: he convinced himself that nature had distorted his mind and soul too. Like Anna, he had called into the void of his childhood and had heard no response. And he had another big problem with it all: Mr Vogel liked fair play, as all children and simple, innocent people do.

He liked everyone to have an equal chance. But religion never gave anyone an equal chance, because people had very different powers of belief. He had said that to Dr Jackson, who hated the primordial primitivism of pigs. Jackson went to the American Baptists in town because he liked to sing like crazy and speak in tongues and generally let it all hang out. He kept it very secret, but as he said to his wife, you had to let it out somehow. Primitive men did a spot of trepanning to release the spirits, and after all, in the lifespan of the universe man was only a few seconds away from woolly mammoths and cromlechs.

'Isn't it strange,' said Mr Vogel to the person next to him, who happened to be Sylvia the Hoover, 'that the very people who mock the old gods are the same people who sit in stone huts and sing hymns to the spirits. *Plus ça change*, don't you think Sylvia?'

Sylvia asked him if they could go to Downing Street, since time was getting short.

Mr Vogel looked at the group, sitting quietly, all with their own little preoccupations, like himself. They were a strange bunch. The human genome had spent a day on the piss when it created this lot.

He continued making his will. He would have to include *Myfanwy*, and a bit of harp music from Llio Rhydderch, and perhaps that plaintive little song by Meinir Gwilym. As for money... well, he simply didn't have any to leave. He lived in a council flat, and he'd never had a proper job. He'd put chains on wash-basin plugs at the day centre, but after a while they'd told him not to go again. It was his own fault – he'd simply gone missing too often. He couldn't help it, somehow. And sometimes he'd been drunk, and they didn't like that either.

Mr Vogel sat outside the unit in clear, cool sunshine, wrapped up in a coat which smelt reassuringly of peat – it belonged to one of the staff members, who had taken pity on Mr Vogel. He and Gwydion daydreamed together about the end of their perfect mission: the end of the walk around Wales. By now their friendship had settled and hardened like cement. It was a strange alliance, certainly, but then again, most friendships are. Gwydion had talked of friendship in terms of longitude and latitude.

'All those segments created by Mercator, vacuums waiting to be filled by explorers – we're like that too, divided up into empty bits, all of them waiting to be mapped and recorded. That's where our friends live – in the empty bits between the lines. They help us to map our contours. Don't you think so, Mr Vogel?'

They decided, after much consideration, to finish the walk around Wales in two stages on the same day: at Nab's Head in Pembrokeshire in the morning and at the little church of St Beuno's in Pistyll in the afternoon. It was their tribute to the north-south divide, to the duality of Wales, and the duality in Mr Vogel. It would have been convenient and logical to end at St David's, at the end of the southern pilgrims' trail, but since they were both pagans they paid tribute to their ancestors by ending at Nab's Head, a perfect example of a Mesolithic fort above the sea. Mr Vogel would tell his friends that he'd found an Iron Age spear-head nearby, though it was probably a finial from an iron railing, not the real thing at all. Still, pretending had been good enough until now; only certain people got to see the real thing anyway. Gwydion had told him about the Bedeilhac caves in France with their prehistoric paintings.

'It's a sham, what they show you,' he told Mr Vogel. 'They make copies of the paintings and mouldings so that people can see them – most of the real stuff was done in recesses and crannies at the back of the cave. They were not for public consumption – they were for a select few to see and experience.'

One of Mr Vogel's acquaintances had gone on holiday for a week on the Gower and had spent a futile day looking for the famous cave at Paviland, home of the Red Lady.

Perhaps it's best to make it all up, thought Mr Vogel, safe in his slippers.

Some people – no, perhaps many people – could walk around Wales for a hundred years without seeing anything of interest; zilch, just a boring and repetitive shoreline.

But through other people's eye they could see all the glories they might have missed.

When he was an old man (not so far away, he thought) he could sit by the fire and remember. He would be tempted to embroider, he knew that. Slowly but certainly small details and fictions would be added. If he reached a hundred the tale would be magnificent, epic, superhuman. He would have created his own myth. It was the way of mankind, especially the Celt.

Matthew Arnold had said of the Celts that they were hopeless at the big picture, at making a constructed whole, but very good at the small detail; they had been expert at illustrating the capitals and rubrics on their beautiful manuscripts, but they had been unable to construe an empirical whole.

Back on the ward, Mr Vogel continued to think about the walk around Wales.

'Damn it all,' he said to Sylvia, 'the walk has a completeness about it. A symmetry – don't you think?'

She sidled away to do some hoovering.

'It has a wholeness – a beginning, a middle and an end,' he said, switching his conversation immediately to the next pair of ears, which belonged to the Walrus Man.

'Don't you think so?'

The Walrus Man also got up, and lumbered off towards the toilets.

Mr Vogel felt isolated, so he moved up alongside a new woman, who had dog-hairs all over her clothes.

'You may wonder if I cheated,' he said to her, 'but no, I was completely honest with myself. I may not have done it all in the same direction, and not all at the same time, but I walked along the whole route. I did get slightly lost in Monmouth because I'm a bear of little brain and I confused the two bridges, and a man gave me a lift in his car to the right spot, but I was still within the town so that's not cheating, is it?'

The woman regarded Vogel for a few seconds, then clumped

off to her room.

The next person along was Peter, the man who spent all day shaking hands with people.

'Hia Peter,' said Mr Vogel, and he shook hands with him continuously whilst he talked, so that Peter could top up his batteries.

'Some people, the doubters, will pour cold water on my claims and ask for proof. Some people will turn their backs on me and deny they've ever had anything to do with me. But I have no proof. I did it for myself, you see. I don't care if there are doubters – there always will be, people are either believers or doubters, basically. Don't you think so?'

Peter was off to greet Dr Jackson who had appeared in the doorway. Mr Vogel waved to him and smiled.

'Frankly,' he said across an empty seat to a little man with a glass eye, who had a very menacing stare, 'it would have been far easier to fake it. Car, camera, a few days in the library – easy. I could have been the next...'

He couldn't remember a famous faker – what was the name of that man who copied old masters and nearly got away with it?

The little man with the glass eye walked off, down to the quiet room, where he stood and stared at a patient who was reading a book, *The Island of Apples*, another book about the Welsh, about myths.

Mr Vogel thought of the Madog myth – did he, didn't he sail to America? But Madog was Welsh, so Mr Vogel put aside his doubts.

'When was Wales? Wales has never been, it has always been,' he rambled on to his next victim, Myrddin the schizophrenic, who (fortunately) was asleep. 'I'll tell you something for nothing,' he said, 'true Wales is never more than a field away, and true Wales is always a field away, like Rhiannon's horse in the Mabinogi. Get it?'

Myrddin woke up and called for the nurse.

Mr Vogel sat alone. They had all deserted him; the party was over. It was time to pay the piper. He would linger with a few images from his mini-epic, which nestled inside him like a miniature ship in a bottle.

Seeing the Severn Estuary for the first time, shimmering

through the trees, from a break in the trees on Offa's Dyke – feeling like Cortez when he saw the far-off Pacific from a silent peak in Darien; seeing the ponies in the marshes at Llanrhidian and going back in time, to Epona, to the sparse landscape of early man; sleeping on the sands at New Quay, dreaming of dolphins.

He nodded off, and was woken by a hand shaking his arm.

'Mr Vogel?' It was Debbie. She was such a lovely girl.

'Mr Vogel – Dr Jackson will see you soon. He wants to talk to you. Don't worry. Just tell him everything. He'll understand. If you tell him everything he'll be able to help you.'

Mr Vogel looked round at the room. He felt a strong urge to visit the Blue Angel; he wanted to sit on the stool in the corner and talk to the barman, who would understand everything. He would be just like Gwydion, a man who could listen patiently for hours.

Mr Vogel's stories were so interesting, said Gwydion.

Mr Vogel felt good about that. Being interesting.

'Tell me a story about the Jews,' he said to Mr Vogel. 'We must put something in about the Jews and the gipsies, they're the world's greatest travellers, after all.'

Mr Vogel stroked his chin. 'The Jews,' he murmured, 'the Jews...

I'll tell you a story about the Jews,' he said finally, 'and about the gipsies, and why they're condemned to a life of wandering.'

He settled in his chair and cast his mind back to a fine-looking wanderer, a man called Roland who wore a beret and had curly auburn hair and a van Dyke moustache and a gold earring in his ear, a man of verve and romance. This man had played his fiddle and told them stories, one of them about his own folk, the Romany people. 'This is what he told us,' said Mr Vogel.

'When Christ was being crucified the Romans sent two soldiers to buy four strong nails. But they spent half the money on drink at a tavern. Incidentally, did you know that the Grapes at Maentwrog was probably a Roman tavern...'

'Just tell it straight, for God's sake, otherwise we'll never get there – I'm not a young man either,' said Gwydion.

'Right,' said Mr Vogel.

'The two Roman soldiers hurried to an old Jewish blacksmith, who refused to make the nails when he was told how they would be used, so the soldiers killed him.

They went to another blacksmith, who said he could forge only four small nails with the money that was left. The soldiers tried to frighten him by setting his beard on fire, but the blacksmith heard the voice of the first murdered man and also refused to do the task. They killed him also.

Then they went to a gipsy blacksmith who made three nails, and was working on the fourth when the soldiers told him what he was making. At this point they all heard the voices of the two dead blacksmiths, and the soldiers ran away.

The gipsy finished the fourth nail and waited for it to cool, but it remained red hot no matter how much cold water he poured on it. The terrified gipsy fled, and after travelling a great distance he pitched his tent. As soon as he had done so he spied the glowing nail at his feet, and although he poured sand and water over it the nail remained hot. An Arab asked him to repair a wheel on a cart, so he drove the nail, still glowing, into the wheel, and then the gipsy fled. When he reached his next stop the gipsy pitched camp again and his first customer was a man who wanted the hilt of his sword repaired. When the gipsy took the sword, what do you think he saw glowing in the hilt?

'The nail repeatedly visited the gypsy's descendants, and that is why they're condemned to a life of perpetual wandering. And that's why Christ was crucified with three nails – the fourth nail is still wandering around the Earth, chasing gypsies.

'Like it?'

'Good story,' said Gwydion. 'Yours?'

'Good grief no,' answered Vogel.

'Now let's see if you can spot a bogus story,' said Gwydion, who was enjoying himself. 'Let's play *True or False*.'

'Fine with me,' said Mr Vogel.

'Is it true,' asked Gwydion, 'that India has something like 60 million people, called the Denotified Tribes, who were labelled criminal by the British because of their nomadic way of life and who were either forcibly settled or shot on sight?'

'True,' said Mr Vogel, without hesitation. 'I know about them. I've heard this story too. Apparently, when the British went to India these tribes, who carried salt and honey between the coast and the inland forests, were a great help to them because they knew all about the geography and customs of the country. But once the British knew their way around these people were seen as a threat and were made into social outcasts.'

'I see that I can't fool you,' said Gwydion approvingly. 'Seems to me that we're quite a match.'

Mr Vogel liked this Gwydion man, increasingly. They sat there, like Castor and Pollux, fixed in an orbit around sanity. Sylvia was hoovering around Mr Vogel's feet. He thought about his love for Anna, who had stayed in her room for days now. *I love her*, he thought. *I want to be with her for ever – for the eons it will take Sylvia to hoover the entire universe into her paper bag.*

'Of course it's all to do with Cain and Abel,' said Mr Vogel, leaning over.

Gwydion looked at him like a teased dog.

'They were Adam and Eve's sons, right?'

Mr Vogel looked tired. 'Tell you what, I'll leave that with you. Have a scratch around. See what you come up with. I'll give you a clue: Cain was a settled farmer and Abel was a nomadic shepherd. One brother killed the other. The human race gave up wandering. That's when our problems really started.'

Mr Vogel had another vivid dream last night: he awoke in darkness, sweating, crying out; a shadow flitted from the staff station to his bedside. It was another whale dream:

> That fateful day, February 29th, again: A great battle was fought out to sea between the northern and southern whaling fleets; all ships sunk. One survivor carried to the shore on the back of a giant boar, a cabin boy travelling under the name of Arthur, who upon closer examination was revealed to be a lovely young girl called Emmeline, fleeing her stupid, puny husband for a Welshman of wondrous virtue, bravery and beauty...

I have talked to Mr Vogel about the monster who sucks his toes and fills him with yellow heat and desire, who tries to pull him into the off-licence and video store.

I will ferry my friend across the Whisky Monster's yellow river.

THE THIRD STEP

GWYDION was furious.

'Hates pigs? What kind of man is that,' he muttered to Mr Vogel, who said:

'Apparently he was chased by a pig when he was a kid.'

'Probably annoying it. Pigs are beautiful. Pigs are pretty gruntled beings on the whole.'

'And he doesn't believe a word of our story,' added Mr Vogel. 'Thinks we're porky pie merchants, through and through.'

'What?' Gwydion was enraged. 'The cheeky bastard. Professor of pig poo, I'll make him pay for that. This is bloody war.'

He sat down in a chair alongside Mr Vogel and thought great big chunks of thoughts. Mr Vogel felt the mass of the room change dramatically, as if the floor under Gwydion was going to give way; with a roaring, rushing sound they would be sucked through a chute of mega-gravity, to join Snowdonia's fossils, swimming forever in the cold, hard, basalt waves deep below. He felt a cloud envelop him, black and cold. He'd never seen Gwydion like this. It was terrible to see, the wrath of a doubted Welshman.

'Right,' said Gwydion after a few minutes.

He straightened, smiled, and the sun came out again.

'I've got it. The perfect plan. The sow-bellied, mud-brained pill-pusher. He's pulled the wrong pig by the ear now, hasn't he?'

'I think we've got the point,' said Mr Vogel, 'but what of it?'

'Revenge!' said Gwydion vengefully. 'He's going to pay! We can't have our honour impugned and fine Welsh pigs maligned by a jumped-up little medicine man with the wrong blood inside him and a head full of scats, or whatever pig droppings are called. When are you seeing him again?'

'Some time this morning, apparently.'

'Excellent. I'll be back before then. And we'll need a man with a van. Know anyone like that?'

'Well there's Waldo, I'm sure Waldo will help out...'

'Fine. And we'll need a pig. And a Polaroid camera. Got that?'

After jotting Waldo's phone number on the back of his hand he was off, trotting down the corridor, leaving a mystified Mr Vogel sitting in his room, wondering what on earth was going on.

Gwydion was back before Mr Vogel had finished his breakfast. He shoved a small bottle in his hand.

'There, that'll do the trick.'

Mr Vogel looked at it, turning it round in his hand.

'Well, what is it?'

'It's a drug.'

'A drug,' said Mr Vogel, feeling as if he'd already taken a swig from it.

'Can you be a bit more specific, and when do I take it?'

'You don't – he does.'

'Eh?'

'Dr Jackson – you've got to slip it in his tea when he's not looking. Good dollop. Get him to leave the room or something. Then whop it into his tea. Got it?'

'What the hell is it?'

'It's a date rape drug, actually, and he should be out for some time. I want him to lose twenty-four hours. Non compos. Out of it, completely.'

'A what? Date rape drug? Are you out of your mind? Where the hell did you get hold of this stuff, anyway? You really are a sex maniac, aren't you?

'No. I am not a sex maniac. And you know this town – you can get hold of anything. It's that sort of place, isn't it?'

Mr Vogel knew exactly what he meant. It was a transit port, with all the associated seediness and grubbiness of busy ports; they seemed to attract runaways and derelicts. Alcohol, drugs... Gwydion was right, they were as accessible as bread and milk.

'Whoa,' he said, trying to slow everything down. 'Just you wait a minute whilst I get hold of what's happening here. You're telling me that I am going to go into the interview room with Dr Jackson and I am going to slip him a date rape drug. Is that right?'

'Right.'

'And then we're going to do something with a man in a van, a pig and a camera?'

'Correct.'

'Go on,' said Mr Vogel, 'for God's sake put me out of my misery.'

'Fine,' said Gwydion patiently.

'You're going to spike professor pig poo's drink, he's going to lose a day in his feeble little life, you're going to escape and get into a van with me and a man and a pig and a camera, and we're going to go round Wales in a day. Got it?'

'Oh, is that *all*,' said Mr Vogel. 'Fine, I feel better now I know I'm going to go round Wales with a pig and a camera. Sounds perfect.'

Gwydion headed for the toilet.

'See you in an hour. Oh, and don't fluff it. We want to make that jumped-up know-all, Mr Medical Bloody Marvel, to look so big [he held his finger and thumb half an inch apart]. Don't lose the plot – you're in charge of the storyline from now on. See ya.'

'You've used the word *trauma* – can you tell me a bit more?'

Dr Jackson was looking out of the window, at the hospital chimney, which loomed over this side of the complex; a plume of white smoke was pouring into the air, and he wondered what they were burning. The psychiatric unit was set aside from the rest of the wards; it was a little enclave, like lepers' huts outside a medieval church. He noticed that a group of children had climbed through a hedge surrounding the water tower, away to his right, and were playing around its legs. He phoned reception to warn them.

Each ward had a little square garden, with paths and benches and flowerpots around a central patch of lawn. There were neat, sane little borders, logical little shrubs and completely rational flower-beds. It was a place where a few of the patients went no matter what the weather. They somehow made it clear that they wanted to be left alone. An angry Pole often sat there in the rain in his shirt.

As he looked at the patients today, huddled in various isolations, sunning themselves, Mr Vogel was reminded of his own retreat into no-man's land. Philip Roth had talked of men standing in the wilderness because they were angry; this was how they wore away their anger, by standing with fishing rods in remote places far from anywhere or anyone.

'Trauma?' he echoed Dr Jackson's word, whilst wondering if Gwydion's philtre was working yet. Fortune had smiled on him; Dr Jackson had brought in a glass of orange juice with him, and although he had remarked on its sweetness afterwards, he hadn't noticed Mr Vogel's sleight of hand as the doctor stood with his back to the room, looking out on the water tower. Today, for some reason, it reminded him of a pagoda.

Mr Vogel went along with the catechism.

Trauma... his mind tried to focus.

Mr Vogel thought of an evening, some time ago, when he'd been in a pub in Laugharne, the New Three Mariners, and a dog, a little Labrador-cross called Penny, had come over to him and sat on his lap. It was young, maybe six months old, and sweet. He noticed that it had a disfigured forepaw, but forgot to ask how it came by it. The dog was very well looked after and seemed comfortable with its disability; it must have been born like that. He had seen dogs with a missing leg, but he had never seen a disfigured dog before. As their friendship grew, Gwydion had told him a story from his own childhood. He had been sent, literally, to the doghouse by his father and ordered to beat the dogs 'to show them who was master'. It was a very cruel thing to do; he had thrashed them – there must have been four or five – until blood streaked their flanks. He had felt a terrible power quivering in his body, and a strange release from guilt because he was doing it under orders; later in life he realised what drew the Nazis to human cruelty. He hadn't felt remorse as such; he had been a child, and if he hadn't beaten the dogs he would have been beaten himself. He'd also had to shoot dogs, and he could remember their eyes spurting out of their sockets and lying on their cheeks after the shot. He could remember the pungent, acrid smell of the cartridge, the limpness of the dog's still-warm hindpaw as he dragged it to a place where it couldn't be seen.

This early, enforced brutality had turned Gwydion into a gentle man; others, he knew, went the other way, became sadists and murderers because they had been taught an advanced lesson in depravity early on in their lives, and would re-enact the scene over and over again. That was the nature of trauma. One cruelty begat another. Cruelty propagated itself like an organism, each succeeding act bearing the code, the stigmata of the last.

The garden was busy now: a nurse had involved some of the patients in a gardening exercise; the little man with a glass eye was hacking at the privet, and others were weeding and raking. One of the newer patients, the little white-haired woman with dog hairs still clinging to her clothes, returned the doctor's stare and he looked away.

Mr Vogel went back to his own childhood; cripples had been much more common in public then. Callipers, platform shoes, crutches, sticks – all these had been everyday sights. Now it was less common to see physically handicapped people other than wheelchair-users. Mr Vogel felt very glad about this, but he also felt, secretly, that western society had an unhealthy infatuation with physical perfection, with beauty and slimming; he kept thinking of the Nazis' preoccupation with calisthenics and eugenics which presaged, somehow, a sickening society.

'Trauma,' he repeated again. He thought of a car by the side of a road, its front windscreen cracked and milky after being hit by a flying pebble. The basic shape of the car remained the same; its function, however, had been annulled abruptly. That's what trauma was: a sudden, shocking experience; a big bang which hummed in the ears for ever afterwards. One always drove a little slower than everyone else; the eyes were constantly on the move, waiting for another happening...

'Does that make sense to you Dr Jackson?'

'Yes, that makes sense to me – though traumas are very personal, and your picture isn't standard.'

'Does my trauma seem large or small in comparison with other people?'

'There's no sliding scale with trauma,' he answered. 'We all maximise our own pain. Like our genes, we have to explore every possibility; we have to probe the full spectrum of pain and pleasure.'

Vogel was beginning to wilt, and was cheered to see Dr Jackson yawning and settling into his seat.

Mr Vogel looked out at the garden, and saw a new figure shambling among the patients, helping with the gardening. He had a primitive, hirsute appearance and a prehistoric gait. His shape seemed strangely familiar.

It was Waldo, the Sumo-bellied builder from the pub, in a white coat reaching right down to his feet. Somehow he had inveigled himself onto the ward, and had come for Mr Vogel.

Relief spread like alcohol through Mr Vogel's body; he'd had enough of this internal probing; he felt as though his head had been opened like a tin of sardines.

Dr Jackson noticed the change in his mood, but was so visibly soporific by now that he didn't care.

'I think that's enough for today, don't you?' he said wearily.

'Thanks doc,' said Mr Vogel, getting to his feet. 'It's been great,' he lied. It was no good talking about it. Talking about it was like a rondel, a constantly repeated song:

> *Kookaburra sing in the old gum tree,*
> *Kookaburra sing in the old gum tree,*
> *Sing, Kookaburra sing,*
> *Kookaburra sing in the old gum tree.*

It was like Paddy pissed, singing by the bar.

There was a knock on the door, and Waldo popped his head round.

'How's it going?' he said gaily. 'Nurse said to have a word. I'm ready to see you about those feet of yours any time you like. I'll be waiting in the staff station. Cheers.'

Mr Vogel mumbled a goodbye to Dr Jackson and beat a retreat. He knocked at the staff station window and waved to Waldo, who was regaling the staff with some story or other – he could hear gales of muffled laughter through the glass. Waldo emerged, winking.

'Right Mr Vogel, I think we'll go to my clinic in town – need a good look at those plates of meat down there.' He turned round. 'That all right staff?'

'Yes, fine,' said Debbie. 'Take him away, give us a rest.' She was still laughing from Waldo's joke. Gwydion popped his head round the door and asked if he could walk his friend to the gate. The suddenness of his request took her by surprise: they were in the van and off before she realised what was going on. Mr Vogel sat in the middle, between Waldo and Gwydion.

A very strange sight greeted Mr Vogel when he looked behind him into the back of the van. Right up close to him was the Blue Angel's pink plastic pig, the one children played on when it stood outside the bookshop. To make the scenario yet more improbable Paddy was curled up next to it, asleep. And curled up against Paddy's belly there was another pig – a live piglet, small and pink, also fast asleep.

'The Three Little Pigs,' joked Mr Vogel, weakly. The piglet looked quite content, and a satisfied smile hovered on its lips, as if this was the entire pig population's idea of a perfect day out, in transit with four men and a plastic pig from the otherworld. The piglet had tried to suckle the bright pink god-pig but had failed to get any milk from its divine but unteated belly.

'Please get a grip on this story,' Mr Vogel pleaded with Gwydion, 'it's running out of control – it's becoming too surreal.'

'Mr Vogel my friend, this is no story,' replied Gwydion crisply, 'it's the real thing – this is reality mate, it's happening to you right now. Touch those pigs and see what I mean. Besides, can't you smell the authentic perfume of a real live pig?'

'I thought it was coming from Paddy, to tell you the truth.'

'Nope. This is all happening to you, so hold on tight and enjoy the ride.'

Mr Vogel allowed a few more miles to drift by in case a more pleasing version of reality asserted itself. In vain, he struggled with the concept of two pigs and a drunkard lying in the straw behind him.

There was another thing. His scalp prickled hotly: what was that in front of him on the dashboard, pressed against the windscreen? Did it really have one eye, glaring balefully at him – and were its ears rising slowly, even now, as they dried in the heat of the van's engine?

He pretended it wasn't there – his body was already overloaded with shock.

'The two pigs,' he mumbled in Waldo's direction. Waldo had got rid of the white coat and was back in his normal speckled garb.

Mr Vogel croaked again. 'The two pigs..?'

'We thought you'd enjoy the symbolism,' replied Gwydion. 'The live pig is from the old world, the one that's gone forever – and besides, we need a realistic-looking porker. The bookshop pig – that represents the modern world. It's plastic and pretentious. We're living in an age of euphemisms, after all – double speak, double standards, so we thought we'd bring both of them along.'

The piglet squealed in the back, and a new odour joined them in the front of the van.

'I wouldn't fret too much about the pigs – you've other worries,' teased Waldo. 'You realise that you've done a runner, don't you? Police'll be after you...'

'Actually, technically I'm being abducted,' answered Mr Vogel.

'Nope. You didn't put up any resistance. You've gone AWOL mate. Fled the scene. Done a bunk. Run scared.'

'Yes, well that's how I like it,' growled Mr Vogel. After all, he was in good company – the Buddha and Christ had both abandoned their homes and their families. 'For God's sakes,' he said. 'Can we go walkabout?'

'Nope,' said Gwydion. 'We're on a mission, and we have to be back by midnight.'

As a joke, Waldo was whistling *On the Road Again* by Willie Nelson, but Mr Vogel didn't know the tune.

They motored on, and Mr Vogel couldn't ignore the bear on the dashboard any longer.

'The bear,' he croaked.

'Bear?' asked Waldo, with mock innocence. 'Want a bear as well, do you? – we'll have a zoo at this rate.

'No, the *bear*,' rasped Mr Vogel again, pointing a distorted finger at the teddy bear on the dashboard.

'Oh,' said Waldo, 'I wondered how long it would take you...'

The bear had arrived out of the blue, a few days previously. Waldo had been sitting in his kitchen, eating his tea, when there was a knock on the door. Walking along the hallway to answer it he'd seen a little face in the lower panes of his front door. Opening it, he found a woman outside, in a wheelchair. She had a parcel on her knees. Her name was Esmie Falkirk. She'd seen the article in the newspaper, headlined *mystery 'walker' puzzles hospital.*

Waldo had been astonished, almost lost for words. He thought Esmie was fictional – a figment of Mr Vogel's imagination. But here she was to confound him. There really was an Esmie. Disconcerted, crashing into things, he invited her in.

She refused a cuppa, wanting to get down to business straight away – she had to be off as soon as possible. She merely wanted to tie up some loose ends.

'I didn't actually want to see David again,' she told him.

'David?'

'Yes, I think you all use his nickname, Vogel, is that right?'

'Oh yes, that's right.'

'I hope you don't mind me calling on you like this. The hospital gave two addresses – the bookshop down by the docks and yours. There was no-one at the bookshop.'

'Fine, that's fine,' said Waldo.

'I've got a gift for him, something from his past. I've looked after it for a long time.'

'The bear?'

'Yes.'

'He's mentioned it a lot.'

She looked round at Waldo's gaff, a shambolic Edwardian villa with stuffed birds and animals, old artefacts, paintings, sculptures and books. Sitting there with her hands clasped across her lap, Waldo saw that she'd retained her childish attractiveness. Life had failed to dent the upturn in her mouth. Quite clearly, Esmie was the girl who'd arrived outside the Blue Angel at the end of the Vogel Papers, when Sancho Panza was delivering his drunken address to the pub before sitting in a pot of geraniums. She had fine hair stylishly cut and was modishly dressed in black cord trousers and a purple top, startlingly like the garb Vogel wore. Altogether, she wasn't quite what Waldo expected; he had got used to her as a fiction; seeing her in the flesh was a real shock.

'I feel as if I've known you for ages Esmie,' said Waldo. 'Or should I call you Little Bo Peep! Mr Vogel would love to see you after all this time.'

'I'm afraid I couldn't contain myself, once I saw that newspaper story. I just had to get Rupert to his rightful owner. The thing is, you see, I don't actually want to see David again.'

She explained. She told Waldo about the party at the hospital all those years ago, when she'd won all the prizes and Vogel had been given his bear.

'It was all a clever ploy,' she told Waldo. 'But we didn't spot it, and we were both happy bunnies. Old Agnes Hunt was a very smart woman. I still celebrate my birthday on March the first, and I still have a bonnet for old times' sake.'

'Did you get any better? Surely you feel some bitterness – it was such a cruel twist of fate, to catch polio in a hospital.'

'No, not really. I've been in a wheelchair for as long as I can remember. It's hindered me in some ways, but you just get on with it, don't you, after the tiresome twenties. David seems to have got on with it himself – bit of a free spirit, I hear, dreaming great dreams about Wales. He didn't get much better either, by the sound of things.'

'Oh, no... but he's a lot better since his stay in hospital. Much better, actually.'

Waldo tried to make small talk.

'Did you get married, that sort of thing?'

'Yes, accountant. Got his own firm, very successful. He's called Jeffrey.'

So she'd ended up with an accountant. Bloody hell.

'Children?'

'Yes – three, all with degrees, all doing very well, two boys and a girl. How about David?'

'No, never got married. No children.'

'He always was one to keep himself to himself. He didn't answer my letters, you know. The little tinker. Broke my heart he did, me all alone in the hospital looking after his precious Rupert, not a blinking word from him. Never mind, it was a long time ago. Tell him I forgive him, thousands wouldn't.'

She reached for the package by her side, unwrapped it, and put a scruffy old one-eyed teddy bear on the table. It was Rupert. She'd kept him on her own bed all her single life; he had been moved onto the bedside cabinet when Jeffrey came along. Sometimes, when Jeffrey was asleep, she reached over and tugged him into bed. He always went on holidays with them; Rupert had been all over the world.

She'd put him through the washing machine and put a bright red bow tie around his neck for his big reunion.

The two of them studied him in silence. He looked old. He'd obviously seen a lot of action; his fur was thin in places and he bulged oddly around the middle.

Waldo asked her if she wanted anything to eat. No, she had a taxi waiting for her. She merely wanted to deliver the bear, to sort things out. She hadn't particularly wanted to see Mr Vogel. He was just a figure in the Bayeux tapestry of her childhood. He was long ago. She didn't want to break the surface of the water, to rupture the shimmering image of her long ago past either. Then was then. Now was now.

Soon she had gone. The hallway mirror rattled as Waldo closed the door behind her.

Now, in Waldo's van, as they drove onwards, Mr Vogel looked at the bear and felt absolutely nothing. This jumble of fur had occupied hundreds of hours in his mind, but now that he was back, here in front of him, Mr Vogel dried up completely. He was scared to look at him. It was like seeing a ghost. He almost felt uncomfortable. Could it be that he didn't want this to happen? Would the film in his mind, the whole delicate fabric of his fictionalised life, come to a grinding halt because he was actually being confronted face-to-face by part of the myth he'd constructed over many years?

'Welcome back, Rupert,' he said to the sky outside. He didn't want to touch him.

Mr Vogel sat in dusty silence and pondered as the van sped onwards. Where did he want to go first? Like his memories of Rupert, perhaps the old Wales of his childhood should also remain untouched. It wasn't a golden age. But it had disappeared now, and he was filled with nostalgia. He was almost a fossil. He could feel the mud of new Wales hardening around him. Soon he would become part of someone else's toy epic; for two generations he would last, and then he would be gone. He had thought once, in a dream, of a word to describe the moment when the last vestige of a memory which had been shared by many people disappeared. He had lived in a house, a large house, which had been demolished to make way for part of Wales's brave new world, a new Expressway. It was a much-loved house, and a handful of people could remember its doors, its stairs, its windows, its rooms, its smell, its laughter, its tears, its accumulated history. One day, with the death of the last of them, perhaps in the night, many years from now, the last memory would go; it would be a tiny sadness. There should be a word for this.

Mr Vogel thought about where he really wanted to go.

To the west coast to hear the choughs, perhaps. To the north to see the seals. To the east to see the badgers' metropoli on the dyke. To the south to see the great rusty cliffs of Glamorgan. He wanted to walk past the power station at Aberthaw, on the southernmost tip, and smell coal on the salt spray; to walk past Penarth's implausible pier and see Flat Holm change places with Steep Holm; to meet the men in the bar of the Prince of Wales at Kenfig; to shout from the blessing stone by the netpool at St Dogmael's and wait for the echo. He wanted to see the medieval pilgrims' graves at Llandilo-abercowin and feel the springy green moss on their stony feet; to sit in secretive Porthgain and imagine the lime kilns in full

flow; to stand on Mawddach bridge in the spring when the
sapphire tide swirled seawards; to walk on a sad day by Dysynni –
he wanted to see a bluster of April dog-winds shepherd sunshine
down Cader Idris and chase spindrift clouds along the raven
ridges. He wanted to visit his Garden of Eden: to watch the Ursula
C loading her cargo at the pier in Llanddulas; to get away from all
nonsense and fashions and politics and human misery; he wanted
to sleep in the church porch at Tallarn Green and watch the bats
and the shooting stars; to drink frothy coffee in the pavilion café –
where the minstrels once sang – in Llanfairfechan when the yacht
stays clanged in the breeze; to see the ancient corn-weighing stone
in the church at Mainstone; he wanted to stand on the devil's pulpit
high above the Wye gorge and look down on Tintern Abbey's ruins,
pitted like caried teeth; to tiptoe past the empty lighthouse buildings precarious on Nash Point, wondering if the world would
tumble into the sea; he wanted to walk along heron-priested shores
and smile at names like Ogmore-by-Sea; Mr Vogel wanted to see
the faded pictures of Richard Burton and Peter O'Toole in the bar
of the Ship in Lower Fishguard; to sleep in the youth hostel lofty
in an eyebrow of gorse above Pwll Deri; to talk to an artist in
Llansteffan and watch the blacklegged kittiwakes nest on
Mumbles' creaking pier. He wanted to swim like a fish in Wales's
containable beauty; she was not so vast as to be incomprehensible,
but big enough to be mysterious.

He told Waldo about his dream.

'I get your drift, Vogel,' said Waldo. He also wanted to see
these places, courtesy of the combustion engine. 'Not today
though,' he said.

Rupert's ears were rising slowly as they dried in the heat.

'Look,' said Gwydion. 'His ears are going up, just like the bear
in the Vogel Papers.'

Mr Vogel closed his eyes and basked in the cab's hothouse
sleepiness.

He daydreamed, briefly, a new scene in the story he and
Gwydion would complete soon. It went like this:

March 1: As we speed away in his van Waldo points to the locker
in front of my seat and says:

'Couple of postcards for you there.'

'Postcards?'

'Open the locker. One from John Williams, our man in Tasmania, and one from Anwen Marek.'

I open my eyes grumpily and scrabble in the locker.

The first postcard shows the great cathedral at Santiago del Compostella in Spain. It says:

> Hi! I've finished my great pilgrimage as promised. Dr Williams is here to see me home. We've become friends during your quest. He has played Ahab to my Moby Dick – though I've lost a huge amount of weight on my trek. Have you finished yours yet? Fondest regards – your little sparrow has brought me unexpected happiness. AM.

'Well fancy that,' says Waldo ruminatively. 'Williams and Marek getting it together. Truth's stranger than fiction for sure. I wouldn't have put a pound on that at a million to one.'

Waldo has been to Santiago and has seen St James's pilgrims arrive in the cathedral. No-one, not even the most hardened atheist, could fail to be moved by the aura, the supernatural frisson around them as they touch the great pillar in the cathedral; so many have touched it over the centuries that deep holes have been worn by their fingers and thumbs in the stone column.

'St James the Greater,' Waldo says. 'Son of Zebedee and Salome, known for his quick temper and his vehemence. He was one of the sons of thunder. Killed by Herod but his body was miraculously transported to Spain. Big Daddy of the pilgrim saints. Made his name by bringing a boy who was unjustly hanged back to life. Good for street cred, bringing a kid back to life. He'd be pretty sure of a job with the social services.'

I am dismissive. 'No Christian icons for me, OK? Mine's a pagan walk. I will hunt the comb and the mirror and the shears between the wild boar's ears for Culhwch, or I'll search for Mabon or Rhiannon.'

Williams's card shows a picture of Lourdes, and bears the message:

> Miracle of miracles! Getting married to Anwen – wedding in Wales (which brought us together) after she's done the St David's pilgrimage. Look forward to seeing you. John.

'Just a bit sickening, don't you think?' I say. 'All that bloody joy and well-being and I'm to blame.'

Waldo admonishes me. 'Don't be such a sourpuss. Let them be happy.'

They were flowing down the A55, Paddy stirring grumpily in the back. They heard a bottle-top being unscrewed, and a couple of splutters as Paddy coped with the sudden intake of raw alcohol.

Gwydion explained everything to Mr Vogel. Whilst Dr Jackson slept for 24 hours Mr Vogel and his loyal band would dash around Wales, visiting as many pigtowns as possible. They were taking part in their own version of the story of Gwydion and Pryderi's magic pigs in the Mabinogi. They would take pictures at each place and present them to Dr Jackson as proof that Mr Vogel had indeed walked right round Wales.

They turned off at the Black Cat roundabout and headed for their first pigtown – Mochdre near Colwyn Bay. Waldo drove into the car park of a big double glazing factory and stopped the jalopy. The engine ticked as they sat in silence.

Waldo lugged an old rucksack from the back, and an Ordnance Survey map.

'What size feet are you?' he asked Mr Vogel.

'Five.'

'Christ, I knew they were small, but I didn't think they were *that* small. These are mine – size 11, but you won't be wearing them for long, so don't fret.'

He took off Mr Vogel's special Velcro-strapped shoes and quickly replaced them with his own jumbo walking boots. He jammed a walker's hat on his head, a floppy broad-brimmed canvas hat which fluttered forlornly in the breeze, like an early, experimental aeroplane plunging off a church belfry. Waldo got out and opened the back doors; the piglet ran around in crazy zig-zags before he could catch it. There was a general melee as everyone got out of the van. Waldo tied the piglet to a length of rope, and Paddy rolled out into the road in a shower of straw. The scene was deteriorating into farce, and Mr Vogel saw a line of faces appearing in the windows of the factory, staring at them.

Waldo helped him into the rucksack straps, then rammed the map into a prominent place between his puny chest and a strap. In his huge shoes and voluminous black trousers, Mr Vogel looked like Charlie Chaplin in *Gold Rush*. After lugging the piglet to the Mochdre road sign and tying it to a stanchion, Waldo arranged the scene so that Mr Vogel and the piglet both faced the camera, with the road sign behind them and a tolerable smile on both their faces. Mr Vogel joined in the spirit of things – he jutted his chest out, and placed his right leg forward in a manly and stirring pose, trying to look like Hillary about to unfurl his flag on the summit of Everest. By now a line of cars and lorries, fronted by a busload of people, had halted to look at their antics. Realising they had to be quick before the police were called, Gwydion took a picture of the scene and waited for it to emerge from the Polaroid. When it did, he gave a manic thumbs-up and ran to the pig, untied it, and swept it back into the van with a swift scooping movement. It was then that they realised that Paddy had lurched off in search of a pub. They passed a police car as they fled the scene, and a worrying period ensued as they searched for Paddy, who had unerringly found the only pub in the village, the Mountain View, and disappeared inside.

They finally got away and settled down to a long drive to the English border; by lunchtime they were nosing along country lanes towards Llanrhaeadr-ym-mochnant, home of the country's highest waterfall. As any self-respecting Welshman will know, this is one of the seven wonders of Wales: the 'moch' in its name is one of the pigs in this story, and our heroes' antics deserve to go down in history as the eighth wonder. You will be troubled for only a short while longer with this last madcap journey around Wales, our mother country, sweetest of all the Earth's dominions. We will pass over this higgledy-piggledy day, though we must reveal to you, in passing, that Paddy pretended to be a film director, preparing for a shoot, at the waterfall, and a tourist became so engrossed in events that she fell in the water and nearly drowned.

Also, in yet another moment of confusion, they ended up on the Mochdre Industrial Estate in Newtown instead of the nearby village of Mochdre; Waldo turned this to his advantage however by buying a large tin of cut-price industrial paint stripper from Confederate Chemicals – he said it would be ideal for a project he had in mind. Also, when they reached Nant-y-Moch near Ponterwyd they somehow got caught up in the annual skyline fell race as the runners came home: when Paddy got out to jeer at the runners he forgot to close the door and the piglet escaped. It finished a very creditable third in the race and it made the front pages of most of the local newspapers. *The Cambrian News* showed a picture of the pig in Mr Vogel's arms, with a yellow rosette pinned to Mr Vogel's lapel, under the headline: '*Well Done Del! Boy, what a shock as Trotter runs away with Olym-pig title*' and the *Western Mail* had a similar photograph under the headline '*Mystery runner hogs the limelight*', whereas the *Daily Post* managed only a paragraph, headlined, '*Rind-up of today's sport*'. An item on the television news showed Mr Vogel and the piglet surrounded by a horde of children on the finishing line chanting '*Hoggy Hoggy Hoggy, Oink Oink Oink.*'

Finally, I must disclose that when they left their twelfth and final porcine destination the pig was briefly forgotten when they drove away and was nearly lost for ever.

They arrived back at their home town as midnight approached, in an intoxicating medley of smells: pigshit, alcohol, sweat, hot engine oil and diesel fumes. They deposited the live pig in its normal abode, a farm on the outskirts (Waldo had useful friends everywhere), leaving it with a host of memories – its visit to the otherworld would be passed on from pig to pig unto the last vestiges of recorded time.

The plastic pig was likewise returned to its normal home, the Blue Angel bookshop, and Mr Vogel, Gwydion and Paddy all managed to snatch some sleep in spare beds or on sofas in Waldo's house.

Mr Vogel went to bed with twelve fresh Polaroid snaps in his piggy bank.

'THERE!'

Mr Vogel was jabbing Dr Jackson in the chest.

The doctor had woken up in one of the general wards, and the nurses had giggled when his wife arrived with a pair of silk pyjamas for him, monogrammed with the initials SJ.

He felt very ill, as if he'd fallen into the pig-pen with Dorothy at the beginning of *The Wizard of Oz*, before her journey along the yellow brick road; in fact, he felt as if he'd been trampled by a whole herd of enraged pigs.

'*Believe me now?*' said Mr Vogel in a near-hysterical screech.

Dr Jackson tried to focus on Mr Vogel's face in the murk; he looked like a Munchkin, thought Dr Jackson, whose vision still hadn't cleared properly. Dr Jackson looked ill. Somehow he'd lost a day: one minute he'd been talking to Mr Vogel, and the next he'd woken up in a hospital bed. It was baffling. They were doing tests.

'That'll teach you to doubt a Welshman,' said Mr Vogel, who was still jabbing uncomfortably at Dr Jackson's monogram. Twelve piggy Polaroid pictures were scattered on the bed, each showing Mr Vogel standing by a proud and happy piglet, beside twelve different versions of the Mochdre roadsign; Mr Vogel had tossed them onto the coverlet, dramatically, when he burst into the room. He was sitting, now, on the side of Dr Jackson's bed, his nose only a few inches from the doctor's.

'Proof,' said Mr Vogel triumphantly, 'if proof were ever needed, that the great walk around Wales was a FACT [he almost spat the word], an ACTUALITY, as REAL as... as...'

Mr Vogel spluttered. He couldn't think of a suitable comparison, and he was so worked up he could hardly control himself. Gwydion stood behind him, nodding. And behind Gwydion stood Waldo, also nodding, and behind him stood Paddy, also nodding, and behind them all, in the window, other faces could also be seen nodding.

'Believe me now, you stupid Anglo-Saxon, you dreamer of steals?' said Mr Vogel, getting his sentence horribly mangled. He was shaking.

'What's the 'S' for anyway,' asked Gwydion behind him.

Dr Jackson stared uncomprehendingly.

'The 'S'?' he asked.

'Yes, the 'S' in 'SJ' on your pyjamas.'

Dr Jackson was cornered; this was a very delicate topic – his father had also been a psychiatrist, and had wanted his son to follow in his footsteps.

Gwydion saw the fear in his eyes, and twigged.

'Sigmund, isn't it?' he cried triumphantly. 'It's bloody Sigmund, isn't it?'

Dr Jackson closed his eyes and wished them all away.

He stuttered. 'Yes, it is Sigmund, and yes, I do believe everything you've said, now please, please go.' He shrank so far back in the pillows he almost disappeared.

Mr Vogel got to his feet and prepared to leave, but he couldn't go without one last parting shot. 'So now you know, Dr Bigshot, what it's like to be on the other end of a periscope,' he gibbered, before turning away. 'I mean stethoscope,' he added weakly. There was an episode of pushing and shoving before they could all get out.

Dr Jackson was very glad, and went back to sleep.

Mr Vogel sat in Waldo's van, which still smelt strongly of pig deposits. He was still cross, and he was having an imaginary conversation with Dr Jackson, in which he got his sentences right and defeated the doctor completely with incontestable arguments.

'You can't invent a past for yourself,' the doctor was saying, dismissively.

'I wouldn't put a bet on that,' answered Mr Vogel suavely. 'That's what everyone else does, all you so-called normal people. Even if you honestly believe you're telling the truth you're making most of it up to cover up your inadequacies or bad behaviour. You try getting a sensible version of a divorce – you'll find two perfect people who married crazy psychopaths. Anyway, that's what history is – a big jumble of facts and fables. Whole books written about Wales but you can hardly find any two authors who agree. So I'm going to do the same.'

Gwydion had told him about Welsh poets of long ago who had apparently shown a great knack for prophecy – but they were merely fiddling the books. If the Welsh lost a battle, let's call it Battle X, the poets would write a great poem, hide it in the back of a cupboard for a while, then 'find' it, pretending it had been written long ago in the past. They'd say: *cripes, look what we have here, a poem predicting we would lose Battle X and get wiped out big style, but the poem says we'll paste the pesky English in our next battle and live happily ever after.*

It was an early form of propaganda.

Mr Vogel had discussed this with Gwydion.

'Sometimes you've got to talk yourself up,' he'd said to Mr Vogel, sitting by his side. 'Give yourself some good publicity. Look at the Tudors – they were the biggest spin doctors of all time. What's wrong with a bit of exaggeration? It's one of the Celtic talents,' said Gwydion. 'And you've got them all.'

'Anyway,' said Mr Vogel, 'our version of events is all true, with real people and real happenings, so it's not a fiction. All we've done is fiddle about a bit with time and space. And the universe itself does that, so sod the lot of them. If the bloody universe can have wormholes then so can we. We're just two charmed blue quarks acting strangely.'

~

'Now I've one last favour to ask you,' Mr Vogel said to Waldo later that morning, when they'd had some breakfast (for Paddy, that meant raiding Waldo's drinks cabinet).

'You're always asking for one last favour, and I always give in,' replied Waldo. 'Must be because I like you. You're completely off the wall, but the world wouldn't be the same without Mr Vogel. Come on, what is it?'

'Just take me back to the hospital, one last time. I need to see Anna.'

'That's going to be difficult – remember, you did a runner from the place.'

'I know,' said Mr Vogel. 'But I really must see her – I've got something I want to give her.'

The time had come. At last, Mr Vogel was ready to start a new chapter in his life.

He felt hope rising slowly inside him like bubbles in a bottle of lemonade waiting to be opened at a summer picnic. The time had come for the dream to end and his adventure to begin. The world around him hummed with choices. Now he had an abundance of possible fates, not just one miserable option.

After the initial shock of his admission he had felt quite at home in the psychiatric unit, when he knew they weren't going to strap him to a frame or carve him up again. The ward was as busy as a factory, with people coming and going with amazing rapidity: sometimes, when he got up in the morning there were two or three new people, who had come like owls in the night.

After a few weeks Mr Vogel felt like an elder statesman, and often he could be heard giving gentle advice to a new migrant. And then people began reappearing, and after a few days they would disappear again. Mostly they shadow-walked in silence, hunched and defensive. Some weeks there was hardly anyone he could talk to, because they were all in a parallel universe, which was quite frightening by the looks of it.

The ward also had a silent host of characters visible only to the other patients. By comparing himself with those patients, Mr Vogel realised that he was quite well. He took to a lightweight walking stick, on which he proved to be quite nifty.

He had stopped composing a grandiose alter ego for himself.

When he first arrived on the ward people who commented on his limp might have been told, with studied insouciance: *I picked it up during the last hundred miles of my walk around Wales.*

Mr Vogel had a fine eye for bathos and hyperbole, and he loved the attention. He basked in the wan limelight of his brief fame, knowing that the thudding dullness of normal life was an ever-present danger, and that a whole line of men in suits was waiting to stuff him behind an office desk and bury his soul under a pile of fatuous mission-statements.

Nowadays, he told the truth.

He had harrowed his past as a puzzled historian might try to unravel early Welsh poems of epic and heroic bravado. He was proud of his own mini-epic, his pocket *Iliad*. It was a part of him now. The future, he surmised, would need no major remodelling, only minor embellishment. He had spent a suitable period feasting and drinking and telling stories of epic adventures, as the Welsh warriors of *Y Gododdin* had done in the old Northern Britain before their famous but doomed mission to steal Catraeth from the enemy; now it was time for him to take his place in the quest.

Mr Vogel washed and shaved. He flattened his hair as well as he could and buffed his shoes. His breakfast weighed rather heavily on his stomach, and he realised suddenly how nervous he was. He became irritable. His work had to be done before he could calm down.

He really was very nervous. He wondered to himself: why, exactly, am I so shaky?

It wasn't the teddy – he knew that it was going from him, that it was finally and utterly part of his past; now was the time to put childish things aside, to stop replaying his childhood video, to make a new one – to create another life. Perhaps he was nervous about his impending rendezvous with Anna.

Though doomed and childish, it had been the only love he had ever felt for a woman. He'd had feelings, certainly, but not feelings like everyone else, the sort that seemed to grow back instantly like shark's teeth when they'd been ripped out. He had seen how quickly love turned to hatred, and he feared deep emotions. He'd just wanted to be friends with everyone. Now he knew what love was like, and it pained him. He didn't regret the experience, it was part of living, but now he wanted to put it back in a giant storeroom with all the other powder-kegs which had been rolled towards him down the dark alleyways of life.

Waldo and Paddy took him there in the truck, to help him and to give him moral support. It was raining, and the wipers had broken down. The three of them sat outside the psychiatric unit, listening to the light patter of the rain, broken only by the noise of Paddy unscrewing his bottle and taking swigs.

'You all right? You're very quiet,' said Waldo.

'Yeh... fine. Just want this over with,' said Mr Vogel.

Rupert was still propped up on the windscreen in front of them. His ears had risen high in the air and the effect was slightly comical. Paddy got lyrical.

'D'ya realise me boys, this is the last drop in the bottle, the final party in the pox clinic, we're over and out, it's time to sing goodbye to mission control, it's a giant step for Mr Vogel, a small yawn for mankind. It's the end of the affair, me little farticle.' He roughed up Mr Vogel's hair. 'You've gone and done it now smelly-pants, you've got yourself in the papers, you've met a bint, and you're finally getting rid of that manky bit of fur. Bout time too. You say your father gave it away? Silly bastard should have given you away the same time, would have saved us all a lot of trouble.'

'Don't push it,' said Waldo. 'Remember, he's paid for your extravagant habits for quite a while.'

'Yeah, paid for my finishing school – my bloody liver finishing school,' cried Paddy. He lurched forward, grabbed the bear in front of him and flung it through the window in one movement.

Waldo retrieved it. Rupert's ears were damp and dusty, and his single eye looked sorrowfully at them.

'You all done with this quest now Vogel?' asked Paddy. 'No more cripples, horses, travellers, damn silly notions, messages from Tasmania, letters from Amerikee. I'm up to here with it all. OK?'

Mr Vogel said nothing. He looked through the window ahead, at an imaginary view. They were on an island, by the sea. An old jalopy was rattling along, and he could smell that heady mix of hot engine oil and the daisy-splattered verdure around them, and the smells of farming – cowpats and silage, and he imagined the aromatic smell of wild flowers prinking the green meadows with fine shades of yellow and cyan and magenta; in his dreamscape he imagined that he lay with Luther in the timothy, the emmer and the spelt under the soporific drone of insects, with the heat of the day glowing on lizard rocks.

Mr Vogel shook the drying dust off the teddy and toyed with him, turning him round and round in his hands. He had bought the biggest box of chocolates they had in the shop, and a hundred cigarettes. It was the price of unrequited love. He had made theoretical mental sums but still didn't know what he would have bought Anna if his love had been reciprocated.

For once, Paddy was useful. Spotting a rake lying on the grass, he rested it over his shoulder and slinked along the path which wound under Anna's window. They could see him as he tapped on the glass and gesticulated towards the garden outside the ward. He returned, whistling.

'Job done – she'll be here as soon as she gets herself together,' he said. 'That'll cost you a pint down the pub,' he added. Mr Vogel said nothing: he was rattling with tension.

Eventually, they could see Anna coming through the main door. She looked up at them, and then walked to a bench well away from the ward, in the lee of some bushes. She sat waiting. Mr Vogel could see her legs shaking. He straightened his hair and dusted some dandruff off his collar. He looked himself up and down, from his Velcro shoes to his fading Oxfam shirt. Then he stuffed the bear into the front of his jacket, so that just its head peeked out.

He left Waldo and Paddy and walked down towards her, as quickly as possible so that no-one would spot him. After giving her the chocolates and cigarettes he sat on the other side of the bench, leaving a gap between himself and Anna, and they looked at each other for some time without saying anything.

The ward was probably quiet right now, thought Mr Vogel. Sylvia the Hoover was probably doing a post-prandial trawl; maybe she had found a tiny piece of reddened tissue paper which had dropped off a shaving cut on the Walrus Man's chin.

Anna cried silently and tearlessly, and trembled spasmodically. There were new blood lines on her forearms. Vogel dug into his jacket and put the teddy on the bench between them. Rupert looked small and exposed. Some of his stuffing was straggling from his armpit.

'Well, here's that teddy bear I promised you – I'm sure you

didn't expect him to be as old as the hills, but he was a great pal to me and I'm sure he'll be a great pal to you,' said Mr Vogel.

'Yes,' she whispered. Mr Vogel loved the way she said 'yes'. She sounded so small, so vulnerable. She looked at the bear, and the shaking around her knees got worse.

'It's like this,' he said purposefully. 'Rupert means a lot to me. I've told you about him – remember?'

'Yes.'

'My father gave him away when he took me home from hospital. I've got him back now. But it's time for us to say our goodbyes. I see him in a different way now. Sometimes it's best to let go of the past. Make a fresh start and all that, you know what I mean. Swap your troubles with someone else. Sort of helps.'

'Yes.'

'Will you look after him for me?'

'Yes.'

'I'm letting him go, but I want him safe. I want him to go to a good home. Perhaps you can keep him in your bedroom – would that make things a bit better?'

'Yes.'

'Fine. I'm glad about that. You're really doing me a big favour. There's one little thing. I want to change his name, because he's going to be living with a new family, and I want to help him put his past behind him. I want him to be called Mr Vogel. It may sound silly, but it's important to me. Laying ghosts to rest, and all that. Understand?'

'Yes.'

'Can I come and see him now and again?'

'Yes.'

'That's great.'

Anna didn't touch people, so they looked quietly at each other for a while. They'd found a great deal in common during their talks. Another time, another place, things could have been different. The last thing she said to him was 'Yes.'

He never saw her again. He thought about her often; he searched for her face in crowds and on television. The bear, too, disappeared with her. It was a suitable ending.

Mr Vogel walked away from the ward, for the last time. Even if it meant becoming a fugitive, he would never go back. He had too much to do. It was a clear evening, with little more than an hour to go before darkness. The sun stirred molten poppies into the sea. Waldo and Paddy were waiting for him and drove him, without saying anything, down the hill, to the docklands. They stopped by the Blue Angel bookshop. Paddy was in an alcoholic haze.

'Bloody hell,' he said. 'I thought I saw a parrot flying into the shop.'

'It's a toy parrot, you pillock,' said Waldo. 'One of those stuffed toys hanging in the window.'

They got out, and stretched their legs outside the shop. A baby robin, speckled and lost, hopped clumsily through the threadbare privet hedge alongside the bookshop, onto the pavement, and wobbled in front of Mr Vogel. It was unaware of the danger: lorries and cars were thundering past it, only inches away. Putting down his stick, Mr Vogel crept up to it slowly, bent down, and scooped it up in his hands. Slowly, he struggled through the hole in the hedge and took the chick to the far end of the garden, away from the traffic, where it would be safe. He felt a wave of relief – he'd saved a little life; he had done one important thing in his slender existence.

Suddenly, the door of the Blue Angel shook; they could see a face in the window. It was Gwydion, rattling a big bunch of keys in the lock. He stepped out and stood in the doorway with the keys swinging in his hand. He smiled and beckoned them into the shop, and they sat down. It smelt musty in there; the books and their various stories had deteriorated in only a short time, as though the characters had detected a lack of interest in them and had started pining and wasting away.

Gwydion opened a drawer in the desk and reached inside. He took out a thick sheaf of paper. It was a document of some sort, and it looked like a manuscript, or a report. He turned to the last page and scribbled for a while with a chewed-up pencil, then drew a line and put a last full stop with a flourish, so that the pencil made a pleasing blip on the paper.

'There,' he said, 'a good ending. We've finished it, Mr Vogel. It's the end of the story.'

Mr Vogel looked at the document in Gwydion's hands. It looked like a big story, much bigger than he'd anticipated. He knew what it was, without asking.

'Our story,' he said. 'Is it good?'

'Best ever,' said Gwydion with a broad grin. 'Now it's your turn.'

Mr Vogel looked quizzically at him.

'Remember the lame ant? The ant which brought the last seed of flax so they could make a head-dress for Olwen?'

'Yes.'

'Well we did agree that you would bring in the last seed of our story, didn't we?'

'That's right.'

'Well come on then.'

Mr Vogel took the pencil, thought for a while, and then wrote:

March 1: The end of our mission. My story is told. We have travelled many miles across many hundreds of years: I believe I can take the last few steps unaided. We will see. Goodbye. Mr Vogel.

When Mr Vogel had added his final sentence he sat in silence, imagining the scenes in the Blue Angel in days of yore. Gwydion thumbed through some of the books, and Paddy went up to the window with Waldo to examine the stuffed parrot; Paddy stood on a chair to poke it about and have a silly conversation with it in the who's a pretty boy and pieces of eight tradition.

It was at this point that Mr Vogel noticed something which startled him: between Paddy's legs he could see a face gazing at him through a bottom pane in the window. He gave a cry and stood up; his stick clattered along the slate floor, but he hobbled towards the doorway without it, his hand outstretched and flapping with emotion. 'Esmie!' he cried as soon as he'd opened the door. 'Esmie! It's you, isn't it?'

Paddy fell off the chair, ripping the parrot from its peg and sending a shower of petals into the air as he fell against a dying geranium in the window.

By now Mr Vogel was in the street outside, on his knees, his arms around Esmie and the wheelchair. They were both crying.

I think you can imagine for yourselves, much better than I can describe, the scenes which followed. After Esmie had wheeled herself into the shop, and order had been restored, amid much laughter and tears, Esmie revealed that she'd been unable to go without saying a last farewell to Mr Vogel. He, in turn, was so emotional that he sprained her back with his constant impromptu hugs. She was surprised, and pleased, that he'd wanted to see her so much. Time had changed him. She had remembered an austere, unemotional person who was capable of great remoteness. This Vogel was quite different: warm, expressive. His eyes had seen a great deal, she could tell – they held a rich store of experience.

After the reunion, during a lull, before everyone became self-conscious and started detaching themselves, Gwydion jerked his head towards the interior of the shop.

It was dark inside, and they could smell its accumulated history enveloping them. All those books, all those words... and before that, all those travellers coming and going, all those tales, the laughter and the gossip.

Gwydion dragged a stepladder from a corner, put it in position under a hatch in the ceiling, and then opened the hatch.

He climbed down the ladder and gesticulated upwards with his thumb.

He held out a packet wrapped in twine, and indicated upwards, again, this time with his eyes.

'Go on then,' he said. 'You've got to take it to its rightful place. You know where that is, don't you?'

Mr Vogel realised, with a hot flush of blood to his brain, what Gwydion meant.

Of course. The finished story. It had to go into the roof-space of the Blue Angel, in the gap in the wall by a purlin. Of course. It all made perfect sense now. Gwydion was a genius. Where else would they put it? The story would be there for the future – for anyone who found it, many years from now, the story of the cripple and his quest, the great walk around Wales, all of it... and he would put it there, no-one else. Gwydion passed the parcel to him, and he jammed it into his jacket, just as he'd jammed Rupert there when he went to see Anna.

He climbed, slowly and shakily.

In the last few minutes of the day, after Esmie had gone, Mr Vogel and Gwydion and Waldo sat looking at the boats. Paddy was out cold.

Gulls dropped to the ground around them, expectantly. A lone sandpiper sped across the mouth of the estuary.

Waldo had driven down to the port, and they had sat in wonderful, glorious, happy silence together.

'I've got a little surprise for you,' said Gwydion after a while. 'The idea came to me a year ago, but I didn't do anything about it. It's been dormant since then, but you've acted as a catalyst – I'm going to do something about it. Perhaps you'll come with me!'

Gwydion had been walking in Abercastell Bay and had seen a fantastically fat man struggling miserably into a wetsuit. He had diving gear, and a chic look-away couple, trying hard to appear cool, were waiting for him. Gwydion had felt an intense dislike consuming him. He repressed it and moved on, but his eye was caught by a sheet of paper covered with cellophane which had been pinned to a stile. A proud local had typed out some neighbourhood history for passers-by: this bay had been the landfall on August 12, 1876, of one Alfred Johnson, the first man to sail across the Atlantic single-handed; he had crossed in a boat which was a mere 15 feet six inches in length. Gwydion had started thinking about all the other adventurers who had helped to write the story of Wales. Suddenly the sea filled with galleons and flats and schooners and sloops. And there were Welsh footsteps all over the world; he thought of Edgar Evans, the Welshman who had died with Scott in Antarctica's drifting snow, now buried in Rhossili's drifting sands.

'Come on, I'll show you,' said Gwydion, and they got out. Waldo also descended from the van. They walked along the harbour wall, and then they all stopped and stared in unison at a boat tethered to a stanchion.

'Come and have a look,' said Gwydion chirpily. 'This is why I need the industrial paint stripper.' He dropped down into the boat.

'It's an old lifeboat,' he said – needlessly, since the orange and blue colours gave it away, despite the fact that someone had painted over the RNLI logo.

'I was really intending to buy a new one,' he said lamely, 'but I didn't have enough money. It'll be fine after a coat of paint and all that.'

'Well don't expect me to come anywhere near it,' said Paddy from behind them – he'd woken up in one of his blustery moods. 'Not bloody likely. I'd rather sail with the owl and the pussy cat in a pea-green boat. Get real Vogel. If you're thinking of going on a trip with Huw Puw in that frying pan you're madder than I thought...'

Waldo jumped down on the deck and nosed around.

'Mmm,' he said, 'don't shoot any albatrosses. You're going to need all the luck you can get in this tub. What's the plan anyway?'

'Sail round Wales,' said Gwydion. 'Completely round. Including the canals.'

'In your dreams,' said Waldo.

'I've dreamt about it quite a lot, actually.'

'You're mad,' said Waldo. 'Ramsay Sound will make you look like a bit of cherry blossom going down a drain. And Bardsey Sound... my God, it doesn't bear thinking about. Let's go before you tell me any more about it. I'm feeling seasick already.'

They ended up in a pub. Paddy lay down on a seat in the bay window and went to sleep. Mr Vogel found himself a stool in the corner.

'I like this place,' he said. 'Could become a habit.'

They could hear the landlord working his way up the cellar steps, his boots clanking heavily on the old wooden stairs. They waited, in an eerie silence, for him to kick the doorframe and emerge holding his head in his hands. It didn't happen.

The place filled quickly and soon there was an air of bonhomie and conviviality. An artist unfurled a roll of canvasses and started selling them: Mr Vogel bought a crayon drawing of a cliff-top scene, with seabirds wheeling and diving around a headland. Paddy woke and started singing filthy ditties. Soon he was thumping the bar with his boot in time with his hoarse tunes.

Gwydion and Mr Vogel chatted about their story. It was Gwydion who had drawn up the first chapter and they had studied it with their heads together, striking out a word here and adding another there. They had shown it to Waldo, who had read it out loud:

Mr Vogel was the winner.

When boisterous spring sprayed its leafy graffiti in the trees which struggled upwards past his grimy kitchen window, Mr Vogel was given a new existence.

Like the supine earth he had been through a deep winter, distanced from the heat of the sun; like the obscure artist who lived at the end of the street he had sat for too long by his fireside in a torpor, gazing into the embers of the past as his life cooled and dimmed. Now, suddenly, the rising sap jolted him from his stupor; the jumbled fields all around him lay breathing again, like cardiac patients shocked back to life and left to recover; he sat watching them, sprawled under their bedspreads of bright green grass embroidered with warm yellow suns and fresh flowers.

Mr Vogel kept a few truths to himself but the townspeople quickly snatched his news and carried it far and wide, to every attic and cellar, every nook and cranny; swiftly forming themselves into a sinuous street collective they ladled hot gossip from their babbling furnace and moulded nuggets of news about Mr Vogel into fabulous tales for ancient, hairy lugholes and lullabies for tiny shell-pink ears. Cunningly they distorted the daily bulletins radiating from the bar of the Blue Angel and created a misty amalgam of half-truth, tenuous fact and five-pint fuddle. The streets hummed with speculation and Mr Vogel smiled with grim amusement when he heard the various versions of his legendary existence. Indeed, by the end he hardly knew truth from fiction himself, such were the cunning twists and embellishments added to the original plot.

And as the shoots of fiction grew and the tendrils of conspiracy entwined, Mr Vogel paid for the celebrations and started his quest.

After all, he had won a very large sum of money, an island croft, an elegant house, a beautiful garden and an orchard.

'And a pagoda,' said Mr Vogel. 'I want to win a pagoda.'

'Right you are,' said Gwydion. 'Why?'

'Because that's how I became a cripple,' said Mr Vogel. 'I fell from the pagoda at Kew Gardens – that's why it's closed to the public now.'

'Christ, that's awful,' said Gwydion.

'Only joking,' said Vogel.

'You bastard.'

'I just happen to like them. Am I allowed to have a pagoda or not?'

'Fine,' said Gwydion, 'you can have a pagoda.'

'And another thing,' said Mr Vogel, 'you can cross out that bit in the introduction, the bit about the robin chick being run over and squashed in the tarmac, like an ivory inlay in a table.'

'Of course,' said Gwydion gleefully. 'You saved it, didn't you! You saved the robin chick Mr Vogel! Well done!'

It was time to go. They paused in the doorframe and faced the glimmering nightfall. Huge storm clouds were rolling in from the sea. They watched them blacken the sky; then a thunderstorm broke suddenly in the hills around, sending bullets of rain scudding down on them. Offshore they could see a yellow rescue helicopter hovering above the water; a gang of boys sped past on bikes, shouting excitedly that a dinghy was drifting out to sea with two small boys in it. They could see a man – the father perhaps – standing forlornly on the shore, waiting for the rescue.

As rivulets of icy water ran like an electric shock down his spine, Mr Vogel made a pact to go around Wales in the boat with Gwydion. He grabbed an old green hat from the hat stand: a hat with a black band and a shiny rim; it had lain there for as long as anyone could remember. He shook a cobweb off it and banged it on the doorframe to dust it, then put it on his head at a rakish angle. He took an old umbrella with a duck-head handle, which had also lain in the hat-stand since time began, and handed it to Gwydion.

It would be a very fine adventure. They were ready for the real thing now.

CODA

YOU MAY like to know that Mr Vogel ended his long relationship with whisky on February 29th, 2000.

Gwydion is the keeper of the door: if Mr Vogel ever needs him he can find him in the fan of yellow light shining outside the off-licence and video store.

The tamarisk tree in Mr Vogel's garden has prospered and its branches shade him from the sun, like an umbrella.

Mr Vogel often visits Gwydion and the Gang. And this is the gift they have given him. Every time he steps into the light of the wrecker's lantern then moves back to safety again, he can walk entirely around Wales in three steps.

Acknowledgements

I would like to thank Jan Morris, Iain Sinclair, Don Waine, Rob Owen, Brynley Jenkins, Hamish and Jude, Will Atkins, Dafydd Jones, Morus Jones, Erika Woods, John Tanner, the Welsh Books Council, my friends in Llanfairfechan and beyond, and both branches of my family. I would also like to thank the many people I met on my walk around Wales, for their company. Special thanks to Don Waine, for providing some of the ideas in this book, and to John Spink, whose initial review on behalf of the Welsh Books Council saved *Mr Vogel* from the bin.

Acknowledgement is due to the following for permission to reprint work in this novel:

Wales: Epic Views of a Small Country by Jan Morris, 1998, © Jan Morris, reproduced by permission of Penguin Books Ltd; *A History of Wales* by John Davies, 1993, © John Davies, reproduced by permission of Penguin Books Ltd; *Journey Through Wales: The Description of Wales*, by Gerald of Wales, Trans. © Lewis Thorpe, 1978, reproduced by permission of Penguin Books Ltd; *Piers Ploughman*, by William Langland, © J.F. Goodridge, 1956, reproduced by permission of Penguin Books Ltd; *Michael Farraday in Wales*, Dafydd Tomos (ed), reproduced by permission of by Gwasg Gee; *History of the Kings of Britain*, by Geoffrey of Monmouth, trans © Lewis Thorpe, 1966, reproduced by permission of Penguin Books Ltd; *Magic & Mystery in Tibet*, by Alexandra David Neel, reproduced by permission of Souvenir Press; *My Past and Thoughts*, by Alexander Herzen, reproduced by permission of Penguin Books Ltd; *Clear Waters Rising: A Mountain Walk Across Europe*, by Nicholas Crane, © Nicholas Crane, 1997, reproduced by permission of Penguin Books Ltd; *This is My Life* by Agnes Hunt, reprinted in 1965 by A. Wheaton & Co. Ltd, reproduced by permission of Derwen College.

The author would particularly like to acknowledge the use he made of the following volumes:

The Bone-Setters of Anglesey, a lecture delivered by W. Hywel Jones at the Anglesey Antiquarian Society and Field Club's annual general meeting at Amlwch on May 3, 1980, published in the 1981 transactions; *The Life of Sir Robert Jones* Frederick Watson, published by the Robert Jones & Agnes Hunt Orthopaedic and District Hospital NHS Trust; *A Book of Traveller's Tales,* ed. Eric Newby, published by Picador; *Spoken Here: Travels Among Threatened Languages,* Mark Abley, published by William Heinemann; *Vanishing Voices: The Extinction of the World's Languages*, Daniel Nettle and Suzanne Romaine, published by Oxford University Press; *Revd John Parker's Tour of Wales and its Churches,* Edgar W, Parry, published by Gwasg Carreg Gwalch; *Wanderlust: A History of Walking*, Rebecca Solnit, published by Verso; *The Pioneer Ramblers 1850-1940*, David Hollett, published by the North Wales Area Ramblers' Association; *Healing & Hope: 100 Years of 'The Orthopaedic',* Marie Carter, published by the Robert Jones & Agnes Hunt Orthopaedic & District Hospital NHS Trust; *Landor's Tower*, by Iain Sinclair, published by Granta; *Don Quixote*, by Cervantes, published by Penguin; *A Tour in Wales*, Thomas Pennant, abridged by David Kirk, published by Gwasg Carreg Gwalch; *Selected Letters of Leo Tolstoy*, published by Macmillan.